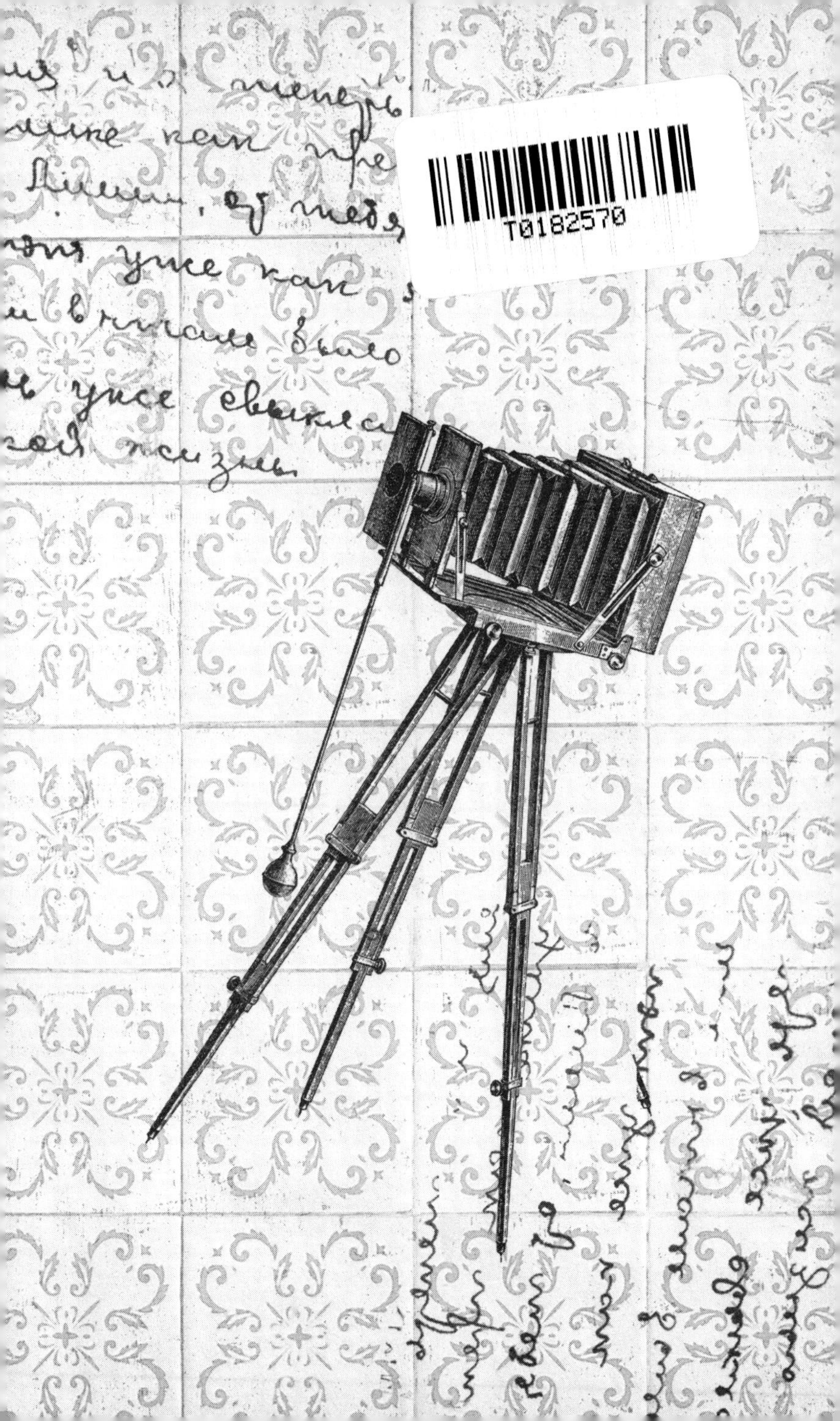

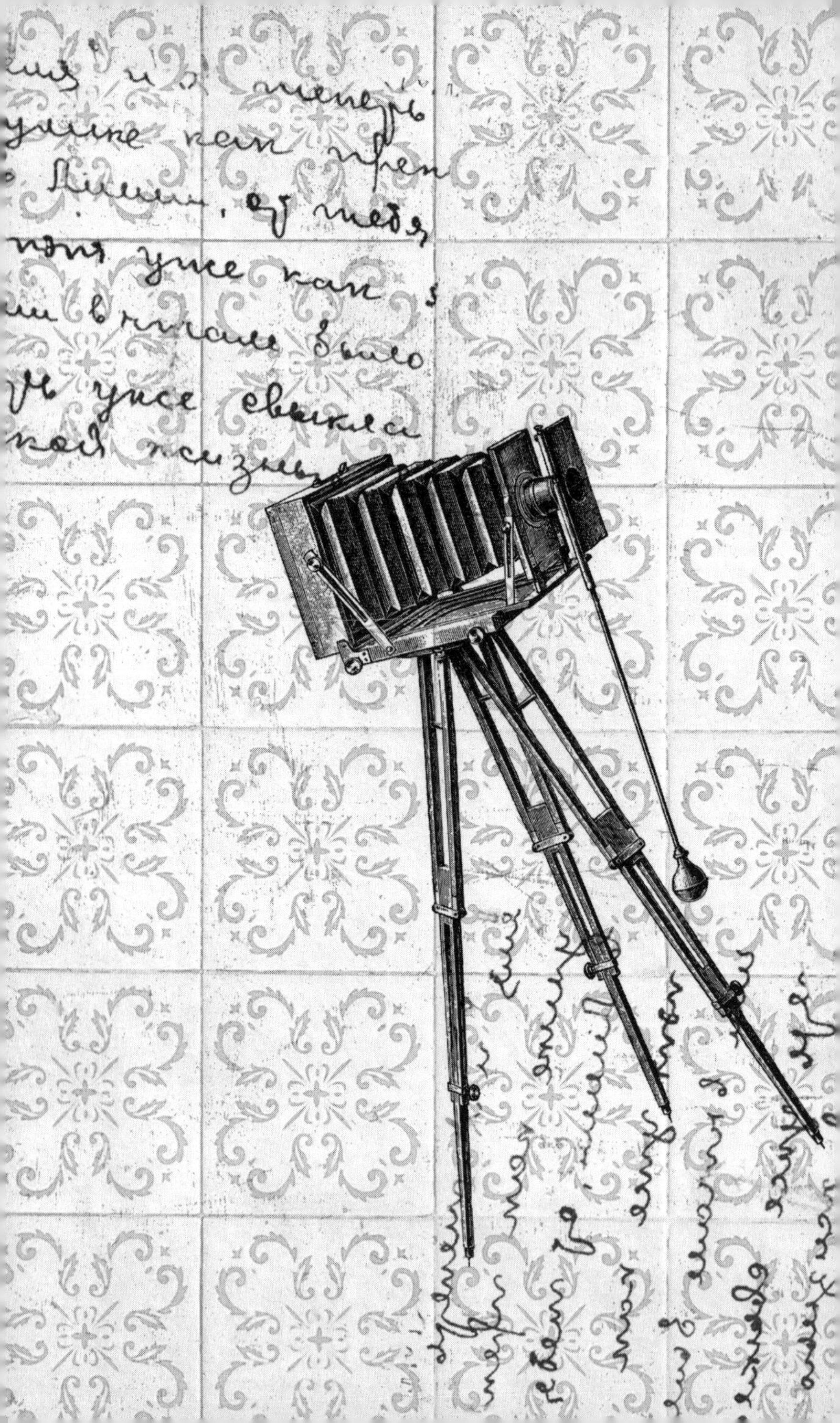

The Light Between Us

Elaine Chiew

The Light Between Us

Elaine Chiew

Neem Tree
PRESS

Published by Neem Tree Press Limited, 2024

1 3 5 7 9 10 8 6 4 2

Neem Tree Press Limited
95A Ridgmount Gardens, London, WC1E 7AZ
United Kingdom
info@neemtreepress.com
www.neemtreepress.com

A catalogue record for this book is available from the British Library.

ISBN 978-1-915584-77-9 Hardback
ISBN 978-1-915584-67-0 Paperback
ISBN 978-1-915584-20-5 Ebook UK
ISBN 978-1-915584-68-7 Ebook US

Printed and bound in Great Britain.

For S., T., & Z.

Table of Contents

Map of Singapore, circa 1920

Prologue: The Q.E.

A flash of lightning strobes across the clerestory of the Singapore Centre of Photography. The flare in the cloistered gallery reveals a portrait of a woman. She is decked out in ceremonial robes, embroidered with peonies and phoenixes; her feet, encased in beaded slippers, rest on a pouf. Her hands lie on the arms of a Chinese straight-backed chair, each finger distinctly displayed. There are no shadows on her face. Her visage is grim and stern, no semblance of a smile, as befitting an ancestor portrait. Ear-splitting thunder follows, as if the sky is being rent asunder.

A shadow dances above the portrait's wall label. Visible and then not: a man hovering before the panel lens of a large-format camera from olden days.

A thin ray of light—faint illumination from the emergency lights—stretches between the shadow and the ancestor portrait. Within the portrait, a visual effect takes hold: a separation of the membranes of oil from glass, a sliver of space, in which a bead of light sequesters and begins to glow. Gaining strength, it becomes a yolk of light, gorgeous. A sulphuric, astringent smell pervades. The emergency lights flicker, then wink out.

Through a Foreign Glass

Tian Wei starts his mornings with a breakfast of fried *you tiao* and a bowl of sweet velvety bean curd. He buys it from the *taufufah* seller, who balances on his head the tray filled with bowls covered with zinc lids. The *taufufah* seller's cries blend in with the pork porridge vendor, the *char kway teow* tink-tonk man, and all the other itinerant peddlers hawking all manner of breakfasts in the morning with banging metal rods or bicycle bells or hammers and tinplates. After breakfast, Tian Wei folds back the *pintu-pagar* shutters to let in light through the windows, and tropical heat invades. Lifting his face up to the sun to soak light into his being is almost a ritual. These fingers of heat remind him how much he depends on light to make his living, and how lucky he is to be alive. He stops still, listening to the sounds of his assistants bustling about, opening for business. These are the sounds that fill him with quiet joy. Like other Chinese photographers, he doesn't permit his assistants to touch his camera. He dusts and cleans and operates the cumbersome camera by himself. He glances at the clock: 7:15 a.m. The most propitious hours for photograph-taking in the morning are between 7:30 and 10:30 a.m.

Eight-year-old Kee Mun tugs on his sleeve near the elbow. "Xifu, you have an early morning booking. It's Mr. Teo Eng Hock's wife and two nieces, coming for a group photograph."

An important booking indeed—the wives and daughters of the elite or wealthy Peranakan Chinese tend to frequent Lee Brothers Studio up the road, but a houseboy from Mrs. Teo's had run over yesterday to notify Tian Wei that they couldn't accommodate them, and so he finds himself with a much-coveted booking. If he delivers to the ladies' satisfaction, it might pave the way for more upmarket clientele. He has every reason to believe his business is on the up and up.

He instructs Kee Mun, "Please make sure to dust all the furniture. Yesterday there were three dead cockroaches in the sireh spittoon. We can't have fine society ladies picking out cockroaches when they spit betelnut juice into the spittoon, can we? And bring out the footstools from the back room."

Kee Mun nods, getting to her chores with vim and vigour, her two pigtails swinging. She is a good egg; although her twin brother Kee Lung is tasked with clearing out their nightsoil for collection, it is always Kee Mun who does it. She also ensures all the kerosene lamp wicks are trimmed, the morning grocery shopping is done—selecting the freshest fish or vegetables from the Telok Ayer market—and still finds time to write her calligraphy as Tian Wei instructed. This is what he admires: her fighting spirit. He wants her to learn her letters, even if she is a girl.

From the ground-floor storage, his darkroom assistant Peng Loon yells out, "Xifu, come see this! Something strange I found!"

He hopes there wasn't a problem with mixing the chemical bath, which Peng Loon still struggles with. Or with the shipment of glass negatives. They sometimes come with cracked glass or flaking emulsion.

What Peng Loon shows him is indeed hardly believable. Holding a glass negative by its rough edges up to the light, he squints, making out the barely discernible image of a letter he himself had typed and sent to the Secretary of Chinese Affairs, Mr. D. Beatty, a few months ago. On the negative is also a scribble. Peng Loon can't read English, but he recognises numbers. He is pointing to a number—in date format at the bottom: *5.1.2019.*

"Xifu, this is strange. I think it's a yat ji, from the future." Peng Loon regularly has his future prospects read by a temple oracle that serves the Tua Pek Kong, the Earth Deity that protects and blesses businesses, and he is superstitious to a fault. When Peng Loon gets the shivers, he rubs his bulbous nose. "It's written in white-man language. Is it an omen? Is it from a ghost?" He looks around, rubs his nose.

The scribble is barely legible on the dark glass negative. It also looks unnatural, as if written by a ghost-child unable to control their writing implement. Even as Tian Wei tells Peng Loon to develop the negative post-haste, his mind cycles through various possibilities. As with other big questions in life, he prefers to be the proverbial Cantonese grass on the wall, a fence-sitter, neither believing nor disbelieving the existence of ghosts. He simply has no truck with them—too *ma fan* bothersome. If the letters are by a human hand, he can't imagine how any person could have gotten access to his negatives; all his employees, including himself, sleep on the ground floor on *mengkuang* mats and any noise would have awakened them. It is certainly not from D. Beatty, who had kindly asked his attaché to make an introduction for him to Mrs. Marjorie Brodie at the Poh Leung Kuk, to enquire about young girls sold into slavery or prostitution. He shudders at the thought that this might be what had befallen Aiko when she disappeared. Hopefully, Aiko-chan had escaped this fate, unlike Sansan who hadn't. Whose death was on him. However, the more dire possibility now looms, that Aiko might already be dead, but her body hasn't turned up yet. Some nights, he sleeps drenched in night sweat, mosquitoes buzzing ill omens near his head despite the net canopy. *Please. Please be alive*, his heart prays.

But how did his letter to D. Beatty end up on a dry plate glass negative?

Melancholy Realism

The portraits in the main gallery look spectral in the dark, these long-dead people who remind me daily that I keep company with the departed more than the living. I swing my torch to the front and side, its beam straight and strong. The storm has caused the fuse box to trip again— it happens often in old colonial buildings with tired electricity circuits. As my archival assistant Mahmood says, the bank of the Singapore River is one of the oldest city sectors, dating back to colonial entrepôt days, when Singapore formed part of the Straits Settlements under British colonial rule. These are places presided over by historical ghosts.

Ping. One text, then another, slide in on my three-generations-old iPhone.

> 7 p.m. tonight at Apophenia. Be there or be square.

> Seriously, can't wait to see you.

My adopted brother Sebastian has been away for seven months in Shanghai, setting up his online art brokerage, The Artistique Village. His plane must have just landed at Changi. My heart gives a small, jagged leap. Seven months is the longest period that we've not seen each other since college.

Passing the portrait I have dubbed "Mother", something flits past the corner of my eye. A cold draught along my skin; my entire being goes on high alert. I'd seen something in that split second; the image in the basin of my mind clarifies, coming into view. A man hovering before the panel lens of a large-format camera. I shake my head to clear it—*this is what happens if you stay late, staring at portraits of dour-mouthed ancestors, researching mass purges and summary executions of Chinese citizens during the Japanese Occupation, you end up seeing things*. It is but a short step from that into the void—what I call the Q.E. It stands for Quantum Entanglement, where not everything is perceived by the naked eye.

Shivering slightly despite myself, I stride through the main corridor and take the stairs down to my office, my smart brogues ringing against the Carrara marble floor.

The blue light from my computer casts an illuminated cone across my desk. Hadn't I left the overhead lights on? I flick the switch on and off—it's dual operated from both sides of the room, driving me nuts sometimes, because I never know which position is "on". The fluorescent bars flicker on, then off, returning the large room I share with my two assistants to its bluish eerie pall. There is a metallic smell.

It's then I see it: a scrim of sharp yellow light underneath the lid of the flatbed scanner sitting next to my mainframe. As if someone has pressed a button and it is xeroxing itself. My breath escapes in a hiss. I grab my handbag. Time to exit; no more trusting of electrical devices for the night, thank you.

*

Silver needles of rain lash down sideways as I sprint across the courtyard, the security guard in his hut waving at me and shouting, "Wait, miss! I can lend you an umbrella." I shake my head, tell him about the lights. He gives me an OK sign, mouths that he will look into it. As I cross the road towards the National Gallery, across from the historic Padang, a crimson red Porsche roars up, making me skip up on to the pavement in a hurry. The driver leans over and pops open the door.

"Sebastian! I wasn't expecting you." Our dinner at Apophenia isn't for another two hours and I thought I'd head home to change, to freshen up after a day spent combing the maze-like photography archives at the Centre. "You're early!"

"Took the earlier afternoon flight." He grins. "Can't let my sister get soaked in the rain now, can I?"

To be clear, Sebastian and I are not biological siblings. We trade the brother–sister endearments between us in ironic jest.

"In that case, why didn't you come five minutes sooner, brother?" I indicate my soggy hemline.

He reaches into the back and pulls out his raincoat. Spreads it over the bucket seat. Proffers a Good Morning Towel (which he happens to have) and gestures at my wet hair. "I came prepared for you."

Oh yes, the wreck that is me, double entendre fully intended. "So kind."

"Always."

Me and sports cars don't get along, because they involve all five-foot-seven-inches of me collapsing in ungainly fashion into a bucket seat, which I then must figure out how to un-collapse from.

Once inside the cramped compartment, Sebastian pulls me in for a tight hug. "Oh God, I haven't seen you in ages and you've had a growth spurt, squirt."

"Oh God, you've shrunk, you old fruity." The gearbox is grinding into my chest, but Sebastian is still hugging me.

"Is this how you talk to your elders?" he mock-growls.

"It's so good to have you home, Seb."

"It's good to be home." He releases me finally, eyes sizing up all the changes he sees in me: approval and appreciation noted. "The short bob becomes you. But you need to acquaint yourself with a hairdryer more regularly."

"Hello? I'm wet."

His side profile showcases his deep dimples to good effect; he looks very much like Bruce Hung.

"You're looking mighty dapper yourself," I say. Sebastian is wearing a midnight-blue velvet suit and sharp white shirt. A little outré, but Sebastian can make a lizard suit look chic. "Ta for the invite to TAV's vernissage. I'm sorry I couldn't make it.

Congratulations, though. From all indications, I hear it was a total success."

Sebastian smiles proudly. "Let me humblebrag for a sec. The whole thing was a snap, and you missed the show of the season."

By the time we get to Apophenia, a classy restaurant in South Beach Tower, full of glass chandeliers and dim lighting, leggy socialites and cigar-smoking bosses, Sebastian has regaled me with tales of the Chinese celebrities that showed up at his launch—Angelababy and Zhang Ziyi; the who's who of the Asian art circuit who attended—M+ Museum's major donor Uli Sigg and the chief curator of the previous Gwangju Biennale; what each VIP wore; whose flesh was pressed; who made snide comments about Takashi Murakami's work; and who got caught shagging one of the tuxedoed servers in the broom closet of the dolled-up warehouse in M50 Art District where they'd held the launch.

Seated now at a banquette, Sebastian has already ordered a bottle of Dom Pérignon. Dinner is solely liquid. I stuff my mouth with free Japanese cracker nuts.

The highlight of his launch, Sebastian crows, was that internationally famous Chinese artist Zhou Zhen had commissioned a few of his photographic bricolages to be auctioned with TAV. Zhou Zhen's artworks are brilliant. They look like traditional Chinese shanshui paintings, assembled not with brushwork but with thousands of collaged digital photographs of Shanghai's urban sprawl—from electricity cablescapes to dumpsites—to simulate a "fabled" reality. A space where old and new, the fictional and the real, collide and defy inner logic.

"Zhou Zhen invited me to his studio on Xisuzhou Road," Sebastian enthuses. "A lot of digital artists don't go in so much for concept and all that highfalutin' theory, but it doesn't faze Zhou Zhen. He was quoting John Tagg back at me about melancholy realism! How many artists do you know who do that?" Sebastian runs a hand through his hair, making the forelock curl like a becoming comma. "I mean, his whole demeanour was intoxicating. For sure, he could use an image consultant—the French beret and velvet Mandarin jacket thing must go, so clichéd—but his words were pure gold. He was talking about how, in the past, people had to ferret out information from library catalogues, information stored on index cards housed in wooden cabinets. If you wanted to look up a newspaper article, you had to do the microfiche hunt, sticking everything up on a lightbox, turning knobs left and right to magnify print and words. Today, everything is digitised. Time and space collapsed by jabbing a few keyboard tiles. Instamatic history. Zhou Zhen's works try to reflect the loss of physical effort. His laborious Chinese landscapes using instant images take months to finish." He slaps one cheek. "What a dope I am, preaching to the converted. When it comes to digitisation, you're the vinegary queen, aren't you?"

"Hey, watch who you're calling 'vinegary'. I just need to be taken off the shelf and dusted now and then."

Sebastian likes to tease me about being holed up in a museum basement, working like a mole. He has me pegged: the work of a photography archivist entails hour upon hour of sorting, staring at images, conducting condition reporting. Work not as glamorous as a curator's, and far more solitary. But it allows me to skip social-climbing shindigs with the Sze-Tohs and art events full of fake smiles and hidden conversational traps.

I clock the speed with which Sebastian is talking. His constant wiping of his hands on his trousers. He's probably popped a couple of mood enhancers on the plane. Sebastian's therapist also prescribes Xanax for his anxiety and sleep problems. Something's off, I can tell.

The online art brokerage is Sebastian's brainchild, a business idea he has nursed since our Stanford days. Every customer fills out a questionnaire, and TAV's high-tech Amazon-like algorithm recommends the best market price for an artwork within the client's budget parameters, as well as other artists they might like but might not necessarily have heard of. Key-in a range of criteria—artist, medium, price, size, region, time period—and voila, an instant, tailored, well-researched list. Additionally, he offers a bespoke consultancy service for corporates, which sends him jetting around the world and staying at top-notch hotels on their dime.

"How is Adnan?" I ask.

Sebastian shrugs, "I wouldn't know."

Warning bells. "Did he not fly back from Shanghai with you?"

"No. He says he has a lot to do. Which is true."

I wait to see if there is more to come. There is.

Sebastian sighs. "OK. I would have told you long before this if you had bothered to pick up the phone and call me in Shanghai. Getting hold of you is like trying to reach Vega."

Emotionally unavailable, that's me, and my heart knots with guilt. A thought intrudes: the other side of emotional unavailability is fear—fear of emotional overreach.

"Anyway, I think Adnan and I are on the outs." His tone is casual, but the look in his eyes is not.

A frisson of something springs up inside me. Furtive, illicit. The sommelier swerves in between tables. Sebastian waves him over, orders another bottle of DP.

Sebastian is bisexual, and I've watched him cycle through a series of partners since I met him. His relationships with women have a usual shelf life of three months, the ones with men a little longer. Even so, Adnan has overstayed, nearing the six-month mark. I'd chalked it up to being friends long before that, and Adnan being Sebastian's business partner for their online art atelier. I've seen how happy Sebastian has been during their time together. Adnan is mentioned in practically every fourth sentence. They buy socks for each other. Cloying snaps of them at various restaurants and vacations populate their separate Instagram accounts. Being in love spurs you to new heights in all areas of your life. Abominable cliché, but, in this case, true. TAV really took off. Untangling the romantic from the business and friendship braided segments of this relationship will not be a snap.

I open my mouth to ask him to elaborate; he changes the subject. I get it: too close, too soon. Sebastian and I are closer than brother and sister. It makes for ambiguous territory, and he draws invisible lines which I can't cross.

"What about you?" he swerves. "How did your exhibition go?"

The launch of the first exhibition I'd been asked to curate in Singapore happened the same week as TAV's vernissage—"(Re) fashioning Female Identity Towards Modernity in Colonial Singapore." I even had a hand in the affected title. As a liminal Singaporean, more diasporic Chinese than local (Sebastian's gentle taunt reverberating in my head—"Charlie, you're about as local as fish and chips in Singapore; accept it already"), I was super lucky to have been invited to collaborate. It was a nod from the art establishment.

"Well received, I think. *The Straits Times* reviewed it, so did *Art Radar* and *ArtAsiaPacific*. Although, nowadays, I'm not sure being called 'on trend' or 'au courant' with #MeToo isn't a diss."

"It's called recuperating neglected histories in the Age of the Anthropocene." Sebastian smirks.

Eloquent eyeroll. "Of course, with the exhibition, I now have more work, not less. New research queries every day."

And just like that, seven months evaporate, and we are soon neck-deep in art lingo, discussing the philosophy of hauntology, name-dropping Benedict Anderson and Hal Foster, throwing out bile-duct-triggering phrases like "imbricated epistemology" and "Age of the Anthropocene".

During a short lull, he asks, "Attending the monthly horror show? It's the full moon."

The monthly dinner at the family mansion at 43A Goodman Road is one family obligation I am expected to fulfil as Cassandra's stepchild.

I down my champagne. Talking about these ghastly dinners has me in knots. "You haven't been to one in months. What do you care?"

"Whoa, whoa! Simmer down. Are the dinners as torturous as ever?"

"You have no idea."

"Just skip them. What can she do to you? Call the police? Threaten to cut off your inheritance?"

The inheritance jibe is ironic, and Sebastian knows it. I shake my head. I can't explain. But I've not said "no" often, and, when I do, I make sure my excuses are iron-clad.

To add insult to injury, Cassandra expects us to call her Yi-Ma, Cantonese for *Aunt*, which, oddly enough, alliterates as *Second Mother*.

"You've said no to Cassandra before?" I ask.

"Good point." Sebastian nods.

The sole consolation of attending these dinners is Atalina, Cassandra's Indonesian cook, who is a genius when it comes to Peranakan food, made in honour of Father's heritage (Cassandra herself preferring the much blander Cantonese cuisine). I absolutely crave Atalina's *ayam buah keluak* and *babi pongteh*—the best in the world, in my estimation. Without Sebastian, however, these dinners have been excruciating.

Sebastian is saying, "I'm coming this time. You won't be alone." He puts an arm around my shoulder. "I'm not afraid of a few fireworks. In art, friction is a good thing. Juxtaposing artworks in the echo chamber to create tension is a fine thing."

"But, in family life, it leads to chaos." I say it quietly and he doesn't hear me.

"Besides, Cassandra isn't all that *garang*," he says, surprising me. What does he mean she's not all that fierce? This thawing towards Cassandra feels out of character. But Sebastian has moved on and is talking now about his expansion plans for TAV.

When Sebastian talks, I don't have to. His words fill up all the empty spaces within me, between us, around our desolate relationships, pushing out the melancholy realism. Sebastian and I are effectively orphans within a family that demands we know our place. This, though, is the predicament of orphans: we want to be loved so badly that we are afraid of our hunger. And so, we draw lines. Lines become fences. Fences provide an emotional husk of protection. Nobody comes in, nobody goes out.

Epistle From the Past

In the middle of the night, I take an Uber back to SCoP (Singaporeans love their acronyms, and I see it as a mark of belonging that I'm beginning to follow suit). The driver tries to engage me in small talk, takes one look at my sozzled eyes in the rear-view mirror, and zips it. The lights are back on as I make my way down the stairs to the basement office.

That look of devastation in Sebastian's eyes when he mentioned Adnan has stayed with me. Sometimes, my closeness to Sebastian confuses me. Could things change between us? They never have. Shame suddenly coats me like grease. I can hear Cassandra intoning, *It is sinful to be harbouring incestuous feelings for one's adopted brother.*

Are these feelings romantic inclinations, though? Or am I just very lonely?

The thing is, I hadn't even known we were legal siblings, or that Sebastian existed, until we happened to cross paths at the Singaporeans-at-Stanford freshers' welcome barbecue. On the green in front of the Hoover Institution, Seb and I picked up the same plastic name-card to pin to our respective lapels—C. S. Sze-Toh. "After you," he graciously said, to which the only acceptable reply was, "No, after you." We proceeded to avoid each other, two suspicious Singaporeans uncomfortable with too much intimacy too soon, but the coincidence of our names hung between us like a *kaypoh*'s question mark, until he thrust a chicken leg with dangling crisped-up skin in my face and said, "I think I might have seen you in a family photograph."

Particularly surreal was when we got to our first names: his first name was Charles, which he never ever used, whereas I went by Charlie, hating the name Charlene.

"Chope," I said.

He shrugged, "Heh, no need to chope—all yours. You can call me Sebastian." And it turned out he knew my Chinese name—Soo Ann—because his mother had mentioned me in the past.

The conversation between us flowed so naturally, it was as if we had always known somewhere in our mutually exclusive DNA that we would become entangled. I told him I was thinking of pursuing a degree in art history. He told me I would have a hard time finding a job and supporting myself (little did he know about my provident fund). But then he gave a dry cackle; he himself was a senior majoring in computer science and economics, with a dream of setting up an online art platform. We went around for the next couple of years being generally inseparable; I sat an economics test for him once and promptly failed it, and he went to an internship placement interview on my behalf, with nobody any the wiser.

My screensaver lights up when I move my mouse. Odd— what's this?

13 February 1920

Mr. D. Beatty
Secretary for Chinese Affairs, the Straits
Settlements
Office of the Chinese Protectorate
Havelock Road, Singapore

SIR,—

It is in the most desperate and dire of situations that I've penned this appeal for your benevolent assistance in locating a young Japanese girl who is the adopted daughter of Baba merchant H.S. Tay. You may perhaps recall that I had the pleasure of making your acquaintance at the showing of The Great Gamble at The Alhambra, in the presence of Governor Sir Laurence Guillemard, where, during

intermission, we had serendipitously engaged in
the most enlivening and animated conversation
about amateur photography.

May I be so bold as to presuppose that
Mr. Sng Choon Yee from Penang, a friend of
mine and your interpreter a few years ago,
might have broached this matter with Your
Excellency in the recent past few weeks? He
has been most obliging in matters related to
my search for Aiko-san. You may well wonder
what my relationship with her is that I should
trouble my conscience so. She comes once a
month to my photography studio on Hill Street
to have her likeness captured, and, over the
years, I've developed a great fondness for her
as a sister, all the more precious as I lost
someone similar growing up in Shanghai. When
Aiko failed to visit my studio for two months
consecutively, I took the liberty of making
discreet enquiries, and suspect that she has
gone missing.

Rest assured that I have exhausted all
available channels of investigation, but,
sadly, have come to no fruitful result. It is
because I am quite at the end of my tether
that I dare enlist your help. I would welcome
a meeting at your earliest convenience.

Obligingly,
Wang Tian Wei

What is this letter and what is it doing here? There's a smell
of rotten eggs in the air that I recognise: one that can only
have wafted from the small, enclosed space of a darkroom—
the sharpness of citric acid, the scent of sodium thiosulphate,
also known as hypo-alum. I wrack my memory: was the letter

accidentally pulled from the folder containing newspaper articles about Sook Ching, the purge of anti-Japanese elements in Singapore by the Japanese military during the Second World War? Had I left it open here?

I click on the folder. Immediately, an article pops up from my search last night about the execution of a Chinese photographer. A buried article in the *Nanyang Siang Pau*—no more than three paragraphs—reporting on his shooting by the Kempeitai using the *genchi shobun* method: disposal on the spot. The accused, Tang Si Nian, had apparently been singing the national anthem of the Republic of China, the "Three Principles of the People" (三民主义), right outside the Ee Hoe Hean Club, the night before. His name was on the wanted list, and he wore glasses, which made him immediately suspect. Specifically, he was said to have fomented violence, organised the boycott of Japanese goods, and fundraised for the Ee Hoe Hean Club in support of the China cause prior to the Occupation. This throwaway detail had caught my eye: upon hearing all these charges, the accused had laughed maniacally and hung his head low for execution. The killing had taken place right outside the Japanese photography studio of Junji Naruto on High Street at 11:11 a.m. on 13 March 1942.

Apophenia. The word jumps into my mind. The tendency to perceive connections or patterns between unrelated or random things.

Message on a Glass Negative

The morning session with Madame Teo Eng Hock and her nieces has gone very well, and lunch is a simple tiffin of noodles with crispy-skinned pork *siu yuk* and wonton soup. Instead of his usual short kip after lunch, Tian Wei takes a cup of *kopi* to his darkroom and peruses the developed negative. What is this word, *apophenia*? He can't pronounce it, let alone understand its meaning. He takes down the English–Chinese dictionary he keeps handy on the shelf above his retoucher Ah Seng's roll-top desk. The word isn't listed. He reads through every single entry for *A*. The section is so bloody long, it is hard not to get booby-trapped by other words. But *apophenia* is emphatically not there. Or perhaps it does not exist. Is it a name for someone? If it is, it sounds posh. English names do sound rather posh; Feng Yu on occasion has asked others to call him by his Christian name, "Philip".

He might consult with Feng Yu regarding this strange English word. Later, they are having dinner together at the Weekly Entertainment Club, where the young blades and leading lights of the Peranakan Chinese community gather. Feng Yu is convinced that birds of a feather should flock together, as he puts it. To be considered that kind of bird, Tian Wei ought to socialise with the right set.

*

The Weekly Entertainment Club is a Chinese club, although it is mainly the Straits Chinese business elites that socialise here, rather than the wealthy new Chinese immigrants. Chock-a-block enough with stuffed shirts that even Europeans gather here on weekends. Rah, rah, Britannia, and all that. Feng Yu, as the son of a banking magnate, and with his charming, insouciant smile, fits into this social scene hand in glove. Fluent in both English and Chinese, Feng Yu has helped Tian Wei with speaking the white man's language so that he can pass off as Straits Chinese if he wishes to. It is also Feng Yu who helps massage his letters in search of Aiko until all the rough edges disappear.

News reports about future food shortages due to the war notwithstanding, the tables in the dining room are half full even at this early hour. Waiters in starched jackets swan back and forth with trays of stengahs and gin pahits. A Chinese orchestra is playing. In the corner, seated at a round marble-topped table, a bespectacled young man half rises as he sees them. He wears a Zhongshan short jacket with four pockets, signalling his affiliation with progressive Chinese politics in the homeland.

Feng Yu greets him in a hail-fellow-well-met manner. "Tian Wei, meet my friend Tang Si Nian." Handshakes all around. Something about his quick eyes and sharp chin puts Tian Wei on edge.

Over a dinner of eggs à la Milanese, grilled mutton chops, and curried fowl, Tian Wei learns the similarities between his and Tang Si Nian's sojourns to Nanyang. They both hail from Shanghai, arriving in their late adolescence when the fall of the Qing government spurred a huge exodus of young lads to the Southern Ocean. To pay off their credit passage in those early years, they did many odd jobs—newspaper delivery boy, houseboy, cook, and finally as employees at renowned photographic studios. Si Nian trained with G. R. Lambert. Tian Wei himself had lucked out—on a newspaper round one day, he'd borrowed a camera from his employer and taken an iconic photo of a rickshaw puller, who was practically all leathery skin wrapped around bones (as the Cantonese proverb went), and *The Straits Times* had used it to illustrate and accompany an article on the rickshaw coolie as a "beast of burden". The photograph had led to his employment with Junji Naruto on High Street. Naruto-san was especially impressed that Tian Wei had apprenticed with the famous Powkee Studio in Shanghai.

Tian Wei exclaims, fork stilled in his hand, "Naruto-san apprenticed with G. R. Lambert also!"

Si Nian looks surprised. He smiles broadly, but not before Tian Wei senses a hood coming down over his eyes. "Naruto-san has introduced me to a couple of his lady friends."

Feng Yu chimes in, winking, "Si Nian is a photographer with an unusual hobby."

Si Nian leans an elbow on the table. "I photograph karayuki-san. Not just for carte postales. Also half-nude. I pay them handsomely for it." Sharp creases etch his cheeks as he smiles, and the slim moustache above his lip almost quivers.

Tian Wei weighs his next words carefully. "For private consumption, you mean?"

Feng Yu smirks. "Not quite so honourable, I'm afraid. An underbelly economy of illicit images, if you like. The Ghee Hin Kongsi are particularly enamoured with these photographs, isn't that so, my dear Si Nian?"

Si Nian flicks hair out of his eyes. "Takes one to know one, chum."

Feng Yu puts down his utensils, tucks his napkin more securely around his collar in readiness for dessert. "Be careful how you phrase that. I don't mind looking at a few dirty pictures, but I certainly have nothing to do with triads." Leaning back, he adjusts his pince-nez. "I introduced you because I thought you could be of help to each other. You see, how shall I put this? Tian Wei has been searching for a missing Japanese girl. Si Nian, with your contacts within the Ghee Hin, I thought perhaps you might be able to enquire if she has been—" he coughs delicately, fist rising to mouth— "if she has come to an unfortunate end."

Blood rushes to Tian Wei's head. "If she's dead, her body should have turned up by now." The waiter serves up bread-and-butter pudding, but he has lost his appetite. He glares at Feng Yu, who raises both hands as if to say he'll shut up now.

"Is she from one of the brothels you've visited?" A knowing look on Si Nian's face.

Tian Wei guesses what he is thinking. "She's not! She's Hudson Tay's adopted daughter. It's true her mother was a former karayuki-san, taken into Hudson Tay's household as a mistress, an ernai. Aiko is a friend, more like a sister to me."

Si Nian's smile widens; again, it does not reach his eyes. "And what do you suppose has happened to her? An adopted daughter of such an elite Chinese businessman as Hudson Tay is unlikely to have been forced into slavery or prostitution, not unless her father had a hand in it."

"Why do you say that?"

"Are you sure she hasn't run away of her own accord?" Si Nian counters.

"Why would she do that? When she came to my studio in July, the last time I saw her, she looked happy and fulfilled; her sole complaint was having her freedom circumscribed. But that is the lot of society girls. She might be courageous, but she's not a rebel. Nor is she foolhardy. How would a young female runaway survive on the streets?"

"True." Si Nian steeples his fingers. "I see you have been much distressed by her disappearance." His fingers interlace. "Do you suppose it has anything to do with the riots and protests in Chinatown last year?"

Tian Wei frowns. "What do you mean?"

Feng Yu sucks on his teeth, gesturing for the waiter. Their glasses are empty.

Si Nian leans over, voice dropping to a whisper. "Your girl is Japanese. Have you not been following events in our Motherland from last May? The students' protests over the very unfair terms of the Treaty of Versailles? Did you not hear that the Kuomintang branches here have been pressuring Chinese businessmen to refuse dealings with the Japanese?"

Tian Wei looks sharply at Si Nian, his unease rising. "I fail to see your point." Does the slick way in which Si Nian slipped in mention of the riots and the Kuomintang mean he knows more than he is letting on?

"All I am suggesting is that perhaps there is a connection." Si Nian takes off his owlish frames, twirls them by the stem. "I could enquire for you with the Ghee Hin. They have eyes and ears everywhere. I'd do it discreetly, of course."

The Ghee Hin! If being pressured by Feng Yu off and on to join the Kuomintang isn't bad enough, Tian Wei is even more leery of getting involved with secret societies. However, not once during the months since Aiko disappeared has it ever crossed his mind that her father might have something to do with it. The thought that Hudson Tay might be complicit in not turning over every stone looking for Aiko makes him sick to his stomach.

Souvenir Postcard

The broadband goes blink; none of us can get internet access within SCoP for ten minutes. I hope the research notes I've spent all morning typing up didn't melt away when the connection dropped. I haven't yet had time to save them in SaneCloud, our digital repository. Ensconced as we are in the basement, we have no idea if another tropical rainstorm is underway. Without sunlight, we've become Minions: Mahmood's glasses give off a Seventies vibe, and Yoo-lin has two pairs—one for distance, one for reading art historical treatises with tiny fonts.

We wait. We reboot the routers. We try again. A message pings from ISP Starhub. *You are experiencing temporary service interruption.* Yoo-lin gets the same message, swears in English, Mandarin and Hokkien. *Si lang gui* (dead fucking ghost) sounds both cute and horrendous in Hokkien. She and Mahmood take the opportunity to head off for their usual morning break of kopi and kaya toast. They wave and ask if I'd like a *dabao* coffee. I shake my head.

Not long after they leave, a door bangs somewhere, startling me, followed by that same metallic odour.

My screen flickers and comes back to life. I sigh in relief, but what shows up on it is not what I had been looking at just before it went dark.

23 March 1920

Mrs. Marjorie Brodie
Poh Leung Kuk
Lock Hospital
Kandang Kerbau, Singapore

MADAM,—

Upon my soul, I received your latest missive detailing your various diligent enquiries on my behalf with gratitude and a fair amount of wretchedness. I sat at the open upstairs window of my studio reading these notes you've enclosed from the Bishop at the Methodist Mission and Matron-in-Charge of the St. Andrew's Mission for Women and Children, and their disappointing replies fill me with a sense of growing despair.

How is it possible that a young girl from a respectable Baba merchant family simply vanishes into thin air?

As more time passes (it has now been six months since Aiko would have come to my studio for a portrait), I fear that the trail of clues to her disappearance has run cold. I fear for Aiko's well-being. Inasmuch as I trembled at the thought that she might have turned up at these missions, or indeed, at the Poh Leung Kuk, I would give anything to know she is still alive.

Dark thoughts indeed, but I confess I feel at ease in sharing them with you. When I came to the Poh Leung Kuk for the first time, you knew immediately that I had not come with nefarious intent, unlike perhaps the Chinese

towkays or coolies you've encountered who
come looking to make matrimonial matches or
licentious arrangements. You allowed me to
enter your confidence so readily that I truly
sense a kindred spirit in you. Your zealous
concern for the welfare of girls and women in
need of protection has touched me deeply.

Alas, my requests to meet with Aiko's
father, Hudson Tay, have been rebuffed time
and again. I've even presented myself at the
front door of his mansion on Emerald Hill,
lain in wait inside a rickshaw to catch him
going in and out. He rides in a chauffeured
Studebaker. Catching him is no easy feat. Only
once have I succeeded in accosting him, and he
warned me with a severe gleam in his eye that
I should mind my own business. To be sure, I
know that Aiko is merely his adopted daughter,
she has many a time bemoaned his indifferent
attitude and neglect, but I ask you, is this
any way for a father to behave?

Aiko-chan is like a sister to me. She loves
the pianoforte and Japanese teaware and hand-
painted scrolls, and she's taken to learning
Malay properly with me by reading Chrita
Dahulu Kala — famous Chinese folklore and
legends, written in Baba Malay. From the first
time she came to have her portrait taken for
Lunar New Year a couple of years ago (I've
enclosed a first photograph of her), she was
impish, asking me many questions about how to
operate my camera, how the box did what it
did—capture the soul of a person on a glass
plate. Over time, she also told me how her
mother, a karayuki-san, was brought into the
household of Hudson Tay as his mistress when

```
Aiko was eight. Prior, she had grown up in the
environs of Malay Street, where the Japanese
brothels are. At six, she learned to slaughter
a chicken. At seven, she helped cook meals
for all the brothel workers. She made her own
yukata. You would not for a moment think she
had lowly origins if you were to see her as
she was dressed in the photograph. Once again,
I beseech you to employ whatever means are at
your disposal to help me locate Aiko-chan.

                  I remain, humbly and gratefully,
                                    Wang Tian Wei
```

An untinted photograph accompanies the letter. A young Asian girl in a high-necked Edwardian frock with blown sleeves and a bibbed front. Her hemline dips just below the knee. She wears a broad-brimmed hat. Her gaze is slightly off-centre; a worldly, wise smile tugs at the corner of her lips. In one hand, a bouquet; the other rests on a rustic fence of twigs and flowers. The painted backdrop behind her is a pastoral scene of the English countryside: open fields, hedgerows, a shaft of light, as in a Turner painting.

I reread the letter. I look closely at the photograph. Impishness. Yes, I see it. Also, her direct stare. Rather than the stiff poses common at the time, hers suggests that she's come in from a country stroll, picked some flowers, and she's now ready for a repast of scones and Swiss rolls. Gracious, refined—a young lady of the world. No hint whatsoever of the "lowly origins" this photographer Wang Tian Wei intimated.

My brain goes into overdrive: what is the meaning of these letters, landing as they have done in my archival folder? In whimsy, I've now dubbed the folder Q.E., to mean *quantum entanglement*, because it's where past and present collide. But, really, where did the letters come from?

I head upstairs for a breather. The sky outside rolls with thick cumulus. It's hot and humid, even underneath the shade of an angsana. With another storm brewing, the sunlight feels heavy. I'm suddenly aware of how hard and fast my heart is beating, blood rushing through my veins thick and full, as if I've not realised before how fully alive I am. Am I imagining things? Like the first letter for D. Beatty, the photo and this second letter appeared on my screen as if by ghostly summons. I've not had dealings like this before; I've had no encounters with the supernatural or occult. But then, the Southeast Asian region is replete—in fact, enamoured— with ghosts and spectres, tales of possession and spirit mediums, *tangki* and *bomoh*. So, why not? Who says it can't happen?

But why me?

*

Mahmood rolls his ergonomic chair up to my desk, eyes narrowing as he scans both the letter and photograph open on my screen. He rubs a perceived smudge on the bottom of his glasses, shaking his head in response to my previous question. "Never seen it before, Kak."

He calls me Older Sister in Malay as a form of respect for my authority. Out of the office, he uses Charlie. Occasionally, he'll call me T.B.—which stands for Taukeh Besar, or Big Boss (not tuberculosis—Mahmood's sense of humour, not mine). I practise my Malay with him, but the way I use it totally cracks him up. "Bosan means bored, Kak, not bossy."

His eyebrows crook above his glasses now like umlauts. "Nice-looking anak dara." His phone pings, and he rolls his chair away. "If it isn't from our archives, maybe it's from the Lim Shao Bin Collection?"

Smart guy. It could well be from the Lim Shao Bin Collection, situated within the National Library, since it and SCoP share the same digitisation vendors. The Lim Shao Bin Collection includes many *cartes de visite* and *cartes postales*, produced by early Singaporean photography studios as souvenir photographs, mailed to and from pre-war Singapore and Japan. An incredible repository of the social life and community of Japanese residents in Singapore before the Second World War. And Aiko is certainly a Japanese name.

However, letters aren't usually appended to these photographs. He's wrong there. The letter's content isn't what would normally be on a *carte postale* either. It makes for quite the mystery, and I intend to figure it out.

Artefact or Forgotten Object

The photograph that had arrived in my Q.E. folder with Wang Tian Wei's letter is a replica of one from our archives. It took hours of sifting through the historical photographs in our digital repository to find her. It is mislabelled in our caption, which identifies her as Chinese.

Aiko.

My thoughts churn. My heart thumps in an uneven cadence. I gaze at the photograph, dated circa the 1920s, as accurate as our archival records can be at present. There are no further identifying marks on the verso of the photograph. No calling card, no stamped imprint of a Chinese studio.

This is the world I live in—a world of historical photographs—but what passes most people by is that the past too could have solidity. Barthes said that the photograph is a forgotten object, we are fixated by its content alone; we forget its physicality. When the past acquires physicality, it brings back what Sebastian said at Apophenia: the collapse of time with space, the return of the real. When history slides up next to us, as easy as the press of a button on a microfiche hunt, it becomes fantasy, an alternate dimension. It becomes sensorial, close enough to perceive: a spectre.

My search within our early photographers' database has yielded no indication of a Wang Tian Wei. There is, however, a listing for a J. Naruto. I will have to look through the year-by-year *Chinese Commercial Directory of Straits Settlements* and the *Anglo-Chinese Directory of Malaya* to ensure I've not missed a listing for Wang Tian Wei. His studio might have been under a different name. There aren't many photographic establishments on Hill Street. If we archivists had a complete register of commercial establishments in the area circa 1920, I'd be able to narrow down the possibilities, but we don't. However, given its proximity to High Street, which during the colonial era had savoir faire, and where another prominent studio was located— Lee Brothers Studio—searching for Lee Brothers might help me locate the names of other businesses close by.

Mahmood is signing off for the day. He pushes his chair up to his desk and slings his satchel across his body. "See you tomorrow, Kak. You've been sibuk like anything all afternoon. Find what you were looking for?"

I reply without glancing up, "Yes and no, tell you tomorrow. Take your brolly."

He nods. "Monsoon season. Don't stay too late. A bit creepy in here by yourself."

"I'm not afraid of ghosts."

"Betul ya, hantu tu, takut Kak," he teases in Malay. Right you are, the ghosts are afraid of you.

Ping. A text slides in. Sebastian.

> Where tf are you? Why are you avoiding me? 我要跟你算账。

He wants to settle accounts with me. When Sebastian uses Mandarin with me, I know that he has worked himself into a lather. My adopted brother has a thing for histrionics—what he calls "putting on a performance". I haven't been avoiding him; I've been busy ferreting through the archives in search of Aiko's photograph.

> Seb: Has something happened?

> Me: In my office. Working late as usual.
> Mysterious letters popped up in my digitisation folder. I only ever keep the digital versions of our historical photographs in there. A prank?

(In fact, until I typed the word *prank*, I hadn't thought any such thing. But it seems saner and more logical than to suppose a supernatural occurrence.)

Me: Who would bother tricking an archive, eh?

Seb: OMG, something exciting and totally incredible has finally happened in Charlene Sze-Toh's life! Your art historian act is being shredded. All those years raving about Gethenians and tesseracts and quantum leaps. Fuck, Charlene Sze-Toh has been Awakened!

(OK, he's not being histrionic. He's upset about something and being bitchy.)

Me: Stop making fun of me.

Seb: Seems like a wormhole has opened up in your brain.

Me: Eff off.

Seb: Easy enough to test if it is real or fake. Write something back to sender.

Me: And how would I do that?

Seb: Use your imagination.

(He key-smashes a row of emojis, which leaves me baffled.)

Me: I'll see you at dinner tomorrow night.

(He sends a GIF of a firing squad.)

*

I imagine a Chinese photographer in colonial Singapore. Most of them were Cantonese, gradually taking over the studio photography market from renowned European photographers like G. R. Lambert (who advertised themselves as photographers of the King of Siam and Sultan of Johore, as well as "the best reputed firm in the colony"). By the time of the Great War, few European studios remained. In colonial Malaya (which included Singapore as part of the Straits Settlements), the Straits Chinese or Peranakans were early Chinese traders dating back to the fourteenth and fifteenth centuries, intermarrying with local Malay women, and therefore prime candidates for key posts such as kapitans (the business intermediaries between the British and the locals) and the only group conversant in English, Chinese and Malay. Their sons were even sent to England for further education. The British differentiated between the Straits Chinese (who had the privileged status of being British subjects) and the *sinkeh* (新客)—the new Chinese immigrants, arriving later, between the eighteenth and early twentieth century—who were mainly cheap labour and could be repatriated at the drop of a hat. Here is my question: how did a Chinese photographer learn to write English so well he sounds like a Straits Chinese speaking the King's English with a plum in his mouth?

Wang Tian Wei grew up in Shanghai. Likely he is Shanghainese. In his letters, he has signed his name using a transliteration from Mandarin; if he were Cantonese, it would have been Wong Tin Wai. That also makes him a *sinkeh*. And he indicates that he reads Malay. Does he belong to the small class of Chinese literati who immigrated to Nanyang from China following the fall of the Qing dynasty? Singapore, as a commercial entrepôt, was aswirl with ethnicities and languages at the turn of the twentieth century. Hill Street was also a prominent address, given its proximity to the Padang and the hub of colonial life. This tells me something about his class aspirations: ambitious, even cocky, if he dared to write to bigwigs like D. Beatty and claim acquaintance with

Sir Laurence Guillemard. And did his affection for Aiko run deeper than fraternal love?

I open up a text box within a PDF. My fingers hover over the keyboard. As a lark, I start out in Mandarin, introducing my name, hoping to put the last five years I've spent devotedly studying it to good use now: 我名字叫司徒苏安 ...

When I next look up, it's past nine p.m. I save the letter as a PDF in the folder in which the first and second letters from Wang Tian Wei had appeared, together with the photograph of Aiko. Return to sender. Go back through the same cervical canal from which you came. As mysteriously as an electron. As unknowable as a tesseract. Or perhaps, since images are stored digitally as a compressed matrix of numbers, deposited in a folder within another folder uploaded on to what we euphemistically call the cloud; this is what the past is in four dimensions: an endless stream of numbers.

Back to Sender

Tian Wei can't sleep. He feels as if ants are crawling underneath his skin. The remnants of dinner dredges the pit of his stomach, as does the insinuation from Tang Si Nian about Aiko's father. Like a serpent's hiss, he hears the question in his inner ear: *Has Aiko been kidnapped as retaliation against her father's mercantile dealings with the Japanese?* Is that why she has been missing these many months and scant action has been taken by her father?

There is also the matter of the letter on the dry plate negative. That word *apophenia* appearing at the bottom of his letter to D. Beatty, and now, no more than a week later, a letter winging its way to him from a hundred years in the future. Can he trust his own eyes? Giving up sleep altogether, he rises silently and walks upstairs to take the print of the mysterious letter to the roll-top desk. He sits on a wicker chair, planking his legs on top of an adjoining cane chair, and lights up a Woodbine. Taking long drags, he rereads it.

Dear Mr. Wang Tian Wei,

我名字叫司徒苏安 ... My name is Sze-Toh Soo Ann. I received two of your letters in search of a young girl named Aiko. I haven't gone cuckoo or anything like that, but thought I'd let you know that your letters were misdelivered not just to place, but also to time. It's 2019 Singapore here, and I work in a museum, archiving old photographs.

Let's be pen pals. In 2019, we don't stand much on formalities, and we write letters averaging between eleven and twenty-five characters to each other on our phones. As short as "R u there?"

If you do happen to get this, I can only deem it serendipitous.

P.S. Please call me Charlie.
7.1.2019

A woman writing to him from 2019 Singapore! Who has received two of his letters, "misdelivered not just to place, but also to time". Most irregular. If she is from the future, he is surprised that she is worried about the misdelivery of a missive concerning a girl, whom, to her, is long dead. There is no doubt that the letter to Marjorie Brodie is his. He typed it out on a black Remington borrowed from Feng Yu—its keys bone-white, its body jet-black—and the ribbon continuously smudged all the rounded curves of the letter *a* because of the stickiness of the button.

He can't wrap his mind around it. How the devil did it happen? Is this a dream? Is she truly from the future? What sort of celestial intervention is this? What is more, she wishes to correspond. Like pen pals. *Wo de tian ah*. Is she proposing that their letters all be between eleven and twenty-five characters? Tian Wei lights up another Woodbine and smokes it to the stub.

Bits of conversation among the literati at Powkee Studio in Shanghai float up in his consciousness—it was how he learned about the invention of the camera—Niépce, Daguerre, William Henry Fox Talbot and so on—how it was reported that, when the camera was first brought to China, the Chinese had feared this foreign instrument, believing it to steal one's soul upon capturing one's image. The literati at Powkee had debated this—not whether the camera could steal one's soul, but whether in fact the Chinese had feared the invention. The concept of capturing light and inverting its image was familiar to Han philosopher Mozi in the fourth century BC, and influential scholars like Kang Youwei and Liang Qichao, whom Master Ouyang entertained at the Studio, had discussed how the Chinese could adapt foreign technologies easily to local practices, and perhaps even surpass their envisioned uses by instrumentalising them as catalysts for social reform. He had listened with wide-eyed wonder, only half understanding the words used by these intelligent men. It cloaked the camera in an aura of mystery that perhaps explains its perpetual appeal to him.

How odd that the occurrence of the letter has managed to displace his worry about Aiko, albeit for a short time. Perhaps the future has more supernatural possibility than he can fathom. Perhaps such a miraculous thing like a letter from the future, whether he chooses to believe it or not, is a lightning stroke in the dark, a glimpse of hope. There are many things we human beings cannot know. But, like a temple oracle, the future has arrived on his doorstep. Or, more accurately, it has been imprinted on his glass negative. He can write back to the future and enquire: Would Aiko be found? Would she be safe? Would all be well and end well?

He hauls himself to his feet and lugs Feng Yu's old typewriter from under its burlap cover, placing it in front of him. Swiftly, he rolls in paper. The first clack of the keys produces a twinge in his stomach, almost of hunger. But the words do not come easily. He struggles with the composition of each sentence. Often, the gist of what he wants to express feels close enough to grasp but floats away just as he reaches out for it. Feng Yu's typewriter chatters long into the night. The floor is littered with curled unfinished drafts. When he rolls the final letter out, the blush of dawn is staining his window and birds are chirping outside. He reads the finished letter with satisfaction. He burps. Then he realises to his dismay that he has no way of sending the letter to her.

Shoot!

The letter sits open, bold as brass, on my computer—the first thing I see when I arrive this morning and jiggle the mouse to dissolve the screensaver.

13 April 1920

Dear Miss Charlie (I think I shall call you Miss C.):—

Thank you kindly for your letter. I ought to set your mind at rest: I don't think you've "gone cuckoo", but I must confess to being awfully surprised when I received your letter on a glass negative. I think you gave my darkroom assistant Peng Loon the most incredible fright. I wager he will be off to Thian Hock Keng Temple post-haste this morning to get a fu lu talisman.

If your letter has come from 2019, and I'm at a loss as to how this could have transpired, thinking about Singapore a hundred years from now makes my head verily spin. Do you still use spittoons and chamber pots? Beg your pardon, I can't help but wonder. The cockroaches love to die in our spittoon; pity the mui tsai whose job it is to get rid of these demons from the underworld.

I am most touched by your concern for Aiko from a hundred years away. There appears, though, to be a misapprehension, for this letter most certainly reached its rightful addressee, who has since replied.

I've also enquired hence at various other missions, churches, and hospitals, and Aiko has not turned up in any of them. At first, I was much relieved, but now I'm not sure if she won't turn up dead.

I have also conferred with the Chief Inspector of Police, who is making enquiries — or, at the least, is on the lookout. What his being "on the lookout" means, I can't guess. The police, he said, in a supercilious tone, whilst stroking his curly moustache, have many important matters to attend to, and if the father himself has not filed a missing person report, then the hands of the police are tied. I had not imagined that the hands of the police could be so easily tied. He suggested that perhaps she has gone upcountry to do a spot of travelling. Just like upper-class missies do, eh? And Hudson Tay is known to have relatives in Malacca and Penang. Upper-class missy! If Aiko had heard, she would have fallen over laughing.

Permit me the liberty to tell you about Aiko. Aiko hasn't always been a missy. In fact, she used to run rampant around the red-light district containing Japanese brothels: Malay, Malabar, Hylam, Bugis, and Tan Quee Lan Streets — she knew them like the back of her hand. She sneaked off to go kite-fighting (not kite-flying) with boys. She spied on

the beautiful taxi girls at the continental
dance halls. She even helped paint some of the
colourful Japanese lanterns hanging in brothel
doorways. She is as dear as a sister to me,
and not just because we are both of lowly
origin. I do not understand why no one else
sees how full of life she is.

After she was adopted by Hudson Tay,
propriety had to be observed. Aiko was sad
when her mother changed out of her beautiful
yukatas and wore koon sahs. Aiko herself had
to be chaperoned everywhere. She could no
longer be with whomsoever she wanted, and she
had to learn to cook and sew in preparation
for marriage. I believe she came to my studio
because it provided a sanctuary from the
confines of her existence. She would bring
her notebook, full of strange drawings of
imaginary beasts. She attended an art class on
Bukit Timah Road every week. Aiko also has a
photographic eye. When I took her to an opera
at Lai Chun Yuen, she drew the lovelorn looks
between the Cowherd and the Weaver Girl with
such exactitude, it made me pilu. I don't know
if you know Malay. It is a remarkably poetic
language, which I learned only when I arrived
on these shores. "Pilu" is a Malay word that
captures sorrow and melancholia, the purity
and essence of both.

I enclose herewith a photograph of myself,
taken by Aiko. I look a right dandy in this
Shakespearean get-up, but I wanted to indulge
Aiko. The banjo belongs to my good friend Lin
Feng Yu, who is not only a dandy, but also an
atrocious musician. Writing this, I remember

that day as if it were happening all over again — how Aiko dissolved into such a fit of giggles she could barely stand up. It did my soul good.

Sincerely yours,
W.T.W.

11.1.11.11

A subsonic buzz invades my mind. Cotton wool in my ears. That sulphuric odour again. I walk upstairs and head out to the cafe on the corner to gather my thoughts. The Blue Mouse sells ferret-pooped coffee beans, and their coffees are severely overpriced. Some have fancy names and unpredictable quality, either as thick as petroleum or so milky it could pass as Earl Grey. I order a Kurasu Kyoto long black—my usual.

I think about the letter I've just received. I am Miss C.—how quaint. His tone is wry, but intimate, his concern for Aiko so palpable it punctures me. Such genuine care. Perhaps it is not simply fraternal love, but I choose to believe it is pure. It's what all the letters have been about. First, he had sought high-up help from the Office of the Chinese Protectorate; next, the Poh Leung Kuk (the Office for the Protection of Virtue), established by the Chinese Protectorate in 1888 and under its supervision. The Poh Leung Kuk's role was to provide inspection and treatment for prostitutes with venereal diseases. Enquiring there meant Wang Tian Wei suspected that Aiko might have been abducted and sold as a *mui tsai* or prostitute, and perhaps she could have turned up seeking protection in one of these missions or hospitals for girls.

The Japanese angle stirs within me an unease, a half-baked intuition: did Aiko being Japanese and going missing have any connection to what was happening in 1919 in Singapore following the Treaty of Versailles, when riots broke out all over Chinatown and Chinese businesses were urged to boycott Japanese goods? These events are well-documented in Singapore's history books. Rickshaws being burned on the streets because they were manufactured in Japan. Japanese goods being thrown down onto the streets from shophouses. Bonfires everywhere. Call it serendipitous happenstance or eerie magick, a Chinese photographer with a link to a Japanese girl has landed on my desk. A mood grips me—a fevered tumbling—and I check the date on my phone: 11 January. I check the time: 11:11. A coincidence of numbers. A beat thrums in my ear.

Overhead, clouds swirl in wild biomorphic formations: a heron, a whale, an elephant's head—a large convoy of moving shapes. A flock of koels dock on the branch of a nearby flame tree. A small aircraft speeds across the blue sky, skywriting in Chinese, 一生一死, 独一无二。

In life, as in death. You and no other.

The Beauty Effect

There aren't many rules for living in Cassandra's Guest Lodge, 43B Goodman Road—adjacent to the family mansion at 43A, although 43B shouldn't rightly be called a lodge, because, after its renovation, it became a tiered cake of four floors, a fake classic revival monstrosity with fripperies. Cassandra doesn't monitor my comings and goings; in fact, other than the sporadic barbs, or petulant requests that I attend more than the monthly ritual dinner, she leaves me well enough alone. Deep down, I'm convinced she is neither as evil nor as bitchy as she makes herself out to be. During the vacations that I was obliged to spend with Father, there were kindnesses from her, usually shown through food or a gift here and there.

Necessarily, as an art historian focused on the neglected histories of women, I understand that women are products of their milieu; they are sometimes complicit with the systems that have helped forge their status in society. Sebastian disagrees. He likes to paint Cassandra as living up to the hilt the stereotype of Shrewish Chinese Mother. He has said more than once, "Just pick up any Malaysian or Singaporean literature—it's replete with at least one dragon mother, one crone mother-in-law, sometimes both, and they can shred your dignity into smithereens even as they toss mahjong tiles." For someone dealing with unbound contingencies in art, how reductionist of Sebastian. In any case, Cassandra is the only mother I have now.

I first met Cassandra with Father at a Japanese eatery near South Ken Tube. Ostensibly, this was to help me make an important decision: to come and live with him and Cassandra in Singapore *or* to remain in England and transfer to boarding school. I was eight; it was the day after Mother's funeral. Thank God he spared me Linton and Laurent's company—it would have been too overwhelming: losing the only family I knew and, in one fell swoop, gaining a gaggle of them that I didn't. Father ordered me a teriyaki chicken bento and a grape juice. I stared at Cassandra, who was all suited in black, including a hat with a veil. Mourning costume. Even then, I knew a spectacle when I saw one. Was she actually grieving a woman she considered her nemesis, or was this a private scoff at the ludicrousness of my existence? Oh, look, practically an orphan, and one with such a rojak upbringing: an absent mother who died, raised by a host of nannies of different nationalities, presented to a father she barely knew. One confused mite. And she'd be right.

I asked Cassandra if she liked Chinese legends. Did she know about Chang'e or the Seven Sisters? At school, I was reading Norse myths and legends; at home, I was reading a book Mother had given me on Asian fables and mythologies. Rather than Cinderella or Sleeping Beauty, the love story I gravitated towards was that of the star-crossed lovers, the Cowherd and the Weaver Girl. Would love be more plangent and pure on account of being able to meet only once a year, on the seventh day of the seventh lunar month, when a flock of magpies would form a bridge symbolising the Milky Way for the lovers to unite? If this story were a myth, why did we make up such a myth, and why do we still tell it so irrepressibly and beautifully every year? Is love, to the rationalists, an equation that demands proof? If so, what suffices as proof?

Deep down is another truth. Perhaps Asian fables appealed to me because they formed the prototype from which Mother emerged: her beauty like the Weaver Girl or a moon goddess— pale snowy skin, long silky hair, almond eyes, cherry lips, and face shaped like a melon seed (the *guazi lian*)—these so-called "objective" Chinese beauty standards that have shaped how women are seen, how they see themselves, and indeed, how they are styled and photographed. And yet, beauty guarantees nothing; it sometimes brings untold misery. Mother chose to exile herself from Father's palatial mansion, rather like Chang'e's banishment from the Emperor's palace in heaven.

In the mundane realm that is London, where no one knew who Mother and I were, and sometimes we didn't either, her decision brought on personal ruin—Mother descended into an alcoholic prison she voluntarily entered, and from which she seldom emerged, until the end of her life.

My question to Cassandra that day had flummoxed her. She looked at me sharply. "Chang'e? Weaver Girl? You're such an odd egg, you know?"

I've often wondered: does Cassandra see me as a hangnail she needs to bite off? Or am I more a reminder of all that she has grubbily gained by virtue of Mother abdicating her position as first wife? Of which the mansion at 43A has pride of place in her heart, with its marble staircase, stained-glass windows, its belvedere and gilt-edged balustrades, garden and swimming pool, the giant chess set on the lawn, the koi pond, every blade of every fan palmetto and every chirping gecko and every pebble in the curving driveway, even the lone saguaro cactus with its arms raised in defeat. I imagine Cassandra sweeping her bejewelled hand in a wide arc to encompass her territory: *see, your mother wouldn't have had to lose any of this if she'd just dug in her heels and held on.*

But no, Mother had to throw toys out of her pram. Breaking Father's collection of Song dynasty celadon porcelain vases. Divorcing him. Diva of the first order. What wealthy man in the circle of Chinese elites in the Eighties stayed content with one woman? By Cassandra's standards, Father was demure: one wife, two mistresses, that's it! Others have singers and models and KTV bar girls and massage therapists and mani-pedi technicians crawling out of every nook and cranny.

Cassandra often said: "Your mother was too stubborn, too proud, too eccentric. Odd begat crazy. Like mother, like daughter."

That day at the Japanese eatery, Cassandra had ripped apart the wooden chopsticks they provided as if they offended her, vigorously rubbing them together so that splinters flew off. She stabbed the California rolls and said, "Call me Yi-Ma or don't call me anything at all." Yi-Ma, or Second Aunt, which also ironically alliterates as Second Mother. I refused. Swung my heels in mute rebellion.

Father tried cajoling, then bribery with a Barbie doll, which I'd already outgrown, before finally adopting a stentorian tone. The moment became drawn out and tense; I felt everyone's stare as if I were being prodded with acupuncture needles. I gave in. I forced out the words, which clawed at my throat: "Yi...Yi...Yi...Yi...Yi-Ma."

And then I vomited out my California rolls. She leaned back in her seat, victorious.

*

What is it like to love someone so much you decide to dedicate your existence to him, only to have him consider you at best as ticking all the boxes for a trophy wife, at worst as one of life's bounteous distractions? What Cassandra experienced when Father brought home Sebastian's mother, Peony, was exactly a repeat of what Mother experienced. I didn't like Cassandra, but I could see how she felt Peony's existence to be a huge slap in the face. When you have over-mortgaged your love, pride is all you have left, and losing that last vestige of dignity can make you mean—mean enough to bypass the Chinese zodiac entirely, where at least the twelve animals are respected, and none are malicious.

The summer after my junior year at Stanford, Sebastian returned to Singapore because Peony was dying of stomach cancer. He asked me to come with him as emotional ballast, and I stayed with him in their gorgeous penthouse overlooking Marina Bay rather than at Father's mansion. Father couldn't deal with Peony's dying; he rarely visited the hospital. When he did, he stayed for only half an hour. Peony was beautiful even in her sickbed. Gaunt from her illness, her waxen skin was still porcelain smooth, her eyes a lovely mocha brown, so full of ache and love for Sebastian. Her thin birdlike wrists made graceful gestures, like a puppeteer. We would visit her at

Mount Elizabeth Hospital, me bringing baskets of fruit to rot away on the windowsill, Sebastian spending evenings massaging her wrists, giving her sponge baths. The intimacy and love—I'd never seen anything like it before. Peony would hold on to my hand as Sebastian read Donne or Neruda to her, her favourite poets. Once, she said to me not to begrudge my mother: happiness comes from within, not from class, status, wealth or other externalities. It doesn't come from being loved, it comes from a spiritual generosity that is the product of loving yourself and another without any expectation of return. "Whatever you may think, Evelyn understood that," Peony said. The words did a number on me. Every fibre of my being stood up in rebellion: was she describing the same person I knew? What was Peony hinting at? It addled my head; it raised the sneaky question of whether Mother gave up everything in Singapore because of me. Was this maternal love? Did it also turn you resentful and desolate, such sacrificial love? Had I known that I would be a child born to be a burden on the one parent who wanted me, I would choose to be unborn.

One evening that summer, I finally accepted one of the numerous invitations to dinner with Cassandra and my half-brothers, Linton and Laurent. Point-blank, Cassandra told me she viewed my choice to stay with Sebastian as a betrayal: "I can understand that Sebastian needs some alone time with his mother, but you're a daughter of this house—you're making your father look bad. People will talk." Nobody talked, nobody cared, and that may have been worse as far as Cassandra was concerned. Money and noblesse oblige entail image-keeping responsibilities, and the Sze-Tohs are fanatic about toeing the line where keeping up appearances are concerned.

That night, as I was about to say goodnight and leave, I stumbled upon Father in his study. His face was a masklike snarl of grief and anguish. I was horrified; I felt as if I'd trespassed on an inner private sanctum. A grown man weeping. Father heard me as I turned to run. He called my name, asked me to come and sit. I felt I couldn't refuse. He dried his eyes with the heels of his hands. He composed himself.

All the furniture in his study was made of Chinese blackwood, sombre and highly uncomfortable. As I perched on the edge of an antique scholar's chair, he showed me what he had been clasping. A silk hankie embroidered with peonies. "Mu Dan sewed this for me," Father said. Mu Dan was Peony's stage name; as a Cantonese opera singer, she was one of the best. He told me several stories that evening: about how they met (at a charity performance for Sheng Hong Temple); their courtship (she refused his advances a total of nine times); and what made her cave (after being refused nine times, he decided he was going to give up, and came to bid her goodbye forever, giving her a scroll he'd painted himself—a drawing of a boy by a riverbank of sedge and rushes, about to release a paper boat in which he had placed fallen flowers, and the inscription 花落知多少, from Tang dynasty poet Meng Haoran's poem titled "Spring Dawn").

Father's voice became hoarse (I squirmed in the chair). "I asked her what made her change her mind after such steadfast rejections of me, and you know what Mu Dan said? 'It's because you can recite Tang poetry, and you recognise how fleeting love is.' "

He took the hankie back and folded it so that the flowers remained visible on top. "She said that, in opera, the beauty of love lies in the dance, the chase. He comes forward, she retreats; he leaves, she goes in pursuit. It's the recognition that, at any moment, love is about to be lost that draws lovers together."

Then, he proceeded to recite Meng Haoran's poem verbatim, like a public schoolboy:

"In spring, one sleeps unaware of dawn
Everywhere one hears chirping birds
In the night comes the sounds of wind and rain
Who knows how many flowers fell."

Despite spending my vacations in Father's mansion, it was the first intimacy he had ever shared with me, and it would also be the last. A raft of emotions swamped and choked me, but the top note wasn't gratefulness or empathy, or even embarrassment for him, although they were present. It was anger. Was he actually sitting there telling me, the daughter of his first wife, that, of the three women, Peony was the one he loved the most? What did that make Mother? What did that make Cassandra? Did wealth bring about this privilege of his to acquire, plunder, colonise, puncture, and shred a woman's emotional geography? Should love be "only you, and no other"? By confessing this to me, what did he expect from me? Absolution? Redemption? What, in the end, was I willing to give? Love and loyalty in exchange for this shred of humanity and vulnerability? I told him never to tell me such things again. I got up and left without saying goodnight.

But something sedimented inside me, the recognition of the similarity between father and daughter. That evening, as much as I hated to admit it, I was pierced by Father's verbatim recitation of a Tang dynasty poem. I could not ignore the cavern of feeling behind it. Mother once said that caring this deeply made you vulnerable; it was as good as walking around the world like a naked toddler. Toddler was fine, naked was brave, naked toddler was asking to be savaged. Cassandra, in response to such vulnerability, believes I need armour. Get hurt, get shot, get damaged—if you don't perish, you heal. A keloid is formed. What is love in this limited realm but a toggle between unavoidable tragedy or all-out emotional war?

It is Sebastian I trust. Between us is a small, lit space, where we can pretend that our emotional needs do not scream an open maw of want. There is no hunger here, nor a need to manifest; we are each other's sanctuary, temporary and elusive.

History is Hysterical

Dinner is in full calamity mode when I arrive. I walk past the monstrous jade sculpture of the characters 和谐—"harmony"—presiding over the entrance; it's by an up-and-coming Beijing artist and had likely cost not just an arm and a leg, but also a torso. Instead of harmony, the characters rightly should be 和平—"peace"—or, more truthfully, "uneasy truce", but Mandarin, which typically loves to push two characters together in marriage to form a compound meaning, such as that for "harmony" or "peace", has no succinct double-character translation that does the trick here. None that I know of. Our uneasy truce is that the family sits down together for a happy meal, while metaphorically poking each other with chopsticks.

All table manners seem to have been abandoned as Linton sits there calmly picking at the remains of a steamed grouper while his wife Madeleine shushes the children: Miles Wee Jun in his tiny tux (and it's so weird that the parents call their sons by their full given names) is rotoring around the dining table as an aeroplane, while Mason Wee Sun bawls in his highchair, rice stuck all over his pudgy cheeks. Neither Eloise nor Laurent is present, but there is a stranger sitting at the table, looking traumatised—Linton introduces him to me quickly as his half-Chinese, half-English friend, Matt Sharpe. Cassandra is talking, her hands waving about, gesticulating, but she can't be heard over Alexa, from which, inexplicably, a Chinese rap song I recognise is caterwauling out—Vava and Ty's "Wo De Xinyi". Sebastian's head rests atop his steepled hands, as if in prayer. This tableau vivant would have made for a perfect staged photograph—channelling Chris Yap's giclée print hung at the Peranakan Museum, *Of Fingerbowls and Hankies*; all we're missing is a puppy indiscriminately peeing—but for the fact that Cassandra immediately stops talking when she sees me.

Linton says, "Alexa, mute."

Sebastian looks up; our gazes meet. Everything is transmitted and exchanged. I take a seat next to him. His hand immediately creeps under the table in search of mine.

Cassandra's eyes land on me. "So nice of you to finally join us, Charlene."

Oh God, the ice.

I'm nineteen again, at Peony's funeral, her Chinese coffin draped with a floral carpet of lilies and chrysanthemums and peonies, the stink of the bouquet of lilies forever associated with the smell of death for me. Cassandra had made a grand entrance in a white suit so sharply delineating her figure she could have been strutting the runway instead of attending a funeral. Vermillion lipstick, kohl-lined eyes. Dominatrix at a Taoist funeral—most unChinese; it had everyone goggling. Father hadn't come and Cassandra was making an appearance on his behalf. When she hugged me, I towered over her, even in her heels, and her vampire-red nails dug into my thin arms. To Sebastian, she'd said in a voice so frigid it would have made all the ghosts believed to be hiding within the folds of the funeral shaman's robe cower: "My condolences. I'm sorry for your loss." We learned that day that we have more reason to fear Cassandra's calm than her storms.

"I'm talking here, are you listening?" Cassandra now says.

Linton sucks his teeth, reaches for a tea-tree-mint-infused toothpick. "Today is Father's birthday."

I hadn't forgotten. A morbid tradition in Cassandra's household: in addition to Sweep the Tomb Day and the Hungry Ghost Festival, ritual days when the dead are venerated, we also celebrate Father's date of birth, date of death, and their marriage anniversary. We celebrate these days religiously every year. There is an ancestral altar in a nook by itself, strategically stationed after consultation with a celebrated feng shui master, on which sits a porcelain urn that Cassandra places joss sticks in daily. She clasps her hands in front of Father's portrait and speaks to him. Love indeed carries on beyond the grave. Or perhaps a grudge does.

"I'm so sorry," and my weird habit of halting words in Cassandra's presence is back in full force, "Uhm... I didn't... couldn't think—"

"But you never do, do you? It's always only about you. We are nothing to you."

"That's ... that's not true."

"Which part? That it's not only about you or that we are nothing to you? How could you have forgotten that it was your father's birthday?"

But you don't allow us to forget, I want to say, except I can't get the words out.

Cassandra throws out a common saying in Mandarin: "you haven't placed us in your heart" (你没有把我们放在你心里), which to me has always sounded more like "you've put us next door to your heart". Its accuracy punctures me. Not in the heart, but pretty darn close.

Sebastian steps in. "It was an honest mistake, Yi-Ma. She has a lot going on at work."

It wasn't a mistake. He doesn't know that I've avoided these dinners exactly twice, only to have been found out by Cassandra. I knew this confrontation was due.

Cassandra arches an eyebrow. "When does she not have a lot going on at work? Truthfully now, what urgent things could there be in a job that takes care of old photos and memorabilia that other people have discarded? Isn't that just a glorified junk-removal service? Dumping it in a museum?"

Linton watches me with eyes that mirror the de-fleshed grouper; Madeleine performs the goldfish-mouth movements she resorts to when Cassandra is in fight-club mode. Even the toddlers have quietened, out of their league. From the corner of my eye, I see Atalina and the help hovering near the connecting door to the kitchen. Atalina is frowning, but the other two are a-titter. More entertaining than a Mediacorp drama.

"Last month, you didn't join us for dinner because you had an exhibition opening. Were you the curator?" I was one of them, in fact, but she wouldn't have cared or remembered, even if I'd told her. And how ironic, neither Laurent nor his wife Eloise were present, but they don't get the third degree. Cassandra may claim that Sebastian and I are her children as much as Linton and Laurent are, but no way are we treated the same; her sons can do no wrong.

"The month before that, on the anniversary of my marriage to your father, you lied, saying that you had a bad tummy. If I hadn't found out, what else would you have tried to get past me? Today, you arrive when dinner is practically over. If I were the sensitive, easily offended type—" Madeleine's expression across the table reveals that she would have rolled her eyes if such a gesture could go unobserved— "I would think you were deliberately avoiding these dinners. Do we make you uncomfortable, Charlene? Are we a demanding lot? Is the food not to your liking?"

At this moment, it's strange to feel a part of me float up, watch my own self cut down to size, note the smirk on Linton's face, feel Sebastian's grip on my hand, and at the same time experience a stupid sense of satisfaction that Cassandra has felt the pinch of my absences. Sebastian interlaces his fingers through mine, his hold tightening, anchoring me. His signal to stay the course. He's said it enough in the past—*Even if you can't find it in you to defy her, don't quail, don't grovel, don't let her see she can get the better of you.* But it's so hard to do this. The pressure in my chest escalates. My mouth opens, my shallow breath bubbles in and out.

Her eyes steadily assess me, the nails of her long fingers making a clicking sound as they come together, and I see that the nail polish on her right pinkie is chipped.

"You don't speak much even when you're present. You choose not to communicate with us. Yet, I'm getting a message loud and clear." She taps her fingers on her temples, as if receiving a transmission. "Ah, I see. You don't like us, but you're quite happy to leech off us. Isn't that so?"

A gasp escapes me. I often marvel at Cassandra's preternatural gift to slice through bullshit: when she senses an architecture of multi-layered truths, she zeroes in on the sliver that shows the other in the most unflattering light. Sebastian and I have discussed it in the past: was there something I was hoping to redeem in my past with Father? The job at SCoP, when it was offered to me five years ago, had come with a housing stipend. But Father asked me to move back to the Goodman Road mansion instead of getting an apartment by myself. I demurred, but then Cassandra called to tell me what my own father couldn't say—he was dying. Three to six months at most. Even Linton and Laurent called me, echoing her refrain like prepubescent choristers—*he's dying, he's dying*—and I acceded. Ultimately, Father and I didn't become closer, though we spent a lot more time together—it was an opportunity that came too late; his illness had seized hold of his lucidity. Not long after he died, the innuendoes that I'd overstayed my welcome began. I couldn't understand the abrupt switcheroo. I was hurt and confused, until Sebastian enlightened me. They'd wanted to stay on Father's good side on account of the will. He wouldn't have been of sound enough mind to have had it changed, but they weren't going to run that risk.

All this presses upon me now and my blood rises. The sentences roll out of their own accord, sudden, unexpected. Or perhaps they have been benignly accreting for years. "You don't have to kick me out. I will move out immediately, if that is what you wish." No tripping over my words. I astonish myself.

Cassandra's eyes change register; an indecipherable emotion takes hold. She tilts her head. Her mouth flattens. "My dear, did I say that? How like your mother you are. So proud. So prickly. Chinese underneath all that British gloss."

Cassandra is mercurial: when she sees that she has got under my skin, perhaps even hurt me, she mocks my Western upbringing. Or worse, references Mother, comparing us, knowing that I don't see myself in her, but wish I did. In these moments, I sense a dark connection between them, a shadowy history.

Her eyes are tracking me carefully. "We care about you, Charlene. What I want is for you to treat us more as family. Don't be a stranger. Is that too much to ask?"

Is she backing down because I've not taken her on before? Not that this is a full take-on, which I imagine to be a Chinese martial-arts spoof—a sharp slice of the sword and your clothes fall off instantly in two neat halves. "No, of course not. I'm sorry I made you feel that way." I lower my head, receiving a kick in the shin from Sebastian. I know what the kick means—*Stop being so non-confrontational*—but it takes more than one altercation for this zebra to change its stripes.

Cassandra smiles. She calls out, "Atalina, we have more chinchalok and ikan masak merah, don't we? I'm sure Charlene is famished. She always has such an appetite when she eats here."

Sebastian harrumphs. All shoulders relax, breaths exhale. Except for Linton, who has somehow picked up his iPad to read *The Wall Street Journal* during the interrogation (not the first time he's flouted table manners in open resistance). My eyes refocus on Cassandra. Scales fall off: everything about her strikes me as no longer sharp and shrill—folds have gathered under her chin, her eyelids droop at the corners, there are milk spots on her face that weren't there before. When I met her for the first time in South Ken, she had impressed me because she didn't fit the standards of a Chinese beauty—all sharp angles and pencil lines, which Mother, quoting a Chinese matchmaker, had called "misfortune-riddled". Fortunes, however, rise and fall. Age softens even the harshest of features.

Miles Wee Jun begins clamouring for dessert—"Bubur chacha! You said we could have dessert. WHERE'S MY BUBUR CHACHA?"

Mason Wee Sun kicks his little legs and thumps his fists on his tray table.

Linton leans over to whisper, loud enough to catch, "We put on quite a show, don't we, Matt?"

Madeleine touches the butterfly pin securing her bun, averting her face.

Our visitor—I'd completely forgotten about him. My eyes cut across to Matt Sharpe. Twin pools of shame are reflected there. So, this is what it feels like to be humiliated in the presence of a stranger.

Quantum Entanglement

13 January 2019

Dear Tian Wei,

May I call you Tian Wei?

I am pierced by your despair about Aiko. Though I don't know the full situation, why do you suspect that something has happened to her if her father hasn't reported her missing? Reading what you wrote about Aiko made me care about her too. I have spent two days trawling our newspaper archives and have found no mention of Aiko: dead or otherwise. This means she is probably alive. I hope this brings you a small measure of comfort.

How you feel towards Aiko is how I feel about my adopted brother: an overabundance of affection that escapes boundaries. Why, though, should love be categorised? Sebastian is the only family I can trust. With Sebastian, I can be myself.

Did you know that, in Chinese mythology, it is believed the world was created from a brother–sister pair following a cataclysmic disaster? They wanted to marry but were worried about the consequences of offending the natural order, and so, they set themselves a test. From opposite perimeters of a large plain, they would each build a fire; if the smoke from their fires should meet in the middle, they would marry. It happened as destined, and they married. However, the offspring of this union was deformed, and the foetus was broken up into disparate pieces. From these lumps of discarded flesh came human beings.

See, we were flawed from the get-go.

What is it about star-crossed lovers in Chinese mythology that makes it so romantic? Is it because they were banished to opposite sides of the heavens and could only meet once a year? As if love has to be doomed before it can be pure? Why do real-time relationships so often fail to obtain the Ideal? I yearn to know if love can be pure. Of course, I also sometimes wonder if I love the Weaver Girl mythology because I can't handle real-time relationships.

A bit about me. As an archivist digitising historical photographs, I upload and store them in a system called SaneCloud, in a folder I've cannily titled the Q.E. These must seem strange mechanics to you. Your initial letters to D. Beatty and Marjorie Brodie showed up in my Q.E. folder. Imagine minuscule atoms and particles sharing space, jostling and manifesting across vast distances. I know it sounds dorky, but is it possible that my letters reached you through a quantum entanglement, like Schrodinger's cat, appearing in my computer and a hundred years ago in your studio at the same time? I hope I won't wake up one morning and find that all I've been doing is hallucinating. Gone absolutely round the mountain and there she comes.

From nowhere, your letters arrived, colliding my past and present. My heart has been beating so fast these days, I can't catch my breath. Have you ever had this feeling of deep familiarity towards someone you've just met, like meeting the other half of yourself across the celestial realms? In fact, we have not met, nor are we likely to, are we? But I can't shake this sense that we know each other, that we have always known each other. Our epistolary connection is a warp that has bent time. If time isn't linear, this could happen, couldn't it? Our timelines could slide up in parallel, like an alternate dimension? A singularity. An enchantment.

Regards,
Charlie

P.S. Despite not appreciating being handled like a dandy, you looked like you had a blast in your Shakespearean costume! I would love to meet your friend Lin Feng Yu, who sounds like a riot. I bet he wears a pince-nez.

P.P.S. What is the name of your studio?

A Measure of Numbers

Another letter! Nothing for months and he had almost written it off as an inexplicable aberration.

Again, sleep deserts him. These mind-boggling terms. Quantum entanglement? Warp? Atoms? What are these bizarre words? What does she mean that time isn't linear? Is an "alternate dimension" something along the lines of what the Taoists believe, i.e. that the underworld exists alongside ours? Does "quantum entanglement" explain the fiddly, supernatural processes of how her letters seem to have dropped from the sky? Or, more technically, dropped onto dry plate glass negatives in his shophouse. Why in the world would this man Schrodinger own such a spooky cat? Cats jumping over coffins is one of the *pantang* phenomena Peng Loon fears about attending Chinese funerals. If a European man's cat materialised like a ghost from the future, Peng Loon's eyes would roll back into his skull and he would faint. And how does she know that Feng Yu wears a pince-nez?

She had called him "the other half of herself". Said she felt this familiar sense that they've always known each other. *Enchantment*. What a word! It invites daydreams. It invites hope. It invites mischief and licentious thoughts.

This morning, when her letter had shown up on yet another glass negative, a flock of swallows had divebombed the top of his tiled roof and sent up such a ruckus that he and his employees trooped outside to catch a glimpse. They saw the birds lift and land, bobbing on air pockets, and Tian Wei barely managed to talk his glass negatives assistant Yip Kee out of climbing on to the roof to scatter them. The birds had remained fluttering all morning, chittering up a concerto. Is this another omen?

He had quizzed Kee Lung and Yip Kee about their cleaning and storage of the silver gelatin glass negatives imported from Eastman Kodak, and there had been nothing unusual about the shipment batch. Then, a stray comment from Yip Kee—that both Charlie's letters had appeared in the same shipment box— had the three of them, arms on hips, scanning the box and the plate holders the negatives were encased in. Yip Kee noticed something peculiar, exclaiming and pointing to the numbers printed on the side of the box: *1314*. Peng Loon, bent to his waist, immediately straightened and clasped his hands in prayer, shaking them at the sky, ululating. Where the number four was concerned, which rhymed with the Chinese word for "death", Peng Loon was ultra-superstitious. Kee Lung simply shrugged, jotting down the number on his wrist for luck. There is no doubt Peng Loon will have gone to the temple this evening, to ask for another paper talisman to banish evil spirits.

One more thing: the first letter from Charlie had been dated 7 January, which he received back in April. This second letter was dated a mere six days later, 13 January, but it is now August. Their time trajectories—or, as she called it, "timelines", he notes wryly—aren't exactly parallel. Her time passes more slowly than his.

One thing is certain: these letters appear and disappear without recourse to ordinary processes. When he types out his letters to her, he places them in a glass negatives box repurposed as a letter holder, from which Kee Lung takes the letters to the G.P.O. on Fridays. He never could have imagined that depositing the letter there would do the trick. He remembers the night her first letter arrived. How he had spent all night writing back. The thought he hasn't quite acknowledged is that this is no message from the celestial realm; minor gods surely don't sit around eager to be pen pals. He wants to tell her how touched he is that she has searched for news about Aiko on his behalf. He imagines them—he and this woman from the future—face to face, having an ordinary conversation, perhaps having a meal together, even though nothing about the set-up is ordinary. He wants to tell her how cold he felt after his meeting with Hudson Tay. The man did not care about Aiko, he saw that. He wants to tell her that her letters have done something miraculous: they've managed to dislodge his worry over Aiko for a short time.

He hauls out Feng Yu's old Remington again, the sound of the roller over paper producing a satisfying crunch. Typing with two fingers, willy-nilly the words come, as if they've been dancing underneath his tongue all this while. He will attach another photograph with it. This one more representative of the young, well-bred Chinese gentleman that he aspires to be, *zhi shi fen zi* (知识分子). One versatile with his letters, able to converse in many languages. If she receives his letter, will she be impressed? Desire rises in him sharp and quick, desire that manifests under the skin and makes a man ache for touch.

The candle has burned down to its wick, a puddle of grease at its base. Tian Wei reads the letter one last time, and can't help admiring his own sentence construction: *I should like to tell you...* What a fine example of upper-crust English. See how he has progressed by slaving away at infinite drafts. He puts the letter away in the repurposed box. Yawning, his eyes land on a courtesan novel—Li Ju-Chen's *Flowers in the Mirror*. Written in the 1800s, the novel tells the story of the downfall of the Fairy of a Hundred Flowers, cursed to become human because of her arrogance. Tian Wei is partial to well-written fantasies, but then look what life has brought him—quantum entanglement! Perhaps this is all a dream, as the Buddhists believe. If it is, how lovely the illusion. He hopes he will continue dreaming.

He yawns again. Time for bed. As he creeps under the mosquito net and rolls out his mat next to a loudly snoring Ah Seng, he thinks about the far-sightedness of Li Ju-Chen. The author had railed against female foot-binding, creating a fantasy land where men suffered foot-binding instead of women—putting the shoe on the other foot, literally! If every person is constituted of yin and yang, didn't the suppression of half the population because of their perceived predominant yin nature also mean the suppression of half of oneself? These are thoughts that must be repressed because they are at odds with the order of his world, at odds with his ambition to own a high-class photographic establishment.

His thoughts fly far and wide, crossing the hourglass of eras in search of a woman from the future. What do rooms in the future look like? What does she look like? What kinds of food exist in the future? Does she care for *chee cheong fun*, which is what he loves best? Do they still use chopsticks in the future? Why did she go round a mountain? Does she have a window to look out from? Wherever she is, can she see the crescent moon, the same moon winking through slits in his *papan* window?

Words are building up in his heart, this deluge of things he wants to pour out to her, and he feels as if he could churn out letter after letter, but in this moment, there is one sole realisation. Out loud, he says, "Your letter, Miss C., brings a touch of wonder. It births hope. I am inching ever closer to finding Aiko. Because of you, all will be well."

A Camera Keeps You Honest

Feng Yu has dragged him to a meeting of the Chinese Philomathic Society in Ann Siang Hill. A large sign is propped on an easel. It informs him in Chinese that this is a fundraiser for the newly opened Chinese High School on Niven Road. A charity bazaar. A man dressed in nondescript white shirt and black trousers—the school principal, presumably—is roundly berating several teachers in a mixture of Hokkien and Mandarin about how to make attractive arrangements of the student-made embroidery (reticules, tea cosies, pillow covers) and amateur paintings (coconut-fringed beaches, houses on stilts in a Malay kampong). Tian Wei buys a handkerchief embroidered with qilin for Kee Mun, then wonders if Kee Lung might accuse him of favouritism. So, he buys Kee Lung a batik book cover. Not that he can see Kee Lung using it; the boy has yet to bury his beak in a book.

Feng Yu waves to him. Behind him is a man wearing a long Chinese tunic and a hat, and he looks vaguely familiar. Ah yes, it's Pastor Cheng Ping Ting, leader of the Young People's Christian Group. The group is rumoured to be a front for the Kuomintang after the British government's curb of much Kuomintang activity in the Settlements; there is no knowing how much of it is true.

Feng Yu becomes expansive. "Let me introduce you. Pastor Cheng, this is my good friend Wang Tian Wei. He owns a photographic studio on Hill Street. Mind you, his studio is a cut above the rest."

Pastor Cheng shakes Tian Wei's hand, shrewdly assessing him. "Nice to meet you. Are you married, young man?"

"No." Tian Wei stifles his annoyance. Without fail, marriage is the first question asked of any young man in polite society. At the Poh Leung Kuk, Marjorie Brodie had remarked that marriage was a social control mechanism to rein in men's indulgence in the four vices that form the pillars of entertainment for Chinese clan communities: gambling, whoring, opium smoking, and drinking to excess. Hers is an unorthodox opinion, but one he finds himself agreeing with. Even liberal-minded Feng Yu is scandalised, calling him an irredeemable romantic: *Marriage is how you acquire status, duncehead.* Duncehead he may well be, but he would rather marry for love—love here being synonymous with the freedom to choose. If not love, he would prefer being yoked with a woman because she can challenge his mind, and not because the lady is fair of face or can cook up a sambal storm so good it melts the stomach lining.

"Not yet, you mean." Pastor Cheng smiles. "All in good time. Which part of the homeland are you from? Let me guess: Canton?"

"From Shanghai. I grew up in Hongkew," Tian Wei says.

"Now, that is quite the city." Pastor Cheng drums his fingers on his chest. "Unrivalled in many things. Singapore may be the Clapham of the East, but Shanghai is the Paris of the East, don't you agree? Well, this is convenient. I was about to enquire at a couple of studios about having a portrait taken with my Methodist youth group. Do you do field work? Take portraits outdoors?"

He does. Tian Wei hands his calling card to Pastor Cheng, who nods. "I shall call about the portrait. Come for a meeting at the Reading Society next Thursday. Young Reverend Goh Hood Keng is giving a talk about all men being equal sinners before Christ. Some of these young men are bound to agitate about the colour bar within the Malayan Civil Service and at places like the Singapore Club. While they're at it, I hope they discuss the size of the 200-foot-long bar and how it might spur indecorous quaffing of liquids, but I suppose I shall mildew alone in my concern."

After he leaves, Tian Wei prods Feng Yu with an elbow to his stomach. "What was that about? I told you I won't be joining any political society."

Feng Yu tucks his hand into his waistcoat. "The Kuomintang can be an ace in the hole, you know."

Feng Yu himself is a member, but Tian Wei is reluctant. Many a Kuomintang lodge is hidden as part of a network of reading societies and vernacular schools, politicising young men through the spread of revolutionary ideas while providing spaces for them to congregate, gain education, and share mutual interests in the Chinese classics. For years after he first arrived in Singapore, Tian Wei himself had gone religiously to Tung Teh Reading Room—he still does—it was where he met Feng Yu, made other friends, socialised, and grew his business. Also, it was where he learned his letters, gained culture and knowledge, learned Mandarin. He owes much to the good work that reading rooms do. How painstakingly he read in those early days, working by lamplight, copying out each character, each Chinese, Malay, and English word, filling in notebook after notebook, building his own lexicon. From a street urchin, he became someone who could appreciate exquisite *bai jiu* and fine words. He even read *Oliver Twist* under the tutelage of a *xue zhang*, a senior member. However, joining the Kuomintang is a double-edged sword: if caught by the British as an anti-colonial agitator, one is deported back to China lickety-split.

Feng Yu says, "Look here, aren't you still searching for that Japanese girl? The Kuomintang has an extensive network. They could put out feelers for you."

Indeed, searching for Aiko in the past few months has accustomed Tian Wei to odd behaviour: lounging behind pillars, spying on the Japanese brothels in Malabar and Malay Streets; playing *chap ji kee* at gambling parlours; even once making the rounds backstage at the Cantonese opera house Lai Chun Yuen, pretending to pay homage to an opera singer. Fellow Chinese photographers spotted him there. They'd mentioned it later when he ran into them, winking salaciously, having a good jest at his expense. He wasn't prudish, but he instinctively recoiled from the flesh trade. Sansan had died because of it. Sansan, who had been a sister to him and saved his life when he thought the world was a hellish place run by hoodlums and bruisers, where life was so tawdry for urchins it made Oliver Twist look like a princeling.

"I don't want trouble," he says. "The Ghee Hin is already making discreet enquiries."

"That's well and good, but you should bear in mind that even the Chinese Protector Mr. Beatty wasn't of any help."

"That's where you're wrong. He was of help. He connected me to Ms. Brodie at the Poh Leung Kuk."

"Fat lot of good that did you. A powerful organisation like the K.M.T. is different. You might consider doing things the Chinese way, eh?"

That's rich coming from a Straits Chinese who can pivot and switch loyalties, depending on which direction the wind is blowing.

Sensing his reluctance, Feng Yu prods him in the ribs. "Oh, loosen up, old boy. Come for a meeting. It'll be a laugh."

It won't be. He has no objections to attending church like Feng Yu, or even attending the odd Kuomintang meeting, but Tian Wei believes that, just as studio photography is best left to photographers, religion is best left to believers, and politics is best left to politicians.

The talk is set to begin in the hall. A man with a well-trimmed goatee and European suit stands near the podium, his hat clasped against his chest, conversing with a number of eager young men.

"That's Dr. Lim Boon Keng," Feng Yu says. "You do know who he is?"

Is there anyone who doesn't? Within the social set of compradors and Straits Chinese elites, Dr. Lim's fiery oratory is well known. He founded the Chinese Philomathic Society as well as the *Straits Chinese Magazine*, which Tian Wei has picked up and read from time to time to improve his English and learn more about how the Straits-born Chinese think. Dr. Lim also founded the Chinese Girls' School with Song Ong Siang and others. He had advocated for the cutting of the *towchang* (pigtail) of Chinese coolies, which had had the *sinkeh* traditionalists within the various pangs up in arms.

At first, Tian Wei doesn't listen too carefully, preferring to look around at the well-heeled young men, some in European suits, others in the long tunics of Mandarin scholars. They carry their place in the world with an easy entitlement he can't imitate.

Soon enough, Dr. Lim's words infiltrate: "Our forefathers weren't all learned men. Most of them were probably illiterate. But they came from a land of culture, imbued with an unbounded confidence in the excellence of Chinese literature. They entertained for it a patriotic passion that led them to provide for their children instruction in the classics of the Middle Kingdom. That the Chinese Babas have been able to maintain their integrity as a people is largely due to this wise and laudable policy of the early Chinese colonists."

Dr. Lim preaches as though he were a sage, not a politician. Though a British subject, who has pledged allegiance to His Majesty the King, he is eager for the Peranakan Chinese to reclaim their Chinese heritage and identity. Well aware of the stark differences between *sinkeh* and Peranakan Chinese that are more to do with social and material status, education, and language adoption, rather than culture or race, he stresses that there isn't just one kind of Chinese in the Straits Settlements, nor one way of being Chinese, nor even necessarily one history pertaining to all Chinese. His tone rises an octave: "The Straits Chinese may be British subjects, but one thing is clear: we cannot lose our connection with Chinese proper, our locus of origin." He goes on to extol the importance of female education. "Suffice it to say that no great progress can be made by any people if one half, the greater half it may be, is perpetually kept in a state of ignorance and degradation. Keep your women in a low, ignorant, and servile state, and in time you will become a low, ignorant, and servile people—male and female."

It is as if Dr. Lim has sneaked into his dreams from the night before. His words don't just resonate, they toll. A Chinese citizen in a colonial entrepôt like Singapore has a duty to be faithful to the British, but Tian Wei's loyalties toggle between a distant homeland that grows ever more distant year by year, and this adopted place he now calls home. Modernisation in China is good. Social reform for women's rights is a great thing. But shouldn't he work towards these good things here in Singapore? He catalogues the changes within himself. What would he do without the dirty, crowded, stench-filled roads of Chinatown? He grows wistful at the sight of the Singapore river jostling with bumboats, tongkangs, prahus, and harbour masters abusing all and sundry within earshot. Travelling over to the beach in Katong, the image of coconut trees and the fishermen hauling in their catch is pastoral enough to make one break out in lullaby. This is home, a place that has welcomed him, a place that has given him a four-square inch to eke out an existence. Not just any existence—it has turned him into someone respectable. A merchant photographer. When he photographs the local scenes, what he wants to capture is the blood, sweat, and tears of the common man. The camera keeps him honest.

Studium

17 August 1920

Dear Miss C.:—

Thank you kindly for your letter. To be
honest, I did not dare hope for a reply from
you. Receiving your letters has been wondrous
and surreal, but I must draw your attention to
the following: for you it appears to have been
but a few days, but it took over four months
for me to receive your reply. I must say, this
quantum entanglement you mention is slower
than the pony express.

You rightly ask why I should suspect that
anything untoward has happened to Aiko. Many
months ago, I ran into her chaperone, whom Aiko
calls Sister Yuk, at a noodle stall on Upper
Chin Chew Street. I asked her why Aiko hadn't
come to my studio for a couple of months.
Yuk-jie ran away, waving and muttering, as
if I'd threatened to tickle her nose, yelling
that this was bad luck and more bad things
would happen. This caused me misgiving. If
Aiko is well, why has she not written? Why has
she kept away? An absence of correspondence
for so many months is unlike her.

I should like to tell you that, as recent as
a week past, after months of hounding Hudson

Tay, the tycoon finally agreed to meet me,
and invited me into his magnificent mansion.
We sat at his garden terrace while a majie
dressed in a white top and black trousers
served tea. The entire time he spoke to me,
a peregrine falcon sat on his upheld wrist,
jerking its head left and right.

The garden was exactly as Aiko had described
it — a verdant dreamscape, with a bird bath,
flowers, and shrubs I don't know the name
of it in English. Oh yes, sculpted bonsai
and trees providing welcome shade. It put
my painted studio backdrop to shame. Now I
understand why Aiko couldn't stop chattering
away about her garden whilst I was taking her
photo. I see how my garden backdrop quite
pales in comparison to hers.

Tucked into a border wall is a secret
garden, her sanctuary. Aiko mentioned it many
times. In it, there is a round double swing
and a Chinese-style pavilion. I've seen Aiko's
sketches of it. There is also a miniature
arched bridge across a koi pond. Aiko told me
she would read her Chinese classics there for
hours, or hide when she didn't wish to attend
to her tiresome needlepoint lessons.

Hudson Tay informed me while we sat on his
garden terrace that he had had his syce motor Aiko
up to Malacca, where he has extensive business
holdings. He wishes her to spend time with
her cousins there, and to meet her betrothed,
a young man of promise from a respectable
Baba Malaccan family in the rubber business,
a potential business partner for the Tays.

Though much relieved to hear Aiko is alive,
I am uneasy. I have no goodly reason to suspect

her father's probity, and yet I do suspect it. When asked when this wedding would take place, he could not answer. Unlikely that a meeting would have been allowed between a man and woman of elite Chinese parentage unless a date has been set. Even more peculiar is the fact that, when I congratulated him on making an excellent match for the fine young intelligent woman that Aiko is, the tycoon looked away and re-hooded his falcon. With a brusqueness of manner, he ended our interview, when seconds earlier he had been gabbling on about his shipping interests. He warned me to let sleeping dogs lie. The phrase fills me with trepidation, but I have even less of a leg to stand on now in this matter.

My mind keeps turning this over. The Aiko I know is not someone who would submit so readily to having her fate determined. She doesn't care a fig for convention. A girl who swore she planned to teach music or open her own photographic studio isn't going to be content being married off to a rubber magnate. Nor even if he were the King of Persia.

I suppose I sound rather on edge. Feng Yu's friend, Tang Si Nian, has enlisted the help of the Ghee Hin Society on my behalf. Since then, I suspect I'm being followed home at night. But I shall persevere. I shall not rest until I find Aiko.

If it's going to take months before I receive another letter from you, I must beat hay while the sun shines. Though sleep has abandoned me, writing to you about Aiko has brought me peace of mind. It is a tonic. I must thank you for it. I am incredibly

touched that you have spent time "trawling
your newspaper archives" for news about Aiko.
It's quite puzzling, but I suppose it to be
a library of some kind that houses newspapers
of the past. How you managed to search through
all of them in two days is quite beyond my
comprehension. You must have magic fingers, or
a thousand pairs of eyes!

It is odd to confess that I anxiously await
your next letter. Your confidences about your
brother Sebastian, and about the Chinese
legends you know of, bring you close, making
me think you and I could meet, share a meal
together (chee cheong fun, mayhap?), and we
would have much to say, without feeling like
a hundred years separate us. Over the course
of the last few months, your words have come
to me at various moments of my day, unbidden.
What you said about deep familiarity — I feel
it too. So very quickly, you seem to have
taken residence in a corner of my mind. Is
this what enchantment is?

I enclose hopefully a nicer photograph of
myself. Will you kindly append yours in your
next missive?

> Obligingly yours,
> W.T.W.

P.S. The name of my studio is Pun Lun. I
bought it from a Cantonese gentleman who has
since returned home to Guangdong. I inherited
three of his assistants. He also left me
his mahjong table. It is why I have learned
Cantonese, so I can communicate easily. I mean
with my assistants, not the mahjong table.

It's rather a hassle to retype a whole letter because of this one gaffe.

    P.P.S. You wrote several strange terms I don't understand. For the time being, a couple of questions: Do clouds in the future behave so strangely as to store photographs in addition to creating rain? Is "warp" similar to a fly-killing device, the netting of which bends when it meets a fly in a resounding thwack?

The (Re)Framing of History

This afternoon, I am giving a curator's tour to an entourage of women tourists, mostly European, faces bright and eager, a little caked with suntan lotion. The first photograph I stop in front of is the ancestral portrait of Mother—a woman in ceremonial robes, her feet encased in slippers and resting on a pouf. The caption confirms her feet were never bound. I point out the lush surroundings she is photographed against: the leafy potted plant, the Venetian staircase backdrop, the many accoutrements on the side table next to her—the Chinese almanac, the porcelain teacup with lid, the *sapu tangan* hankie (finally, a clue that she's not simply Chinese, but Straits Chinese).

"This woman is the embodiment of tradition and culture." The nickname I've given her—Mother, with a capital *M*— isn't as fatuous as it seems. As Tian Wei described in his letter, the unmarried cloistered Straits Chinese girl's life was one of intolerable monotony: her virtue had to be guarded at all times. Even at home, she was not allowed to be alone with her brother-in-law, for it would be unseemly. After marriage, she often suffered the tyranny of her mother-in-law. As Mother-with-a-capital-*M* evokes through her stern visage, a circumscribed life in the public domain often translated into ruling home and hearth with an iron fist. At least there, she had unbridled power. "The rightful place of such a portrait is on an ancestral table for worship, and hence we know she must have had progeny. The Chinese adopted a practice of *chuanshen xieying* to replicate exactly on a portrait all the human features of the subject, because the soul is believed to transmute to the portrait for veneration by her descendants."

The expressions on their faces shift as they enshrine this woman, alive a century ago. Bizarrely, this talk, which I've given a dozen times now, is making me out of breath, as if I've been running up and down heedlessly. My lungs are filled with thick air. Bubbles of heat surface in my body like energy swells. I feel slightly dizzy. Strange emanations puncture my mind, and a headache is beginning. I do not feel well.

My thoughts stray. They wander to Wang Tian Wei. Aiko! Aiko! So much about Aiko. I would rather hear about him. Those well-formed sentences describing bonsai and bridges in Aiko's secret garden: is he trying to impress me? Then that last paragraph: *So very quickly, you seem to have taken residence in a corner of my mind. Is this what enchantment is?*

My heartbeat increases to a staccato. The world stops moving, distilling itself to a point of stillness, a pinprick of light.

His letter has come accompanied by another photograph. It shows him in a dapper light-coloured suit and a dark bow tie, seated on a European-styled curule seat with a cushion and curved armrests, his light-coloured socks setting up a nice contrast to his dark leather shoes. His hair is slicked back, as was fashionable in the 1920s. He is smiling slightly, a kindness etched across his pleasant features, arms loosely cross-wrapped across his midriff, young and handsome. A bone of feeling lodges itself in my throat; something has punctured my perimeter.

The women are looking at me with mixed expressions. I have stopped in the middle of a sentence. I am a recidivist daydreamer. As a child in boarding school, whenever I got bored, which was often, I time-travelled in my head. A friend at school, now a lauded writer, once shared an Orwellian insight with me: during our youth, we often craft distorted maps of the world, fabled countries we revisit incessantly. As writers, we don't just invent places, however; she explained that writers also remap time, carving out segments of history, retelling and reframing them, so that we see things differently. We think that inventing narratives belongs in the domain of fiction, not in art history. Yet, in my dialogues with budding curators and esteemed art historians, I've found myself listening to their assertions rooted in fact, while wondering at the imaginative leaps they take to bridge the gaps in historical records. I wondered whether this kind of storytelling is not so far removed from the art of fiction after all.

I begin afresh. "History as told through photographs is accepted as fact. And yet, despite all our grand theories of sign, signifier, and signified—Lacan, Derrida, Barthes, and what have you—" throwing out these names always impresses at least a couple of them, and today is no exception (quick thinking on my part)— "a photograph actually tells you little. It masks reality. We make much meaning out of a photograph, extend such meaning backward and forward in time to narrate what is essentially a freeze-framed moment siphoned from the river of time. Consider this: we use photographs of the past to discern and interpret history; yet, if a photograph masks reality, can we ever know the past at all? What is history but a story told from a particular viewpoint, usually the victors'—or, in this case, the colonialists? What then do we know of untold history? When we reconstruct the past through the lens of the future, how much illusion is involved?"

Some of them nod, some purse their mouths in rumination. I've struck a chord. A silence settles around us like a cloud. Buttery sunshine lights up dust motes in the air.

In front of me, what I see is not Mother-with-a-capital-*M*, but a garden. A garden of sculpted bonsai and flowering jacaranda and herbaceous borders. Tucked into a border wall is a secret garden in which a young girl frolics and chases butterflies with a net.

The image about to happen—it will take in the pavilion, the profusion of foliage and flowers, the girl posing, arms and legs flung wide. An image in which you can almost hear a garden waking up. The snip of secateurs. The clang of a gate. The clack of geta or slap of slippers. The image reels you in, transports you to a duplicate world.

Then I see the man standing behind the camera with its square bellows, front panel, back lens. Even in the tropical heat, he is attired in a handsome bow tie and a crisp white shirt. He adjusts the shutters. He waits. What is this elusive state of mind? This dreaminess? This betwixt and between?

*

It's well past six when the tour ends. I head back to the office. Mahmood and Yoo-lin have already gone home. I switch on my phone, and multiple pings alert me to many received texts. Sebastian. The beginning of it signals calamity.

> He wants me to buy out his 50% of the business. Where would I get that kind of money right now? 😩😫

> 🙀 Shit. It's happened. Adnan says he wants to break up.

> For the record, he says he broke up with me. It's so fucking immature.

> We just LAUNCHED! Could he not have either done this before, or waited until six months after? Using bad timing to get back at me, it's so immature.

> CHARLIE?? Remember *The Great Gatsby*? Unfamiliar sky, frightening leaves. How grotesque the rose, how raw the sunlight. Where tf are you? I'm dying here.

This last message galvanises me to call him immediately. Gatsby is S.O.S. language between us. Scanning my phone, I see that he has called twelve times. After an uncountable number of rings, he picks up.

"Dammit, Charlie. Why do you always do this?"

"I'm sorry. I was held up. I'm such a bad sister."

"Don't hand me that 'sister' card. What I need is my best friend. Present in mind and body, OK?"

My tone is contrite. "I shall be very present in mind and body."

"Did something happen? Where have you been?"

Indeed, where have I been? Betwixt and between, in no-space, or is it a third space, a realm that gains reality because it beguiles the senses, a corridor in which a fire stream of emotions flow, heedless and headlong?

Timed Exposure

Sebastian and I are ensconced at his condo in Marina Bay that he inherited from Peony; I am seated on his plush sofa while he lies with his head on my lap—his favourite position, because it makes him feel like a child again. His sofa faces the panoramic night view of Marina Bay Sands and the Supertree Grove of Gardens by the Bay, all lit up in incandescent colours. I've changed into a pair of Sebastian's PJs and I've got my black-tea hot-toddy in hand. After his revelation about breaking up with Adnan at Apophenia, the next day they were back together. Broke up, got back together. It follows the pattern of Sebastian's break-ups. If it happens a third time, it's finished. Three is a fabled number, but neither Sebastian nor Adnan cares for fairy tales. So here we are. Yay me—I get to hear about the final straw.

Their quarrels had escalated back in Shanghai with the stress of THE LAUNCH, ever after memorialised in all caps. Sebastian had entrusted all the tech elements to Adnan, given Adnan's tech whizz. "Schmoozing clients isn't his forte, he hates all that interfacing with artists—too temperamental, too moody, too suspicious, too everything for him." I'd considered Adnan a foil for Sebastian's sentimental side—sometimes, I'm even a little jealous that Sebastian has someone like Adnan in his life, while all I have, having acclimatised to Singapore culture, is a tubular pillow historically known as a Dutch wife.

Adnan takes zero notice of me. He thinks I'm worse than Sebastian when it comes to being a sap. Also, despite being a bona fide member of the chi-chi art world and an heiress to boot, he considers me to be a little unhinged and too unglamorous. Adnan is one cool cucumber, as hybrid as they come—born in Morocco to wealthy British-Indian parents of the Ismailli sect, he attended boarding school at Eton, obtained a PhD in computer engineering from Caltech, and then spent half his working life bouncing around Taiwan, Hong Kong, and Shanghai. He speaks fluent Cantonese and Mandarin, and—unlike Sebastian, who teases me in good humour about my mangled phrasings—Adnan looks at me with disdain when I use my rusty Chinese, as if to say, *If a mongrel like me can master the nine tones of Cantonese, so can you.* Aptly, Sebastian and Adnan met at a Zhou Zhen exhibition, five years ago, at the Singapore ArtScience Museum.

"I can't help being suspicious of Adnan's business plans." Sebastian's brow furrows. "I'm worried that he might insist on the intellectual property rights to the algorithm."

I'm debating whether to have another hot toddy, but need to stay mentally alert in case I inadvertently let slip my animus towards Adnan. When Sebastian gets anxious, he doesn't want validation of his feelings. What he wants is someone who can help him unravel the tangle in his head. "Did you not sort out those legal details beforehand?" I ask.

Sebastian sighs. "He's my business partner. There's a thing called trust? The algorithm was part of the capital he invested; we thought we would get to all the rights stuff later. Our partnership agreement is seriously bare-bones. I'm not sure we considered disputes or buyouts all that thoroughly. After all, I thought we would be an ironclad item forever."

You did? But I don't voice this. "Did Adnan say he was going to take the algorithm with him?"

"Well, he's been making noises about using it as a template to develop a different version, but it'll probably be more sophisticated rather than different. I wonder if he has another art entrepreneur in the wings. He is required to sign a non-compete if he leaves. It's not that easy to transfer the algorithm."

"Isn't there a way you can stay as business partners, even if you're not together? You've recently launched; surely he can see that it's not in his business interests to be bought out now?" I pat Sebastian's hair—its springiness makes me wonder what new organic sulphate-free shampoo he is using. He grabs my hand and pulls it to his chest. Fouling up his hair is prohibited.

"That's the thing: he's smart; he's super logical; he's self-interested. That's why I'm wondering if another art entrepreneur is courting him. Offering megabucks perhaps. The algorithm is the heart and soul of our platform, it was how we secured funding from seed investors, and we have reps and warranties and covenants that tie us down; I honestly didn't think it would even be an issue. Adnan knows that, if he takes the algorithm with him, my business is kaput and I'm so screwed where the investors are concerned." Sebastian raises a knuckle to rest across his forehead. His eyes swim with worry.

"Is it about money? Can't you offer him a bigger share of the business?" I'm toying with the idea of offering financial help, but Sebastian can be uptight and sensitive about this, as he has been in the past. His pride is quick to injure, thin as onion skin, although the issue isn't merely about pride.

Sebastian sighs. "That would be counter-intuitive when he has asked me to buy him out. He doesn't want a larger piece; he wants cold hard cash, which I don't have. My one way out is to convince him to wait six months to a year. I wish we hadn't broken up just now. Negotiating gets sticky." He sits up suddenly, dead-staring at the lights of the bay. His irises have turned light chocolate by reflection, and I sense distance and withdrawal. A line being drawn.

I bite my lip. It's on the tip of my tongue to say I never liked Adnan all that much, so maybe breaking up isn't cataclysmic, but this might come across as rubbing salt into a fresh wound. I clear my throat. "Last we spoke, you were going to try to make it work with Adnan."

"He's wanted to buy a place in Shanghai with me since we got together. It makes sense, since our clientele, though online, are predominantly rich Mainland Chinese. Operations would have to be shifted to Shanghai anyway—but I told him, with the working capital so tight, I wasn't ready to consider it yet."

Still, to humour Adnan, he had gone along to all the show-house jaunts—from Pudong to Dapuqiao to Xuhui. Last week, the arguments went a notch too far. Adnan said he didn't buy Sebastian's argument about finances—Sebastian could just take out a mortgage on his Marina Bay apartment or even sell it; besides, didn't he have the whole Sze-Toh conglomerate behind him? And this was what made Sebastian upset. "FIRST." Sigh, all caps again. "Adnan knows my relationship with the rest of the Sze-Tohs is rocky at best. SECOND. This was my mother's apartment; all my memories of her revolve around this apartment. And you know what Adnan said? 'It's a condo, babe. Memories are portable. Your memories of your mother are buried in your head, not wrapped around an apartment. Don't be so fucking nostalgic.' Fucking nostalgic! It's not as if he doesn't know all my personal history. Can't he put himself in my shoes for one second? I may not subscribe to all that ancestral tablet-and-prayer-altar bullshit, but my mother's soul resides in this apartment and always will. Not in some urn in Mandai, OK?"

Heavy underlying note of upset. Deeply furrowed brow. Clenched jaw. Slightly trembling fingers. Pain crouches in the interstices of his words and gestures. I am suddenly furious at Adnan.

I've always believed that collective time may be linear (though even this is debatable), but individual time is cyclical. We trudge each step towards a future trapped by our pasts and our memories. Our new selves will always contain shards and traces of our old. The problem with "fucking nostalgic" people like Sebastian and I isn't that we can't weather a broken heart. Or that we can't acknowledge that everything that happens to us in the future, how we decide what to do or how to act, is tied up with what has happened to us in the past. The problem with "fucking nostalgic" people like Sebastian and I is the stickiness of residues and traces. Crush our hearts, and we don't heal the same way as others. Fragments—pain, trauma, love, moments in which life turns quiet as a pin but with the impact of a cataclysm—these remain embedded as glass shards. Ashes of a past so burnished it becomes mythological. To wit: Peony is gone but Sebastian will never let her go. Adnan doesn't see that and now he too is saying goodbye.

A Semblance of Knowledge

When Father legally adopted Sebastian, a provision was entered into his will. Because Sebastian is not related to the Sze-Tohs by blood, all that Father had granted to Peony—the Marina Bay apartment, some stocks, a bank account with lots of cash—were Sebastian's to inherit. However, as far as the sweep of Father's assets were concerned, there would be no sharing with Laurent or Linton or me. The saying that blood is thicker than water appeals to the Sze-Tohs the way crude oil appeals to oil magnates—it's pure bank; thus, I am not surprised by this heavy-handed, inequitable treatment. Like adding brush dabs to an already ugly picture, Sebastian only discovered this during the reading of Father's will. Whenever this subject surfaces, Sebastian jumps on his standard refrain: Cassandra got the conglomerate, Linton and Laurent the real estate and securities portfolios, and look what the two orphans got—a whole cache of junk. As an exclamation point, Father bequeathed Sebastian his entire collection of old photographs—flea-market memorabilia bought from antique shops in Bras Basah.

But it's not true that I got junk. Father set me up differently. A fund ensures private schools for however many postgrad degrees I have the mental gigabytes for. A fund that continues in perpetuity, from which I draw a healthy monthly stipend, enough to afford a pair of Jimmy Choos and a new Prada bag every month, though I choose to support an orangutan survival fund and Habitat for Humanity instead. In addition to Mother's London flat, I also inherited a rather large portfolio and Father's small chateau in Bordeaux, situated on three acres of land, with stands of spruce guarding prettily the brow of a hillock. If I were to dress better, as Sebastian keeps reminding me, I may tout myself as an heiress, aim to become romantic prey for fortune hunters. *A future sticky with promise, like a honeytrap to catch flies.* Sebastian's words. Even as I wince at his wry metaphor, I see its truth. This is exactly why I don't dress better. I don't wish to be harpooned by fake men on fake dates. I never asked to be an heiress. It gives me impostor syndrome. The reason Cassandra gets away with calling me a leech (what have I done to deserve a part of the Sze-Toh fortune?) is because I sometimes think I am one too.

Sebastian was so angry and hurt after the reading of the will that he didn't speak to me for months. We take our pain out on those we love. He didn't care about any of the other Sze-Tohs, but since I'm legally a sibling, the only one he is close to, I should at least bear that much. I hounded and harassed him with calls and texts, plastered his office window with apologies—then blew up at him with a "How is this my fault?"—and he forgave me finally when I carted in a box filled with La Madeline au Truffe and vintage champagne. I also offered to transfer over the chateau in Bordeaux. I meant it sincerely, but I also knew he would refuse (he accepted the ganache and champagne though). But the gesture mattered. It mattered terribly.

It was Sebastian who saved me from tumbling down the cliff of depression during my undergrad days. In my junior year, Laurent had asked me to help his good pal, Marcus Lo, who had joined a dotcom in nearby Menlo Park as a software developer: could I show Marcus around San Fran and Silicon Valley, acquaint him with the BART system, introduce him to good eats, like where to get a bowl of pho, shop for Chinese groceries—fellow homesick Asians looking out for one another, ya dig? I wanted to get into Cassandra's good books (pathetic, yes, but I did hope for a replacement mother), and I thought buddying up to Laurent might help. Marcus Lo showed up, tall and rangy, sporting a six-pack, with craggy cheekbones I secretly dubbed cliff-face, oozing masculine charm. I've never been the subject of much male attention, at least not until they hear I come from money; I'm awkwardly tall, with the social panache of a giraffe, and having attended a single-sex school all my life till Stanford, I approach dating the way I do fencing.

Marcus bowled me over completely. I believed him when he said he found me "not your normal Chinese beauty," that he "loved a girl with deep thoughts," that he found me "cute, as in good-quirky, not ugly-adorable," and these concocted portmanteaus of his amused me. I accepted the perfumes and flowers. I wanted to kiss and be kissed.

Truth be told, I didn't so much want to sleep with him, as let him sleep with me. The night that we had booked a nice hotel room in Half Moon Bay, I overheard Marcus's phone conversation with Laurent, who was on speaker. I heard my name and the words "ingénue," "simple," and "*chin chai* woman." I didn't know what a "*chin chai* woman" was; I do now. Someone so eager to please, she'll be your slut if you ask her to. Laurent had instigated the whole thing: dared Marcus to ask out his "frigid" half-sister. Marcus's laughter grated on my ears and sank my heart. The clincher was when Marcus lowered his voice and said, "You're not going to rat me out to Daphne, right?" I didn't know who Daphne was to Marcus, but I didn't stick around to find out. I took Marcus's car keys and left him stranded there, letting hot tears salt my cheeks as I zipped all the way down Highway 101.

Two nights later, Marcus busted into Escondido Village, where I shared a campus apartment with a roommate. He sexually assaulted me by forcefully kissing me and wrestling me onto the bed while Owl City warbled "Fireflies" from my stereo. The memory that stings me the most, which I would like to blip out completely, is of him pulling off my joggers and inserting a finger deep inside me. I bit his lip so hard it swelled up like the underside of a snail. For good measure, I whacked him on the head with the handy baseball glove on my desk. My memory is hazy after this point. I remember calling Sebastian. Campus police arrived. Long, interminable hours at the department office. Then, at the hospital. I remember sobbing. I remember trying to joke—*Look what a story I get to tell about losing my virginity*—and Sebastian joking back, "Honey, it's better than the one I got. I lost mine to a boy named David, the *d* at the end is silent."

By the end of term, every time I heard "Fireflies," I broke out in a cold sweat. I failed half my exams. Heartbreak. One word. I didn't know what it meant. And then I did.

One evening before graduation, Seb and I ran up to the Dish. He said he wanted to talk. It sounded ominous. We sat on a tump of grass, surveying the low brown hills before us, inhaling the scent of field and hill and sky. A drought had been ongoing in Northern California, and the sedge looked parched and withered. He plucked at the straggly dandelions. I tried to hold a blade of grass in place between my nose and lips. Sebastian's opening gambit: "Are things A-OK, Charlie? I'm here for you—you know that, right? I'll always be here for you."

I laughed. "What do you mean, asking if I'm A-OK?"

Sebastian waited a couple of beats. "I mean about not pressing charges against Marcus Lo. You should. You have every right to."

"And see my name plastered all over *The Stanford Daily*? No, thank you."

"All right. I would never tell you what to do."

"I'm well over that dweeb. I'm well over *that*."

Sebastian crossed his arms over his pulled-up knees. "So, what's going on?"

I shrugged. I had signed up for counselling sessions at the campus medical centre. All semester long, I'd talked to a therapist about how stupid Marcus had made me feel. How the assault made me feel violated. The therapist had flipped through his notes, not making eye contact. He said, "Hmmm," but not often. I'd always had my armour up when it came to people, a fort housing my inner core, so tender and easily bruised, because I'd grown up with a mother more intent on her drink than on raising me, because I'd had a slew of fork-tongued nannies who said one thing in front of me and quite another behind my back (in their different languages—Chinese, English, French, Catalan!), because I'd learned early on not to trust easily. And yet, I told the therapist, Marcus had somehow snuck through all of that. It galled me that, the first time I fell hard for someone, it had to be for a schmuck with slick words and a treacherous heart. Here, I thought I'd been watching out for all the trope permutations of the wolf in sheep's clothing—but somehow the handsome wolf manipulating his sheep and wolf personas, manifesting the self-consciousness of one while pretending to be the other, still managed to fool me. "Never date anyone who is basically constructed like a set of nested Russian dolls," I told the therapist. He scratched his chin. All in all, I hadn't known I was so susceptible to being taken in, that I could be such a poor judge of character. It shook me badly to think I couldn't even trust myself. The therapist wrote some notes, but offered no advice.

That was when I knew he would be of no help. No one else out there in the big bad world could help me unless I first learned to pick myself up. I survived on coffee and instant ramen one whole semester, I zombie-sat in class so I wouldn't fail outright. My body was present, but my mind did the *wan yau sei kai* and travelled continents and eras. I couldn't get out of bed in the mornings, not because I wanted to die, but because I didn't have the energy to live. Russian-nested-doll metaphor or Taoist nine-levels-of-hell, take your pick—it turned out there were layers to losing; just when I thought I'd hit rock bottom, there was yet another level to fall through.

Sebastian listened to what I had to say about quitting the therapist. He listened without comment. He nimbly took the blade of grass and folded it, as if it were origami, into a blob. "I wasn't sure, but I suspected you had stopped your counselling sessions."

"It was just an assault. No biggie. Lots more fish in the sea. Isn't that what they say?"

Was it the glibness that made him grip me by the shoulders, spinning me round hard? "Charlie, you do remember me taking you to the hospital, don't you? You were inconsolable. You screamed every time the nurse touched you."

I pushed him off angrily. "It was just me overreacting, as usual. I'm not going to allow this one incident to dominate my life."

"Of course it shouldn't. But surely repressing it isn't the answer?"

"When it comes to repressing things, you should talk. And why is it that it's fine for you to overstep the line, but not when I do it?"

His eyes held a look I didn't like. "I just want you to talk to me. Don't shut me out." The deep concern I saw in his eyes brought me close to tears. I felt transparent and raw, as if Sebastian saw right through me. It made me feel completely exposed, and it terrified me. Jitters broke out, increasing in strength. He put an arm around me. "OK," he said.

OK, what? We didn't talk for several minutes. It was all I could do not to scream, not to claw at something until I drew blood.

After another moment, he said, "I want to show you something. Not changing the subject or anything, just redirecting energy."

He handed over a photograph. "See this?"

I made a show of studying the photograph until my tremors subsided. It was a historical studio portrait of a couple—the woman in traditional *baju panjang* (a long tunic with a pleated skirt) seated on a high-backed chair, the man in the white ducks of a colonial servant (the standard white *tutup* tunic and solar *topi* hat) standing with a Malacca cane in one hand and a book in the other. Then, upon closer examination, I realised that it wasn't a couple at all, but the same woman dressed as he and she, produced as a superimposed double print. Or it could have been twin sisters—one cross-dressing so they could pose as a couple. The possibilities explaining this photograph were many.

"Where did you get this?"

"From Father's collection of albums; I filched it after Mum's funeral. He didn't even come to her funeral—what kind of phlegmatic response was that? He doesn't deserve my honesty and integrity. But then, he bequeathed these albums to me, including ironically the photographs I stole. Gradually, the photographs grew on me."

"Who are these people?"

Sebastian leaned his head against the hand resting on one drawn-up knee. "Oh, just *ah beng*s and *ah lian*s of old. Father was buying lots of old photographs, entire collections at one point, from Bras Basah. Don't ask me why. Especially photographs of opera troupes, which is probably more self-explanatory. But you're missing the point."

"What point?"

"Do you see how what you see can't explain what you see?" Sebastian said. "A photograph can dissimulate the truth, project a wishful reality. A space to self-realise and project one's desires and idealised identity."

It took me a second to realise that he had planned this heart-to-heart, even dug up a photograph to make it seem like an off-the-cuff discussion about an artefact he had enjoyed analysing. How annoying—also, how sweet, how considerate: he was making me feel loved without using the word, which had been empty of meaning for most of my life.

"Yeah, OK, so what?"

Sebastian ran a hand through his hair. "I was just thinking—I'm writing this article for an exhibition catalogue—the space in front of a camera is a fantasy space. A place to shed one's prescribed and categorical role in the world, a place to shed troubles and the eking out of daily survival, a place to remake one's own image into that which speaks of desire and beauty and success. In the duplicate world of the photograph, one's self-image—self-homage—is transformed into the cathedral of fire one holds in mind."

"O… kaaay…" I said slowly. "Still not getting it."

Sebastian drew me closer to him, hugging me from the side. "Sometimes, art holds up a semblance of knowledge to navigate real life, know what I mean? What I'm trying to say is this: I love you, Charlie. Sometimes it feels like there are only the two of us. We're stranded on an island of two, but it doesn't feel bad. It doesn't feel lonely. I got you. You got me, babe. Nothing in the world will alter that."

So cheesy, yet those were precisely the maudlin sentiments I had been thirsting to hear. Something sprouted inside me, a tiny shoot, sending up its first tendril. It must have begun then. Transference.

He rubbed my hair. "I'm going to introduce you to some outta-this-world shampoo, because you look like you need it—this frizz has to go, honey. Also, I would like you not to freeze-frame your conception of yourself based on this one—" he paused, then continued— "experience with Marcus. The danger, with people like us, is the trauma narrative locked inside us—it freezes us. Sontag said, 'Life is a movie, death is a photograph'—but a photograph is an oxymoron. My argument with Sontag is this: a photograph freezes a capsule of time, but it also fires the imagination. In front of the camera, people invent new selves, enact their passion and desire and fancy. Faced with the object of the photograph, people freely interpret what they see, use it as a doorway into the past, sparking new imaginings. Do you understand?"

I did. Finally. That pivotal moment at the Dish changed my life, triggered my devotion to photography and photographs, though neither he nor I fully comprehended it then, because we were just beginning to negotiate our identities through images, our personal histories in spite of images.

He tickled my face with a strand of my hair. "Sontag also said this: 'It hurts to love'. But here's a freebie from me: To love is to allow yourself to be flayed. It means giving someone carte blanche to walk off with your skin. Don't ever give anyone that much power over you. You come first, do you understand?"

What he said contradicted how he himself behaved towards love. Time and again, I'd watched him have his heart shattered, pick himself back up, run that marathon called life, will himself to gamble once again in a new relationship. The ability to love again after heartbreak was what made Sebastian glow with life.

It isn't all those smart, sensible observations he trots out about Sontag or Steichen or Lange or Arbus that secures me to him like a loyal subject. Nor is kinship created by sharing the same surname. It comes from a person's mindful care entering the gaps that have left you incomplete. When I talk, Sebastian listens with the utmost attentiveness, his weight canted forward, his entire body straining towards me. It is an incredible skill, not talking in the face of someone else's pain, not talking when you don't have to and letting your body speak instead. It is more articulate than the tongue is. It's also the other side of melancholy realism: talking so I don't have to. Like a photograph and its negative, two sides of the same truth.

Parade of the Immortalised

Déjà vu. Here I am again in my basement office in the middle of the night.

I get down to work, sifting through thousands of photographs and their negatives in the archives, all of denizens of early twentieth century Singapore: men and women, young and old, Chinese and Malay and Tamil and European and Armenian, faces composed into a stillness for the hushed eye of the camera. A parade of the immortalised. It soothes me.

Tian Wei, I am searching for you. The heaviness in my sternum will not lift until I find you. Time is on a loop. When I next glance at the clock, it's five a.m. I get up and stretch. I do my Kegels (a must if you've had a few UTIs in the tropics). I walk down the corridor to the loo; on a whim, I detour to swing by the main hall. It's shrouded in darkness but for the emergency lights casting a shadowy pall across the visage of Mother-with-a-capital-*M*, this woman I know and do not know. I gather the substance of "mother" from the tell-tale signs within the portrait. Just as I do for Mother, whom I know more intimately from her photographs than from real life. But Mother-with-a-capital-*M* seems to be following me with her eyes. She has a message for me. She has far more secrets than I could ever find out.

I wash my face in the bathroom sink. My eyes look engorged, the edges red and chapped. I release my hair from its Alice band. I head to the vending machine on my way back to the basement, but the red light is on for orange fizz and I have to settle for grape soda. The taste is as awful as every beverage the machine offers. But there is the fizz. There is that.

Back in front of my computer, I start again. Click, enlarge, quick check, not him, next photo. I keep doing it until my vision blurs.

And then… There he is.

I gaze at the photograph open on my computer for several long minutes.

Tian Wei, I've finally found you. Damn, you do look ridiculous in your Shakespearean garb. Happiness floods me. I pull the copy on to my desktop. Next click.

You again, in your dapper, light-coloured suit. Full of moxie. Dated circa 1920s. The confirmation of your existence reaches me like light from the stars, an image imprinting itself from a hundred years ago. The caption merely reads, *A Chinese man.* Nothing about your occupation, no other identifying characteristics.

I throw my weight back against my chair, staring up at irregular ceiling stains, feeling indescribable jubilance. Tian Wei, are you the image revealed between lenticular shifts? Are you the sculpture of Galatea made flesh because of the sculptor Pygmalion's deep intense yearning for it? When the unbelievable and mysterious happens, the tug of war with the rational mind begins. The rational and irrational switch places, and the only thing to go on is one's gut. But can you trust your gut when it delivers an open cry to the universe?

I get up and walk over to Yoo-lin's row of cacti under their artificial lights. I can't quite manage what she does, crooning Hokkien oldies to them, but I can spritz them. I pick up her water sprayer. She will be surprised when she sees the droplets, thinking a ghost has watered them in the night. I fold her reading glasses, place them on top of her computer. I checkmate the mini chess set on Mahmood's desk, a game in perennial motion. Spook them a little; these assistants of mine are getting complacent.

For now, I have a long letter to write, and its first sentence curls into my mind.

A photograph does not lie. Once photographed, the subject becomes fact.

A Photograph Does Not Lie

20 January 2019

Dearest Tian Wei,

I write you a letter where I spill my guts and you write me a letter full of Aiko? Watch I don't end up sending you a dissertation about Sebastian! Having said that, I do love your descriptions of Aiko's garden. Her father sounds freakish. I bet he has a room full of hunting trophies, like stuffed falcons and taxidermied harimau. At that time in Singapore and Malaya, there were supposed to be lots of tiger hunts. Also, have you considered talking to her mother rather than her father? I found this in the newspaper archives: in the 1930s, Hudson Tay contributed sums of money towards the Shantung Relief Fund, which aids victims of Japanese aggression in China. Perhaps this doesn't prove where his loyalties lie, but I can't imagine, as a father, he would do anything to endanger her.

The poem below is by Czesław Miłosz, a Polish-American poet. In 1920, he would have been nine years old, and this poem of his hadn't been written, nor yet conceived in his mind:

The bright side of the planet moves toward darkness,
And the cities are falling asleep, each in its hour,
And for me, now as then, it is too much,
There is too much world.

I was two when my mother divorced my father and took me to live in London. It must have been then that she stopped allowing photographs of herself. There are no photographs of us together in London. Not a single one. They couldn't even find a suitable one of her for her funeral. All they found was a photograph when she was still with my father. In it, she looked the starlet—it must have been taken at a charity ball. She was dressed up as a Shanghai diva from the Jazz Age, in flapper dress, complete with a feathered headband, long gloves, a fur stole, and a string of pearls. She was stunning.

I haven't inherited my mother's beauty, in case you're wondering. I'm gawky and tall, instead of petite and graceful. I'm nothing like her, within or without. My sense of beauty is twinned with horror; hers glowed strong and pure. Growing up, I always felt my mother's absence; she was there and not there. Nannies accompanied me everywhere. What I remember is my mother sitting in the dark by herself, curtains drawn, nursing a drink. She said incomprehensible things, or perhaps they were too adult for me to understand, but even a child could discern deep sorrow. That's what I remember—her voice sounding like an ugly cry, her distant eyes, the sadness that cloaked her. Once, she told me that my father had a nickname for her—Snow Flower—because her skin was so pale. The nickname no longer fitted her because the person sitting there in the dark had red, splotchy skin; she didn't in the least resemble a delicate flower; she seemed to me to be made of some rubbery substance, hard to dissolve, harder still to see through.

This version of my mother has the deadness, the finality, of a photograph. The beauty I missed out on is all the different versions of her. Photographs from her hellcat days, photographs pre-marriage, photographs of her in Singapore. All those years, my father kept his photographs of her. I saw them for the first time when I moved back. Her singing karaoke with university mates. Performing at a university concert. Dancing the rumba with my father at a club. A photo of her with a Cantonese opera singer, arms slung around each other. My parents' wedding. A photograph of her at the hospital when she gave birth to me. I was all swaddled in a blanket, you couldn't see much of me except my nose, but she was smiling. I'd like to believe she was happy to have me. That the day she gave birth to me was one of the highlights of her life, one of her happiest days. But I shall never know. Does absent knowledge function like the stories happening out of frame, with the potential to change how the picture is perceived?

I believe that beauty isn't static. The objective standards of beauty miss the boat. In art, what intrigues me is morph, a moment manifested in the ordinary, in the traces and stains of what had passed most people by. If John Berger is right that "beauty inserts us into existence", then what is existence? Does beauty entitle you to love? Is it love that gives us the full measure of existence? Let me redefine beauty. It isn't objective, it isn't what's on the surface. Beauty surely is in that transmission between the object and our perception, all that we felt and comprehended, and realised we didn't and hadn't.

Here's a photograph Sebastian took of me. Behold. I don't look Chinese in it, so I've been told. Would my mother have approved of this photo? Or would she say, "Cover up—I can see too much of your neck and shoulders"?

A photograph does not lie. Whatever is photographed becomes fact. The photographic truth as currency. Lesser truths. Bigger truths. Fragments of truth, as well as untruths that do not equal lies. There are truths that don't matter. Sometimes images of the truth are more important than the actual truth. Sometimes the world only asks that you show it a semblance of the truth, or a claim to truth. As a photographer yourself, I hope you get me. Maybe what I write here doesn't matter. Freedom comes with the ability to (re)imagine history. I can write anything. I can show you all of it. Despite my cynicism, in this space, I create something true. I hope you feel the same way.

The proof of your existence is the photographs of you in our archives. I'm ecstatic that I found you. It brings you to me, face to face. Although we are still separated by glass, I love these glimpses of you.

I wish that I could simply convert body and organic matter into a PDF and plonk myself into my Q.E. folder. Would I miraculously pop up in your studio? In real life, I would never be so forward, but shall we pretend for a moment? You can take a portrait of me in Shakespearean garb, strumming a mandolin. Or maybe even a nude portrait? 😱 Then, shall we grab a coffee afters?

Yours truly,
Charlie

P.S. On needlepoint, the last time I tried to sew, I managed to sew a torn sleeve shut.

P.P.S. We don't beat hay (😊), we make it while the sun shines. I have much to say, hence many postscripts. I am downright impressed with your versatility with so many languages, I had to look up "pilu" in my Malay dictionary. Not to be confused with "malu", I see.

P.P.P.S. Cloud storage, impossible to explain, and I'm poor at explaining technology anyway. The best I can do is give you a glimpse of the future. Someone quite clever will invent something they will call a giant cloud that can do a lot of different things: allow people to photograph what they eat for dinner with their phones and upload them on social platforms, allow people to go into an app and swipe to see who they would like to date based on photos and key information like age and occupation. Allow two people in love, separated by vast distances, to video call each other every day and have a meal together virtually and virtually together. Think of it as Cowherd and Weaver Girl seeing each other every day via a camera, even if they aren't physically together. They can still go on a virtual date, have an ice cream together. He buys his on Altair, she buys hers on Vega, but they will be licking them on different sides of the screen. This version of romance has much to commend itself. Here, I'm brazenly misappropriating Edgar Allan Poe's words—modern romance "scares the birds" out of me.

P.P.P.P.S. Tell me about you.

Punctum

Tian Wei receives Charlie's letter one bright morning on 13 May 1921, and experiences a flash of blinding light. Right after he finishes reading, a shimmering whiteness descends like a cap over his eyes. A moment of shock, an interval of freeze-time, and then the feeling that something has entered him like a gunshot. A presence jarring him out of existence and then folding him back into himself. It seizes him, nestling inside, and begins seething. He reads the letter over and over, as if he should like to swallow the words whole. Who is this woman from the future who speaks with such forthright words? He does not know what to think or do with the thoughts she's laid before him: her sadness about her mother, these incomprehensible things she says about truth and beauty and a photograph. Ah, the future world is indeed full of magic and mystery. It calls to mind a show he saw at the Alhambra: the inimitable magician Denny, who "dealt in necromancy and demonology", as the *Singapore Free Press and Mercantile Advertiser* tooted, and supported by his curvaceous assistant Miss Aero, had made canaries, pigeons, and rabbits appear and disappear from his top hat at will all evening.

Charlie has appended a self-portrait. The colours ablaze in it. Of life and sun. Leaning against a tree, she wears a yellow deckle-edged summer shirt and white shorts; her long legs are bare. Very bare. Green grass. Blue sky. The blurred edges of a field behind her. In her hand, she clutches something. A letter? A hankie? The sun casts a soft glow. The wind feels tender and feathery; strands of her short bob rustle across her brow and cheek. Her eyes rivet him. Large orbs in her angular face. The expression in them. Liquid chocolate. Deep and dense with emotion. His pulse begins racing, his heart thumps violently in his ears. In that instant, he understands what "too much world" is. It is a wounding. An invisible string that has begun unspooling.

Seong–Tai a.k.a. 'Look-See Matchmaking'

A few days later: a commotion outside his studio, right after breakfast. Kee Mun hasn't even cleared up the tray yet, and who should Tian Wei see but Bibi Gemuk bustling in, flapping her hankie at Kee Mun, her wooden clogs clacking loudly against the studio's cement floor. Bibi Gemuk is the matchmaker par excellence of the Peranakan Chinese community. Her cheeks are rouged up as red as barbecue *char siu*. Her chin boasts a small black mole from which a single hair protrudes, and she pulls at this itinerant hair when she's contemplating a match. She finds it scandalous that Tian Wei is unmarried at the ripe old age of twenty-seven. Every week, she brings an album of photographs, all of nubile young *anak daras*—some taken by Tian Wei himself, to his chagrin.

Bibi sashays in, her ample stomach and hips corralled by the tight *baju kebaya* she wears. Her gaze darts about, assessing prospects—which of his four male assistants is looking fatter, more prosperous, coming up in the world; which assistant is lacking in pallor, going about his activities with lassitude, showing the effects of opium smoking or gambling or whoring. Her eyes miss nothing. They fixate now on Tian Wei, as she clucks in Malay, "Hancur hati." Her heart is crushed, because— look at him—he's clearly overworked himself, looking thin and dissipated.

Tian Wei snorts under his breath. Instead of his usual impeccable attire of a Windsor-knotted necktie, waistcoat, and shirt, this morning he's wearing a plain cotton Chinese layman's tunic with frog buttons and deep pockets, which he gathers is less impressive to Bibi Gemuk. The dark rings encircling his eyes certainly don't help. His sleep has been much disturbed of late— ever since Charlie's last letter, in fact. His mind, less preoccupied with finding Aiko-chan now that her father has insisted she is visiting relatives upcountry in Malacca, is singularly dominated by a woman separated from him not by distance but by time. Not just by time, but also by era, history, modernity, mechanics, inventions in technology, the onward march of progress. Points of history for her are events that haven't even yet happened for him. That thought alone halts him in his tracks. Thinking about that, thinking about her, makes him lose time behind the camera, leaving the poor subject seated on a high-backed chair having to hold her smile for even longer than normal. Once, the wife of a British civil servant simply discarded her smile and berated him in front of his shutter for not having his mind on the job.

Never before has waiting for a letter taken him over body and soul like this. Thoughts of her are frequent, tossing him about as if one were frying peanuts in a *kuali*. Random questions crowd his mind: does she go to work in the skimpy attire shown in her photograph? Even swimming costumes provide more cover. How does she see him, then, in his linen suit? Too fuddy-duddy? Does she battle atoms and wrestle the cloud daily, like Guan Gong, the God of War? He has asked Peng Loon and Yip Kee to check the 1314 box every morning. All this ruminating makes his appetite swing up and down, and here, he owes much to Feng Yu, carping at him to eat, enticing him with advertised specials at the Weekly Entertainment Club ("Kedgeree with smoked fish! Chicken country captain! Pickles from Crosse & Blackwell!") and getting shirty when he refuses ("Don't be such a wet blanket").

"You'll have to forgive me," he says now to Bibi Gemuk, making his tone especially apologetic, "but I have a portrait session this morning. Have a cup of tea. We have an extra portion of char kway teow noodles. Kee Mun will bring it for you."

Bibi Gemuk tents her painted eyebrows. "Oh, anyone I know? Who's coming in to have their millionaire portrait taken?"

It would not at all do to let her know that his customer this morning is Teo Eng Hock himself, who founded

Chung Shing Yit Pao and is head of the Tung Teh Reading Room, as well as the Kuomintang branch in Singapore. His bungalow, Wang Qing Yuan, is used as a revolutionary meeting place and headquarters, hosting Sun Yat Sen when he visits Singapore. Bibi would see it as a wide-open avenue to fame and lucre.

He aims for flattery to deflect. "Is there anyone you don't know, Bibi?"

"Betul sekali," she chortles, right you are, settling down in a rattan armchair, placing her clogs on a footstool, fanning herself. Although still early, the heat is rising. "I have a couple of flowers plucked for you, just turning fifteen this coming month. Pretty, with complexions like bawang puteh." She pulls at that itinerant hair.

He flips through the photographs, but instead of admiring the complexions, pale and delicate as white onions, he is thinking critically about the angles at which some of them were taken. Some girls are posing in twos and threes along with porcelain dogs and rustic fences, looking stunned and grim; others seemed to have overdone it with Victorian pompadours and high-necked gowns, looking florid and pasty. Not all photographers care as much as he does about composing the frame. Look at this photograph, crowded with props. If you station the lady next to an overhanging floral bouquet and tall table, do not also add a Roman column, a Dante chair, and a spittoon: more isn't always better.

"Over here, Mr. Wang," Bibi Gemuk says, gesturing at the young lady's face. He realises that his finger has been tapping on the spittoon, giving her the wrong impression. Bibi Gemuk is looking at him with pursed lips. *This will not be countenanced*, her expression says.

He hates to throw his assistants under the buffalo-drawn water cart (he actually saw a coolie labourer's foot crushed by one the other day), but he hollers for Yip Kee. Of his assistants, Yip Kee is the most prepossessing, with his fair face, tall physiognomy, koi-sized eyes, and finely shaped skull (as a European phrenologist had pointed out during a portrait session). With all that going for him, Tian Wei hopes Yip Kee is also eager to be paired off in matrimony.

"Take a seat. Bibi, this is called killing two birds with one stone."

Bibi Gemuk flaps her hankie in the air. "Choi, choi! No killing necessary." Kee Mun brings up a tray of noodles and a cup of tea, and Tian Wei uses this as an excuse to escape, saying he needs to prepare his studio for his morning sessions.

The Spectral Past

Ah Seng is remonstrating Kee Mun for not setting up his pots of paint properly. Even though the twins are tasked with cleaning and sweeping, Kee Lung is learning the photographic trade, so Ah Seng treats him differently. Kee Mun cooks, fetches tea for everyone, and even uses her little knuckles to give Ah Seng back massages when ordered to do so. Ever since Dr. Lim's lecture at the Chinese Philomathic Society, Tian Wei has decided to borrow books for her from the Tung Teh Reading Room. Kee Mun had taken one look and protested. "Xifu, this book is as thick as my clog! And there are so many characters, the page looks like it's crawling with ants!"

Sternly, he had told her to keep at it, that he had enrolled her in a girls' school nearby, and that soon she would be able to read the whole book from front to back in days instead of weeks, and without using her finger to track each vertical line as she read.

Ah Seng had listened to this exchange and snorted, "Money down the drain, lou ban. You don't need a wife who can read. You need a wife who knows how to take care of your cane stalk!"

"She is not my wife," Tian Wei had said quietly.

Ah Seng had sniffed. "That makes even less sense then."

Tian Wei has always had a soft spot for street urchins. It's impossible to forget that he was one himself before he made good, roaming the streets in Hongkew after his mother died of a blood-coughing illness and his father disappeared, either off gambling or assuaging his opium addiction. Turfed out on to the streets, he knew hunger intimately, begging for scraps with pleading eyes before being shooed off by tenement neighbours who barely had enough to feed their own. He was often given a good drubbing by gangs of older urchins hustling the streets of Hongkew and Chapei.

One day, an older street urchin, Sansan, adept at running errands for small coins or food, defended him against a group of them by firing pebbles with a rigged-up catapult; her shots were so fast and accurate that the boys scattered, howling in pain. Sansan took him under her wing. Soon, he was as adept as she was in wheedling food out of teahouse kitchens or food stalls. It was also Sansan who introduced him to the big boss of Powkee Studio on Nanjing Road— Master Ouyang Shizhi. Together with Sansan, he would run errands like buying tobacco, sweetmeats, and melon seeds for Master Ouyang's many important guests. Often, the two of them would huddle by lintels and doorways to share a bao or a bowl of noodles. Sansan told him she was born in the Year of the Ox. She boasted she was as strong as three men put together, her cheeks shiny with grease, her hair wiry and long like porcupine quills.

Master Ouyang took a shine to him and apprenticed him in his studio. Tian Wei only had the courage to ask Master Ouyang once about taking in Sansan too, but his request was rejected unceremoniously. The master had no use for girls in the photographic trade. Sansan merely laughed and waved as she walked away, nonchalant. Then, she did the most amazing thing. She opened her mouth wide. Out of her throat emerged songstress notes, as sweet and melodic as those he'd heard from cabaret sing-song girls around Nanjing Road when the two of them were bootlicking and dodging in and out of kitchens.

The thought did occur to him that he should stick with Sansan. Together, they could tough it out, this business of survival. But the chance offered by Master Ouyang was too good to relinquish. Sansan wouldn't want him to pass it up. That was what he told himself.

Once he started working at Powkee, he didn't see Sansan much. One day, she told him that she'd been taken in by a courtesan house on Foochow Road. They were going to train her as a sing-song girl, she said. She twirled in one of the hutong lanes, laughing and showing off her dance moves.

When he thinks of Sansan now, a shadow flits across his brow—the year she died, 1910, is etched in his heart, as well as the memory of her body dredged up from Suzhou Creek: bloated beyond recognition, the skin purple and peeling, some of her fingers and toes missing. She didn't have a stitch of clothing on. The police said she must have fallen in because she was drunk; the fish had gnawed off all her clothes. He didn't believe a word of it. In his heart, he suspected foul play. This was the lot of sing-song girls, courtesans, and brothel workers, their flesh sold as merchandise for compradors and literati alike. At her death, Sansan had just turned twenty-one. Being as strong as an ox had not saved her.

In 1911, when he was seventeen, the Qing government fell, and he bought passage on a junk under the credit-ticket system and came to the Southern Ocean. Singapore. What he remembers is the hodgepodge scene that greeted him: stevedores hauling cargo at a bustling port; white bosses in colonial uniforms, swinging Malacca canes; Sikh policemen standing at street corners, blowing their whistles; Chinese hawkers in tricorn straw hats, hawking wares from two drums slung across their shoulders with a bamboo pole; and meanwhile, horses clip-clopping along, pulling carriages, and rickshaws trundling past, pulled by strong shoulders. All of it smacking of industry and boom time. A promise of fortune and paradise. And yet, one thing was so different from Shanghai: where were the women?

How time flies; October has begun, and thoughts of Sansan must have surfaced this morning because of his agitation over Aiko. Since agreeing to let Si Nian put out tentative enquiries with the Ghee Hin about Aiko, several incidents had happened to make him quake in his straw slippers. He feels strongly that the shophouse is being watched. He wonders if he is being followed when he walks back after dinner in Club Street. A few times, he distinctly heard footsteps behind him, even detected a lurking shadow, quickly lapsing into the gloom when he turned his head to look. He feels jumpy and anxious all the time. He keeps to the busier streets, especially those filled with roadside stalls raucously offering late-night snacks.

One afternoon, while out with Yip Kee and Kee Lung to shoot an off-site group photograph, the studio was broken into by a band of tattooed hooligans wielding machetes and Chinese cleavers. Glass negatives were smashed, furniture destroyed, his assistants frightened to within an inch of their lives. The hooligans delivered a message written on joss paper—that which is burned for the dead: 井水不犯河水 or *Well water does not cross river water*. In other words, mind your own business. Si Nian had been keeping him abreast of the enquiries he was making with the Ghee Hin. Clearly, Tian Wei was being warned off his search for Aiko. Someone's feathers had been royally ruffled.

Ah Seng isn't so sure this is the work of the Ghee Hin. The hooligans weren't sporting the Ghee Hin's usual green dragon tattoos. "I have a hunch, Xifu," he says. "I think maybe they were hired *samseng*." Ah Seng frequents the opium dens; if anyone knows about skulking thugs, it is Ah Seng.

Then, one afternoon in late September, after months of waiting in a rickshaw in the shade of a large flame tree, a Panama hat over his eyes as the afternoon sun heated up like a furnace, Tian Wei saw a middle-aged lady in a motor car being chauffeured out of the Tay mansion. The hood was down and he could see the lady clearly—she was wearing a cotton yukata with a print of tiny folding fans. Without thinking, he jumped out and bolted straight in front of the motor car, causing it to screech to a halt, its passengers jolting forward. His rickshaw-puller squawked. The horse of a passing gharry startled and neighed. A *majie* dropped her basket of provisions. A dog lying on a square *tikar* in a nearby shophouse barked. A couple of boys playing football nearby paused in their play and the football rolled into a ditch. In the air, the scent of sulphur and rain.

"Here, take all the money," the lady in the car pleaded, thrusting her cloth purse at him.

"I didn't mean to scare you, I apologise deeply, but I've been waiting and waiting. I've sent numerous letters to your residence but there have been no replies. Are you Aiko's mother? I'm Wang

Tian Wei, the studio photographer. Do you remember me? Did you get my letters?" He spoke rapidly, trying to include everything he'd been rehearsing in the few seconds before she drove away.

Recognition dawned but her expression also betrayed great fear and wariness. She waved no, ordering her syce to get moving, but Tian Wei placed a hand on the door. The syce stared impassively ahead.

"Please. Please talk to me. It's been two years. I will not rest until I find out what has happened to her."

He continued to plead, and saw the moment she relented— it was when he mentioned Aiko's drawings and withdrew from his pocket the *pilu* sketch from Lai Chun Yuen she'd gifted him. Aiko and he had gone together for the matinee performance; he'd bought her dried squid and *kacang puteh* snacks, and she had given him the drawing as a keepsake. Tears filmed over her mother's eyes. She gestured for him to get in and they motored their way to Grand Hotel de l'Europe at the corner of High Street and St. Andrew's Road, overlooking the Esplanade.

Seated in the grand dining room, with its chandeliers and draped tables, Aiko's mother introduced herself as Tomoko-san and ordered a cream tea. Her Malay was lightly accented, not as fluent as his.

"Aiko is in Penang," she started off without preamble. "She was kidnapped one evening in July, two years ago. The amah came home frantic, and I suffered a nervous breakdown. My husband was adamant that the police should not be called. He must have already suspected that it had something to do with the threatening notes he had been getting. I accidentally saw one of them in his study one day. After Aiko-chan was kidnapped—" Tomoko-san's voice broke— "I confronted him, and he admitted the kidnapping was in retaliation for his refusal to join the Japanese boycott. The note had told him that in one week something very bad would happen, and still he refused to give them what they wanted. Many of the Japanese imported goods are stored in my husband's godowns at Collyer Quay, especially Japanese textiles. He stands to lose a lot of money if he joins the boycott. So, he refused."

This admission from Tomoko-san caused her to start weeping into her handkerchief.

Discomfort had built up in Tian Wei's windpipe. The clotted cream in the dish glistened and he put down his scone. "Why wouldn't he go to the police for help?"

"I think he received a note following her kidnapping. It must have said that harm would come to her if he went to the police. He promised me he would handle it privately. That he would make sure she was safe."

"What happened next?"

Tomoko-san's fingers gripped the clasp of her handbag resting on her lap. "I had to trust him at his word. I went to the temple every day to recite the Great Compassion sutra and light the oil lamp for her. About a year ago, he told me she had been retrieved from the lowlife who kidnapped her into the hands of the Tua Pek Kong Society and thence into the custody of the Hai San Secret Society. She is alive, he tells me. And safe now. But she won't be allowed back into our house because she is with child." At this, Tomoko-san began weeping anew. Tian Wei felt burdened; forcing her to talk to him had been hugely distressing to her.

People at surrounding tables were casting them curious glances. A part of him was relieved to hear Aiko was indeed alive, and safe by all accounts, but another part of him was suffused with anger. So young, and now Aiko would be a mother? Was this what she had wanted? Certainly, it wasn't. It couldn't have been. Had something been done to her? It didn't bear thinking about. A vision of Sansan dredged up from the creek made him nauseous and clammy. But the meeting hadn't been for nought; the Hai San Society was based in Penang; it provided him with a valuable lead.

"You must promise me to enquire no further," Tomoko-san begged. "If you do, you might endanger her life."

"Why?"

"I'm not sure. My husband has warned me not to ask questions. He says that there is political foment I don't know anything about. He says we live in tumultuous times; our society is on the cusp of change. I am just a woman. A woman who wants to see her daughter again. For her sake, please leave the matter alone."

Arguments swarmed inside him, but he had no claim to Aiko strong enough to voice them.

"It's already dangerous for me to talk to you like this," Tomoko-san said. She hadn't eaten a thing, her fingers repeatedly pleating her handkerchief into a fan. She tucked it back into her handbag and pushed back her chair. "Please don't approach me again, Mr. Wang. If you truly care about Aiko, please do what I ask. I beg you."

The Emulsion Factor

Two weeks later, a letter arrives mysteriously at his studio. The letter isn't addressed to him, but to Hudson Tay. It reads,

DEAR MR. HUDSON TAY:

WE KNOW THAT AT THE PARIS PEACE CONFERENCE OUR FOREIGN DELEGATES ANNOUNCED THEIR FAILURES. WE OVERSEAS CHINESE DEEPLY FEAR THAT FROM THIS POINT, IT WILL NOT BE LONG UNTIL OUR NATION IS DESTROYED. THE STUDENTS' INDIGNATION AND THE BUSINESSMEN'S BOYCOTT ARE FINE EXAMPLES OF PATRIOTIC ACTIVITY ON THE PART OF OUR COUNTRYMEN. YOU ARE PART OF THE CHINESE PEOPLE. WE BELIEVE THAT YOU MUST ENDORSE OUR TACTICS. A FEW DAYS AGO, WE ALREADY INFORMED YOU THAT YOU SHOULD RESIGN YOURSELF TO THE BOYCOTT. BUT TILL NOW YOU STILL HAVE NOT LISTENED. WE ARE GIVING YOU A LAST WARNING, LIMITING YOU TO LESS THAN ONE WEEK TO COMPLY. IF NOT, IN THE FUTURE WE WILL USE RUTHLESS MEASURES TO OPPOSE YOU. WE HOPE YOU ACCEPT OUR WARNING. OTHERWISE, IN THE FUTURE WE WILL USE BLOOD TO REPORT TO YOU.

It is unsigned. It must have been one of the aforementioned written threats that Tomoko-san discovered in Hudson Tay's study. She'd sent it to Tian Wei as a reminder to honour his promise of silence.

So engrossed is he in ruminations over the letter, he doesn't sense Peng Loon reading it over his shoulder. "Xifu," Peng Loon now moans, giving Tian Wei a dreadful start, "there seem to be a lot of letters floating about. Sei foh! This studio shophouse is haunted. There's another one of those lan gwai letters on a negative again."

This jerks him upright; it is all he can manage not to rush into the darkroom immediately. The letters from Charlie are taking longer and longer to arrive, and he suspects there is some mathematical formula at play. But what is this: the last letter he received from Charlie was in May, and it is only mid-October now; surely it couldn't be another letter from her so soon? He whips round on Peng Loon, startling his assistant so abruptly that Peng Loon drops the broom he has been swishing around and throws up his hands in surrender. "Where's Kee Lung? Call him."

Kee Lung comes running—one hand covered with soapsuds, the other clutching a pair of chopsticks—moving so fast his slippers fall off his feet. "Yes, Xifu? You wanted me?"

"It's Friday today; have you already dropped off the letters at the G.P.O.?" His throat feels parched, but his mind is whirling.

Kee Lung looks at him wide-eyed, stunned into speechlessness.

"Well?"

"Not yet, Xifu. I was going to go after clearing up breakfast."

Tian Wei dashes up the stairs to his reception area. He opens the repurposed letter holder, takes out the letters, to which a film of silver-halide residue clings. The metallic scent tickles his nose. He rubs some specks between his thumb and forefinger. It stirs something within him, an inchoate instinct, a flash of insight, and then the thought floats away like a puff of lalang seeds. For the first time, he notices the numbers on the side of the box: *1152*.

Meanwhile, there is a letter from Charlie to develop. Hastening to the darkroom, he mixes the chemical bath himself.

The print that emerges shows a short letter. He reads it under the pinhole light and his entire being wants to go to her, wants to leap across decades and ford eras so he can hold her.

23 January 2019

Dearest Tian Wei,

My brother Sebastian has gone missing. It's been several days since his disappearance. He hasn't returned any of my calls or texts and I am frantic—no, scratch that—I am absolutely bonkers with worry.

The Portuguese apparently have a legend that goes like this: Take a stone and leave it on a cairn. Put the stone under your pillow before you go to sleep. When you wake the next morning, you will see an apparition of a soldier for a brief moment in time, before he morphs back into a stone. Do you suppose, if I did that, Sebastian would reappear?

Yours,
Charlie.

The Spectacle That Is Cataclysm

A few days later, the shit truly hits the fan. The last time we had a heart-to-heart, Sebastian seemed resigned to the idea of the break-up with Adnan, and he had even thought up a couple of possible solutions—find a financial partner to buy Adnan out or raise another seed-funding round. The morning he is flying out to Shanghai, Sebastian sends a text to say I should feel free to use his gym membership, and see if Atalina would be willing to make *ondeh-ondeh* for when he comes back. His mood seems good; he sounds bouncy. Everything is fine. No need to worry.

At work, Mahmood rolls up in his chair and shows me his phone, where he has numerous tabs open. One after another headline screams:

ONLINE ART AUCTION HOUSE TAV CAUGHT IN UPROAR OVER SALE OF FORGERY!

ZHOU ZHEN'S *THE FLOATING MONTGOLFER* IN PRIVATE SALE SAID TO BE A FAKE

SALE OF CHINESE ARTIST'S HYDROGEN BALLOON COLLAGE ALL A PUFF OF HOT AIR

THE AGE OF WONDER OR THE AGE OF PHONEY? ONLINE ART DEALERSHIP PEDDLES FORGERY A MONTH AFTER LAUNCH

"Did you know, Kak?" Mahmood asks.

I hadn't. I hadn't known at all. Shock ripples through my inner being. Followed by alarm and worry. Is this why Sebastian is flying to Shanghai again so soon after coming back? Did he know this shitstorm was about to hit on his way to the airport when he sent that text? I push my hair behind my ears, scan and read all the articles quickly.

A private collector named D. Broussard had bought Zhou Zhen's work, *The Floating Montgolfer*, immediately after the launch. The work, a departure from Zhou Zhen's usual shanshui collages, is a stunning photo-collaged recreation of a *Le Journal* pictorial from 1783, showing the first manned ascent of a Montgolfer hot-air balloon in Paris. Being an outlier from his series, critics had panned it. The articles revealed that Zhou Zhen had indeed commissioned TAV as his online art gallerist for this work, which sold for something like five million HKD (Mahmood, reading along behind my shoulder, gives a low whistle). Broussard, evidently a fervent collector of Zhou's works, was quoted as saying he immediately noticed when he received the work that the Chinese insignia seal of Zhou Zhen was in the wrong place—Chinese scrolls are unfurled right to left, and the seal is imprinted on the left, but Zhou Zhen's seal here appeared on the right, which has never been done on any of his artworks and is an instant tip-off. The articles all said that TAV founding partner Charles S. Sze-Toh could not be reached for comment. Instead, there is a quote from Adnan claiming TAV's innocence. "We will get to the bottom of this. We will give due accounting to the satisfaction of all parties concerned." But the articles all concluded that proper provenance documentation is the basic responsibility of any art dealer, and once public trust is broken, it is difficult to repair.

I dial Sebastian. It rings and rings, then lapses. Did Sebastian find out at the same time the whole world did? Is any of it true? I redial every five minutes. I send numerous texts, increasingly frantic with worry. I dial Adnan, who is also not picking up. Work is impossible. Lunch is impossible. Mahmood brings me a cup of *tieguanyin*—I've never told

him I don't like Chinese tea, but I gulp it down, scalding my
tongue, in search of something warm. He places a hand on
my shoulder. "It'll be OK, Kak." I see Mahmood and Yoo-lin
huddled together at the copier, their voices migrating as
sibilant whispers. I can barely sit still, escaping to the corridor
to gaze at Mother for minutes at a time as I try to figure out
a way to reach Sebastian. My thoughts are spinning. Why did
he disappear like this without telling me? The symmetry of
Sebastian's disappearance to Aiko's strikes me suddenly: it's no
coincidence; shit just became real.

The ringtone of my phone sounds—*Omo! Omo!*—and I
jump to answer it before realising it's Linton, his tone crispier
than *kueh pie tee*: "OK, we're in the news. No such thing as bad
publicity and all that, but what the hell happened?"

"Whoa, whoa, slow down with the charm," I say.

He softens. "Ma is worried sick."

As if. They're obviously more concerned about how
this would tarnish the Sze-Toh pristine noblesse-oblige
image. Linton and Cassandra sit on the boards of multiple
philanthropic organisations.

"Well, I'm sorry to hear that," I say.

I can almost hear a scowl at the other end. "You mean to say
you had no idea?"

"Linton, I don't know what that's supposed to mean. I can't
find Sebastian. I don't have time for this."

"Emergency gathering at home tonight, eight o'clock."

The words escape like balloons: "Not another dinner!"

A stiff silence on Linton's end. "If you can put aside your
dislike of us for a short hour, there are bigger issues at stake."

Why does talking to Linton always make me want to squeeze
his oesophagus? "Fine. But first, I need to find Sebastian. Let's
give him a chance to explain. I'm sure it's a misunderstanding
of some kind."

A loud exhalation on the other end. "Is it, now?"

I hit *End Call*—I simply can't deal.

That evening, just as I am planning to leave for the day, Linton calls to say Cassandra has an evening do she can't reschedule. So much for being worried sick.

"She'll call you, I expect. Pick up the phone." Linton's tone is this side of arch.

I decide to let the microaggression go. My anxiety about Sebastian is driving all other thoughts from my mind. Throughout the day, I've been calling and calling him, but there is no answer. Obsessively checking his *Last Seen* timestamp is doing my state of mind no good. With a shock, I realise there are five half-drunk Styrofoam cups of Kurasu Black on my desk and an empty packet of Loacker's Quadratini. It's all I've eaten all day. In utter desperation, I ferret-type a letter to Wang Tian Wei—as if he were a minor god, with access to the supernatural, and the letter a form of prayer. It is also a deathly honest admission that I have no one in my life I can talk to about my fears regarding Sebastian.

I take a taxi over to Sebastian's apartment. Using the spare key he has given me, I let myself in. The heat inside lets me know the air conditioning hasn't been on. The curtains are pulled back and the setting sun casts the room in sepia. No mugs on the dish rack, the laundry rack in one corner is empty of clothes. In the closet, his overnight suitcase isn't there. Still not back from Shanghai, then.

I call and text Adnan repeatedly. He's likely up to his eyeballs dealing with the media frenzy. None of my various messages—*Any news?* and *Have you heard from Sebastian?*—get two blue ticks.

Before bedtime, I try again. This time, success. Adnan's voice box sounds like it's been dragged over cut glass. He's worn out. But not so worn out that he can't open fire with, "Unacceptable. Absolutely not on."

"Me?"

"Not you. It's been an absolute shitshow. What kind of an irresponsible person disappears at a time like this?"

And breaking up with him right after THE LAUNCH isn't irresponsible? "You haven't heard from Seb then, I see. Where are you?"

"I'm in a taxi, stuck in traffic on Shiji Boulevard. Several major artists wanted to pull out of our online auction next month, and it took every shred of my PR skills to get them to hold their horses till we finish investigating. Investors have been hounding me for an explanation. If they pull out, we're done." His frustration is a smear across trunklines. Then, he starts coughing and it's several minutes before we can resume.

"Adnan, you OK?"

"Oh, just bloomin' marvellous," he says tersely. "Listen, can't chit-chat. I've got another incoming call."

"I want to know what happened."

"I'll call you later."

*

It's a long night of intermittent shallow sleep and wakefully checking my phone.

*

Adnan rings as I'm brushing my teeth the next morning. In a hurry to answer, I drop my electric toothbrush into a shallow sink of water, and, in retrieving it, receive an unpleasant buzz. The morning is well on its way to glory. I spit out globs of toothpaste and put him on speaker.

"Charlie?" Adnan says. "Rough night?"

"A bit. You?"

He sighs. "Oh, erotic dreams all night long. Did he call?"

"Nope. I guess he hasn't called you either."

"When I get my bare hands on him…" Adnan says. But there is no grit in the threat; it's just something to say. Adnan's sigh transmits his weariness, and I can't stymie the twitch of relief that Sebastian didn't disappear on me alone; he did this to Adnan, too.

"What happened, anyway?"

He pauses. I hear him bark directions to the taxi driver in Mandarin about where to turn off for WeWork Weihai. He comes back on: "The digital images we have in our system indicate that we had all the correct provenance documentation. Zhou Zhen's agent swore that he handed over the original artwork. His wife Xueling was on hand to supervise the packing. The art handlers are about to crap in their pants, swearing that all processes were done exactly to specifications. But it must have been switched either in transport or in storage."

"Can you prove that?"

"If I could, we wouldn't be having this conversation, would we?"

"Could it possibly be anyone within your shop?"

An explosive sigh from Adnan. "Listen. We hire the crème de la crème from top art schools. It'd be career suicide if any of them did something so shady. By virtue of taint, it could already be career suicide. Slightly different than mousing about in the archives." I hear him glugging from a bottle of water.

I don't take umbrage. If he is throwing shade, his fighting spirit hasn't taken that big of a hit. "I need to find Sebastian. Adnan, I just hope he doesn't do anything stupid."

"That makes two of us, gurl. Call me immediately if you make contact, please?"

*

A day turns into two, turns into three. Phone calls ring straight into a power-down message, texts whoosh off as delivered, yet none of them are picked up. I go to all the places he frequents. At his gym, a Pilates Reformer workout with a Molly Sims lookalike is in full session, but no Sebastian. I walk over to his favourite eco-conscious cafe, The Squawk Box, and the girl behind the till, with dyed vermillion hair and a ring through one eyebrow—Samantha—says she hasn't seen him for days. The same at his coffee place and dry cleaners. At Apophenia, the maître d' looks at me as if I have recently been diagnosed with amnesia. "Not since you came with him that evening?"

I message his closest friends, Darren Yu, Simon Tan, and Leesa Ganesan. Not one of them has seen him, but, like standard-issue busybodies, they all want to online chat for at least ten minutes to find out what had gone down. By the time I'm done with all these conversations, the director of SCoP is glowering at me from above my computer. I tell him there's a rendang spot on his Hermès tie, which instantly gets him out of my hair.

The next day, it isn't Linton but Cassandra who calls to reschedule the emergency meeting. The strain of it all must have been discernible in my voice, because Cassandra suddenly says, "You don't sound like yourself." Yet more glimpses of the blindingly obvious. She clears her throat. "Atalina has made some hong dou tang. I know how much you like red bean soup. I'll have her bring it over to the Guest Lodge."

"Thanks, Yi-Ma. I'm sorry I don't have news for you."

"Tell me, did he do this horrible thing the papers say he did? Did he create an art forgery?"

"No. I can promise you Sebastian would never do that."

Cassandra makes *hmm* noises on her end, then says, "What's your plan? Are you going to sit there until he turns up or floats up? Shouldn't you fly to Shanghai and do a bit of poking around for him, since you two are so pally?"

Nice. Just when I'm softening a smidge at the idea of the red bean soup. Touché, though—why indeed am I sitting still instead of poking around?

Wind

13 October 1921

My dearest Miss C.:—

I received a letter from you today. It was very short, saying your brother Sebastian was missing. I am very perturbed to hear this. I wish I could be there to provide some comfort, or at least offer you my shoulder to cry on.

So much has happened in the past few months for me as well that I don't know quite where to begin.

You managed to find a photograph of me in your archives? It sounds too fantastic to be believed. It boggles my mind. You mean I haven't made myself up?

Jokes aside, your words also capture much sadness, and I wish I could take away some of it. You write about your mother, and I wish to say, I cherish you. You are not bereft of love. I see it in your photograph. Those colours. As if you leapt across the hourglass of ages and jumped straight into a corner of my heart. I shall carry your photograph and your letters with me everywhere. You do look Chinese — brain the person who said you didn't and maybe the hare inside will come out. Hare-brained: see?

Pardon the very bad pun, I'm not much for wit. Please accept these feeble attempts of mine to try to cheer you up.

How I do wish we could meet. Is it presumptuous of me to call you "my dear"? Is it allowed in your world, where people don't stand on formalities? Here, in our proper society, if a woman stands up, all the men must rise to their feet. It's not that I mind showing women courtesy, but sometimes I get a little confused. I go to the Chinese Philomathic Society and hear lectures about educating women so that they are free of their superstitions and prejudices, but in a world where they are not allowed to work or choose their husbands or go about without a female chaperone, I am confused. Will education be the answer to equality for the sexes? Perhaps we ought to show less manners towards the gentler sex (I can well imagine English suffragists saying, "Stuff your manners!"), and instead give them what they want — freedom. Freedom to do all the things that men enjoy. Or is that too over-simplifying for such a complex matter?

I hope I don't come across as a bore. Writing to you gives me great pleasure and happiness. I used to think in Chinese and then turn the thought into English. I do this much less now, but it still takes me several drafts to get what I want to say down on paper. The wait for your letters is so interminable, it is painful. I clutch at shadows. This intensity of feeling is new to me. It isn't always hopeful or joyous. It is also attended by despair and melancholia. What is the point in prevaricating or hiding in a letter to you, when your letter takes so long to come?

You said that a photograph does not lie.
Whatever is photographed becomes fact. Much
depends on my framing of a photograph, does
it not? A subject may come in all hot and
bothered, but the minute he sits before my
camera, he is all solemnity and importance.
I'm always looking for that telltale expression
that clues me in to who he is. I don't always
find it, but sometimes it's, "Eureka!"

I shall have to ponder what you said about
beauty. The other day, I was watching my
assistant Kee Mun feeding the stray dogs
and cats in the street, of which there are
many. This frame is not suitable for a studio
portrait, but what you said about beauty has
made me think that there is indeed something
beautiful in the way she held out her hand,
glistening with leftover fish bones and fish
heads, allowing the cats to feed off it.
She squatted on her haunches and sang to
stray cats, and they set up an accompanying
hullaballoo. I try to take these kinds of
photographs also. More impromptu, more real.
But I don't know if I had managed to capture
Kee Mun's kindness.

I am much obliged to you for saying my
English is impeccable! Quite chuffed, really.
I shall take you up on your invitation to
write about myself, and hope I won't be a
complete and utter bore. You see, I learned
my letters — Guoyu and English — at the Tung
Teh Reading Room. Having looked up to Master
Ouyang Shizhi during my Powkee days, I try
hard to measure up to the standards expected
of a well-read Chinese gentleman. A zhi shi
fen zi. I have an exemplar also in Freddie

Khoo, a kind Straits Chinese man who was educated in England. He had me read all manner of tomes — Dickens, Shakespeare, Milton — but I much prefer P. G. Wodehouse, Agatha Christie, and Leslie Charteris. From my other upright Confucian scholar-friend, Ting Shixin, I worked through Tang-dynasty poems, read Confucian texts and Mencius. Writings by Kang Youwei and Liang Qichao. Dr. Lim Boon Keng's essays in The Straits Chinese Magazine. Unlike Si Nian, who reads only the Chinese papers, I read The Straits Times and The Singapore Free Press, and also The Malaya Tribune, the voice of the Asiatics. These latter writings are so full of new ideas and current affairs they make my head swim. It changes my thinking. No one is just a cog in a machine. We all must do our part towards building a better society. A couple of lines from Du Fu's poem "To Imperial Advisor Han" comes to mind:

> How dare I ignore our nation's success or failure, to dine amongst the fragrance of bitter decay?

At heart, I am a simple man. However, I do relate to what you say about different kinds of truths. Man manipulates truths, but, if his heart is pure, the camera keeps him honest.

I must tell you that, when I received your letter and your photograph, I collapsed in a swoon. Kee Mun was so worried, she fetched the Chinese doctor from Chinatown. He took my pulse and said I had too much wind. An endogenous wind has attacked my liver, causing

spasms and convulsions. He prescribed a dose
of mulberry and feng xian hua — I know not
what its name is in English, but it is good to
dispel disorders of the intestines.

Though I am fully recovered, this wind
is still inside me, arousing from slumber
suddenly with the force of a tempest. I don't
pretend to understand what it is or why I am
feeling this way. Perhaps it is to do partly
with you asking for a nude portrait, which
made me colour with embarrassment. It also
sparked some quite inappropriate thoughts. I
appreciate the words of this Polish-American
poet you sent: "too much world". Perhaps he
meant it to be synonymous with wind. Wind
and rain and thunder and lightning that seise
hold of one's very soul and shake it about,
until every bit and bob inside (what you call
"atom" and "particle"?) falls out. I fear
I am well and truly poxed. How I fervently
wish we could meet at a kopitiam — it would
be wonderful to get some chee cheong fun
together with green bean and meat dumplings.

It has begun to get light outside my window.
I can hear the rattle of the water cart,
the first clang of the tram, the cries of
breakfast vendors. Kee Mun is folding back
the window shutters. What will the world bring
today?

                              Yours forever,
                              W.T.W.

P.S. It's quite all right that you don't
sew. I myself am quite adept, especially with
buttons.

```
     P.P.S. I have had more time to ponder this
giant cloud you mentioned — it sounds Zeus-
like and I doubt Bibi Gemuk should like to be
put out of business by such strange marriage-
making competition. She doesn't even trust
spittoons, which are practical necessities if
one insists on chewing betelnut.
     P.P.P.S. In your photograph, may I ask what
it is you're clutching in your fingers?
```

With this letter comes a bloom of feelings. A whoop and thump and boom. My breath shortens. The sulphuric scent I have come to associate with these letters tinges the air.

A *kopitiam*! A bit like having a date at KFC. Disbelief settles in my sternum. And a realisation: my heart rate does not escalate near Sebastian. But it does with this man I have no hope of ever meeting. My inner world flips through a jukebox offering of despair and hope and happiness and joy. Observe: my world can somersault and flip 180 degrees in minutes.

From her corner, I hear the sibilant wheeze of Yoo-lin's water-sprayer against her cacti; I spy Mahmood beginning a new chess game, and the lump in my throat dissipates. Desire springs out of nowhere. A want, an ask. An impossibility. A cessation of activity around me.

Mahmood looks up and blinks at me lazily, then he says, "What is that you are reading, Kak?"

In dismay, I realise I've been muttering to myself. "Nothing. Just something I've found."

He taps a couple of fingers on his tabletop. "Most of the plates we sent over to the conservators have accretions and chips on them."

I blink. He blinks. "They've carried out surface cleaning. They are beginning to categorise according to what level of treatment is needed. Some of the plates are in bad shape."

Bad shape: is Mahmood referring to the dry plate glass negatives? It doesn't sound like he is only referring to the plates.

"Shh." I put a finger to my lips. "Send me the report and I'll take a look. Right now, I need to ring the T.T.B. (big-big boss) and ask for a leave of absence." I've decided to fly out to Shanghai on the next available flight.

Shanghai Follies

The aeroplane is half full, and who should I spot but a familiar face, whose name it takes me a couple of seconds to recall. Matt Sharpe. His name is Matt Sharpe. At some point, Linton had informed me archly that Matt is a visual ethnologist, researching spiritual spaces and spirit possession. *He's a proper academic.* I had flipped Linton the bird in my mind.

I squint—I haven't daydreamed; it really is Matt. Coincidence rarely happens in real life, and yet here is one. He's several rows ahead, loading a duffel bag into the overhead compartment, and hasn't spotted me. In that same conversation, Linton told me that he had extended an offer to house Matt Sharpe at the Guest Lodge, so he wouldn't have to continue staying in university lodgings and eating heat-lamp bacteria-proliferated cafeteria food every day—*Matt said that, if he ate any more fried tenggiri, he'll turn into one himself.* I don't know if we are in fact housemates now; I haven't run into him. It would be the neighbourly thing to say hello. But something quails inside me. I put my things away, take out my laptop, and strap myself in.

The plane lands at Pudong International. At baggage claim, as I am lifting my suitcase off the conveyor belt, I hear a voice over my shoulder. "Charlie?"

Matt's smile seems genuine, and he looks very good in his white polo shirt and light grey sportscoat.

"Oh, hi!" I feign surprise. "What are you doing here?"

"I'm giving a lecture at the Shanghai Academy of Social Sciences. East Asian religions."

"How long are you here for?" I ask.

He moves to give me a hand with my luggage, but I bat his hand away. It amuses him.

"A couple of days." He pauses. "Are you here because of…?" He trails off, but if he is expecting me to finish his sentence for him, I don't do that.

"I guess you heard all about it."

He shrugs, but his gaze is curious. "Hard to avoid; it's in the papers. Dinners at your stepmother's have been…" He pauses again, scratches the back of his head.

"Dramatic?"

His mouth crimps. "Heartburn-inducing."

His luggage hasn't arrived. Good time to make my getaway. I pull up the T-bar handle of my suitcase, but he stays me with one hand.

"Charlie?" He fidgets. "I'm guessing you're here because of Sebastian. It's not my place to ask, and I'm not trying to intrude on your privacy. I just want to say that, if you'd like help, don't be shy to ask."

"I don't need help."

"I know you don't, I'm just saying." His shoulders tense. A muscle ticks near his angled jawline. A fluffy minion swings from the zipper of his backpack.

"Would you like to share a cab into town?" he says. He has a well-meaning look on his face, and I'm flung back into a memory.

When I first arrived back in Singapore, a foreigner and I, waiting in the taxi queue on Battery Road, had struck up a conversation, and he told me that the taxis in Singapore were like crickets: when it rained, they all went into hiding. There was no way to assess if what he said was true, and he then ruined the beauty of his observation by following it up with a pick-up line: "If we're headed in the same direction, would you like to share a cab?" Sebastian had laughed uproariously when I told him— "Charlie, I love you, but only you would assume it's a pick-up line. He could be offering to carpool, being environmentally-minded perhaps?" For a month, each time we headed out, Sebastian would quirk an eyebrow and ask, "Would you like to share a cab?"

The memory has caught me unawares and the look on my face must have given me away. Matt Sharpe reaches out to touch my elbow. "Are you OK?"

I shrug away from his touch. "Sure, let's share a cab." Blame it on that swinging fluffy minion. Most men of the Marcus Lo variety wouldn't be caught dead with one.

*

The following evening, we meet up for dinner at a Szechuan restaurant in Tianzifang—the old French concession area, now gentrified with hipster bars and chic restaurants, and lit up everywhere with lights. The restaurant is decorated colonial style, with a tropical long bar and French terrace doors opening on to a balcony. Large electric fans circle languidly overhead. The waitresses wear *qipao*, with jasmine sprigs in their hair. Big-band jazz plays out of the music system. Matt is ebullient—too ebullient—his lecture has gone over well, and he's been invited back already later in the year. He loves Shanghai, all that pervasive jazz-era history and Bund glamour—he holds up his hands as if about to sing hosanna.

I find Matt easier to talk to than I expected. Over spicy *ma la huo guo* and several peach-blossom vodka cocktails, I end up telling him about my relationship with Sebastian and our troubled relationship with the rest of the Sze-Tohs, using self-deprecating dry wit to make him laugh. In Matt, I detect a look—the look a man gives a woman he'd like to take to bed. My subconscious sends a weather warning.

I start babbling, "I hope you don't think I'm crazy or one of those crystal-loving woo-woo sorts ..." But then Matt shakes his head in disapproval, and I'm like, "What? What did I say?"

"I'd never think you're woo-woo," he says. "Rude, maybe—a touch cranky—but definitely not woo-woo."

I roll my eyes.

He laughs. "Also, I'm a Scorpio. Intense about love and relationships. All in or all out, no in-between."

"Huh?"

"Look, Charlie, I've been meaning to ask you. Are you seeing anyone?"

Matt has completely stumped me. My mouth opens and shuts. What would he think of me if I were to tell him I fantasise about someone who lived a hundred years ago? He'd revise his opinion about "woo-woo", wouldn't he?

His eyes scour mine in search of a response.

"Uh, Matt…" and then my words stall.

"You don't have to answer right now. I know you're worried about Sebastian. You have a lot on your mind."

"You have no idea."

I watch his face change expression—a hopefulness to something gentler, kinder. Out of nowhere, a notion enters my head: this is someone with bad timing. Also, this is someone I can maybe trust. Only one way to test this: to come clean.

"I have a scenario for you. Suppose letters start appearing in a digital archival folder, one linked to a metaverse." I watch for every twitch of his response. "These letters are from someone living a hundred years ago, as if a wormhole has opened up in the server, and his era has slid up parallel to yours. You begin a correspondence with this person, enabled through a quantum entanglement. Far-fetched, perhaps, but it doesn't seem a stable connection because your bodies can't materialise in each other's space-time, only the letters toing and froing. What do you make of that, Mr. Religion Expert? Is it some sort of mystical experience, like stigmata?"

Matt takes hold of my hands and turns them palm up.

"What are you doing?"

He studies them. Shakes his head. "Nope, no signs of crucifixion. You're good. But, if things change—pins and needles on your hands and feet, blood spurting from wounds in your sides—let me know. Actually, don't let me know. I'm an expert in East Asian religions, not Catholicism. I get shook by stigmata."

"Smart-ass. I didn't say it happened to me."

He grins. "It happened to a friend, right?"

"No, I didn't say that either. I said, 'suppose'. It's a hypothetical."

"A hypothetical?" A look on his face I can't interpret. His eyes narrow. "Sure it didn't happen to your friend?" His tone is teasing.

In reply, I pile a mountain of cooked enoki mushroom into his bowl. "Eat your food, if you're going to mock me."

He laughs. Stuffs the mound of mushroom into his mouth, along with napa cabbage, wood ear, and an assortment of fast-wilting cooked veggies. Masticates with big jaw movements. At length, he says, "I'm an academic, Charlie. I try to reserve judgement when I watch a *tangki* entering a trance. People have asked me, 'You study ensoulments and spirit possession, do you believe in ghosts?' " He pauses dramatically.

"Do you?"

"It depends."

"On?"

"Observing something has an effect on me. If I happen to observe two or three *tangki* sessions in quick succession, I begin to believe. The rituals around Chinese folk religion are premised on the belief that the dead have social lives. They have wants and needs, same as when they were alive. The world of the dead is a duplicate world. Ignoring their needs can wreak social havoc. Hence, family members burn paper effigies for them in the underworld, and these *kim zua* are darn impressive, from mansions to Mercedes to Rolex watches to whole eight-course Chinese banquets with abalone and shark-fin soup. Next thing you know, we will have Impossible burgers for the vegetarian dead."

"I prefer a sashimi platter," I say, as I chase a fish ball around the cauldron with a spatula.

"The *kim zua* shops have that, and bubble tea also."

Success: fish ball hooked. "Your point is that one would be communing with the dead?"

"The shoe fits. He *is* from a hundred years ago."

"Fair point," I concede. "If, let's say, the person getting these letters is obsessed by them, would you think that person a fool? Would you think they are crazy?"

He takes a sip of rice wine. "I can't answer that." All serious, now. "Charlie, we're all fools of one kind or another. We time-travel in our heads all the time: through books, through photographs. Our souls time-travel in our dreams every night. None of this we consider strange. I believe strange phenomena happen more than we think. When the spirit mediums are possessed by their deities, they have literally abdicated personhood. Their body belongs to another. Souls without bodies now have bodies."

Matt goes on to talk about how the spirit mediums enter trances, the "contract" they have with specific deities like the Monkey God Sun Wu Kong or Tua Pek Kong, and how the *tangki* is robed accordingly and might take on characteristics of the deity, such as scratching himself, prancing about, or sticking his tongue out. Some of them might have their cheeks pierced while in a trance.

He talks about visual anthropology. How he follows several *tangki* and attends their trance sessions, how he senses different energy flows during the Hungry Ghost Festival or the Nine Emperors' Festival. He gets academic on me, explaining his use of spatial theory to highlight the tension between the state-sanctioned use of space and impromptu roadside grottoes or temporary spirit altars, increasingly a fight between old and modern, religious folk practices like these being deemed backward superstition and at odds with the narrative of a progressive technology-oriented modern state like Singapore. I nod along; I eat a lot of fish ball tofu. He explains how those state-provided iron-drum receptacles for burning *kim zua* have become a third space where many things collide: old and new, real and unreal, person and state, rational and irrational. "You didn't know I could deliver an impromptu TED Talk while cooking beef tripe in a hotpot, did you?"

A sea of dried chillies floats above a scrim of oil in the hotpot, a mini cauldron of hell. "This conversation has just turned woo-woo."

He laughs. "You should be able to woo-woo someone you like."

I blush at the double entendre. "Would you believe that, in boarding school, I once told spooky stories so scary someone reported me to the housemistress?"

His eyes twinkle at me. A very bad sign. "I believe it. I knew there was something different about you that I would like." Then he hunches forward, intent, searching my face, as if he has seen something there while I was alluding to W.T.W. "There is more to these letters than obsession, isn't there?"

In answer, I fish out some of the overcooked tripe and place them in his bowl with my chopsticks. As a gesture of care from one Asian to another. It also doubles as a cork.

*

While waiting to see Adnan to get my questions about Sebastian answered, Matt and I hang out. The couple of days I spend with him in Shanghai are restorative. We walk down Nanjing Road together, looking in all the shop windows. The light in Shanghai seems softer to me, caught in glass and steel in an opaque glow; on the older buildings and the leafy trees of side streets, the light sifts and shadows. When the light dances, my thoughts slip-slide to Wang Tian Wei. Over a hundred years ago, he walked these streets as a young boy. This ghostly sense of treading where his feet once trod gives me a feeling of being trapped in and by time, of continuing to miss each other, even though the corners and bends are full of possible encounter.

Matt puts on his pilot shades, drawing a lot of looks from the female quarter. The women eye me with that gaze—a complex mix of envy (*How come she's so lucky?*) coupled with disdain (*He can do so much better*) aimed at the cosmetic inequality of a woman not fitting the "objective" standards of beauty, walking beside a man who does.

Matt takes me to his favourite bookstore on Fuzhou Road. We end up having tea there. We talk inanities. We don't talk about Sebastian. I learn a lot about Matt Sharpe. His mother is Malaysian Chinese, his father English. His mum raised him single-handedly in Kuala Lumpur on her meagre salary as a nurse. Him and five cats. Because of the cats, he was never lonely growing up. (I suddenly had a thought of the vistas of possibility my childhood could have offered up if any of my nannies had thought of getting me a dog. Or a turtle. Or fish. Or even a pet rock.) His father died when he was two. His mother loved his father so much, she kept a boatload of stuff that reminded her of him: Post-it notes, gifts she had left on shelves to collect dust bunnies, photographs with torn edges. Also, a fan from a duende, picked up while they were holidaying in Seville.

"Ma has consulted spirit mediums a few times. She told me my father was disappointed in me."

"Why?"

"Well, if I'd gone into banking, like him, I'd be rich now, and I'd be able to buy Ma a big spanking mansion in Subang Jaya. If he hadn't died so early, it was what he had planned for them in retirement. Instead, she has to continue her work at the hospital and live in a small pied-à-terre overlooking Pudu Jail. Add on an unfilial son, who only visits once a quarter."

"Do you really believe your English father is talking to you through a Chinese spirit medium? That's quite a feat."

"It doesn't matter what I believe." Matt looks at me pointedly. "It's what my mother believes."

I nod. I tell him how I've witnessed Cassandra burning paper Davidoff cigars to my father during Qing Ming. The incineration bucket as quantum entanglement for the dead. "She kvetches to his ancestral photograph every day. He doesn't exactly get to rest in peace."

Matt grins. "Well, my mother has this saying: couples in life, couples in spirit."

*

Matt comes with me to see Adnan at WeWork Weihai.

Adnan is pacing back and forth in front of his workspace. His normally pristine appearance is rumpled, his goatee in need of a trim, his reading glasses perched on top of his head as he asks if anyone has seen them. He looks like he hasn't slept in days. There are coffee-cup rings all over his desk. They've rented a couple of other workstations here, and their assistants are working the phones. Adnan looks at Matt when I introduce them but doesn't comment. As we sit down in the joint conference room, he tells me he's decided to hire a private investigator while the police summon everyone for questioning.

"To look for Sebastian?"

Adnan frowns. "No, to look into the forgery. Sebastian will turn up. It's not the first time he's gone on a binge."

How cold can you get? "I take it you haven't heard from Sebastian."

"Nope. Not a single line of text."

"Me neither." And his radio silence has begun to hurt.

An involuntary shudder works itself outward. In the early days of their relationship, Adnan and Sebastian would lick from the same ice cream, eat pasta from the same platter, go on dates wearing couple outfits. I made mental notes: all the cheesy things couples do are not cheesy when you do them with someone you love. You live in a bubble of two. So, is this what a break-up is: you eventually come to care about externalities before internalities, image before person? What happens to all that love? Does it simply stop mid-flow? Why is it some of us can move from bubbled lovers to friends by a mere flick of a wrist, a wry change of tone, thereby inserting the emotional distance of eons? If "love is for eternity", why do we not see that separation holds the dark promise of eternity too?

Adnan shakes his head gloomily. "Wait till I get my hands on him."

"You already said that. Is there something I can do?"

"To help me get my hands on him? Oh, I think I can manage on my own."

"Not funny."

Adnan runs a hand through his hair. "Did he tell you we broke up right in this spot? We broke up right before the news hit the stands."

I wait a couple of seconds. "Not about you breaking up in this spot, no. He was pretty upset."

"He's upset? I like that." Adnan cracks his knuckles. "It's the best thing for us. I hope he can accept that."

I bite my tongue so that I won't let slip anything that sounds remotely judgemental. A break-up and a forgery scandal would make any sane person go on a binge. For someone as sensitive as Sebastian, emotional wounds fissure him from within. Does Adnan not know this, or has he blown past caring? In a moderate tone, I offer, "With this major debacle, splitting up the business may not be wise."

"Is that why Sebastian has disappeared?" Adnan eyes me warily.

I keep my expression neutral. "He hasn't said anything."

One of his assistants pops his head around the door. He holds up his phone. "I think you'll want to see this."

He hands us his phone. It shows Sebastian's Instagram account. A recent post. No caption. An off-kilter, out-of-focus photograph of a hand against a windowpane stippled with raindrops. I recognise the hand—Sebastian's; I also recognise the windowpane—behind the glass is the fleur-de-lys iron grillwork that adorns many old black-and-white bungalows in the area of Peony's *lao jia*, her childhood home in a Singapore neighbourhood called Joo Chiat. The childhood home where her coffin had lain draped, all those years ago, with lilies that remain an embedded stench in my memory. Softly, to myself, I say, "I know where he is. I've got to fly home."

Old Black and White

Peony's *lao jia* is actually her mother's house, Sebastian's *po-po*. An old one-storey bungalow on Ceylon Road, not too far from the Sri Senpaga Indian temple. After his *po-po* died four years ago, an Indian family had rented it for a while, but then moved out, likely because of all the junk in the back storeroom, full almost to the ceiling. Rattan chairs with the matting punched out, old cabinets missing their knobs, books and records and magazines from the 1960s. Either a collector's treasure trove or a descendant's nightmare. His granny had been something of a hoarder, he said, and she'd also kept all his debate-team trophies, his textbooks and artworks and exam results. She'd even kept Sebastian's old PlayStations.

The grass has grown wild around the house, and a sweetheart dual swing's yellow paint is flaking in patches. I ring and ring, first the doorbell and then Sebastian's phone, but there's no answer. Determinedly, I climb the gate—to the round-eyed horror of a Deliveroo man scootering past. I fib, the words coming easily, surprising myself: "I forgot my keys!" I go round the back, see an open window by the kitchen, and scrape my knee as I fold my length to clamber through. The smell of the house is musty, and it's dark despite the bright sunshine outside, but I don't bother with the light switches.

"Sebastian?" I call as I enter each room, my eyes adjusting to the gloom, pricking my ears for any sound of life. The house seems to have several bedrooms; closed doors line the long, dim hallway. I shudder; the home feels as dead as a charnel house.

He's not in the first or second bedroom. I locate him in the third. He's in a bad way—empty vodka bottles line the windowsill, next to a prescription bottle, half open, from which white pills scatter. Clothes are everywhere, and the whole room stinks. Dry vomit on the bed. When I try to rouse him, he's insensible to stimuli, and that's when I panic. His forehead feels hot to me, his entire body sticky and sweaty. I call an ambulance and rush him to A & E.

The doctors say he's severely dehydrated, it does not look like he has eaten in days. His blood pressure is low. *Lucky to have found him*, they say. *Could have died*, they say. They draw a curtain around him and put him on a drip.

Hours later, he recovers consciousness, and I weep. "Have you any idea how scared I was?"

He turns his head, his voice crackly and thin, his eyes glazed with the medicine for his fever. "Phew—the alcoholic fumes—is that me or you?"

I blow my nose. I take my time, bring my emotions under control. Then, I turn the full force of my glare on him. "You look all puffy and hideous. What were you trying to pull?"

"Oh, honey," he groans, trying to move the hand with the drip needle, "don't glare at me like that. You'll put a bullet hole between my eyes. Do the Cassandra number on me once I've had a bath. I don't suppose I could ask you to give me a bath? I pong, don't I?"

I begin to weep again.

He lets me. Then, softly, "I'm sorry, Charlie. I just wanted to disappear for a while. It felt like everything was unwinding, everything I've worked so hard to build."

The Map of Our Feelings

2 February 2019

Dearest Tian Wei,

I found my brother Sebastian! 😱😵☹️🤕🙏😊 It felt like that Mandarin proverb—*fan tian fu di* (翻天覆地)—heaven somersaulted with dry land. What about you—any luck locating Aiko?

I wanted to say this in my last letter: we seem to be travelling symmetrical journeys. Serendipitous? No, it's not serendipity. Not happenstance. There is something deliberate about this connection. This symmetry is an invisible string between us, a trick of light. I'd like to believe that.

What you said about seeing beauty in Kee Mun's feeding of the cats reminds me of Vincent van Gogh's words about seeing beauty in the "poorest cottages and in the dirtiest corners". If you were trying to impress me with all the literature you've read, consider it done. I am very impressed. And ashamed to say I haven't read any of the Chinese classics you mentioned. I once attempted <u>Hong Lou Meng</u>—<u>Dream of the Red Chamber</u>. I think I snored through two chapters before giving up. Sebastian also gave me Han Bangqing's <u>The Sing-song Girls of Shanghai</u>, and I'm afraid the full extent of use I've got out of it is as a doorstop.

Thank you for Du Fu's poem—I feel sorry for Imperial Advisor Han, who seemed to have been a sad, confused person, withdrawing from political life and becoming a cynical mystic, and Du Fu gave him a proper wigging, didn't he? But I also relate.

How, you ask?

Despite the distance of eras, we are similar, you and I—
transplants to these shores, never fully at ease. I believe a cultural
flexibility comes with migration and movement that allows one
to slip in and out of skins. I have learned to call this place home,
as I suspect you have. We seek out belonging through our social
antennas, and, as an archivist, it's easy to be sucked into the art
hierarchies, to peg one's professional worth on social capital, but
I also catch myself thinking: What are the benchmarks of success
for someone diasporic and liminal, like me? After five years, I'm
still working on my Mandarin and Bahasa!

Powkee Studio—I've come across it in my research on
photographic studios in Shanghai and Hong Kong. It's very
illustrious; it must have been amazing meeting the illuminati
who gathered there to discuss current affairs, all the cultural
and political pressure points of the day. Lately, I've been thinking
how we historicise every moment of our lives by capturing it in a
photograph, democratising the important and unimportant alike.
When we look back at a digital album of our lives, do we see that
we have left maps of our feelings, all our peaks and joys?

I was impressed by your observation about gentlemanly
manners and giving women freedom. In the 1930s, newspapers in
Singapore, like The Malaya Tribune, would have a special section
called "Girls' Corner" or "Women's Corner", and scores of women
would write in with editorials debating what kind of equality,
what manner of emancipation they wanted. How should women
behave? How should they dress? Should they be allowed to
choose who to marry? Should they be allowed to work? Don't we
think their obsession with gambling, especially playing the chap ji
kee, lowers community morale? Men too weighed in to say that
these new-fangled ideas of female emancipation smacked of
Western indoctrination. See, you're ahead of your time.

So. How can you be a bore? When your letters are our only
contact, they don't seem nearly long enough. Now for the best
bit of all—your confession of wind! I sometimes feel as if I have
feverishly dreamt you up. Yearning begins in the body. If two
people are physically in each other's presence, it begins with a

glance, a recognition, a transmission of current. Or perhaps it begins with a swallow, a stiffening in limb and torso, a tremor in the voice that betrays the busy beating of a heart. We have none of this to mark our moment. I have to imagine everything. I have to imagine you, and that is the hardest of all.

Thank you for your photographs. They sit open on my desktop every day. I even have a photograph of you as my phone screensaver. In exchange, I send you a photograph of a curry puff.

Yours,
Charlie.

P.S. In the photograph of me, I think I was clutching a biscuit. If I remember, I think it was a jammy dodger. Or was it a Jaffa Cake? Never mind, I love both. Jammie dodgers and Jaffa Cakes, I mean, not self-portraits and clutching biscuits.

P.P.S. If we were ever to meet at a kopitiam, will one-up you with chee cheong fun and curry pigskin. Curry pigskin is the bomb. Oh, that pigskin texture!

A Photograph To Shut The Eye

The Ghee Hin has sent word that a dead girl matching Aiko's description has turned up at the mortuary at Lock Hospital, Kandang Kerbau. Tian Wei's heart sinks. He debates whether to tell Si Nian what Tomoko-san had told him—that Aiko was safe in Penang—but he's not sure how much to trust Si Nian. If Aiko's mother was speaking the truth, saying anything might endanger Aiko. If she wasn't, the corpse at the mortuary might well be Aiko. He spends a whole night tossing and turning on his mat, causing Ah Seng to flap his hands at his ears and mumble in his sleep about flying bottle caps and *mambang* water ghosts. In the end, Tian Wei decides he needs to check for himself. Better to confront the truth than to be sorry later.

Tian Wei asks Peng Loon to accompany him. On the way there, they are followed by Ghee Hin shadows. The Lock Hospital at Kandang Kerbau is a somewhat imposing edifice, right smack in an area full of bullock pens, hence its nickname as the Kandang Kerbau Hospital, emblazoned across its front archway entrance. The Poh Leung Kuk is located here also. The Coroner is a portly white man with muttonchop whiskers, his neck exploding out of his tightly buttoned collar, constantly mopping his brow with a handkerchief due to the tropical heat. His accent is so Scottish that poor Peng Loon makes him repeat whatever he says five times. But he is a sport, and a compassionate man. Ghee Hin ruffians are outside the morgue, possibly swinging ball and chain; inside, two lily-livered Chinese men are trembling, fit to piss themselves as the Coroner lifts the sheet covering the cadaver. The sight makes Tian Wei and Peng Loon shrink back, gasping in horror. It's not the first time Tian Wei has seen a nude female cadaver, not even the first time he has seen a murdered and mutilated cadaver, but it is the first time the full horror of what a girl-prostitute has had to endure is brought home in such a gruesome manner. Someone sick and possessed had taken a knife to her and skinned her. The surface of the cadaver runs red in rivulets. Peng Loon gives up the ghost and has to be carried out.

The Coroner reads from the chart on the trolley in a monotone. Height. Weight. Estimated time of death. The knowledge slams into Tian Wei. It's not her. This is not Aiko. She's not the one lying there on a slab, an unclaimed corpse, no more than fourteen. The dead body is simply the wrong height. Thank the sky. Thank all the heavenly deities. Tian Wei's horror is eclipsed by his relief that it isn't her.

The Coroner asks if Tian Wei remembers the time he came to take a photograph of a corpse. How could Tian Wei forget? He had gone with Aiko disguised as a boy in a skullcap with a pip on top and a fake *towchang*, acting as his photographic assistant. A dead *ah-ku* was lying on the table, her throat slit, and Aiko didn't bat an eyelid. She was made of stouter stuff than Tian Wei.

"Men can be such devils, eh? Their Hobbesian nature wins out," the Coroner says.

Tian Wei does not know Hobbes, so he offers, "I read Xunzi myself, and he might well have said something similar. Did your office and the police manage to track down the bastard who did it?"

The Coroner strokes his moustache a trifle awkwardly. "The case remains open." He clears his throat. "It's not for detective work—the photograph, I mean. Strictly medical. Used as social documentation for the Colonial Office."

Tian Wei is shocked. "It is more important to study the social order than catch the killer?"

The Coroner coughs, then straightens up. He puffs his chest out. "It's to study the spread of gonorrhoea and syphilis." As if that makes everything better.

Later, outside in the compound, while waiting for a rickshaw, Tian Wei dry-heaves, retching and retching until his nose starts running. Snot and saliva drool out of his mouth on to his handkerchief. His tear ducts smart. As if he were trying to expel the chemicals he had breathed in while inside the mortuary. His thoughts too hiccup along, from the Coroner's kindness to his strange revelations. His own relief that it wasn't Aiko. And his sorrow for the skinned corpse on the slab—this person whom no one will weep for. This person who will be thrown into an unmarked grave, forever erased.

The Third Eye

Tian Wei telephones Si Nian, asking him to stop the Ghee Hin's enquiries about Aiko because he has heard (he didn't reveal that it was through Tomoko-san) that Aiko is believed to be in Penang. In response, Si Nian says he shouldn't be *ban tu er fei*, he should finish what he started; if he doesn't wish to have trouble with the Ghee Hin, he'd better come round to Si Nian's studio, located on Market Street, next to a Chettiar moneylender.

After dinner one evening in Cross Street, Tian Wei sets out on foot. Daytime smells still permeate the streets—heat, pungent *belachan*, food cooked at roadside stalls, labour and sweat, nightsoil collected as vegetable fertiliser. Rickshaws trundle past, pulled by wiry men on sandalled feet, towels looped round their necks. Walking down South Bridge Road past the brothels on Nankin and Hokkien Streets, Tian Wei notices the *ah-ku*s lounging in doorways, beckoning to passing men, calling to him as he walks by. Reminded of the corpse at the mortuary, he looks away.

Si Nian's shop is shuttered when he gets there. It's past ten, the street almost empty. He knocks on the foldaway wooden door panels. A shop assistant opens the door, rubbing bleary eyes, swinging a kerosene lamp. Si Nian himself appears, his shirt wide open to reveal the corded muscles in his neck—rather obscenely, in Tian Wei's estimation. Si Nian's studio set-up is almost identical to his own: furniture and negatives are stored on the ground floor; the reception area, living space and kitchen are on the second; studios and darkroom are on the top floor. Si Nian shows off one of his outlandish backgrounds, which he pulls out on customer request; he had commissioned artists from Surabaya to paint a propeller plane against a large field for his subjects to pose next to, as if they were taking off right from Farrer Park. He has furniture and props to simulate a European boudoir, imitating a G. R. Lambert 1881 albumen print that showed a Malay servant attending to her mistress in the manner of Manet's *Olympia*. Many photographers in the trade had seen it displayed in one of G. R. Lambert's catalogues. No one had dared mimic it but Si Nian.

Si Nian ushers Tian Wei into his hobby room. More a cubbyhole than a room, the floor is lined with boxes of prints and books rimed with dust. Enlarged photographs scale the walls, overlapping because of scarce wall space, all of *karayuki-san* and *ah-ku*s in various stages of undress, their throats angled white and elongated, inviting a stroking, a vulgar one. The looks on their painted faces and the way they lick their lips do not spell desire. Rather, it is the illusion of desire. He doesn't understand it. It is and isn't pornography.

"Why are you showing me these?"

"Do you not find them artistic?"

Tian Wei's breath expels abruptly. "Kai wan xiao?" Are you kidding?

"Tian Wei ah, Tian Wei, you need to liberate yourself from the shackles of moribund Confucian ideals and Victorian prudishness. Have you not heard of surrealism? We are living in an exciting time. Look at the new inventions that distort our reality: the telephone, the motor car, electricity, elevators, refrigerators full of ice installed at Robinsons & Co. Surely you can see that morality and values themselves are in a state of flux?"

"They may be in a state of flux, but what you are proposing seems to be revolution. Have you not heard lectures from the Chinese Philomathic Society about how selected traditional values can help reform our society? Be warned about the dangers of hedonism—drinking, gambling, womanising—these things are dangerous to society!"

"There is but one principle by which we should orient society. Capitalism. The market should determine. If you offer a service that the market wants, the market shall set a value. That is what I am aiming to do. I provide a form of entertainment that the many male immigrants flooding our shores want and need. A release valve." He gives an oleaginous grin at his own witticism. "The future is yet to be written, as are our fortunes."

Tian Wei realises there and then that it matters not a whit whether he likes or trusts Si Nian. Si Nian is a man who bends with the wind, his finger on the pulse of multiple urban currents. He needs Si Nian more than Si Nian needs him. "Right. Let's not waste time. What is it you wish to tell me?"

Si Nian fingers his collar at the opening, darts a look at Tian Wei. "I have it on good authority that you met up with Aiko's mother recently."

Tian Wei's eyes widen. "How do you know this?"

Si Nian leans back against a cabinet, puts his hands into his trouser pockets. "There are eyes and ears everywhere, don't you know? I suspect members of the Ghee Hin spotted you. Perhaps they were spying on the spies you said were following you. Regardless, they wanted you to know that whatever you might have heard from Mrs. Tay is not the truth. Aiko has not been saved by the Hai San. She is still in danger!"

"That's impossible. Why then would her father believe that she is safe? He told her mother as much."

"Who would you rather believe? Her father, who made no enquiries on her behalf and does not wish the police to be involved, or our intelligence network? If she is safe, why isn't she at home? Why is she piao piao lang lang in God knows whose territory?"

Thinking about Aiko adrift in hostile territory, that maybe no one knows where she is, pains him, but he needs to focus on Si Nian's point. What if the Ghee Hin has found out something important? Why else has Si Nian asked for a meeting like this? "So, what has the Ghee Hin heard?"

"They believe she is still being hidden somewhere in Penang. They tell me she is working in a brothel. She might have tried to escape once, but she was found and recaptured. She was lucky they didn't do anything to her. After all, if her father does not try to rescue her, who or what can prevent her from being beaten black and blue, or worse…?"

Si Nian leaves the implication hanging, causing Tian Wei's throat to close up in despair.

"I have a proposition for you." Carefully gauging Tian Wei's reaction, he says, "Join the Kuomintang. We need your help. If you help us, we help you, you understand? I will negotiate a way for the Ghee Hin to rescue Aiko for you."

Si Nian's proposition confuses Tian Wei: what is the relationship of the Kuomintang (a nationalist party) with the Ghee Hin (a triad gang)? He doesn't know, and he senses danger if he asks too many questions. "Look, I don't wish to get involved in politics. I told Feng Yu as much."

"Why would you not care what happens in our guo jia? You yourself have noted the clan division within our Chinese pangs here. Hokkiens don't talk to Hakkas don't talk to Teochews don't talk to Cantonese don't talk to Hainanese and so on. The Babas see themselves as superior, adopting the white man's ways, and they are British subjects anyway. It's people like us—the ones who speak multiple dialects, who flow through society as modern and progressive-looking Chinese intelligentsia—who must carry the torch. We need to organise ourselves under a banner. We need to throw off the yoke of our imperial masters. Luo ye gui gen. Fallen leaves must return to their roots. Otherwise, we wither away and degenerate. Did not Dr. Lim Boon Keng, whom you admire so much, say that losing our Chinese heritage is exactly like a tree severed from its roots?"

Tian Wei feels that Si Nian has twisted Dr. Lim's words out of shape. Besides, he's read in the Chinese papers that the British are quick to enforce the Ordinance governing secret societies, deporting Chinese persons on suspicion of political activities. British policy is why the Kuomintang, though not outlawed, mainly recruits through Chinese reading rooms and night classes. Or clandestinely, as Si Nian is doing.

"I'm a photographer," he begins, "a common man." But then the new facts revealed by Si Nian give him pause. He thinks about what Aiko's mother revealed. Should he be so quick to reject Si Nian's new offer out of hand? If this is all part of Hudson Tay's contemptible plan, rescuing Aiko from his clutches will require a more powerful force than himself.

"Don't be so dog-fart humble! I know how much you read, Tian Wei. It's why Feng Yu hangs around you like a lapdog. Trying to sponge knowledge off you. What do you say? This is not help I offer to just any zhang san li si, you know."

Tian Wei looks at Si Nian. "What would I have to do in the K.M.T.?"

Si Nian spread his palms. "Nothing. Just be a member. You've interacted with plenty of K.M.T. members—Feng Yu is one. All absolutely legitimate and legal, in support of building a new nation within our guo jia. But, of course, the colonial government is being extra cautious. It's got a bee in its bonnet—" Si Nian says "bee in its bonnet" in English— "with this notion that China is trying to annex Malaya."

"Listen, Si Nian, I have heard rumblings that the K.M.T. are being infiltrated by far more radical members—those who are working with the Communists."

"Tian Wei, I'm a capitalist! Why would I side with Communists? Look, I will even waive your entrance and annual subscription fee for the first year."

Tian Wei thinks about this. He can see Si Nian is getting impatient with all the talk.

Si Nian folds his arms. "You'll have news of your Japanese girl soon. I promise."

Tian Wei looks around at all the photographs, and thins his lips. "If I only need to be a member, perhaps I shall consider, but nothing more. And on the condition that you see to it that the Ghee Hin will keep Aiko safe."

Si Nian is all smiles. "The Ghee Hin may be able to do more than that. Let's shake on it."

A shadow passes across the ceiling. Tian Wei looks up. A large gecko scuttles across the speckled expanse, its stomach distended, as if it had swallowed something it shouldn't. Tian Wei's heart fills with misgiving even as he accepts Si Nian's handshake.

The Eye of Yearning

18 November 1922

My dearest Miss C.:—

I am much relieved that you found your brother Sebastian. Shall I just say that I am grateful there is someone like Sebastian in your life? You mentioned you aren't related by blood, and you sound inordinately close to him. I confess to feeling a spot of jealousy!

I wish most fervently that we could meet. Waiting for your letters to arrive is interminable. I should exercise patience. Quite several of my European clients are affianced to women residing in Europe, and only have letters by which to communicate. I should take a leaf out of their book. I did not know that longing for someone could make me feel as if I'm piao piao lang lang, adrift at sea, beset by storm-tossed feelings that change from morning to night. One minute I'm in euphoria, another minute I castigate myself for reading too much into your words. I have read and reread your letter until I've worn a hole through the print. I am not abashed to say that I almost have the whole of it memorised. It's put a song in my heart and my heart has been singing since.

I took the liberty of writing down the dates of the letters you wrote, and the dates I received them, to see if I could discern a pattern.

They are all received on the thirteenth of a given month, spaced further and further apart, and, by my calculations, one month, four months, nine months, sixteen months. Do you not think that strange? Also, why the thirteenth? The one letter that broke this pattern was your letter about your stepbrother Sebastian's disappearance, which showed up suddenly in October 1921.

One more thing: your letters arrive on glass negatives, which are all from a box with the shipment number 1314 on the side. The letters I send out are put in a box with an old shipment number: 1152. Yip Kee noticed a curious thing and pointed it out to me. In Chinese, 1314 sound like the words "in life and in death", and 1152 sound like "only you and no other". Do you not think these similarities significant?

After months of waiting outside the Tay mansion, the tampal kasut man and I have become best mates (he even offered to mend my shoes for free), although no such luck with the chee cheong fun man, who considers me a roustabout (so we shall have to do our seong-tai at a different chee cheong fun vendor, or perhaps over a meal of lor mei — do you like roast pig tripe? Or duck's leg stuffed with liver?). I took your advice to seek out Aiko's mother. Finally, I managed to meet up with her — Tomoko-san — last September, and she says Aiko-chan has been sent to Penang because she is

with child. By this date, she must have given
birth. Since then, Si Nian has told me that
the Ghee Hin believe Tomoko-san has been told
lies, that Aiko is still in the clutches of
the thugs. I no longer know what to think or
believe. This constant fear I have had to learn
to live with is wrecking my inner constitution,
but, out of respect for her mother, who made
me promise not to make further enquiries, for
fear of endangering Aiko-san, I have had to be
cautious with deliberate action.

The other merchant photographers, even my
assistants, whisper about me. They say my
intentions towards Aiko aren't what I make them
out to be. This is injurious gossip, it harms
my business reputation, and makes me question
myself. Perhaps they are right, perhaps my
need to find Aiko and my anxiety for her
safety aren't completely pure or noble, but
neither are they impure and ignoble. I only
know that I am driven to care, especially when
her father seems not to. The dire possibility
of a repetition of what happened to Sansan
haunts me.

Yearning indeed does strange things to the
body. Last night, my soul slammed straight
back into my body from whatever dreamland it
had gone wandering in, and I was jolted awake,
wrapped up in this pounding, surging feeling
of loss and a deep ache in my heart. It was
painful, as if my entire being were sunk in
waves. Yearning does strange things to the
mind. I find myself hearkening back to Li Bai's
poems. And certain lines would stop me short,
enthral me for days ... like wind blowing
through pine trees, "no dust could ever seal

our love", "the autumn wind is blowing through my heart". On certain days, yearning makes me feel I am in danger of losing myself. Will we ever be able to meet? This thought alone sends wave upon wave of fresh yearning.

I feel I am quietly going out of my mind.

Forever yours,
Tian Wei

P.S. The photograph you sent mystifies me. Why have you sent me a photograph of this curry puff? Is it some form of meat pie? One of my clients, Ms. Newton, called it an "Oriental sausage roll, and nicer." I thoroughly concur.

Is this what desire is—a kind of colonising force? Yet, it begins organically, as a seed sprouted from a word, growing to a kernel, becoming shoots and leaves, sending tendrils everywhere. It desires water. Seeks the eddies of rain. It desires sun. Rises from the gully of a belly to drape across bone and flesh and skin, the fissured curves of buttocks, the tapered cleave of the pubis, to snake down the length of thigh to shin to ankle. A desire that gnaws and becomes hunger that squeezes the heart muscles. The lungs release uneven breaths. The belly contracts. The surface of the skin tingles. A feeling of cleaving together, but also attended by a pain that barely allows one to breathe. Tian Wei, I feel it too, this going quietly out of my mind. Because there is no dimension in which you and I could ever meet.

Abetting Desire

If there is one teensy-weensy complaint I have about living in the Guest Lodge, it's that it is, well, meant for guests, and thus it's not uncommon to emerge from my bedroom to find a whole assortment of second or third cousins and related aunts and great-aunts seated at breakfast, munching on toast soldiers and slurping up half-boiled eggs. I sometimes wonder if my father or Cassandra knew they had so many relatives.

The Guest Lodge has seven bedrooms, and about as many bathrooms, but none are en suite—an old-fashioned layout reminding me of Father's ostentatious but outmoded style. What I feel towards the Guest Lodge is ambivalence: it is at once a familiar and unfamiliar place. During my school vacations, sections of 43A were off-limits to me: Cassandra's private apartments, the servants' quarters, Father's hobby rooms, the large kitchen (divided, I was told, into dry indoor and wet outdoor kitchens). One vacation, I decided to rebel. The Guest Lodge's renovation had been completed, and I simply moved there without announcement. At least there I was free to roam the seven bedrooms at will. Other than the daily meals over at 43A—where Linton and Laurent would eyeball me and I would stick my tongue out at them (or they would mock my foreign accent, which fluctuated depending on which nanny I had at the time)—I sometimes spent entire vacations not seeing anyone or doing anything other than reading, watching TV, or playing computer games (or conducting failed experiments—glowing slime that detonated, absorbent polymers that clogged the sewage).

Goodman Road is not far from the Geylang River; in the evenings, before dinner, I would walk the jogging trail all the way past Tanjong Rhu to the open mouth of Marina Bay, where the river flowed out to sea. It remains my favourite spot in Singapore, especially Tanjong Rhu Pier and the Lookout Tower. I would climb the spiral staircase all the way to the top and throw my arms open wide, as if I were on the prow of a ship. If Sebastian and I happened to be back in Singapore at the same time, we would make a point of meeting here late at night, dangling our feet through the railing, sneak-drinking chilled beer that Sebastian had cleverly stored in water bottles, and talking cock (as the Singlish phrase went).

Sebastian's relationships with Cassandra and Father were different from mine. All our birthdays were celebrated at Cassandra's with an eight-course Peranakan meal and a birthday cake with the correct number of candles, but not Sebastian's. He said he couldn't care less. Every year, on 29 November, his birthday, I take him to a gourmet Peranakan restaurant and attempt to spend a fortune on him. It doesn't make up for the differential treatment or the neglect, but, truthfully, I much prefer a birthday celebration where it is just Sebastian and me. Because he is not related to the Sze-Tohs by blood, his presence is not required at the monthly ritual dinners. His voluntary joining of the awful monthly dinners is an act of solidarity beyond compare. If Cassandra says anything too mean, he either sasses back or turns it into a joke, and somehow she tolerates this from him. Cassandra confuses me—fooled by her sudden kindnesses, I would melt and long for another kind word or gesture, until her razor-sharp admonition or brutal criticism cuts me to the quick.

None of the Sze-Tohs went to see Sebastian while he was hospitalised, not that I expected them to. After helping Sebastian with check-out procedures, I escort him back to his apartment at Marina Bay, but he declines my offer to stay overnight, saying he needs to talk to Adnan, having been laid-up for several days. I'm worried about him being on his own, but I don't push the issue. Two things Sebastian hates: scolds and *kaypoh* busybodies. However, I do take with me the two remaining bottles of Armagnac from his cabinet before leaving.

When I get back to the Guest Lodge, sticky and sweaty, I head for a shower and find my bathroom door locked because someone is evidently using it. I knock. The running shower turns off. Sounds of movement. But, five minutes later, the guest shows no sign of coming out. As I raise my fist to knock again, intending to be more vehement, the door is thrown open and someone barrels out, causing a collision of naked chest with fist.

I jump back. "Oops. Hairy."

"Hey," he says.

It's Matt, hair dripping water down a hairy, albeit washboard chest, a towel wrapped mid-waist, another around his shoulders. The unexpected skin contact sends a tripwire current shooting through my bloodstream. Glancing up, I see Matt clocking it. I avert my eyes, but can't help giving him a quick body scan, though I pretend I'm checking to see if all that extra surface area is making the floor wet. He's not fooled, judging by the glint of a smile in his gaze. Is this how our bodies betray us?

"I moved in," he says. "Nice pad."

I scoff. "Pad? I note you can be observant."

He twinkles at me in amusement. "Have you eaten?" The standard Singaporean greeting, but, in that tone, it has somehow been massaged into sounding seductive.

I shake my head. "Sebastian checked out from the hospital today."

"Is he OK?"

I nod. "Yes, feeling a bit weak and all that, but he's going to be fine. I forgot to thank you for all your help in Shanghai. Thank you, I mean it."

"No biggie, I was there for work anyway. And I enjoyed our dinner together. No chance of a repeat of that colon-blow ma la huo guo, I suppose?"

I look at him. The late evening light slanting through a side window is throwing a swath of liquid amber across his chiselled ladder of ribs, his eyes seem to be cradling light itself, and all of it makes me suck in my cheeks. His hand, which is flicking water from his hair, stops moving. The naked arrival of desire stretches like an invisible hammock between two bodies, and it utterly flummoxes me.

"Charlie—" his voice drops to a lower register— "you haven't replied to the question that I asked you in Shanghai."

"Which question was that?" It's somewhat difficult focusing.

"Whether you're seeing anyone. Would you like to have dinner together?"

Momentarily thrown by the double-barrelled question, I opt for the easier one. "You mean tonight?"

He slips the towel from his shoulders, up and over his head, and slings it around me. He doesn't try to draw me closer, but the towel has given expression to tangible circuitry. A sphere of intimacy. "I borrowed your shampoo, by the way," he says softly. "I hope that's OK. White grapefruit and mosa mint, mmm… I like. The smell reminds me of you."

My cheeks go hot. I take a step back, but the towel keeps me tethered.

"I had no idea when Linton offered for me to stay, and mentioned his half-sister also staying here, that it would get this interesting."

I scowl. I don't stay here, I live here, but trust Linton to make that distinction. And I intuit it rather than feel it—a sudden jet stream of cold drifting into the space between our bodies. A sentence dancing into my mind: *It's put a song in my heart and my heart has been singing since.*

He notes the sudden shift. "Did I say something wrong?"

I duck underneath the towel and pull away. "Matt, I'll take a rain check on that dinner. I'm knackered. All I want is a bowl of noodles—it's my comfort food. I love it more than anything."

He purses his lips. "I wouldn't mind a bowl of noodles myself."

I edge around him for the shower. "I'll probably have mine while working, since I took a whole afternoon off to deal with hospital procedures. I'll text Atalina, shall I, and a bowl of laksa will magically arrive in fifteen minutes. You do like laksa?" I'm speaking rapidly, even as I make to shut the door. "That's one of the perks of living in the Guest Lodge." It's really the only perk of staying in the Guest Lodge, but to mention this would be petty, wouldn't it?

Matt's face is shaded with disappointment. "Sure, sounds great. Rain check it is, then."

I lean my back against the closed door: there will be no rain check, no foreseeable dinner date, is what I can't say out loud. To respond to that call of the flesh would entail a betrayal of my own heart.

Behind the Frame

Cassandra's summons to the main house is delivered by Atalina the following evening; Atalina does it with a quiver in her lip. "Mam say you come, she want to know about Sebastian, miss." Obviously, Cassandra can call Sebastian herself, so it's clear this meeting has an agenda behind it.

In the palatial living room, Laurent is in his golf kit, pulling on white gloves, a cap tucked under his arm. When he sees me, his eyes narrow; no love lost here. I walk past without a word and head for the sweeping marble staircase. He heaves up his golf clubs. There isn't even room for functional words between us.

Cassandra's bedroom is on the second floor. In fact, the entire second floor is hers, housing her bedroom, a study/office, a home gym, a massage room, and her dressing room full of gowns and shoes. This is my first time in this off-limits area, and I'm curious why she has made an exception. The hallway is dark wood, carpeted with rich Persian rugs. The furniture in the hallway is a mixed bag of Malayan dark teak or Chinese *huang hua li*—opulent, ornate. Jasmine, jacaranda flowers, and chempaka are crowded into vases, their perfume cloying despite the open windows. White muslin curtains flutter in the light breeze. A butterfly has flown in from outside, lost, and I watch it flit above me, hover around the bouquets, and dart towards the ceiling as I walk down the long hallway. The lighting is muted and dim; I feel like I'm entering a cloistered sanctum. I don't belong.

Cassandra's bedroom door is slightly ajar. I knock gently, but there's no call to enter. Through the slit in the open door, I glimpse movement: Cassandra in a diaphanous pink peignoir. As she hunches down, the light through her window pierces the material. She is naked underneath. I gasp and withdraw, but my gaze is arrested by the sight of Cassandra taking off her gown, draping it over the bed. One hand rises to cup her breast, as if weighing fruit. Her breasts are tiny pears; her naked body is pale; her stomach has a little bulge, and there are slight creases of adipose in her buttocks and the backs of her legs. But her figure is well maintained. She is still a desirable woman.

She turns and sees me through the crack. I lower my gaze, mumbling, "I'm so sorry, I didn't mean…"

Cassandra makes no move to cover herself. "Come in, Charlene; don't stand there gawking."

I push the door open gently. Naked women abound in art, and I'll be damned if an art historian like me should act bashful in front of a little nakedness, but there's something entirely bold and brazen in Cassandra's leisurely exhibition of it. She saunters over to a big almirah wardrobe, huge enough to hide a family of four, and opens it, taking a dress off a hanger. Casually, she makes me watch as she hooks up her bra, slips on panties, and then throws the long linen shift over her head.

I sit down on the edge of the huge four-poster bed, two entwined naga dragons carved into the wooden bedstead. Above me is a white canopy scarf. My hand grazes the softness of the white duvet. Hard wood, soft duvet—this meeting of opposites, yin and yang—a true matrimonial bed. The floor is not wood, unlike the hallway and other parts of the house, but Peranakan tiled, a lovely blue and yellow curling-vine design. The roomy bedroom is sparsely furnished: other than the imposing bed, the almirah, a low dressing table and a cross-legged divan, there is little else. Cassandra seats herself before the two-tiered dressing table, stares at herself framed in the oval mirror, and picks up a hairbrush. Vigorously, she rakes it through her hair, making *scrape-scrape* sounds against her scalp, catching strands within the bristles, which she gathers into a ball and flings into a wastebasket. On the table is a paraphernalia of hairbrushes, lotions, and a cloisonné organiser for her lipsticks and make-up. An iron tree is draped with necklaces. There is a shell-backed Edwardian sofa chair in deep pink suede. She points to it and says, "Sit here, Charlene, and stop staring. I don't bite."

I don't move from the bed.

"Water, Charlene?" A glass pitcher is on a tray, condensation pearling the sides. Cassandra pours me a glass. "I don't know if I ever told you," she says, "but I had a lump in this one breast—" she cups the breast again— "and, after the removal, I thought my breast became smaller, although the surgeon said it was in my head, because the tissue they removed was but one centimetre. But I couldn't stop thinking that way. It even looks lopsided in the mirror to me."

This unexpected confidence throws me off balance. I'm not sure what Cassandra is getting at. "Was it…was it before Father died?"

"It was around the time Peony was dying. At first, I thought I was imagining it. Like how you get paranoid that you'll get sick if someone else close to you is sick."

She and Peony were close? "Close" is a curious choice of word.

"But then, the mammogram confirmed it. You know, your father was so consumed by Peony's dying that, when I told him I had to go in for a procedure, he didn't even bother asking what it was for." Cassandra laughs, a bitter sound that echoes in that capacious bedroom. "But, luckily, it was benign."

"Father was many things, but…uhm…but considerate… wasn't…does not seem to have been one of them."

Cassandra's eyes flick up at me; a small smile touches the corner of her mouth. "You see, we do understand each other, do we not?"

I wouldn't go that far. I avert my face. I watch a drop of condensation slide down the glass surface and become formless on the table.

"I called you in here to ask about Sebastian. I've had Atalina make some chicken soup and jook. Can you take them over to him?"

Surprise must have galloped across my face, because Cassandra lets out a laugh. "We are family, Charlene, and we don't have to be sayang-sayang to look after each other."

I steady myself with a breath. "Sure. I'll be happy to…Well, I'm visiting him later."

"Now, will you tell me what happened with the atelier?"

Was this why she had called me? To get inside deets on the art forgery scandal? The emergency meeting that didn't happen turning into a private interrogation? "Adnan has hired a P.I. …uh…I don't know all that much. It's best to ask Sebastian yourself."

Cassandra looks at me long and hard. She opens her compact, proceeds to dab her face with a puff. "I wouldn't trust Adnan quite so much. What is Sebastian doing entrusting the investigation to Adnan?"

I bite my lip. Whenever she can, she makes a dig either at their relationship or at Adnan.

She addresses the mirror. "Are you sure Sebastian isn't implicated in any way?"

I become aware of how the lines have gathered not around her mouth, but around the base of her neck. It's an effort to remain seated. Anger rises in a slow burn, then grips me around the throat. My eyes return to hers, baleful. "I trust Sebastian. He's innocent."

"I never said he wasn't." She uncaps a tube of lipstick and lines her lips. She sprays perfume on her wrists, rubs them together and dabs them against two points underneath her earlobes. "Charlene, you don't have to look at me like that, as if I'm out to get you. I have a right to know as an investor in Sebastian's business."

The information she has just casually dropped leaves me dumbstruck.

Cassandra's smile is sardonic. "Oh, you didn't know?"

Indeed, I hadn't known, and it pricks me that I hadn't known.

"And here I was thinking you two tell each other everything." Her tone taunts me. "A word to the wise, Charlene: sometimes a P.I. finds out things you'd rather not know."

"I'm not sure what you mean." Has Cassandra hired a P.I. to spy on Sebastian? It would be the sort of thing she would do.

Has the P.I. found out something? Does she know something more that I don't?

"A long time ago, when your mother was still living in Singapore, I hired a P.I. to see if your father was cheating on me. Imagine: what a nest of snakes we had made ourselves. Your father was carrying on an affair with me right in front of your mother, and I was trying to see if he was also carrying on an affair with someone else. The P.I. had his hands full. Not only did he show me photographs of your father's pursuit of Peony, visiting her with all those pathetic Tang-dynasty poems and huge flower arrangements more suitable for a restaurant opening than for courtship, but the P.I. also found out something else. It's about your mother."

The revelation has me mutely staring at Cassandra as she tucks her hair into a bun and secures it with gold pins. The semblance of a smile on her face makes me suspect she's secretly enjoying these surprises she's lobbing at me.

"Your mother has taken her secret to the grave, so it is not my place to say anything." She spritzes a bit of coconut oil on her palm, then smooths her hair. "These dark secrets are best left undisturbed. She cared a lot more about you than I thought, I'll give her that. You young people are so quick to judge. You form your opinions based on what you see. Yesterday, I saw you walking up the driveway back to the Guest Lodge as if you were carting a load of stones. Why so sad? You're young yet, and you have such willowy grace on you, so tall. If I had a daughter, how nice it would be if she looked like you."

Our gazes meet in the mirror. I'm not sure what to make of this moment. It isn't the first time she has said "if I had a daughter," but is the sentiment sincere, or is she performing "Mother" with a capital *M*? Here she is again, dropping hints about Mother. Her mouth says secrets are best left undisturbed, but her body language says she is dying for me to know. I have a sense here that Cassandra has lit a match, and if I flutter too close, I might get burned. What skeleton has Mother hidden in her cupboard? If I find out what it is, will I be able to weather it? Can ghosts come back from the grave to devastate me anew?

A Duplicate World

Tian Wei and Si Nian catch the steamer to Penang. From the harbour, their guest house on Chulia Street is but a short rickshaw ride away. Si Nian had offered to front the expenses for the luxurious E & O Hotel, but Tian Wei had refused. He doesn't wish to be more in Si Nian's debt than he already is. Si Nian's kindness comes with strings attached.

Tian Wei has never been to Penang before, and he stares wide-eyed as they walk down the gangplank to the bustling port. Ocean liners jostle cheek by jowl with dodging sampans and *kolek*s. Quayside, a flurry of activity: stevedores haul cargoes, passengers and sailors stream past, vendors and urchins wander in and out trying to hawk wares and make a quick buck. The salty tang of the sea mingles with dried fish and fried foods from the vendors. The blazing sunshine shimmers as Tian Wei takes in the godowns lining the quay, the shops along the intersecting streets, the palm trees waving their fronds in the gentle ocean breeze. A silhouette of a blue hill winks in the distance: Penang Hill. Although Weld Quay is not as big as the ports in Singapore, it is no less thriving and busy.

Si Nian wastes no time hailing a passing rickshaw. They clamber in, their travel valises resting between their legs as the rickshaw puller weaves in and out of streets at a steady jog. They pass a clock tower. A Malay woman with a sarong wrapped around her breast is bathing her child by the beach. A roadside vendor washes his bowls in a bucket of water. The coconut fronds swish in the breeze. The gossamer twist of joy among poverty-stricken faces, homeliness and comfort. He leans his head out to soak in the sun-baked air. He hasn't travelled much in the past few years since his shop opened—the proprietor of a small business is yoked to it year in, year out—but travel offers such fresh experiences; it liberates. One can slip out of the tether of one's mind, think new thoughts, gain a new self. And then he realises why he feels this immense sense of freedom: it temporarily relieves him from the interminable wait for a letter to arrive. With each missive, fresh feelings swamp him. They run the gamut: from despair to euphoria. Does she feel the same? This is what separation is: a kaleidoscope of emotions from bending one's soul towards that special person on different shores—he in his world, she in hers, without hope of intersecting, of their feelings being shared. All they have are letters. What if she stops writing to him one day? How long can this supernatural connection last? What is the point of these eddying emotions when there is no destination in sight?

A month ago, Si Nian came by his studio on Hill Street with a note. It said that a young girl fitting Aiko's description had finally been located in a brothel in Penang. In fact, this wasn't the first such tip-off from the Ghee Hin. There was the mortuary episode, then a couple of sightings in Japanese brothels in Singapore, and each time Tian Wei had diligently chased it down. He would go with Si Nian, who perversely relished these outings. Tian Wei endured the checks in the lobby (the Japanese madams were meticulous now about checking their clients for crabs and sexually-transmitted diseases), sitting in the reception-room boudoir while a number of the *karayuki-san* brought them tea and snacks. A quick scan would immediately reveal that Aiko-chan was not among the girls present, but to leave immediately upon arriving would horrify the *mamasan*, not to mention trigger all sorts of speculation and gossip.

So, while Si Nian took his time choosing a girl, and then went upstairs with her, Tian Wei refused the rice wine and *okonomiyaki*, drinking cup after cup of tea until his bladder almost gave out. He let himself be entertained with song and dance. He did find the girls attractive—they were beautifully made-up and splendidly attired—but one simply could not have witnessed a dead *ah-ku* lying on a cement slab in a mortuary and then proceed to revel and make merry with another of them, heedless of one's participation in this extreme farce of sex. It was an economic transaction in which desires were relieved, like defecation or urination, and he had no illusion that the girls enjoyed these transactions. In fact, what he saw, hidden behind the cosmetics and beautiful silk robes, was a sheen of sadness; sometimes, in profile, one of them would look absent even as she plucked the samisen, another's voice would quaver in wistfulness as she sang. There in body—fingers dancing over strings, red-lipped mouth rounding to issue forth beautiful notes—but not in mind or spirit. The thought of Aiko's joy in life being threshed and throttled in such a manner was an affliction upon his soul, and after any such visit to a brothel, he would be off his food for days. Kee Mun would worry, thinking the wind which came that day he fell into a swoon, a wind she regarded as ill, had once again returned. She would hurry to the market to get a kampong black chicken to make soup with ginseng to revive him.

But this recent tip-off felt different. For one thing, it came attached with a grainy photograph. Si Nian said the Ghee Hin didn't take it—triad members didn't own cameras, he smirked—but how they came by the photograph, he hadn't asked. His philosophy in life was simple: advantage, information as barter. The photograph showed a young girl wearing a yukata, twirling a paper parasol. Said to be taken at a brothel called Cherry Blossom in Penang. Tian Wei perused the photograph, but still couldn't make out if it was indeed Aiko. It didn't look like her, and yet it could be her. It had now been almost four years since she disappeared, and she must have grown from child to woman. Would he even recognise her if he were to meet her face to face?

They check in at their guest house. Si Nian wants to have an afternoon kip. On the steamer, all Si Nian seemed to do was laze about or play fan-tan or mahjong with a group of eager gamblers, while Tian Wei spent much of that time either on deck gazing out to sea or reading. Watching the horizon of the Straits of Malacca change had done something to him—the fiery hues of dawn in contrast to the settling violet dusk, the emerald wash of the sea, the occasional sighting of swordfish breaching the waters—all of it made him long for his slim, slight love from the future. He hadn't known the heart could have such cavernous chambers, full of nooks and crannies, and at every corner, he was confronted with fresh want.

In his studio, he had seen her in the eye of the camera when he had taken photographs. He had wanted to show her the sample portraits hung up in his reception room that he was especially proud of. When poorer customers had asked to dress up in the Western or Chinese robes he provided on a rack, he had understood suddenly what it was to indulge in fantasy. Many of them wished to send home to China photographs of themselves in splendour and prosperity—*Look how well I'm doing in Nanyang*. He had recognised, without being quite able to articulate this, that the space in front of a camera is a duplicate world.

Standing behind his camera, he had indulged in fantasies of make-believe interactions. What they would say to each other, what glances they would trade. Where else they might travel together. The ability to converse without limit. The intoxication of being in proximity. To touch and be touched. Would an actual meeting dispel or inflate this cloud of feelings? Feelings seemed strangely more real and trustworthy than the physical. Yet, they were also clouds of thin air, changing constantly, igniting at the smallest trigger, evaporating at the slightest puff. Was Charlie a castle in the sky he had built up?

To give himself some reprieve from his constant ghost, he steps out of the guest house and goes for a walk. From Chulia Street, he wanders down side streets. All these different sections of town—Malay, Chinese, Indian—the enclaves segregated, as in Singapore. The guild halls, the clan buildings, the row upon row of shophouses. A street full of coffins. A domed white-stuccoed mosque. Then a Taoist temple with its curved tiled roof

and stone lion at the front. He reads the name: the Temple of
Kuan Yin, the Goddess of Mercy. He goes in and lights a couple
of joss sticks, the acrid incense stinging his nostrils. The serenity
of the temple buoys his spirit. Although his faith in religion is
shaky at best, and he doesn't know how to pray, still he clasps
his hands together, pleading for mercy in his search. What with
supernatural happenings and mysterious winds, he's not sure of
anything with certitude anymore. The last building he sees on
his walk is St. George's Church on Farquhar Street—its white
façade of imposing Palladian columns, its sharp protruding
spire—and his energy wilts within him. Let this not be another
wild goose chase. Whether Aiko be dead or alive, he would like
to know, so he can stop the forage in his heart once and for all.

*

Evening descends. Si Nian has brilliantined his hair; he comes
downstairs with a skip in his step. His linen suit is neatly pressed,
his tie slightly askew for a rakish look.

"Ready?" Si Nian dons his hat.

They hire a rickshaw to take them to Cherry Blossom on
Japan Street, as the street is known unofficially, and it is as if they
have entered Little Japan: young girls dressed in yukatas lounge by
doorways; a Japanese barber snips the hair of a customer in open
view; a Japanese dispensary and Japanese sundry shop are doing
brisk business. They are also right smack in the red-light district:
dance halls, gambling dens, and restaurants are cock-a-hoop with
patronage. In Singapore, Tian Wei has heard talk in the reading
rooms that the Japanese government considers prostitution by the
karayuki-san a huge disgrace to national prestige and is planning to
clamp down, if not eradicate it altogether. The Japanese brothels
have been given a date in the near future to close, and several of
the workers have already been repatriated home; but, in Penang,
it seems to have had little effect yet.

The Cherry Blossom brothel is a handsome-looking
establishment, its *pintu-pagar* ornately painted with birds and

flowers, a red velvet curtain hanging over the doorway. Beautiful yellow lanterns and a vase of pussy willow adorn the brothel veranda, extending into the five-foot way. Three women in yukatas, with elaborate hairdos, are sitting on round-backed rattan chairs outside, languidly fanning themselves. As he and Si Nian alight from their rickshaw, one rises to usher them in immediately. None of them is Aiko.

Inside, the décor is ornate to the point of fussiness— Chinese and Japanese motifs jumbled together. A tiny trickling fountain hosts a single finning goldfish in the vestibule, and a phoenix is embroidered on a double-panelled cloth hanging over what looks to be the entrance to the back of the house, through the seam of which Tian Wei spies a curving wooden staircase. A painting dominates one wall: Mount Fuji rising out of a foreground of cherry blossoms on branches. A Japanese silkscreen panel decorates one corner. They are invited to sit at a round, marble-topped Chinese dining table, and a *mui tsai* they call Ah Lan quickly brings a tray of tea and watermelon seeds. The *mamasan*, introducing herself as Ohatsu-san, is a woman dressed in a vermillion yukata with a painted mole on her cheek. Her make-up is so heavy it pantomimes opera. The girls call her Okasan—Mother—as one by one they troop in to be ogled at and hopefully picked, resplendent in their yukatas like cut flowers, their obis tight underneath their breasts. They introduce themselves shyly:

Okiko, fifteen, from Kusumoto, Amakusa.

Onatsu, twenty, Futae, Amakusa.

Oichi, eighteen, Gryoo, Amakusa.

"They all seem to be from Amakusa," Tian Wei whispers into Si Nian's ear.

"The Amakusa Islands must be full of cherry blossoms," Si Nian whispers back laughingly.

A phrase comes to Tian Wei, oft-whispered among his Cantonese assistants: *jou gai*—"becoming a chicken"—a Cantonese derogatory term for ladies of delight or those prostituting themselves. So much opprobrium was attached to this phrase that, as he looks at these young, beautiful women, he can't suppress the pity and shame he feels. The men who buy their flesh are pitiful, photographers like Si Nian who purvey sexual images of them are pitiful, but even more pitiful are the men like him, who sit and silently observe, doing nothing.

Si Nian taps two fingers to his lips. Quietly, he takes out from his waistcoat pocket the photograph said to be of Aiko and slides it over to Ohatsu-san. "Do you have this woman?" The conversation is being conducted in Malay.

Ohatsu-san leans down to inspect, and her mouth crêpes. Her eyes crinkle with suspicion, her breath hitches, a stillness drops over her facial expression as she surveys their faces, assessing their intentions.

Tian Wei's heart rate notches up. Clearly, the *mamasan* recognises the face. A moment of reckoning is at hand. Is it Aiko? Has he finally found her?

"Why do you have a picture of Ohime?"

Si Nian quickly adds, "I hear she is one of your best."

Ohime? Tian Wei's expression flattens. But could she be in disguise? Ohatsu-san looks once again from Si Nian to Tian Wei. "Tak boleh. She is not available. Another client has booked her for the night."

Tian Wei, no longer able to keep still, blunders in: "May I speak to her for a few minutes, please? Sekejap sahaja. I think she is someone I know."

Ohatsu-san bursts out cackling. "You know Ohime-san? You are sweet on her, yes? You must wait in line. Mr. Yap Kin Loy— he owns a pawnshop near Chowrasta Market—you know him? He wants to marry her. Mr. Ki, do you know Mr. Ki? Mr. Ki is rich man, works in big shipping business, he is the one booking her tonight. Ohime is his favourite. Ohime plays the samisen and also the tsuzumi. She can recite poetry. She reads Chinese and Malay. She is most talented. And beautiful. Kulit macam salji. Pipi macam itu buah kuning-kuning apa nama…Bukan pelacur biasa." Skin like snow, cheeks like peach (he supposes). Not your normal girl for hire.

Is it Aiko-chan? It must be. It has got to be. His voice trembles: "Please, allow me just five minutes of her time. Tell her that Wang Tian Wei is here to see her. Please, could you give her my visiting card?"

Ohatsu-san considers this. To sweeten the offer, Si Nian quickly slips over a couple of Straits dollars. From Si Nian's past encounters, Tian Wei knows this is almost a quarter of what it would cost to bed a *karayuki-san* for the night. Ohatsu-san's eyes gleam with greed, and then, sly as a fox, she pockets it. She pulls the whorl of Ah Lan's ear, whispers into it, and the girl scampers behind the phoenix curtain.

Moments of heavy dread mix with anticipation. Tian Wei doesn't know what to look at. His pulse ticks in his ears. Si Nian chats up one of the *karayuki-san*; she simpers and tips her eyes at him.

Eventually, after what feels like ages, but is just twenty minutes, a reply comes back with Ah Lan. Ohime-san does not wish to receive other visitors tonight, only Mr. Ki. Disappointment bites into him. Desperation etches his jaw. What if he simply barges into the inner apartments, charges up the stairs? All it will take is one look to confirm if it is Aiko, to finally put years of concern and worry to rest. So close now, how can he bear another moment of waiting?

Si Nian cajoles Ohatsu-san, but she shrugs. Her eyes track them carefully. Si Nian slips a few more dollars over. She makes no move to take it. Neither does she offer to return their money. "I'm sorry. Come back tomorrow. Maybe she changes her mind then."

No amount of persuasion will do the trick. Si Nian turns to Tian Wei to confer. "What if I stay here tonight? I might be able to spot her in the corridors."

Ohatsu-san seems to understand their whispers in Mandarin. She shakes her head in warning. "Ohime-san is special. She is not your average prostitute," she repeats, her voice mysterious. "If you are not here to sample the goods, go away now."

Is she afraid, although nothing has given her away? For her to turn them away so impolitely, she must be hiding something.

"We have no choice," Si Nian says. "Let's not push too hard now. We can come back tomorrow. And the day after that. Until she relents."

Aiko

In the middle of the night, loud knocking at their room door wakes Tian Wei. Si Nian is snoring soundly in his own canopied bed, draped with a mosquito net. The knocking continues. Urgent. Rapid. Whoever it is won't go away until there is a response. Tian Wei gets up, rubs his chest, and walks to the door.

A Chinese boy in tattered shirt and shorts stands at the threshold, fist raised to knock again. He is one of the servants working for the guest house. "A lady downstairs waiting for you, sir." Then the boy blushes to the roots of his hair. "Not lady. *Xian shui mei*." He beckons to Tian Wei to follow him.

The boy's term—salt-water maid, the derogatory term for prostitute—galvanises him to don shirt and trousers in such a hurry that half his shirt is buttoned wrong. On soft-slippered feet, Tian Wei follows, his heart rate doubling once again.

The hotel proprietor behind the reception desk glowers at him, opens his mouth—to chastise him, Tian Wei supposes, but he has no time to stop right now.

In the lobby, a young woman in a yukata stands with her back to him. He hesitates, not entirely trusting his own instincts. Nothing about her reminds him of Aiko, the girl he used to know. The elaborately styled hair sits on her head like a hat sculpture, the drape of the yukata at the back revealing a swan-like neck. Hearing his approach, she turns slowly.

This face. Who is this? His heart makes a jagged leap into his throat. Aiko. Recognition is in her eyes too. They are the same—dark brown, still lively, in fact more intense, burning with desperation like live coals. Her mouth—that cupid bow, so quick to flip into an impish grin. And yet. Nothing else is the same. She has grown tall, a woman now. A layer of powder cakes her face, her eyebrows are pencilled in thick lines, her cheeks rouged. The yukata she wears looks expensive—a motif of crane and bamboo leaves. Her feet are encased in beautiful wooden clogs. If she were to pass him on the street in this get-up, he would not recognise her.

"Aiko-chan?" he says uncertainly.

Tears rush into her eyes. And his. They step towards each other, clasp hands. The proprietor behind the desk looks on from above his glasses and tsks in heavy disapproval.

"Is there some place we can talk?" she whispers, fear in her voice. "I can't be away for long."

A conundrum. There is nowhere he can take her. Not upstairs, not with the proprietor eyeing them askance. It would generate a lot of loose talk. Not to a restaurant, where there might be flies on the wall. A young man and a lady at this hour! Not to mention the eyes of the Ghee Hin or Hai San or Mr. Ki's men tracking him. But another chance might not come again. Resolutely, he steps outside, in time to spot a rickshaw. Without thinking, he hails it. Quickly, they jump in.

Aiko-chan gives an urgent order to head for the beach.

The beach is dark and deserted. She walks quickly, despite being hemmed in by clogs and clothes. The stars are bright in the night sky, a black velvet glove studded with jewels, shedding just enough illumination to allow them to make their way. Together, they stumble over soft sand in the direction of the ocean. The surf pounds feelingly through his veins; the breeze carries a musky brininess and combs his hair back in gusts, silhouetting her yukata against her frame. Cicada cries pierce the night; the moon hangs pendulous above them. Sand crunches underneath his shoes. He's walking in a dream. She finds a big rock near a headland. There, huddled between it and the thread line of lapping waves, he learns the full story.

One evening in late June 1919, on her way home from art class, two men had jumped across the path of her rickshaw on Bukit Timah Road, and her elderly chaperone, Sister Yuk, had screamed. Aiko had heard about the anti-Japanese boycotts all over Chinatown because of some major conference in Paris that granted territorial rights in China to Japan. The concessions had made the Chinese upset, even in Nanyang. Her stepfather had told her not to go out, but she was stubborn. How could she miss her art classes—the one activity she loved? Her freedom of movement was already severely curtailed. Father and daughter had had an argument. He told her people were throwing down made-in-Japan utensils and earthenware, Japanese beddings and fabrics. Shops were being wrecked. In the Japanese brothel areas of Malabar Street and Malay Street, rioters armed with staffs, lead pipes, daggers, and bludgeons swarmed and smashed property and people alike. Rickshaw drivers known to have carried Japanese passengers were set upon mercilessly. An entire rickshaw was set on fire on Upper Chin Chew Street. Aiko had shouted back that none of this had anything to do with art class.

Martial law was imposed. That evening in June, the streets were relatively deserted. One man grabbed the startled rickshaw puller, threw him to the ground, sat astride him, and pummelled him. The rickshaw puller simply curled into himself, allowing the *samseng* to punch him senseless. The other gangster pushed down the hood of the rickshaw, and as if he were bagging a *lap ngap* for a customer, slid a gunny sack over Aiko's head. She felt herself lifted bodily over his shoulder, heard his whistle, and felt herself carried and dumped into another transport, with no idea who the men were, where she was being taken, or why they were doing this. She heard the sounds issuing from Sister Yuk, round and rolling—*"Aiiko! Aiiko!"*—and it sounded to her like a dirge.

After being kidnapped, she was locked up in a house for months. At first, she had to remain hooded and tied up. This was the hardest of all to endure, not knowing what or who or why they had done this to her. Time was of no moment, sand trickling through an hourglass, measured not by seconds but by intermittent sounds she strained to identify. When light disappeared, life itself was reduced to the simplicity of sleeping and eating and defecating. The reason she kept her sanity then was because she recited all the things she had read with Tian Wei in her head—all those stories from *Chrita Dahula Kala*—

narrating them over and over. If she forgot details, she would keep working at her memory until she remembered.

Gradually, however, she was allowed freedom in her room and to go out twice a day to use the bathroom. She was allowed no news of the outside world. What she heard outside her closed window were the sounds of hoodlums playing mahjong—the clack of their tiles, their swearing, their ruffian loudmouth curses when they lost money. They were drunk all the time. Yet, no one touched a hair on her head, for which she was grateful. She was fed well—*nasi lemak* every day, imagine! She even gained a little weight in captivity from the rich diet and lack of exercise. One day, she asked for pen and paper. She asked if she could have books. She asked if her diet could be varied—how about some noodles? It flummoxed her kidnappers.

They conferred with each other in Hakka and spoke to her in *pasar* Malay. "What say, what you want?"

She asked for *mee udang*.

They had to get Cookie—a wizened Hakka man wearing a floppy hat—to talk to her. "You want prawn noodles?" He was dumbfounded. "You think prawns dangle from trees? I go catch with bare hands?" She had to settle for noodles with cockles.

Once, she managed to escape, wrapped in a sarong from the bath she was meant to have, running like a headless chicken across open fields with lalang grass and curling liana, bordered by wild jungle. Taking off her clogs, she ran as fast as she could for the nearest structure or habitation, and she almost made it to the pig farm before they caught her. This time, they stationed a guard outside her room. She shed tears of frustration, but at least she now had an inkling of where she was. A dilapidated *papan* house next to a river. Over the tops of trees, she thought she saw a mill. Next time, she would head for the river.

Then, one day, several *samseng* burst into her room, threw a gunny sack over her head, lifted her bodily and carried her away. Again, she didn't know who they were or what they planned to do with her. She didn't know anything. There followed a long,

long ride in a vehicle. Jostled, bumped, trundled, she suspected she was being transported in a lorry upcountry into Malaya. The pungent smell of rubber engulfed her and made her sick. She was afraid, but she figured, if they meant to kill her, they would have already done so.

The long journey ended. What day was it? How long had it been? Her life from before felt like eons ago. She was adrift in a land of no coordinates. Someone removed her hood, and the light that greeted her was blinding. She found she was in a room bare of furniture except for the rattan chair she sat on, hands and feet bound.

In front of her stood a man.

He looked like a pig to her—thick in the neck, thick in body, thick in his swarthy arms. He had a fat nose like a hippo. An expansive forehead. Small eyes. Fleshy lips. On his pinkie, he wore a signet ring with the head of a serpent. He said to call him Mr. Ki. "You don't need to know my actual name. Your father sent me."

For the time being, she had to remain in hiding, he said. This was for her protection, and he, Mr. Ki, would protect her. Aiko laughed. She became hysterical in her laughter. Mr. Ki merely watched her with piggish eyes. Aiko laughed till tears bathed her face.

She said, "Here I am, tied up like a hog in front of my kidnapper—who looks like a hog."

He placidly told her to calm herself; there would be no going home. She had been rescued by the Hai San and entrusted to his safekeeping. She had two choices: to work as a girl-servant or to work as one of the ladies of the night in a brothel.

Aiko joked, "How about being a girl-servant in a brothel?"

Mr. Ki said, "That can also be arranged."

Thus, she found herself washing dishes and cooking food in front of a charcoal burner. The work was back-breaking. The chores were unending. Sweep the floors, mop the staircases, clean the toilets, feed the chickens, fetch this and that for the *karayuki-san*. Time had come full circle; she was back to her eight-year-old self, slaughtering chickens and draining their blood. She knew that *karayuki-san* had more freedom than girl-servants. The higher-paid ones could go out in the afternoons. Learning that her father wished to keep her in captivity for his own ulterior purpose broke her heart. She missed her mother, but her mother had little power in Hudson Tay's household. Aiko took time to think things through. After all, she had all the time in the world on her hands. She resolved not to go home. She would need a plan. To execute this plan, she would need Mr. Ki's help. In exchange for her promise that she wouldn't try to escape, a promise she had no intention of keeping, she asked to become a *karayuki-san*, but Mr. Ki would be her sole customer. To her surprise, he agreed without demur. He kept her in seclusion at the Cherry Blossom brothel. There she has been ever since.

Tian Wei finally interrupts, "Your mother said you were with child."

Aiko laughs. No one has touched her. Not Mr. Ki. Not a single customer at the brothel. Ohatsu-san is paid a handsome sum every month to keep quiet, and to keep bars around her. When Mr. Ki comes to stay for the evening, he sleeps on a tatami mat next to her bed. However, if she intends to escape, she suspects that she will need to do it soon. Mr. Ki hasn't divulged anything, but she has now known him for close to three years, and this state of affairs will not continue indefinitely. She suspects her father intends to marry her off. She guesses from Mr. Ki's hints and evasions that it will be to someone important back in Japan, and this connection will facilitate her father's businesses.

Mr. Ki's work is mysterious to her. Ostensibly, he works in shipping, but he also seems to do other things. Once, she peered into the canvas bag he carries with him always, and saw a map of Penang. Maybe he was a cartographer or surveyor. The map indicated it was made under the auspices of the Imperial Japanese Government Railways. Why would the Japanese

Imperial Railways need a detailed map of all of Penang's official buildings?

They sit in darkness. The sounds of the ocean waves and night-time insects obscure their low whispers. The matches he lights every now and then help keep the mosquitoes at bay. He smokes as he listens. She has talked so fast that he hopes he will remember everything come morning. Aiko is gazing out to sea. The ocean shifts in billows of pitch-black slate.

"I don't wish to go home," she states flatly. "I'm not sure what deal my father has struck with Mr. Ki, but I'm a pawn in it. I am basically an orphan, Tian Wei Ge Ge, like you." *Older Brother Tian Wei*, an endearment she used to call him, and it nicks his heart. "I have neither father nor mother," she declares, even as her lower lip quivers. "When Ah Lan brought your card to me earlier today, I thought I must have surely died and gone to heaven. But I felt so ashamed. I couldn't let you see me there, dressed like a prostitute. When I was growing up around the Japanese brothels, it was all the life I knew. I didn't know it was shameful until I became a tycoon's daughter. Until I became a karayuki-san myself and saw the way the customers looked at me. As good as daging babi hung up on a hook."

Aiko pauses. He can't see her tears in the dark, but he sees her hands swiping at her eyes.

"And yet, I knew," she continues. "Finally, here is my chance. It was so unbelievable to me that you had come all the way to Penang to look for me. It is a fairy tale. My fairy tale is wonderful, isn't it, if it has you? Help me escape, Tian Wei Ge Ge."

His mind is a blind maze, but he hugs her to him. Unshed tears, mirroring hers in deep sympathy. A lump lodges in his throat; it is difficult to get his words out. "Of course I will help you, Aiko-chan. I shall do everything in my power to help you. Or I shall die trying."

Wedding Portrait

At breakfast the next morning, Si Nian listens to his retelling with bland equanimity, although his gaze moves about restlessly. When Tian Wei is done, Si Nian says, "If the Hai San is involved, this is as far as the Ghee Hin will go, given the Larut Wars of 1861. Bad blood runs deep." He speculates that Mr. Ki might be in cahoots with the Hai San, not actually working for them. He knocks out a Players cigarette and taps it against the packet. Lifts it to his lips and lights it. Smokes and finishes his coffee.

Tian Wei puts his head in his hands. No rest for the wicked. The cottonwool feeling in his head makes it hard for him to see the end of the tunnel, to devise a plan. Anxiety rushes hot and cold in his bloodstream. What if he were to kidnap Aiko like a thief in the night, like the Hai San had done? When he gives voice to this, Si Nian immediately rejects the idea— who knows what the arrangement is between the Hai San or Mr. Ki and Hudson Tay? It is too dangerous, and she has already been recaptured once. Secretly, Tian Wei suspects that Si Nian does not want to risk his own neck, and who can blame him?

"There is one option," Si Nian eventually says.

Tian Wei looks up.

Si Nian's gaze on him is sombre, also containing a hint of devilry. "Ask Hudson Tay for Aiko's hand in marriage."

Tian Wei blanches. "How can I do that when he says she is betrothed to another? He informed me himself."

"Then perhaps you should elope together."

"But that will compromise her marriageability forever. It will create a scandal."

"It will compromise nothing. She will be married to you. You will be her husband. Isn't that what you want?"

"No! Aiko is like a sister to me. How can I be married to someone I regard as a sister?"

"Oh, come now—she is not your actual sister." Si Nian leers. "Can you not perhaps envision that, over time, you will come to develop feelings for her of a different sort? You have gone to impossible lengths to find out where she is—all this for a 'supposed' sister? Really, who are you lying to: me or yourself?"

Tian Wei stares at Si Nian. It is impossible to get him to understand. Which part should he reveal: that love can be pure, that his love for Aiko is indeed brotherly, because he too was once cared for like a sibling? That he carries the letters from Charlie and his own unsent letters in a pouch even here? Si Nian would say that Tian Wei should be committed to an asylum, and he would be right. It doesn't matter. He knows where he stands. Only Tang poetry is adequate to express this love, its purity, its distilled essence, and the cleaving of mind from heart. What is a man if he cannot own up to the truth of his own feelings? To him, the hundred-years distance between him and Charlie is as if she were writing to him from a faraway continent. Even if they never meet, it doesn't diminish what he feels. Love can be true and pure, and he feels blessed to have felt it in his life.

Yet, it is sensible to consider Si Nian's elopement proposal. He has come too far to give up now. What other choices present themselves? Si Nian can help obtain a marriage certificate, and, by the time Aiko's father sends henchmen to catch up with them, they will be married. In fact and law, if not in reality. Aiko-chan will come under a husband's protection. He shan't tie her down; if she wishes to be independent thereafter, he will do whatever within his power to grant her freedom, to enable her dream. But will Aiko-chan even agree to an elopement?

"There is nothing more to ponder. Do you have a better plan?" Si Nian asks. "It is your only choice if you want to help her."

*

Once decided, things move swiftly. They head over to Cherry
Blossom that evening. While Si Nian selects one of the girls to
go upstairs with, Tian Wei asks for Aiko, going through the
elaborate procedure of persuading Ohatsu-san. Word is sent up
to Aiko. To Ohatsu-san's astonishment, Aiko agrees. Ohatsu-san
follows him with shrewd, speculative eyes as he walks upstairs,
accompanied by Ah Lan.

Aiko is shy, seeing him again, as she lets him into her room.
There is a massive Chinese-style platform bed with an ornate
headboard, a dressing table full of cosmetics and jewellery,
a beautiful painted Shanxi cabinet—full of her yukatas,
she says. Hers is the best room in the house. Her father has
seen to that. Over by the window, an easel stands, on which
are several drawings of the women from the brothel, looking
like mythological beings: face of a woman, body of a snake;
Chang'e flying to the moon as a crane. At least one thing hasn't
changed: Aiko still loathes drawing flowers, although she is no
longer averse to wearing them. Her hair is crimped in waves
on her forehead, knotted with pins into a bun at the nape of
her neck, a frangipani tucked into the raven folds. Her painted
face makes her seem far older than her years, and he stymies a
sudden urge to wipe her face clean.

"Would you like to eat something, Tian Wei Ge Ge?"

He sits and reaches for her hands. "Listen, we don't have
much time." His elopement plan is simple. Si Nian will return
post-haste to Singapore and obtain a marriage licence on his
behalf. Meanwhile, he will take Aiko to a studio to get their
wedding portrait taken. As soon as this is done, they will set sail
for Singapore. When they dock, they will be as good as husband
and wife. He will present the photo and marriage certificate
to Hudson Tay as a fait accompli. The merchant will have no
choice but to accept it.

"You can come live with me in my studio. I will telegraph
ahead to have Kee Lung and Kee Mun set up your own room
for you. You may live with me for as long as you wish. And,
if you should like to become a photographer, I will teach you

all the skills of the trade. Perhaps, over time, after your father accepts the reality of your situation, he may help to set you up with your own studio."

Aiko's hands in between his own have become sweaty. So intent has he been in outlining his plan in full that he failed to notice until now that her cheeks have reddened considerably. He is struck by a sudden thought: she is a maiden still, despite having lived in a brothel for three years, despite having grown up in one when young, despite having heard and seen things no proper young, chaperoned girl should. The things that happen between man and wife behind closed doors must be causing her consternation.

"You don't have to trouble yourself that I would ever…" He feels horribly embarrassed himself. "What I mean to say is—" he clears his throat— "this won't be a real marriage. I wouldn't expect that we should act as husband and wife. I would respect…" He stops because Aiko is giggling. "What's funny?"

Aiko-chan leans over and plants a soft kiss on his cheek. "Oh, but I want you to. As my husband." Charmingly, after this peck and confession, she hides her face behind her palms.

What in the world can she mean? He stares at her cupped hands; then, as she gently parts her fingers to peek at him, he is flabbergasted. God, no! This must not happen. Dismay lines his face, words flee. He opens and closes his mouth. At a future point in time, perhaps it could have been a possibility, but, to him, she is still a child. Rather, those fervid nights when he can't sleep, parsing through his memory those words in Charlie's letters that he holds in his heart like gems, realising the pleasure he derives from reading them, feeling that pall of emotion that strains every fibre of his being: those nights have brought but one conclusion. For him, there will be no other. If he stays lonely as a sparrow forever, it cannot be helped. He knows this the way he knows his camera—knowledge ingrained into muscle memory.

His dismayed expression semaphores itself to Aiko. Her impish delight and blushing coquettishness give way to gradual awareness. Her eyes rove his face for the truth of his feelings. And she is crestfallen when she learns it.

"Is there someone else?" she asks quietly.

"No, it is not like that. There is no one else."

But she withdraws her hands, because they both know a lie when they hear it.

*

They don't speak about this knife-edge moment, as if by tacit agreement; plans proceed apace. Si Nian takes the train back to Singapore, though it is a less comfortable journey compared to the steamer and involves several changes. Tian Wei books an appointment with a Japanese photographer on Northam Road, rather than at a Chinese studio. More than once, he senses himself followed. Shadows and ghouls. Hai San or Ghee Hin, no way to tell. Mr. Ki might have his own lackeys. The sooner they set sail, the safer he will feel.

Aiko does not want to wear a kimono; kimonos remind her of her time in captivity. The Japanese photographer has a selection of robes, but none are bridal wear. Tian Wei rushes from fabric shop to tailor, to get a European bridal outfit ready in time. Her measurements have to be done stealthily, but Aiko manages with Ah Lan's help. Ohatsu-san is getting highly suspicious, so Tian Wei curtails his visits to Cherry Blossom, which makes communication with Aiko hazardous and difficult. Fortunately, they have already set the date for their wedding photograph for the following week. He secretly buys her clothing and toiletries (she told him some things she needed: Kaloderma soap, iced hair lotion, lily of the valley eau de toilette), packs them in his valise for her. Their tickets on the steamer *Renong* lie on top of the armoire.

The day of the wedding photograph dawns with black thunderheads rolling in the sky above. Heat suffuses the town like a blanket. Tian Wei wakes with pins and needles wracking his body, pain in his joints, a crackle in his throat. It hurts to swallow. His head pounds. When he touches his forehead, he realises he has a fever. Instead of breakfast, he asks the servant-boy to get him medicine from the Japanese pharmacy. For the photograph, he has bought a white satin bow tie and felt hat, and the one other suit he brought comes back from the Indian laundry dhoby ironed and pressed. A cream linen suit. As he dresses, he notices a large creamy yellowish stain on the side of his jacket near the vent. The stain strikes him whimsically as resembling the shape of a constellation of stars. He scratches at it, giving it a sniff. Metallic. A feeling arrows through him: disappointment. A thought enters his mind: betrayal. Charlie. He parts his hair in the mirror, applies pomade. This wedding feels dead wrong, but he hopes doing it to save Aiko is the right thing. If he can secure another person's freedom and happiness in this world, will it be enough? Will Sansan's lost wandering soul finally be at peace? Will it repay some of the debt he owes her for saving his life? Is this how inner redemption is negotiated?

When he gets to Nikko Studio on Northam Road, Aiko hasn't yet arrived. Hatsumoto-san, the general manager, is a genial, apple-cheeked fellow, his manner hearty, overly chatty. He speaks passable Mandarin, but his Malay is nonpareil. When complimented, Hatsumoto-san digresses into a long explanation of why Japan needed to modernise after the Tokugawa era ended, and how its efforts to do so have been stellar, a clear message to Western powers steaming up shorelines in gunboats and demanding concessions, not to underestimate the might of the East. Consider the Meiji government's naval development, its industrial and shipping industry expansion; consider the strides it has made in embracing all things technological, all things Western. Even in the arts, the changes have been spectacular. Has Tian Wei read *Ukigumo* by Futabatei Shimei? How marvellous its revolutionising of literary language, how the turn inward to the psyche reveals so much about a man living in his time. Tian Wei lets the man babble on, occasionally nodding. It camouflages his own stormy thoughts.

Aiko arrives in a rickshaw, flustered and tense. She has had to get ready without the rest of the house knowing what she was up to—no mean feat, sneaking out the back door in full bridal gown, accompanied by Ah Lan. Her European wedding dress is high-necked and comes down to her ankles, the sleeves and hem trimmed with lace. She is beautiful; on any other day, he would have been proud to stand by her side, as a brother should. He holds out the bouquet he asked Hatsumoto-san to provide, from which he has snipped off a tiny sprig for his buttonhole. Aiko takes it; her eyes dip down to her feet in the manner of a blushing bride. The heels he bought her patter as they walk into the studio. Inside, Ah Lan helps Aiko don her veil, transforming her into a seraphic creature.

Hatsumoto-san positions them against a simple backdrop—behind them is a large gilt-edged floor-length mirror, reflecting the opposite backdrop: a window opening out to a range of low hills. In front of the painted window is a painted desk. On it, a goose-necked lamp. Something about the mirror and its reflection makes Tian Wei think of a photograph and its negative, the yang and yin forming a composite whole. That is marriage as well: there can be no bride without a groom. Aiko-chan slips her gloved hand into the crook of his elbow. They pose, facing the camera, solemn and still. They hear the snap of the shutter. Change pose: him standing, her seated. *Snap.* And again. What a definitive, teeth-clenching sound.

It is done.

Come collect the photograph tomorrow.

*

They return to the guest house together, now husband and wife, as the skies break above. They rush indoors, sheltering their heads from the big, fat drops. He signs her in, introduces her to the proprietor, who looks thoroughly bewildered, in the middle of spooning *nasi ambeng* into his mouth. Throughout the entire photograph session and the ride back in the rickshaw, they barely spoke. Tian Wei is sunk into a welter of knotty thoughts; Aiko too has lapsed into a stagnant silence. The atmosphere between them is strained, not at all celebratory.

They face each other in the middle of his room. Aiko-chan looks around, lost. The bouquet in her hands is fast wilting from the heat. Wind whips and rain lashes in through the chik blinds, and Tian Wei rushes to close the windows. "Are you tired?" he asks her. "Would you like to change and lie down for a rest?"

She shakes her head.

"Are you not hungry, Aiko-chan?" he says.

She doesn't answer. She wears a dejected expression instead, as if a dismal thought has bubbled up. He moves to help her with her veil. Ah Lan has gone back to the brothel to fend off enquiries from the *mamasan* with the excuse that Mr. Ki has requested Aiko to accompany him across the Straits to Province Wellesley. It is not untrue. Mr. Ki is indeed in Province Wellesley on business; Aiko has made sure of it. They needed his absence to carry out their plan of elopement. To make their getaway.

As Tian Wei lifts the veil from her head, their proximity makes Aiko freeze. Her breath slows. Tian Wei notices, and his heart rebels. *I have given her the wrong idea.* In his mind, what he sees is a quick glimpse of another face underneath the veil. The jumping heart makes you see things that aren't there.

Aiko raises herself on to the balls of her feet. It throws her off-balance, and he reaches out to steady her. He isn't expecting that, for the split second she is in his arms, she would plant a peck on his lips. Colour floods her face as she rights herself. Contrition, embarrassment, but also a measure of determination. "Tian Wei Ge Ge, forgive me for being forward, but maybe this will change your mind. I've come too far to give up now."

Everything converges: not having eaten all day, the stress and worry he has been carrying, the pins and needles in his joints, the fever. He is overcome with dizziness and nausea. The room tilts; Aiko-chan's image wavers and then blurs. The fever flares all over his sinews and muscles like a bed of nails. His knees buckle. Like an extinguished candle, a pop, he feels his spirit being lifted, and then sucked out. The light goes out in his mind.

Sand of Time

21 December 1925

My dearest Miss C.:—

Today, I thought of you endlessly, and I suppose it must have something to do with watching Feng Yu get married yesterday. This waiting for your letters is harder than you know. I shall do as you ask and meet you by the lake. The days of waiting feel so empty sometimes. Nothing goes smoothly. Business has been slow, and I think about how I failed Aiko-chan. Memories bring loneliness. Also, happiness. They are curse and blessing both. I had not realised — a photograph is made from glass, and glass is made from sand. Therefore, a photograph is...

I am completely mystified. The letter ends here, without his signature, and alludes to something I have no knowledge of. What lake? The astringent scent is especially sharp. I try to scroll down. There is nothing more. It is a letter fragment. Not only that, it is dated 1925, and the last letter from him had been in 1922. Could it have popped up in my Q.E. folder out of sequence, perhaps referring to a future that hasn't yet happened for me? Is the Q.E. becoming unstable? Is the sand in the hourglass finally trickling to its end? Is the time-continuum enabling our letter exchange in sequential order breaking down?

And what has happened to Aiko that his letter is bleeding such desperation and sorrow?

A Temporal Hallucination

A break in the case: the P.I. Adnan hired has discovered something interesting, and Sebastian is leaving for Shanghai again. I don't confront him about Cassandra's involvement in TAV. It isn't the time. Besides, when it comes to confidences, there is no quid pro quo between nominal siblings, even if they are best buddies.

Sebastian sounds harried on the phone. Apparently, Zhou Zhen's marriage has been on the rocks for a while—with his philandering ways, it is only a matter of time—but Xueling, his wife, also his business manager, has recently taken out insurance on all his artworks. While unclear what it is she hopes to gain from a forgery of his work, this at least suggests motive, and gives the investigators something to mull over. On the day of the artwork's transport, she had been on hand to supervise the packing and shipping personally. Thus, she had plenty of opportunity to swap the real for a fake. Meanwhile, in a bizarre turn of events, the exploding news of the forgery drives up the value of Zhou Zhen's works, simply because another collector, a competitive friend of D. Broussard, has made a bid on TAV for another of his works. In one single gesture, faith returns to the platform. The online art community has already leaked the possibility of Xueling's involvement in the forgery; the gossip mill goes wild. She becomes the scapegoat, tarred and trolled, without so much as a whiff of concrete proof.

These are the days when the shallowness of the art world, of which I am a part, disgusts me.

*

Another day, another curator's tour.

Today's group comprises teenage students from Ching Hwa Junior College. As usual, I start at the portrait of

Mother-with-a-capital-*M*, then move over to the famous photograph of Sophia Blackmore and her female students.

"Sophia Blackmore was the principal of the Methodist Girls' School, one of the earliest girls' schools founded in Singapore, with the help of the American Methodists, in 1888. As you can see, this photograph shows Blackmore seated among her girls, the Straits Chinese girls wearing baju panjang with the standard hairdo of sanggul encircled with a floral tiara, the Tamil girls in saris or European frocks. The photo is dated 1915, taken at Lee Brothers' Studio, and in contrast to the usual photographs of women in stiff poses, the girls' poses here are relaxed and smiling, some with heads tilted, others leaning or turned slightly sideways in their postures. Blackmore herself is the photograph's focal point, depicted in quite an extreme leaning pose that not only indicates her attitude towards formal photographs—a bold intrepid spirit, not afraid to 'lean away' from orthodoxy—but, by extrapolation, also offers clues to her style of leadership, her influence on and affection for her students."

I tell them about the female education reform drive in early twentieth century Singapore, in which Sophia Blackmore was a key player (going door to door in a *becak* to convince parents to send their girls to school). How the banner of female education reform was really part of a broader progressive cultural reformation.

"This movement, started by Dr. Lim Boon Keng and other Straits Chinese leaders, arose out of the Peranakan Chinese community's need to redefine their hybridised identity. To reorient towards a more solid sense of Chineseness. To revive elements of Chinese culture within themselves—such as language, classical literature, and Confucian values—while abandoning more regressive aspects, such as folk religious rituals and pigtails for male coolies."

One of the girls raises her hand timidly. "I have a question."

"Sure," I encourage her. "Ask as many as you want."

"Did the Chinese clans at the time have an understanding of what it means to be Chinese?"

"Excellent question. We don't yet have a full picture of how much the various clans at the time—Hokkien, Teochiew, Cantonese, Hakka etc.—had economic, social, and cultural dealings across clan lines. Thus, Dr. Lim's early consciousness-raising efforts—founding *The Straits Chinese Magazine* to debate social and political issues, founding the Chinese Girls' School—undoubtedly had a great influence towards a collective sense of Chinese solidarity, one that is distanced from the ruling British elite. But one must understand that it also served colonial interests to lump all the Chinese clans together as one ethnic category, doing the same for the Malays and Indians. It made for easy governance. So, you see, the driver of female empowerment within this larger cultural reformation also helped build Chinese solidarity, because, after the May Fourth Movement in China, it signalled Singapore's status as a cosmopolitan port city aligned with the female-empowerment movements happening in East Asia as well as in the Western world. In the 1930s, there would be a proliferation of male and female voices in the newspapers vigorously debating the proper roles of women."

One girl with her hair plaited in two, wearing thick glasses, raises her hand. "Excuse me, Miss Sze-Toh? Can I ask a question?"

"Of course." I smile at her encouragingly.

"Aren't all the photographers during the colonial era male? Aren't we also talking about the male gaze here?"

Just like that, I'm lost, adrift in inner captivity, where all my thoughts are of Wang Tian Wei. As if my soul has escaped and is floating somewhere above me, I hear myself tell them about the first female doctor in Singapore in the 1920s, also an avid photographer-hobbyist, Lee Choo Neo, grand-aunt of Prime Minister Lee Kuan Yew. I point at the photograph of her sitting in a roadster with a friend, hear myself say how I believe that there were other ladies of the Peranakan social set who similarly took up photography, thus their albums formed a private, cloistered economy of gazes where women were consuming each other's photographs. Within me, two things percolate: yearning and waiting. Two things that elongate time. Two unbearable things. My voice sounds tinny and far away, as if a tunnel of air were trapped between my ears.

The girls ask if they can take photographs. A photograph of a photograph—how much more meta can we get? Frissons of energy are bubbling within my body, hot and cold, and I sense the shift in elemental energy flow before the singularity happens.

Above the corridor is a domed skylight. Light falls through it to lay a filigree pattern within a circlet of fire on the grey-tiled floor. The contour of this cone of light sharpens to a shimmer, suspended slightly above floor level. Sun rays create a minuscule aurora. Gossamer rainbow colours shift and glint. Do the girls in the tour see it too? They murmur among themselves, intently studying the museum brochure guide.

I turn back. Still there, unmistakable, a hovering forcefield, tightening and gaining an outline. I blink. A man is silhouetted within the glimmer. A man in a three-piece linen suit with a small bouquet in his buttonhole. The vision is only there for a moment. A strong astringent scent infiltrates. My steps falter. My gaze collides with his. I get the feeling he sees me too. I stare at the mirage, transfixed. I suddenly remember that ghostly image of a man hovering before a camera with bellows that I saw a month back. These two occasions are related. The thought grows from a muted whispering in my mind to a kind of certainty: the mirage in front of me is none other than the man I have been writing passionate letters to—Wang Tian Wei.

My entire being goes rogue. Goose pimples along my forearms. I break into a light sweat. Pockets of cold alternating with heat travel up and down my spine. I walk the group up to and underneath the domed skylight, but the mirage does a strange thing. It does not gain perspective, it does not get bigger as I approach. It stays equidistant from me, as if light years away, and the principle of perspective cannot alter it. My body suddenly feels feather-light, then awash with a warmth I know is love. Absolute, eclipsing, unconditional love. It infuses me from top to toe, as if I'm standing before Michelangelo's *Pietà*. My vision is pricked by tears. I am riven.

As we pass from light into shadow, the mirage vanishes. In its place, a placebo of light.

That night, back at the Guest Lodge, I am shaken to my inner core. Truth dawns on me. Anything I have felt before this was but a pale reflection of the real thing. Awash in tears, sobs are wrenched from the body like wind-driven rain, as if the body is releasing oceanic washes of emotion. The body fissures to release the light within.

Magic Maths

My dearest Miss C.:—

There has been no letter from you for over
a year. I feel my soul is shrivelling. Did you
receive my letter dated 18 November 1922? You
haven't replied; I must assume you did not.

We found Aiko-chan. I shan't go into all
the details, but it was exactly as Si Nian
said — Aiko was working in a brothel. Without
the Ghee Hin's help, we would not have got
this far. Aiko-chan is much changed. She has
become a young woman. Although she was working
in a brothel, she was under the protection of
an unsavoury character in the employ of her
father. It grieves me deeply to realise the
depth of treachery a man reaches in his heart
when his kingdom of riches is threatened.

Aiko-chan was happy to see me and asked
me to save her. Si Nian and I made a plan,
but alas, we failed. Aiko has once again gone
missing — although, this time, by her own
choice. I hope that, wherever she has escaped
to, she is safe.

Charlie, I am too ashamed to write the
details of what happened, but I am greatly
conflicted. I have betrayed you. Separated
as we are by time and place, there are
no promises I can make to you. Thus, the
betrayal that punched me in the belly was not
a betrayal of you, nor even the promise of

you, but of myself. In the deepest, truest
part of myself, I had a dream — all the more
fantastic for its implausibility — but the
dream was to be face to face with you, to
tuck your hand inside my arm, to be the one
to lift up your veil, to have a photograph
taken with you.

Perhaps wishes sent to heaven echo and
reverberate. Just before Aiko disappeared, I
became unwell. I do not know what happened,
but I had such a high fever the doctor had
to be brought. I dimly remember Aiko taking
care of me, putting cold towels on my forehead
to help dissipate my temperature. The hotel's
houseboy — I saw him too, carrying a shallow
basin back and forth. The doctor came and went.

But none of this is important. What's
important is what I saw. Perhaps I was dreaming
about you. I was in some dark, pitch-black
place, and then I saw you. You walked towards
me. There were young girls around you, all
wearing what looked like a school uniform —
white top, green pinafore, neat as a pin. You
were in a big hall full of large portraits on
the walls. The sounds of all your footsteps
rang like temple bells. But it was you — you
looked exactly as you did in your photograph.
You wore a white studded hairband, a white
blouse, and long grey trousers that a man
might wear. Your shoes made you seem as if you
were balancing on small stilts — you towered
above the girls. I treasure this glimpse of
you. This vision confounds me — was it a
hallucination, or did my spirit travel this
far in search of you? When I recovered, Aiko
was gone.

In the lowest of spirits, thence I returned
to Singapore. During the time I was away,
Peng Loon was so terrified that there would
be another "ghost-letter" from you, he stayed
awake at night, sitting in a corner surrounded
by a dusting of flour. If a footprint should
emerge, or if the flour so much as blew
sideways, he would straightaway mumble the
charm he had received from the Tua Pek Kong
Temple.

Peng Loon thinks all the letters arrive on
the thirteenth because the number is related
to the number 1314 on the box. Some sort of
evil magick. It has got me thinking. Not evil,
but magic maths. An esoteric doorway: what
if the square of any number is a celestial
doorway into the unknown?

If indeed that was a glimpse of you, I am
so grateful for it. I didn't think it was
possible, but it makes me greedy for more.
I am overcome whenever I think about you.
我真没想到我会 爱上一个我从不见过的人。

Forever yours,
Tian Wei

Ghost Photographs

This morning, I had a meeting with Luo Sin Yee, the curator for an upcoming exhibition, on the early twentieth century leading lights of Chinese descent, at the Sun Yat Sen Nanyang Memorial Hall in Balestier. It is one of my favourite museums—quiet, unsplashy, offering moments of reflection. A statue of Sun Yat Sen presides in front of the building. Its history is remarkable. Teo Eng Hock built it as a villa for his mother in 1905, then named Wang Qing Yuan. Sun Yat Sen stayed here during his visits to Singapore.

Sin Yee was really impressed with all the research I'd done on the Chinese intelligentsia existing in the colonial entrepôts of Penang and Singapore. Though numbering at best a couple of hundred, most were in the merchant classes, of which photographers were included, while a few dozen were schoolteachers, doctors, pastors, newspaper editors, translators, writers, and monks. Many were bilingual or trilingual, but little has been written about them, these denoted *zhi shi fen zi.*

The role they played in the re-Sinicisation of colonial Malaya and Singapore was critical. They maintained ties with China; they formed philanthropic organisations, *hui guans*, night schools, and reading clubs that promoted a sense of Chineseness; some of them opened bookshops; some of them helped bring in Chinese books and magazines as textbooks for schools; others supported library services for schools and reading clubs. Many also became members of the Kuomintang. After the Jinan Massacre in 1928 and the Mukden Incident in China in 1931, fundraising efforts and donation drives to help victims of aggression in China intensified in Singapore. The overseas Chinese communities rallied to the China cause. The Chinese intelligentsia were key in agitating for their vision of China. Even those who worked for the British government kept a close alliance with

Chinese organisations and participated in Chinese-related activities.

"Is this for an academic paper," Sin Yee asked, smiling, "or for another exhibition?"

"Neither," I replied honestly.

"Then what is it for?"

"Purely my own personal interest." I didn't say that, because of a quantum correspondence, I've delved into this research with new fervour. To help me understand him.

She nodded, but I could see from the gleam in her eye that she didn't quite believe me. No such thing when you work in the art world. Perhaps she is right.

Sitting in the park opposite after the meeting, the Zhongshan Gongyuan, I watch a mother chasing her toddler, and the toddler chasing their dog. Round and round they go. In front is a pink-marbled rock with the inscription, *One Man Changed China: Dr. Sun Yat Sen.* A connecting walkway is dotted with factoids, inscribed on slates, about the nine visits Sun Yat Sen made to Malaya and Singapore to raise funds and build solidarity for his new government. A man and woman sit on a bench, bits of their deep conversation drifting over to me. How uncanny, they are talking about photography. I catch words and phrases, like "privileging of the scopic regime," "ethnographic mise-en-scene," and "historical juncture," and names like Rosalind Morris, Christopher Pinney, and Sebastian Dobson; they mention past photography exhibitions held in Singapore, one of them at the Nanyang Memorial Hall: *From Brush to Lens.*

My kind of people.

I take out the printed copy of Wang Tian Wei's letter to read slowly. I sense something terrible has happened and it has to do with a botched rescue of Aiko. I also sense that Tian Wei is hiding something. I don't have to think about it too hard. From the few facts he shared alone—especially that she was with him while he fell ill—the plan must have had something to do with either marriage or concubinage (one, if not the only, way to rescue a woman out of prostitution). My heart is unruffled. He must have hidden the details because he thought they would upset me. Does he not know that I come from a complicated modern family that is a cycle of olden-day concubinage arrangements for wealthy men? *I forgive you*, I sing out in my heart. *I have already forgiven you, Tian Wei.*

Those Chinese characters in his last sentence—*I never imagined that I could be so in love with someone I can't possibly meet*—upend my world and make me crush his letter to my chest. Why does it echo so when written in Chinese? This feeling—a lyric dancing through stardust, a song embedding itself in the heart—I couldn't have imagined it would feel like this. A singularity throws logic out of whack, breaks into mindsets and rhythms, cracks molecular lines, opens pastures of feeling, sparks wonder at the mystery of the world. Over and above all is the realisation that our entanglement, slim and slight as it is, allows for more than letters. It allows for the spectres of us. All the different manifestations of us beyond the body. These futures of us can meet. What if we can make a manifestation happen deliberately? It has already happened twice. Without meaning to, I jump to my feet, startling the two scholars on the next bench. I turn to them and solemnly say, "Baudrillard says illusion is not the opposite of reality, but another more subtle reality... Now, why didn't I think of that before?" They stare at me round-eyed, conveying that they think me slightly mad. What do they know? I want to run and shout. Howsoever the energy of matter from a hundred years ago may have travelled across an hourglass of ages, it has brought joy. An avalanche of it. Didn't Mary Oliver say, "Joy is not meant to be a crumb"? How do I get Wang Tian Wei's spirit to come again? How do I get him to stay?

I text Matt Sharpe:

> Do you like Hainan chicken rice?

> Matt: Adore it.

Me: Wanna go get some for dinner? There's this place on South Bridge Road. Literally three generations of a family making it. The bees' knees.

Matt: OK, let's go.

Me: 7 p.m. Send you a Googlemap Loc. Oh wait, I can't, phone's too old. I'll text you the address.

Matt: Are we dressing up?

Me: For Hainan chicken rice? 😳

Matt: I don't know!? This could be a date?

Me: *typing…*(pause) *typing…*

Matt: Hello? You still there? Did I put my foot in it again?

Me: I'm coming from work. Also, I need to ask a favour of you.

Matt: OK. Got it.

*

When I get there, Matt is perched on one of the stools in the small cafe, scrolling through his social media.

"Hey!"

He glances up. Good grief, he really is so good-looking. Too bad I hanker after people from a hundred years ago.

"A colleague at Nanfang has passed. I didn't even know he was ill. His office is two doors away from mine. We were having a good old natter just last week at a kopitiam."

"I'm sorry to hear, Matt. These things are never easy."

"Thing is, when a colleague you're not all that close to dies, you don't get to grieve. In an instant, something changes to nothing, presence becomes absence. You're sad he is gone, but, in a day or at most two, you're back to getting pissed off that Facebook is sending you ads for tongue scrapers or penile enlargement, or that another colleague is always bragging about his achievements online, down to how many mentions he gets in Academia." Matt rolls his eyes. "Nobody gives a fuck about Academia."

I suppress a chuckle. He says everything with such solemnity, it's hard to tell if he's joking, which in turn makes whatever ridiculous thing he says even funnier.

"Look at this. His Facebook post, here, says his funeral is tomorrow. It doesn't say who posted this; ostensibly, he posted it himself. There are 369 likes that he died. Insanity."

Matt is only now catching up to irony expressed on Twitter a decade ago, and I thought I was the misfit with my hermit-crab life and three-generations-old iPhone. I channel Sebastian: thoughtful, ruminative. "Ghost photograph. When we die, one of the most prominent traces that remains will be our social-media profile—photograph after photograph of what we did, what we ate, who we did what with, all the whats, whys, and hows of the way we chose to live our lives, memorialised now and forever. *Amituofo*. Amen."

Matt grins. "No shit, Sherlock. Let's get some chicken rice before they sell out."

The tiny shop sells a limited number of plates every day, and lucky us, we have managed to grab the last two plates of the day.

We sit down with our food at the window counter side-by-side, and I launch straight into the reason I asked him to meet me. "What I want to ask is this—" my voice wavers, turning into an embarrassed croak— "do you think a *tangki* can help a spirit from a hundred years ago manifest in the present? Or send my spirit to the past?"

Matt's eyes saucer. "Jesus Christ," he says. "Are you serious?"

"Very serious. Can you help or not?"

He looks away. Fear bites into his features. "I photograph what they allow me to. I've never tried asking them for anything. I'm not sure the *tangki* himself can be possessed by just any spirit from a hundred years ago. They are beholden to a particular deity, like the Sun Wu Kong Monkey God or Goddess of Mercy, or to an ancestral spirit of the overseas Chinese. It's a sort of religious contract."

"Assuming it is an ancestral spirit of sorts from the 1920s, can he manifest in our space-time?"

If Matt notes my use of the present tense, he does not comment. He clocks the determination in my tone. "Well, Derek Tsai is a *tangki* I know, whom I've been following, and he does channel the spirit of the Tua Pek Kong."

"You think the spirit of Tua Pek Kong can help?"

"I didn't say he could. But it doesn't hurt to ask. Tua Pek Kong is believed to be an all-knowing Taoist deity embodying the spirit of overseas Chinese pioneers—and, supposedly, one can ask anything. Mainly, people ask advice about health matters, like how to realign vertebrae or cure an irresolvable bunion, or domestic troubles, like how to entice back a cheating spouse or get a son to be more filial. While he is in a trance, you could ask him what you want to know."

I spoon chicken rice rapidly into my mouth, not tasting, barely chewing. "OK, how do we do this?"

Matt spins my stool around to face him. He leans forward, one hand resting on each side of me. His eyes on me are solemn, no bullshit. "This stuff can be dangerous. Are you sure about this?"

I nod, spoon aloft in my hand. "Very sure." I suck on the spoon.

"May I ask why it's so important?"

I let my eyes do the pleading for me. A slim, slight love may seem pathetic to others when voiced, but it is vital for me to see it through. I have this image of myself holding a bag of leftover love—dregs from my mother, my father, and the modicum of care I sometimes receive from Cassandra. Only Sebastian would understand. To be the recipient of such focused, pure love for the first time is to allow for the possibility of movement after stasis. Where once no one could come in and nothing could go out, some fenced-in part of me is now being prised wide open. All I know for sure is that the intensity of the connection means it is something more than loving someone at a remove. I'm not sure he gets it.

Matt's eyes stay on mine a long time. He caves.

The Spectral Economy

The date set for our visit to a *sin tua*, a makeshift home temple run by a *tangki*, is the ninth day of the Lunar New Year celebrations. Which happens to be 14 February, Valentine's Day. Surely auspicious. I have high hopes and feel as if my feet are bouncing on pockets of air as Matt and I head off to the M.R.T. at dusk.

The makeshift temple where we will catch Derek Tsai in action is in Ang Mo Kio. A low-slung building has a huge tentage set in its compound. The entrance is a rusty green gate, the perimeter is fenced with barbed wire and decorated with lots of yellow and red prayer flags. Inside the tent is a three-tiered main altar, all draped in gaudy red and yellow silk cloths. Banners are tacked up along the tent walls, some with Chinese talismanic writing, others with pictures of generals on horses with flying hooves, and yet others with pictures of underworld deities. A massive painting depicting the San Qing (三清)—the Taoist triumvirate, which represents the emanations of pure Tao cosmic energy—hangs on the centre back wall. A large figurine on the altar represents the Tua Pek Kong—looking benevolent in his flowing white beard, a dragon staff in one hand, a gold ingot in the other—flanked by a number of sacred artefacts and heavenly deities, candles and a massive urn for incense. There are food offerings: oranges, *fatt-gow* buns looking soft and pillowy, bowls of rice, bottles of rice wine, cellophane-wrapped baskets of goodies. In celebration of the Lunar Festival, red lanterns have been hung everywhere. Rows of red plastic chairs are placed behind the ceremonial chair in front of the altar. Followers bustle to and fro, all of them wearing yellow polo T-shirts with Taoist images imprinted on their backs, a kind of unofficial identification. Devotees are streaming in through the gate. There are easily a hundred people milling around. Incense smoke wraiths the air, and the night is overly warm without the faintest breeze.

Matt points out Derek Tsai to me, arriving in a singlet and shorts, almost as if he had rolled out of bed, attire as unlike a *tangki* as a saint without his halo. He doesn't look over twenty.

"He gets robed later, and the enrobing is completed after he enters his trance," Matt explains, then tells me Derek's life history in brief. He began entering trances when he was eight, but resisted his calling to be a spirit medium for a long time, and it wasn't until he turned twenty-one that he embraced it as his destiny and began giving consultations and advice. In addition to the Tua Pek Kong, he channels a couple of deities lower in the celestial hierarchy. "Derek has a day job fixing computer motherboards," Matt says, enjoying my raised eyebrow of surprise. He points to a couple of men with charcoal faces. They channel the Di Ya Pek, the Second Brother of the pair of hell guardians, who wears a black robe. The story goes that the two brothers—Tua Di Ya Pek—lived in a southern province in China centuries ago and were upright citizens who would rather die than accept bribery. Tua Ya Pek, who wears a white robe, died by hanging, hence his tongue hangs out, while Di Ya Pek died by drowning, hence his inky face. The two of them ferry souls to the underworld.

The beating of gongs and clashing of cymbals begin the ceremony, followed by low, monotonous chanting. A couple of followers are walking around the area before the altar, cracking a snake-headed hessian whip. Matt explains that they are performing a ritual called the *huat-soh*; the thunderclap sounds produced by the whip scare away evil spirits, and cleanse and secure the area for the arriving deities. Today's festival is a big one; in addition to Derek, several other *tangki* will also be entering trances and channelling their deities. Off to the side, I see a woman all in white.

"She channels the Goddess Kuan Yin," Matt whispers. "If we stay long enough, we may see some of them in a trance, bleeding their tongues or walking on burning charcoal." While the prospect of witnessing this is potentially gruesome, the scene before me is festive and loud, like a big party.

Derek comes back to the tent partially dressed. His trousers look like those worn by Cantonese opera singers—balloon trousers in bright yellow embroidered silk, tightened around the ankles—but his chest remains bare. He sits in the ceremonial chair, his head hanging low. The chanting and banging continue for several minutes. All of a sudden, Derek's head swivels from side to side, increasing in speed, and one leg involuntarily shakes. His head continues to swing side to side but so violently now that a couple of his followers have to hold on to him. Derek leaps up, begins pogoing on one foot, his hands rising in an arc around his head. In front of the altar, he dances, and Matt tells me Derek is performing a ritual dance tracing the zig-zag pattern connecting the Eight Trigrams of the Luo Shu (洛书), the magic map of the seven stars said to be imprinted on the shell of a turtle from the Luo River. Yu the Great, founder of the Xia dynasty (2070-1600 BCE), had received this magic map and danced this zig-zag pattern unceasingly for thirteen years to combat the demons of a great flood.

When Derek finally calms down, his *toh tao* (main assistant) drapes him with a decorative *du dou* (肚兜), a diamond-shaped cloth, over his bare torso, and helps him to don his headgear and a false long white beard. Derek receives lit joss sticks from them and plants them in the urn.

We watch him, mesmerised. Someone is filming this sequence. Matt has his camera slung around his neck but does not seem to be taking pictures, saying in a low voice: "Derek is no longer Derek, his soul has vacated. The Tua Pek Kong has taken possession of his body."

We watch Derek in his trance walk down the main aisle towards the tent where he will be doing consultations, accompanied by his followers and devotees. A small table has been set up for him there.

"Come on!" Matt says, "It's like a clinic, you've got to get a number if you want a consultation."

I look behind me to see that another man has now taken the ceremonial chair.

"He channels the Sun Wu Kong," Matt whispers. "Want to stay and watch more?"

I shake my head. All of it is ethnographically fascinating, and it's doubly sweet to have a dishy sociologist-cum-ethnologist running through all the sights and sounds, but I'm on a mission. The incense is thick and acrid, making me tear up. The banging, the cymbals, and the chanting are also drilling into my head. If I stay too long, I will be touring the nine levels of hell in my sleep. We wait and wait, seated in the plastic chairs—but there is plenty to observe. Some of the other *tangki* in trances are writing charm papers for those wishing to ward off evil; one *tangki* channelling the San Taizi (the Child God) is sucking on a milk bottle. The minute hand creeps towards the hour, and I am famished enough to eat a small horse. My calves have been bitten by so many mozzies, they are a hotbed of itchiness. Finally, our number is called. Matt and I take seats to one side of Derek, who doesn't acknowledge or look at us.

"Go ahead and ask your question," Matt urges. "No need to stand on ceremony."

Other than his eyes being closed, and a shiver now and then riding his body, it's hard to tell that Derek is in a trance. Matt has told me that, even though Derek himself is well-versed in English, when in a trance, he speaks in dialect or in Mandarin, but it doesn't matter what language I use to ask my question; Tua Pek Kong can understand.

Here goes nothing. "I would like to meet a man who lived a hundred years ago. Can his spirit travel here?"

Derek's eyes pop open briefly, but all I see are the whites of his eyeballs. He closes them, doesn't speak for several seconds. Matt has become very still beside me. Derek speaks Mandarin in a guttural voice: "His spirit is already close. He is on his way." Then he grabs a sheet of silver joss paper and scrawls numbers on it in red felt tip. The people around us scramble to write down the number on their palms or their phones.

1314—I know this number. Tian Wei has written about its homophonic meaning. *In life and death.* Derek's eyelids flutter, but there is nothing else forthcoming.

Matt makes to rise.

"Wait," I say, desperate. "Is that all? How do I find him?"

Derek's eyes open, but all I can see are the whites in them. He doesn't answer. It doesn't look like he will.

"The deity can choose not to answer," Matt says.

Right. How is this helpful? What does it mean that Wang Tian Wei's spirit is close? I can make neither head nor tail of the advice I've been given. What do I do with *1314*? Am I supposed to buy 4-D lotto with that? Reluctantly, I get up, about to turn away in disappointment, but then Derek gargles his throat as if hawking up sputum. I lean back, slightly alarmed. Derek's eyes remain closed as his mouth moves. No sound emerges. Matt's hand stays me. The *tangki* frowns, taps his breastbone. "What you seek is right here." Then, he shakes his head side to side violently, blowing raspberries with his mouth. "*Phroo! Phroo!*" Matt springs back. Derek spits, then says, "Right place, right time. A place that hasn't changed with time, a time of shifting light."

I gasp. But there is nothing more, and the assistant calls the next number. There is no payment for the *tangki*'s services. Instead, Matt puts a red packet into a brass bowl as a donation to the *sin tua*. We don't stay for the bidding of the *fu pin*—the "lucky items" that have received the deities' blessings (apparently, what fetch the highest prices aren't the goody baskets or fruits or charms, but the charcoal and the bowls of rice). We don't stay for the celebratory feast. We don't pick up a charm to ward off evil. My clothes reek, my hair is plastered to my scalp from sweat, my ankles are a hive of bites, but my body is full up with smoke.

Meet Me By The Lake

15 February 2019

Tian Wei, my dearest,

If your theory is correct, that my letters are all destined to arrive for you on the thirteenth, spaced further and further apart—one month, four months, nine months, sixteen months—then I suspect it is through some temporal distance of squaring—one squared, two squared, three squared, four squared. In which case, I would hazard a guess that this letter might arrive for you on 13 October 1924. I can't be sure, it took me quite a lot of combing through our letters to figure this out, but it's worth a gamble.

I visited a tangki (乩童) (God forbid, am I beginning to sound like Peng Loon?) during the Lunar New Year Festival, and he gave me advice which I interpret as follows: it is possible for your spirit to manifest in my time. I have already seen you twice: once when you were operating your camera, and the second time, exactly as you describe in your last letter. It's completely uncanny, but I was indeed leading a tour of young schoolgirls and they wore green pinafores. I was dressed exactly as you described.

The tangki also said that we have to be at the right place at the right time. While I'm not sure what this means, I believe him because he wrote down 1314. If magic maths is at work here, what if we were to anticipate that you will receive my next letter on 13 October 1927 (six squared)—and, instead of writing, we meet instead? I know this must be such an interminable wait for you, to wait three years, but think about what it means for us:

we may be able to meet face to face! It may be our one and only chance to do so.

Shall we try? Do you think, on 13 October 1927, at 7 p.m., you could go to Goodman Road? I have checked the road directory of 1927, and Goodman Road exists, formerly called Grove Estate. The present location of 43B is opposite and not too far from a huge natural freshwater lake with an island in the middle. Meet me by the lake.

All my love,
Charlie

Life Through a Stroboscope

The year 1924 dawns, and the Chinese community celebrate the Year of the Wood Rat with loud firecrackers set off in public streets and offerings of *nian gao* (glutinous rice cake) to the Kitchen Deity to seal his lips so he won't report all their wrongdoings to the Jade Emperor, king of all the deities in the celestial realm.

Tian Wei subscribes to a new Chinese paper—the *Nanyang Siang Pau*—which is pro-Kuomintang and gives him news more favourable towards the homeland than the English papers. At Tung Teh, he hears from the rumour mill that, despite being financially strapped, the Chinese-medium schools are reluctant to apply for grants, available to them since last year, seeing them as a form of colonial government surveillance. Gossip spreads that the British colonial authorities believe the Chinese-medium schools—including vernacular and night schools, as well as reading societies—are hotbeds for radical left-wing politics, fanning fervour for Chinese nationalism. When Tian Wei attends the Kuomintang meetings, he realises that the meetings are increasingly dominated by strident voices, and he wonders if they are in fact Communists, despite Si Nian's protestations.

Tian Wei sits at the back of these meetings full of young men, shrouded in the thick fog of cigarette smoke emanating from them, not saying much. But it is impossible to ignore the things he hears and sees, nor can he be insensible to the fact that a rift seems to be developing within the Chinese community, between those who are Straits Chinese and those who are China-born. The latter are more loyal to homeland concerns, more extremist in their views. At Ee Hoe Hean Club, he hears rumblings among the merchants about the secret societies recruiting for the Kuomintang from the Hainanese coolie ranks in their factories. Meanwhile, despite the colonial authorities clamping down on the Chinese schools and societies, the British police seem to behave ever more erratically, and are susceptible to bribes. Instead of law and order, street fights break out almost daily in Chinatown, and murders are frequent.

A European planter who comes in for a portrait dubs Singapore "the Chicago of the East." Tian Wei attempts to dissuade Kee Lung from wandering around after dusk, one of his favourite pastimes. "More entertaining than Cantonese opera, Xifu," he says. Without scaring Kee Lung unduly, Tian Wei tells him there is a hue and cry in the papers about *kway teow* sellers causing congestion in Chinatown streets. "Makes for ma fan," he advises. But Kee Lung shrugs off his worries about *ma fan* with a boyish grin. Tian Wei asks Ah Seng to curtail his visits to opium houses, but Ah Seng also receives his warnings with sangfroid. Tian Wei hopes Ah Seng's habit won't become a deadly addiction.

Yip Kee, thanks to Bibi Gemuk's strenuous efforts, is about to be wed to a lovely young woman whose father is in the tin-mining business. After the wedding, Yip Kee will be moving to Ipoh, where his father-in-law owns a couple of tin mines in the Kinta Valley and is head of the Hakka *hui guan* there. Yip Kee plans to start his own studio in Ipoh, and Tian Wei is sorry to lose his assistant, though he truly wishes him well. With Yip Kee betrothed, Bibi Gemuk zeroes in on Peng Loon next. Tian Wei does not disagree with Bibi Gemuk— indeed, young men should settle down, so they won't be tempted by the brothels—but he asks Bibi Gemuk to consider finding a match for Peng Loon from a Singaporean family. It would be dreadful to lose Peng Loon as well, so soon after Yip Kee leaves.

He changes the backdrop he had had painted in Shanghai—an outdoor scene of a lake, bamboo trees, and a Chinese pergola—to a simpler one, with dark painted drapes, opening to reveal a curving staircase. Instead of the many props of old—European-style spoon-backed armchairs or console tables with cabriole legs—clients chasing a modern look these days prefer no props. The women come dressed in a hybrid of fashions: one dons a Western frock, while her companion wears a *koon sah*. Many of them are also not as eager to have jewellery painted on by Ah Seng; rather, they wear their own.

A letter arrives from Aiko, postmarked from Tokyo. The letter is in Malay, her written Malay being her stronger suit, and it is brief.

25 June 1924

Tian Wei Ge Ge:

Are you well? I am safe. I hope I have not caused you worry. Apologies to brother for how I left you that day in Penang, when you were ill, without saying proper goodbye. I was much upset. My heart was pained. I should not have read your private letters with Miss Charlie. I do not wish to tie you down. I do not want to be your fake wife. Does brother remember the Malay proverb brother taught me? Hutang emas boleh dibayar, hutang budi dibawa mati. Money debt can be repaid, but a debt of gratitude is forever. I do not want life with you of being close but still not close enough. A life of waiting and wanting for brother to love me. I couldn't breathe thinking that. That is not freedom, but a different bondage.

I am married to a Japanese army colonel now. Mr. Ki arranged it. It is father's wish. Something tore inside me, too hard to fight. Maybe this disappoints you. But maybe father is right. Girls like me have too much want. Girls like me must find own place in life. Girls like me should count themselves lucky. One day in future, perhaps we will meet again.

Aiko

The letter brings Tian Wei tremendous pain and sadness. To think that he had set out to help her, and instead had had a hand in breaking her resolve. He had failed Aiko in a deep, unconscionable way. As he did Sansan, all those years ago. Aiko is alive and safe, for which he is eternally grateful, but he hasn't been able to guarantee her happiness. His thoughts return to that fateful day, harkening back to how his soul had wandered so far that it traversed the Milky Way to Charlie as in a dream. That glimpse of Charlie in her element. But this happy memory is also now freighted with pain. Love is selfish. Love has unintended consequences. Is joy forever thus, half-blighted by guilt and pain? Perhaps he shouldn't have brought those letters with him, but how could he have known Aiko would find and read them?

The sheaf of letters he carried with him had been placed on top of the jacket in his suitcase. When he was packing his wedding suit away, his gaze had fallen once again on the stain shaped like a cluster of stars. Its metallic sheen like an irregular patch of microscopic sand. Perhaps the miracle that happened has something to do with the stain. He rushes to his desk to retrieve the cotton pouch. Opening it, he withdraws the letters. His hand brushes over the crackly paper, staining his fingerpad with a sprinkling of silver halide residue too fine to be visible to the eye. He wonders if the residue from the boxes with the magic numbers might have something to do with how his soul had managed to travel such a vast distance that day.

His thoughts zigzag back to Aiko. He has hurt Aiko terribly; how had he not seen that his attentions to her in the past could have been misinterpreted? He hopes that she will find some modicum of happiness in her married life. Does her husband, the army colonel, treat her well? These days, he spends a lot of time being nostalgic about the past, especially that day on the beach with Aiko, remembering her story, their moment of closeness. Having their wedding portrait taken at Nikko. What a picture she made. How happy she had seemed. He has saved that photograph from Nikko. Even though it tells a bald-faced lie.

Perhaps to assuage this sense of failure and guilt, he acquiesces when Si Nian asks him to help canvas for donations from Chinatown residents for the Weihaiwei Famine Relief Fund. For a few scorching days, he walks the sour-smelling streets of Chinatown from Hong Kong Street to Sago Lane, where the death-houses are, then down Teluk Ayer Street to the run-down shophouses by the wharf, following the meander of the Singapore River, which is crowded with prahus and bumboats, tongkangs and sampans, collecting a few cents here, a dollar there. Coolies eking out daily survival have little to spare. He witnesses their living conditions—three to four per rented room in a Chinatown shophouse—and understands how lucky he has been. But for a twist of fate, from meeting Sansan to being taken in at Powkee Studio, coming to Nanyang and working for Junji Naruto (who seeded him capital), he might not have become a photographer at all, and instead ended up loading cargo at shipyards, or smoking rubber at one of Tan Kah Kee's factories, the man called the "Henry Ford of Malaya". But for a twist of fate.

Writing back to Aiko is much, much harder than he anticipated. For months, he tarries until the torment proves too much for him, this guilt that slowly eats away at a man's self-regard.

17 September 1924

Dear Aiko-chan,

I am grateful to receive your letter. There is nothing you need to apologise for. In fact, it is I who should beg your forgiveness. Your Tian Wei Ge Ge has failed you enormously. I am sorry that I could not reciprocate your feelings, sorry that our plan did not come to fruition, sorry you found the letters. I feel much to blame for how everything turned out.

```
You have every right to hold it against me. I
do not know if I can ever make amends.

   Are you happy in your married life, back
in Japan? I don't feel I have a right to ask
if you are happy. I dearly hope that you will
find some happiness. At least inner peace.

   Whatever happens, I shall always remain
your Tian Wei Ge Ge. If you visit Singapore,
I hope we will meet again.


                         Your affectionate brother,
                                        Tian Wei
```

Initially, he adds that he has kept their wedding photograph from Nikko, an indelible memory, then he whips out the draft from the typewriter and scrunches up the letter. For her, that wedding photograph can only bring bitterness.

In September, he sees the *Angel of Crooked Street* at the Gaiety. Starring Alice Calhoun and Ralph McCullough, it is his first silent film at a cinema and it is a highlight of his year, though he is no clearer, as the credits roll, as to why the film was initially banned. It seems like any other story about shenanigans and shams—and, in any case, he much prefers his Chinese courtesan romances.

Also in September, Feng Yu finagles an invitation for him to attend a grand dinner in honour of the Secretary of Chinese Affairs, D. Beatty, returning to London on home leave. In attendance are the esteemed officers from the Chinese Protectorate, the Poh Leung Kuk, and various members of the Chinese clan communities. Merchant banker See Tiong Wah gives an ostentatious speech. Having joined in with their fundraising efforts of late and helped them set up charity bazaars, Tian Wei enjoys reconnecting with the officers of the Poh Leung Kuk. He hasn't forgotten their help during his search for Aiko. His friend Sng Choon Yee can't attend. In their exchange of letters, Tian Wei had apologised for not looking him up while in Penang, but didn't want to go into the whole business about the Cherry Blossom, Aiko, and Mr. Ki. The esteemed Sng Choon Yee would probably be scandalised.

In December, he reads in *The Straits Times* that Japan is preparing its aviation and naval arsenal for war. That evening, he has dinner with Naruto-san, who dismisses the report out of hand.

"China is in disarray, my friend—don't believe everything you read in the dailies. None of the foreign powers, neither European nor Japanese, wishes to 'carve up China'. It's a cock-and-bull story. The concession areas are about mercantile interests, and if mercantile interests are protected, it is good enough."

Indeed, China is in chaos. A northern warlord named Zhang Zuolin has seized power and installed his own far-right government, but in the southern provinces, K.M.T. and Communist forces are gaining control and clout.

In March 1925, Sun Yat Sen's death is reported in the papers, and public grief spreads all the way to Nanyang. The papers report that the Kuomintang are fomenting anti-imperial and anti-Western propaganda in major Chinese cities. Fights and demonstrations are also taking place at Japanese-owned cotton mills there between Japanese and Chinese employees. Si Nian disappears for a couple of months to the interior of Malaya.

At Lee & Fletcher, where Tian Wei goes to get his photographic equipment and collect his shipments of dry plate negatives, the manager introduces him to "safety film"—more convenient than glass plates, and safer than nitrate films, which are apt to catch fire. Tian Wei tells the manager that soon photographs might come alive blazing with colours caught by the camera, rather than painted on, and the manager looks at him with surprise and not a little admiration. He hadn't known Tian Wei was so up to date, the man says. Several new models of camera are also on show in their showroom—cameras without plated parts and which use roll film.

At the Malaya-Borneo Exhibition in 1922, he and Feng Yu had spent a happy day wandering around the railway godown on exhibition grounds, looking at amateur and professional photographs put up for competition prizes. He had learned about roll film then, and autographic cameras by Eastman Kodak that allowed one to make notations on the film through an opening in the back of the camera using a stylus on backing paper and a strip of carbon tissue. Film was as yet not popular or widely used by the studios in the Straits Settlements, but Tian Wei had roamed happily through the showroom for a couple of hours, perusing each model. Though unsure of the quality of the image produced and how it would be impacted by the technical skill of the photographer, he imagined one day upgrading all his cameras. For the time being, he didn't yet possess the capital, what with the handsome wedding *angpau* he had dished out for Yip Kee and his bride, the payment he had made to bail Ah Seng out of his opium debt, and his contribution to Kee Mun's school donation drive so the school wouldn't close.

Bibi Gemuk also dangles her album at Feng Yu. In mid-1925, he is introduced to an eligible young maiden who is a relation of Aw Boon Haw, the tiger-balm merchant, and if Feng Yu playing music is atrocious, Feng Yu in love is insufferable. He worms the words "my lovely Diana" into every bit of conversation, rhapsodising about her virtues and qualities until Tian Wei is convinced that a more angelic being cannot be conceived. Feng Yu waves his pocket watch containing an oval photograph of Diana at every opportunity; if not the pocket watch, then a handkerchief Diana has embroidered for him. Overnight, his favourite haunt changes from the New World Cabaret (where Feng Yu had enjoyed gambling and ronggeng dances) to the Botanic Gardens, so that he can take his lovely Diana on strolls designed to broaden her mind and energise her body. Properly chaperoned, of course, by what Feng Yu calls a martinet of a *majie*, with her beady eyes and blunt scolding. After strolling, he takes the lovely Diana to enjoy the scrumptious iced teacakes at the newly opened kiosk of G. H. Cafe there. The *majie*, too, is now well and truly stuffed with teacakes and on his side.

The highlight of 1925 is most certainly Feng Yu's December wedding, officiated by Reverend Goh Hood Keng at the Straits Chinese Methodist Church. The guests easily number more than two hundred. The choir sing hymns, the day becomes stifling hot, the guests fan themselves vigorously in the pews, and a fugue state of bliss settles on all and sundry. Tian Wei, as official photographer, doesn't get a moment's rest as he busily takes photographs of all the *who's who* of the elite Peranakan community in attendance. A journalist standing next to Tian Wei keeps licking his pencil, enunciating each note he takes down of everyone's attire for his article, so that Tian Wei too has these details imprinted on his torpid mind for eternity. The lovely Diana wears a beautiful gown of ivory georgette with three-quarter sleeves. Her sister, Adele, as bridesmaid, wears a gown of green georgette with a beige hat, shoes, and stockings.

Afterwards, the reception is held at the ostentatious Lin bungalow on Chatsworth Road. A feast of indefatigable proportions continues well into the night, and how much one eats and drinks can be measured by one's stagger about the grounds. Feng Yu is so drunk that he crashes into a couple of tables, vomits into a water cistern with floating lilypads and snapping turtles, and tries to sing "Yes, We Have No Bananas" to a coterie of Teochew merchants. How he is going to embark the next day on his honeymoon cruise to Europe with the lovely, but now looking quite infuriated, Diana, Tian Wei can't fathom.

Towards midnight, Feng Yu slings his arm around Tian Wei. "When will you give up your bachelorhood, old man? Time for you to get hitched, you know—a stalk needs tending."

Tian Wei doesn't answer, but no answer is needed, because Feng Yu crawls underneath a draped table and promptly falls asleep.

Without Feng Yu, the first part of 1926 is quiet and dull. Tian Wei stops going for dinners at either the Ee Hoe Hean or the Weekly Entertainment Club (and misses its mulligatawny soup and plum duff the most!). In any case, he has never felt he belonged; there is a studied indifference and cool mockery in the stances of those in the upper echelons that, try as he might, he can never adopt, despite his literate leanings.

A Cantonese photographer who has travelled to Shanghai brings back a new hot glossy magazine—*Liangyou huabao* (*The Young Companion*). Leafing through it, Tian Wei takes note of the form-fitting *qipao* the women are wearing. He has seen a couple of women promenading the fancier part of Orchard Road dressed in this fashion, but had assumed they were foreigners. Yesterday, however, a young woman came in dressed in a full-length *qipao*. Instead of the usual case of wanting to be photographed with her friends, she wanted to be photographed alone. When he suggested a pose, her eyes held a flicker of lively tease, and she ignored his suggestion. She showed him the pose she wanted from *The Young Companion*: back towards the camera, body twisted sideways to draw attention to her face and the jewellery on her hands, accentuating her curvaceousness. Yes, he can feel it—change is in the air. Si Nian was right, after all.

All meetings of the K.M.T. have halted for the time being, ever since the ban by the British government last year. Waiting makes his mind the devil's playground, besetting it with doubts. To calm his wayward thoughts, Tian Wei takes to his books. If he is to make that date of 13 October 1927 with Charlie, he wants to impress her as a *zhi shi fen zi*. He reads Lu Xun's *Outcry* and is struck when Lu Xun writes in the preface that he studied microorganisms on photographic slides while at a medical college in provincial Japan. During leisure time, the lecturers also showed war-time slides, and one showed a Chinese man about to be decapitated by a Japanese soldier for being a Russian spy during the Russo-Japanese War. The Japanese students around Lu Xun cheered and clapped, appreciating "the grand spectacle."

Tian Wei realises two things then: in war, one has to choose sides, no such thing as being Chinese grass on the wall; in war, all fates of Chinese men, homeland or overseas, are yoked together. He also reads Lu Xun's essays in *Hot Wind*, and finds himself ruminating over what Lu Xun wrote about the condition of the spirit being as important as the health of the body. Not enough people worked on elevating their spirit through literature, succumbing instead to ennui and dissipation and emptiness. Most of the *sinkeh*—even those learning a skill or trade—are guilty of the same. Toiling with the body, wasting the mind. Zhuangzi has written about winds and the piping of the earth and music being the harmony of the universe. Tian Wei neither comfortably counts himself with those in the top elite class nor belongs to the coolie and labourer class, but all this reading alienates him further from the merchant photographer community who own their studios—he is a lone stork among a flock of cranes. At night, he sleeps soundly and long, his dreams full of mysterious twists and turns. In the morning, fragments snag in the basin of his mind. His body feels hollow, a song wafting through the idle spaces, carving its tributary through bone, skin, and sinew. What is a soul if not a melody that nightly escapes its bodily mortal tether?

He writes letters to Charlie, but doesn't send them. What is the point if he won't receive any reply? If the exponential maths has fidelity, her next letter will not arrive for approximately four years; the next one after that, five years and four months; and, at a certain point, it will take twelve years! He will die waiting for the next letter to arrive. His heart contracts with pain, the feeling of loss sharp as a blade. Those words in her last letter: *Meet me at the lake.* At once a promise and a dream. What keeps his feelings alive is the date, 13 October 1927, scrawled on a sheet of paper and circled in red, then tacked to a portrait advertisement on his wall. Call it intuition, but he has a feeling that his ability to travel to see her in 1927 will be impacted by the granular residue on the letters. He gives Peng Loon an order to save the remainder of the glass negatives in the 1314 box.

A couple of weekends, after buying some fishing tackle, he heads out to the lake Charlie mentioned was on Goodman

Road. The lake is a gorgeous and extensive body of water, fringed by reeds and wild grass, *nipah* and tall coconut trees, its waters as still as a mirror. The air feels fresher and cleaner here, the trill of birds reminiscent of Tang-dynasty poems. He even catches a couple of sultan fish. However, other than finding a lake abundant with fish, nothing else happens. No emanations. No time travel.

In early 1927, a massive commotion occurs outside his shop, people rushing about in a frenzy. Tian Wei walks outside to try to catch some of the flying rumours, but can't make head or tail of what he hears. Later that evening, Si Nian drops by. They have a simple dinner together, and Si Nian tells him that six people have been shot outside the Kreta Ayer police station following the memorial march to mark Sun Yat Sen's death. The British government had allowed a memorial service at the Happy Valley Amusement Park on the condition that there would not be a procession. A march had indeed occurred, mainly comprising Hainanese K.M.T. members, waving K.M.T. flags and distributing anti-imperialist pamphlets. Si Nian had helped organise this, and he was proud of it. The march had proceeded through Anson Road, Maxwell Road, and on to South Bridge Road. Passing the Kreta Ayer police station, a clash ensued between the police and the marchers. What strikes Tian Wei is that Si Nian seems more upset by the number of wasted leaflets, trampled underfoot in the commotion, than he is about the six people shot on the spot.

The night of the incident, Tian Wei has another vivid dream. In it, he has transformed into a large mud-brown toad with sleepy eyelids and grotesque webbed feet, and he is jumping around a temple compound festooned with red lanterns. He hears the distinct tolling of bells and the chanting of monks. He inhales the sweet pungence of burning incense. Birds twitter overhead. The sky is powder blue with wispy clouds. Then a lady's voice, sweet and girlish, quickens his breathing and beckons to his soul. As if he is watching himself from above, he sees his throat pulsate laboriously. Distending, contracting, distending, contracting. But his toad legs are wound tight as a spring. No matter how hard he tries, he can't get to her. Since he is in a temple, perhaps he can transform himself.

He becomes a uniped, but his one muscular foot is too slow. So, he becomes a millipede, a bristle of a few hundred furry legs, though that too is insufficient. Next, he becomes a snake, slithering along on his flank. Faster, now. He transforms into a flying frog, darting and leaping towards her voice, its gentle cadence calling out to him, each leap sending him longer distances and higher off the ground. See how he takes off flying, legs spread-eagled, adrift on tailwinds. Finally, he has become the wind itself.

He jars awake, with no resolution as to whether he reached the voice. Is the dream significant? Is it an oracle foretelling his future? What does it mean to dream yourself a frog? Technically however, it wasn't a frog, but a toad. Feng Yu is fond of frogs— he considers them mythological. Si Nian would probably smack his lips and think of them braised in Shaoxing wine and ginger. For him, it is a dream congruent with all the others, stitched together like a quilt, and he must write it down before it too disappears into the fog of his unwritten memory.

In this way, three years pass.

A Story Escapes Its Frame

Sebastian video-calls me from Shanghai—he's standing in the WeWork conference room, his sweatshirt tucked into his trousers. I tell him it's not a good look—too dorky—and he jibes that taking fashion advice from me is like being styled by Kim Jong-un.

"Why are you standing?"

"Why, can't you hear me OK?"

"I hear you fine, but your face is a moon hovering in the horizon."

He doesn't laugh. "I'm all puffy from fluid retention. Drank too much last night."

"Watch the alcohol intake! You just got well." I wonder if he's overdosing on the Xanax as well.

Sebastian folds his arms. "OK, Miss Nag."

He has colourful news. Xueling, Zhou Zhen's wife, arrived at TAV's offices yesterday with an entourage of bodyguards in black suits and ties—*Men-In-Black*, P.R.C.-style—and threw a massive tantrum. She swanned in, dressed in a romper with a matching long overcoat—white with black polka-dots—looking more Cruella de Vil than Cruella de Vil herself, Sebastian says, shaking his head ruefully. In a screechy voice like pulling a cat's tail (扯猫尾)—Sebastian slipping in a Cantonese proverb here—she put on quite the show, accusing TAV of framing her to save its own hide and threatening to ensure Sebastian and Adnan would never be able to do business in China again. They tried talking to her, but she wasn't amenable to reason. She flew around the room in her clicking high heels and gave an order.

I can tell that Sebastian is stressed, despite his wryly subdued telling of how it went down.

Her bodyguards then lugged in two cases of champagne—vintage Ruinart, no less—popped them, and, together, she and her bodyguards aimed the bottles. Champagne arced across the room, sloshing on the floor and over the office furniture, drenching everyone and everything within their parabolic trajectories. Sebastian tried to make light by saying that such good stuff goes in the mouth and not on the dowdy WeWork corduroy sofas. Adnan tried to restrain her by wrapping his arms around her.

"Big mistake," Sebastian says, "because she has slapped him with a charge of assault." To get the charge dropped and the office disturbance sorted with the police, the paperwork requires Sebastian's old passports, which contain information about his previous China visas. "Do you think you can get them for me from my apartment, Charlie?"

"Of course. This all sounds like it will take time to settle. When are you back?"

"As soon as this is sorted. I'm not staying an extra day for Xueling to come back at us with another trumped-up charge. I don't wish TAV to be a pawn caught up in the power game between Zhou Zhen and his wife."

"It sounds like it already is? Perhaps Zhou Zhen can help talk to his wife?" I suggest.

"Are you kidding? Right now, he's preparing to sue her for negligence, if not fraud. There might also be divorce proceedings. How all this will play out in mediation, I have no idea. Our lawyers are on it now. At least we are cleared of the forgery."

"What about you and Adnan?" I ask. Or perhaps I shouldn't have asked.

I hear him blow out his cheeks. His voice falters. He glances quickly to the side. "Can't talk now. I need to find another partner quick. Or get me a bailout loan. Adnan is definitely out."

*

The light crashes into Sebastian's apartment in waves. Its lambent quality through the curtains throws a dappled effect, creating eclipses and haloes across the dots and swirls of his carpet. The bay is spread out before me: an apron of verdant foliage dotted with the rooftops of tall buildings, before land meets the electric blue of the sea. Large tankers float on its surface like animated GIFs. A helicopter speck moves across the sky.

Sebastian said to look in the bottom drawer of the antique chest in his bedroom. The camphor smell of this chest that Sebastian has fondly dubbed "Big Ben" tickles my nostrils as I lift the lid. It is big enough to be a coffin for a small child. Another piece of furniture inherited from Peony. Inside is a plethora of documents encased in plastic pouches. It takes me a good long while to locate the old passports he needs.

My glance falls on an old album with a vellum cover. I take it out, wipe off the slight film of dust on the cover. I recognise it; the album contains the old photographs of Mother that I saw for the first time after Father's funeral. Photographs of Mother from her university days: in a flapper costume at a fancy-dress party, singing karaoke, performing at concerts, at her wedding. A photograph at the hospital, holding me swaddled in a blanket. I was but a few hours old.

Opening it, the first photograph I see is Mother dancing the waltz with Father, her back to the camera, her face turned sideways. He gazes at her with an expression of unmistakable fondness. I notice Mother's dancing heels, a butterfly buckle adorning each side. Each time I look at these photographs, a new detail punctures me, giving me back a mother I didn't know. Where there is no memory, a vacuum exists; fantasy and imagination rush in to fill the gaps, gaps that are pregnant with ambiguities and slippages, and I don't always know how to process what I feel. Over time, these photographs of Mother bring nostalgia. The nostalgia has less to do with Mother as the root cause than it does my own repetitive act of looking at the photographs. The person my mother was remains as elusive as before, and my affection for her as attenuated as the past.

Here is a photograph of Mother with a Cantonese opera singer, their arms forming a heart around each other. The singer is in full opera regalia, with painted face and elaborate tasselled headpiece. Mother looks a bit older here, closer to the image I have of her in London. Her hair is a long braid draped to one side. Her dress has massive shoulder pads, giving off Cher vibes. It's then I notice the unicorn locket around her neck. I remember playing with it on the rare occasion I was allowed to sit on her lap. Mother slipped it out of my grubby hands and said that I should be careful not to tug too hard; she wore it for special occasions. Was this a special occasion? A date is imprinted on the bottom right: *14 February 1985*. Just before I was born. On impulse, I slide it out of its cellophane protection and turn it over. On the back, an inscription: *To Our Happily Ever After.*

Singular, not plural.

14 February—Valentine's Day.

I look at the photograph again, slightly perplexed. Who is this Cantonese opera singer that my mother was with, photographed together to commemorate Valentine's Day? Then, a suspicion forms, slowly and unmistakably. I begin taking out some of the other albums—sorting the personal from the photographic collection Father amassed in his treasure-hunting jaunts through Bras Basah memorabilia shops, now bequeathed to Sebastian. My focus is intense as I flip through one family album after another, scanning, looking for one particular face: Mother's. Here she is again, at a university club, making a speech at a podium. Here with a group of friends, dining on a patio next to a swimming pool. Standing in front of the Victoria Theatre with Father, holding a playbill. Sitting on the steps of Clarke Quay with two other female friends. But there are no more pictures of her and this mysterious woman.

Somewhere in the middle of another album, I know I have found it. My mother kissing a woman full on the lips. Although I have only a side profile, I know the face. I know who she is. The Cantonese opera singer. I slip it out of the cellophane and turn it over: *14 February 1986. To our forever and happily ever after.*

The secret Cassandra said the P.I. had found. The penny drops. The clandestine affair Mother had with another woman. I am not as shocked as I should be. Did some part of me already know? The past reels by my eyes in fresh revelations, flying jigsaw pieces assembling themselves into a composite. All those nights she sat alone in the dark, nursing her drink, I thought her unhappiness was because of Father, but what if all along Mother had been pining for someone else? I thought she left Father to start a new life in London, but what if I was wrong? What if it was to escape desolation instead? What was Cassandra's role in all of this? Cassandra's words to me in her bedroom return anew: *These dark secrets are best left undisturbed. She cared a lot more about you than I thought, I'll give her that.* What did she mean exactly? Did Mother shun me because I was a reminder of an unhappy marriage, or because I stood in the way of her happiness? What if her unhappiness had nothing to do with me at all? How am I supposed to feel about this? Relief, or an even deeper sadness?

The next photograph in the album leaves me gobsmacked. It's Peony, Mother, and this opera singer, the three of them laughing into the camera. It must have been taken at a birthday party because they're wearing triangle party hats on their heads and holding party blowers. The inescapable truth: the three of them had been friends. Does this mean that Peony knew all about the affaire de cœur my mother had with this singer?

I see the edge of a folded piece of paper peeking from behind the folio. It's a letter. How ironic: my life these days is being governed almost entirely by letters. Trepidation enters, as if I'm about to cross a threshold that cannot be uncrossed.

15 March 1992

My dearest love,

You may say that I am cowardly, breaking things off with a letter instead of face to face. You may say that I don't love you enough because I choose freedom instead of you. I won't deny either of those charges, but the truth is that it does not negate an iota of my love for you. I love you so much that the force of it leaves me shaken and helpless. It leaves me vulnerable to my core. I love you so much that I am in danger of losing myself and my sanity. I love you so much, I prise your happiness above my own. Can you understand this?

You do not need to be afraid of Cassandra's threats or how she would expose us, but I am afraid of the damage a scandal would wreak on your soon–to–be–born child. Do you really want her to grow up in an atmosphere of jealousy and acrimony? Don't be conflicted any longer; go. As soon as you're able, fly to London, protect what's yours. There is no written destiny that lovers have to be together. Being apart will not change my love for you. Not one bit. Because I never had any expectation in the first place. Who would sanction our love in this society of ours?

Live your life to the fullest, my darling. Be free. I will be thinking of you as you wander London streets, visit Buckingham Palace, watch the Changing of the Guard. I will think of you as you adapt, as you change, and London becomes your home. I will think of you with your little one, hand in hand visiting museums and the zoo. I hope she won't be a stranger to the stories you love—give her books on Asian mythology, tell her the story of the Seven Sisters, or Chang'e and the elixir of immortality, help her feel in whatever way you can that she belongs to this island city.

She has a home here. Let her know there is no shame in love, no matter who it is, how it is, why it is.

Know that the moments I shared with you were truly the happiest of my life. I was more honest and unfettered than I have ever been at any point in time, and it utterly changed me. As I know it did you. We share something that passes most people by and which they have never experienced. It is enough, so much more than I ever expected.

I love you truly, madly, deeply.

Forever yours,
Oriole

Here the truth has been all along, right underneath my nose, in these old photographs. No wonder Cassandra intimates that I'm dumb and slow, and Linton, too, that I prefer to mire myself in my "Cinderella syndrome" instead of being part of the family.

Tears gather even as I pocket the photographs and the letter. This will take time to sink in. This is opening the hatch of Pandora's box. A heaviness settles somewhere in the region of my stomach—sadness, too.

A photograph does not lie; once photographed, the thing becomes fact. But a single photograph may not yield a complete picture. It may shed grave rubbings, a partial truth. When the truth emerges, when it escapes its frame, dare we face up to it? This feeling slamming into me is not a feeling I've had before. It cracks reality wide open; in doing so, it liberates. The truth is bigger than a single life. The truth is feeble in the face of the intensity of love. Oh, Mother, I understand now what you gave up. How lucky you were to have been loved this intensely. But we pay the price too for the love we are given, don't we? We and our offspring.

Standing in the Right Place at the Right Time

In 1947, Chung Cheng School (named after Chiang Kai Shek) bought the nine bungalows on thirteen acres of land, which included the lake, from Crédit Foncier D'Extrême-Orient for a cost of $120,000. The main edifice has a Chinese-style double-tier green roof, similar to a temple, and its façade contains Chinese symbols of clouds and bats. If one surfs online, there are stories about it being haunted.

The lake is natural, though reduced in size by two thirds following building extensions by the school. It is the one geological feature near me that hasn't changed through time.

Dusk. A time betwixt and between. A time of shifting light. The school has emptied for the day, and it is lonely here.

Getting permission to visit the school premises after hours had taken some doing. I had higher ups write to even higher ups, citing historical research, archival authentication, anything work-related I could come up with. It wasn't a smooth process, there were a lot of quirked eyebrows, but, with grim determination, I made the improbable happen.

For the past five days, I have frequented the lake, my heart filled with hope against hope, a live wire snaking beneath the skin. Every evening that I go home unfulfilled, my spine loads with dejection. The next day, hope suffuses me again. If waiting one day is this hard for me, waiting three years must feel like eternity.

In my letter to Tian Wei, choosing this time and place had felt uncannily right. Is this what coincidence is—two souls trying to reach each other, the cries from the hearts forming a bridge, a transient, illusory Milky Way?

The water of the lake does not ripple. Stone steps lead down to a grass verge by the water's edge. A cement strip circles the perimeter of the lake; in previous visits, I walked this cement strip as exercise. Today, I am not in the mood. Thoughts percolate. My spine tingles. Would today finally be 13 October 1927? Can one control a mysterious connection this way? What is life lived in compartmentalised chunks between letters? Oriole's words echo in my head: *I love you so much that the force of it leaves me shaken and helpless. It leaves me vulnerable to my core. I love you so much that I am in danger of losing myself and my sanity. I love you so much, I prise your happiness above my own.* These words form pitted stones in my own heart, longing to be released. A cocoon has cracked open, and I am moulting, a moth seeking the dusky twilight, that realm of evanescence betwixt day and night.

I have so many questions that will have to wait till Sebastian gets home. Did Mother and Oriole correspond by letter after we moved to London? Oriole's letter referred to Cassandra's threats. What was the nature of those threats? Had she threatened to expose their relationship? By creating a scandal? If so, why? Did Mother move to London to protect me? Or was it because she had no choice? One letter and one photograph have changed everything I understood about her.

A text pings on my phone. Sebastian.

> Arriving ETA 30 mins.

> Oh God, I'm so exhausted.

> Can't wait to see you.

My phone vibrates as if a call is coming in. A box pops up. I'm asked if I would like to allow voice-over notification. Mystified, I hit *Don't Allow*. Bizarre. The notification request disappears, but my screen reverts to locked mode and freezes.

I shut it down, turn it back on. It remains frozen. Fiddling with the buttons on my phone, turning it off and on, nothing works.

A barely perceptible sigh of wind, fingering the hair on my arm.

Goose pimples. Or not goose pimples exactly. A sixth sense that something is hovering above me. I look up from my phone. Adrenaline swamps my body. My feet stay rooted to the spot. The dusky, falling light shifts and darkens—a shadow is passing overhead. Transfixed, I look straight ahead as a figure gradually emerges from a gelid membrane in which I can see the surroundings of the lake as if through a ripple of water. The contour of the figure becomes a man—an Etch-A-Sketch coming to life—and details begin to fill in: the white suit, the tie, the buttons of a jacket, the shoes, and finally, the face. An avatar, retaining the drawn quality of a caricature, which gradually sharpens and becomes flesh. Is flesh. I gasp. Goose pimples now, for real.

My hands fly to my face. I have wanted him to come so much and now he has. The tingling in my spine flares, ignites, and I'm flooded by a moil of emotions: shock, excitement, joy, dizziness, disbelief. A word I picked up from somewhere, floating into my mind like confetti: thraptured. A cross between *enthralled* and *enraptured*. The larger-than-life impact someone has had on your life that is completely out of kilter with the duration and amount of contact. He looks straight at me. Not speaking. He smiles.

I smile back. My heart is about to supernova itself.

Gradually, a corner of a desk emerges in the glow in which his mirage is sequestered. Picture frames outline themselves, filling in with granular detail. His hand clasps something to his chest. A pouch? A piece of paper? Peering, I see that it is a sheaf of letters.

I have prepared for this moment. I have prepared so many lines, written them down, but now they all seem silly beyond words. Tongue-tied and awkward, I am bereft of words to suit the import of the moment. We simply gaze at each other. We take in each other fully. I have never looked at another or been looked at like this, this looking that is not so much gazing as it is a drinking in of each other's features. His face on my screensaver has become so familiar, but I now notice a tranquillity in it, like a pool of still water. An open, calm, clear gaze. Sadness and joy, alleles of emotion in the gathering dusk. Fireflies flitter and dive among the reeds.

I wave. He waves back.

"Did you have trouble getting here?" OMG, stupid! I smack the side of my head.

He's surprised. He can't hear me, I realise. Visual OK, no audio. We are communicating through soundproof glass. Schrodinger's-cat frequencies are not powerful enough.

I make a gesture of a duck quacking, put a hand to my ear, flip my hands up to signify *No sound*.

He comprehends, holds up his hand—*Wait*. He turns to write something down on a piece of paper, shows it to me— the characters 没关系 appear in reverse, as if reflected in a mirror.

It doesn't matter, he is saying. He came prepared. I look down. I have nothing to write back with; my phone remains frozen, disabled by the wave disturbance.

He's writing something else—I squint: *You look better than in your photograph*. An infinitesimal moment between reading and comprehension, and yet another before feeling joins it, like a series of burst shots. I laugh, the sound of it ironic. I did not know that the joys of Tinder dating apply also to quantum entanglement. Warning: one's reality may shock when matched against the image.

He scribbles furiously. One after another, messages from across dimensions.

You are a dream come true.

I have much to say but there is not enough time.

Words are not important.

You are an illusion I long for. 我爱你.

Three Chinese words that are cardio jolts to the heart. Far more powerful than the English equivalent could ever be.

Too soon, his mirage dims. He sees my look of distress. The sun has set, darkness swiftly descends. The glow around him is fading, getting smaller. "Wait," I whisper. "Don't go." The clogged feeling is back in my throat, a greedy gnawing. Even as I send up my fervent wish, his outline is dissolving into smoke.

And then he is gone.

My watch tells me that about eleven minutes have passed. Forever and an instant. A gasp and a wince. I look up at the sky. It is night. But how pendulous the moon, how bright its glow. How dark the night by contrast. Is the rabbit up there? Is it pounding its millet still? Is Chang'e looking down at me with pity in her eyes, or commiseration and understanding? Here, the night has just been kissed by the breath of immortality.

Transference

Sebastian alights from a taxi outside 43A Goodman Road, and I simply fly into his arms.

My hug is so tight that he drops everything he's holding. "Arrgh…" He makes a strangled sound. The skin on his neck is damp and hot. I rub the shirt on his back, also damp with sweat, and that's when it happens, a series of jumping sparks between our bodies that must have been a residue from my encounter, a residue also of the electro-magnetic storm that has besieged my phone. Which still isn't working. "Ow!" Sebastian retracts. "What was that?"

"Static, I think. Or maybe not. I need to talk to you."

We walk into the house. In brief strokes, I tell him about Oriole's letter. The photograph I found of the three of them: Oriole, Mother, Peony. We are standing in front of Father's altar. His portrait stares down at us, his eyebrows beetled, mouth turned down. This stern-faced ancestor of mine: was he ever genuinely happy in his life, despite having so many wives? Laurent and Eloise are tripping down the grand staircase. The flow of my words pauses. Eloise is wearing a black *qipao* with red roses; she's been to the salon, her coiffeur is a beehive. Laurent's gaze wanders to us; he lifts up a hand. It hangs there, the gesture incomplete. He feels the animus emanating from me. He sails past, hand still aloft. Eloise gives us a nod.

Atalina is bearing into the dining room one steaming platter after another, animal anatomy visible: the raised crab claws, the full-roasted duck with plump drumsticks, the salted egg-yolk and cereal-battered prawns like curled apostrophes. The fragrance of her cooking wafts over to us. We hear the piping voice of Miles Wee Jun being taught by Madeleine how to set a dinner table. We hear Laurent order Alexa to queue up a playlist. Teresa Teng. Long Piao Piao. Oh God, Cassandra's favourite balladeers. Laurent sure knows on which side his bread is buttered.

A second later, Matt Sharpe strolls in through the open front door, dressed in khaki slacks and a long-sleeved shirt with a floral print, looking so good it has Sebastian and me ogling.

Matt's face lights up upon seeing me. "Hi, you!"

Heels tapping down the grand staircase; the three of us turn as one. Cassandra. Lime-green kitty heels with a pink pouf on top. Her billowy white kaftan is made of silk, and shimmers as the light of the chandelier falls on it. Tonight is the celebration of the fifteenth day of the Lunar New Year, also known as Chinese Valentine's. The first night of the full moon.

"Well, well, so you've come back at last, Sebastian," Cassandra says.

"Hello, Yi-Ma. I haven't been dragging my feet, if that's what you're implying. I'm sure you'll want to know how everything has been resolved."

"My, we're testy, aren't we?" She folds her arms. "I expect a full report. As a partner."

"Silent partner, or did you forget that part?"

I look at Sebastian. He isn't usually this abrasive. Light beads of sweat dot his brow. He looks haggard, his eyes are bloodshot. I reach out to touch his hand—it's burning hot. Sebastian is running a high fever. He has never handled stress well, and there is more stress now than he's ever had before.

When Cassandra made her appearance, Sebastian had instinctively moved closer to me. A part of me feels it before it happens: one minute, Sebastian is standing; the next, he's swaying on his feet and crumpling to the ground. An almost imperceptible energy drain, the cognitive dissonance of having time slow itself in the mind while speeding up in reality. For a few seconds, none of us reacts. Then, we all hunker around him as he enters into a semi-conscious state, eyes rolling white, mouth mumbling a string of incoherent words, producing strange sounds, the clicks and chirrs of someone in a trance.

The tendons on his neck knot in relief, his arms go rigid. His whole body tenses.

Panic and pandemonium. A short, sharp scream. Linton tells us to give Sebastian's prostrate body a wide berth. He has served as an auxiliary emergency responder in the past. We comply. Expertly and gently, he crosses Sebastian's arm across his body, brings his knee up and turns him over to his side. He barks at us to call for an ambulance.

In the urgency of the moment, I'd been oblivious to everything except Sebastian. I realise that I had been frantically calling his name. I was the one who had emitted a short scream. Images imprint themselves in my mind: the metallic spoon appearing in Matt's hand (Linton waving at him to say, *Not needed*); the hair on Linton's arms as he rolls up his sleeves; Eloise covering Miles Wee Jun's eyes; Laurent, one hand on his hip, the other slapping the back of his neck—his way of demonstrating distress; Cassandra uttering things to my father's portrait—no, actually praying!

Sebastian mumbles incoherently. His body jerks, and Linton leans his ear close to listen.

"One, three, one, four?" Linton repeats, a frown forming on his brow. "What the fuck is he talking about? Does that have something to do with TAV or Adnan?"

I can feel Matt's gaze on me, but I steadfastly refuse to meet it.

Whatever the spell is, it leaves as abruptly as it arrives. As Linton holds open Sebastian's jaw to ensure clear airways, Sebastian's muscles suddenly slacken. The tension in his body deflates. The jerking stops. His eyes close. He stops mumbling.

"Sebastian!" Linton calls his name loudly. "Sebastian, can you hear me?"

Sebastian's eyes open. "No need to shout, I'm not deaf." Though weak, there is no mistaking his dry tone.

Nervous laughter. We all feel our anxiety evaporate.

The ambulance is called off. Instead, Cassandra decrees that their private G.P. Dr. Woo will attend to Sebastian, who is now sitting on a couch, wrapped in a blanket. His body continues to have the occasional shake and shiver. Cassandra instructs that he should be helped upstairs to one of the guest bedrooms on the third floor.

"I'd prefer to go home to Marina Bay," he says.

Cassandra impales him with a stern glare. He opens his mouth to resist, then relents.

The room he is settled in is beautiful—the wooden floor has a large faux tiger-skin rug, and a four-poster bed is made up with down pillows and a soft white bedspread. It's otherwise known as the Camera Room, because a collection of olden-day cameras—Father's hobby—populate its shelves. There are repurposed movie lights from the 1950s and huge lightbulbs adorning a large mirror, as in an actor's dressing room. The double terrace doors open out to a small belvedere.

Atalina is lighting incense in an incense holder. Sandalwood. On the wall behind the bed, a large black-and-white photograph depicts an Indian temple door, sectioned in squares, embedded with lotuses and studded with brass bells. The air con has been turned off, but there is a draught in the room. The windows are open.

Dr. Woo arrives, mopping sweat from his face. His family gathering has been disrupted. He is a rather corpulent Chinese fellow with hangdog jowls, his glasses perched at the end of his nose. He takes Sebastian's blood pressure and temperature, gives him an injection to bring his fever down. "Nothing bad." He lowers his stethoscope. "Have you ever had an episode like this before?"

A slightly guilty look enters Sebastian's eyes, but he shakes his head. Shoots me a warning look. He wants me to keep mum about the episode at the hospital. "This kind of fainting spell? No. I haven't slept in days, though. And I just got back from Shanghai. Aeroplane food has never agreed with me."

The doctor asks a couple of questions about his travel, and if he felt unwell before this. He fingers his ear, thinking. "What prescriptions are you taking?"

Sebastian shoots me another glance, but asks me to get the prescription bottles for him from his briefcase.

The doctor turns them over in his hands. "I would advise that you come in tomorrow to get a full check-up, and we can review your medical history. For now, you're not in any danger, and your mother is right—full rest at home will be better for your convalescence than in a hospital."

"I'm fine. Tomorrow, I'll phone my doctor who gave me the prescription, promise. Charlie is here. You'll stay with me, won't you, Charlie?"

"Of course."

Sebastian tells me that Dr. Woo was his physician when he was a boy. He was the one who thought something was wrong with Peony during a casual conversation in which she mentioned feeling full when she'd eaten just a smidge.

Dr. Woo nods, sight softening with the memory. "A talented, beautiful soul. Gone too soon."

Atalina pops her head in to say that dinner has progressed without us. She offers to bring up a tray. "I don't want any food," Sebastian says.

"I will bring up soup for you," Atalina says.

I tilt my chin at the doctor. "Doctor, would you like to join us for dinner?"

Dr. Woo shakes his head. "Time for me to get back to mine."

"Can you bring me a tray, Atalina?" I ask.

Atalina nods. "Shall I set up another guest bedroom for you, miss?"

"Let's worry about that later."

After they are gone, I turn to Sebastian. I'm beside myself, and it's with utmost control through clenched teeth that I keep my tone level. "What did I tell you about taking care of yourself?"

He puts a finger to his lips. "Ssh… Don't. I'm ill. Go have dinner."

"I'm not leaving you."

Sebastian pats the bed. "Crawl in here and give me a hug, then. I need one."

I climb in beside him, drape one arm across his shoulder, and he settles his head in the crook of my neck. His eyes close and the muscles of his face relax. Love for him fills me. I'd been terrified when he started convulsing. I stroke the forelock on his brow. Just as I make to climb out, Atalina comes in with the tray of soup and dinner. She startles. An expression enters her eyes. An expression I can't make out.

"I was helping him relax." Oh God, it came out wrong.

Atalina nods, but doesn't look at me. She places the tray on the small table next to the terrace doors. "Enjoy your dinner, miss."

"I'm going to stay with Sebastian tonight. I'll look after him."

"All right, miss," Atalina says, closing the door behind her.

The cool draught slides like a whisper in the room. That look in Atalina's eyes: do I need to worry about it?

Click, That Voluptuous Sound

Sebastian wakes up. The time on my phone says 10:30 p.m.

I rise from my chair and sit beside him on the bed to feel his brow, which feels cool and dry. His fever has subsided. "How are you feeling? Would you like me to get Atalina to reheat the soup?"

He shakes his head. "I had the weirdest dream," he says. "I dreamt that I was a toad in some kind of temple, and a voice kept calling out to me—a woman's voice—and, for some reason, I thought the voice belonged to you, Charlie. But now that I'm awake, the voice doesn't sound like you at all." He seems to be trying to recall more from his dream. "Too sweet and innocent to be you," he teases, getting a poke from me.

"What can I get you?"

"Some water, please."

I walk over to the small table and pour him a glass. He gulps it down and asks for more.

"Try and go back to sleep," I say.

"Are you going to sit there and watch me sleep all night?" His tone is slightly drowsy. "How about you read to me awhile?"

There isn't a single book in the room to read from. But then I remember that I always have an academic tome in my voluminous bag—usually on photographic theory. "Care for some Walter Benjamin?" I offer.

Sebastian lifts one eyebrow in wan acknowledgement of my feeble joke. "Come here," he pats the side of the bed. "You're too far away."

I move to sit next to him.

"Don't you love this room, Charlie?" he whispers, eyes closed, drawing my arm back around his shoulder, snuggling in. "This used to be the room I played in when my mother brought me over here to visit Father. Father and I had little in common—

he cared too much about making money and womanising—but I do remember a game of hide and seek he played with me once. I hid in here, and when Father found me, he showed me the cameras, and also some of the photographs he collected in albums. Must be why Cassandra asked to have me moved up here. She knows I am fond of this room."

I sigh. "This is what I don't get about Cassandra. Just when I'm all set to write her off as a termagant, she'll show these momentary kindnesses. What am I supposed to think?"

"People are complex and contradictory. I wouldn't beat myself up over it."

"I'm trying to do what you advised all those years ago—not freeze-frame my conception of myself, or others."

"So, don't. She's still mighty scary."

His head is heavy on my shoulder. "Goodness, what do you carry in here?" I retrieve my arm, pushing his brow off with a finger.

"Grey matter, love. You wouldn't understand." For this, he gets another poke in the ribs. He leans against me.

"Speaking of which…" I cross my arms. "How come you never told me that Cassandra is a silent partner in TAV?"

Sebastian looks sheepish. "Did I not tell you? I thought I did."

He is not getting off so easily. He relents when he sees my expression. Lays his head back on his pillow.

"I was seriously strapped for cash. I knew, if I told you, you would say it's a bad idea, asking Cassandra for money, being beholden to her. To be fair, she has been quite hands-off until now." Seeing my unconvinced look, he reiterates, "Honest. She hasn't been that bad. I may have to do the same thing again—ask her for money. Either as a loan or as an increase in her share, so that I can buy Adnan out."

"Are you mental? You could have asked me!"

Sebastian rests the back of his hand over his eyes. "It's a very, very large sum of money, Charlie. We're talking millions. Adnan and I have come to a mutual agreement. As soon as I can get the funds together, I'll buy him out in return for the algorithm. I'll relocate the offices to Singapore. Perhaps it's time to court local corporate clients, diversify our client base."

"And you think Cassandra will agree to help? With no strings attached? Why have you suddenly abandoned all your faculties?"

A spark of anger enters his eyes. "Stay out of this, Charlie. You don't understand business loans."

"Maybe not, but I can't believe you chose to keep this a secret. Why didn't you tell me?"

He puts one arm behind his head. "Trust me, OK? I know what I'm doing." He gives a wry laugh. "Never thought I'd hear you spouting the same thing as Linton and Laurent. They too advised against it." He mimics Linton's voice: "'You don't know much about art, Ma—' and he said this while pointedly gesturing at the Beijing sculpture of *Harmony* in the dining room; I'm surprised Cassandra didn't take umbrage—'and online art auctions are risky ventures, technology-dependent, low returns.' Dick-brain. He should stick to his ETFs and REITs."

I don't say anything for a few minutes, a medley of unvoiced concerns in my head. We have been here before; if Sebastian wants my financial help, he will ask for it. His pride is at stake.

As if sensing my thoughts, he changes the subject. "You said you would show me Oriole's letter?"

I get up and retrieve the letter I've been meaning to show him. "Here's the thing. What do you think Cassandra's involvement is in my mother's affair with Oriole?"

"Read it to me first."

Sebastian closes his eyes to listen. Something happens as I read the letter from start to finish, as if words of love must perforce be spoken aloud to work their magic. A surfeit of emotion coats my voice that I can't stymie, regardless of how many times I clear my throat. It demands that I give in to it. I raise the page to hide the sudden film of tears obscuring my vision. Silence settles like a mantle when I'm done. I thought

Sebastian must have dropped off, but his eyes are wide open and staring directly at me.

I clear my throat again. "What do you make of it?"

He shifts his posture. Looks away. "There isn't much I can tell you, Charlie. Secrets from the past are finicky. I'm not sure one ever gets the whole picture, because the people who can tell their sides of it are gone. All I know is that Oriole and Mum were in the same Cantonese troupe and staged several operas together. I suspect your mother met Oriole when she came to one of the performances." He pauses, and I can sense him searching his memory bank. "Ah, I remember when Mum first told me that I may be adopted into the Sze-Toh family. I was five. She said that I would have to change my last name. A new baby had been born into the family—I remember her delighted words, 'Evelyn is having a baby,' which must have been you—and we were going to help take care of it. I was a kid—I didn't think to question why this entailed having to change our names."

I'm surprised. "But I didn't meet you until college!"

"That's the thing. I think Mum understood her place as a mistress, a xiao san. She didn't want to cross paths with Cassandra. So, you and I never met. Father came to us in Marina Bay; we hardly ever went to him. I remember meeting Father for the first time. It was at a restaurant overlooking the bay. He was so formal, in a suit and tie. I remember thinking he looked like a nice man. Serious and withdrawn, but with a kind, intelligent, and sensitive face. Before he sat down, he gave me a present—a set of toy cars—and shook my hand. Then, he made some long, solemn speech, the gist of it being that it was a shame I never met or knew my own father, that a man should not shirk his responsibilities, but if the heavens would allow it, and if I missed having someone to call 'Father', he'd be more than willing. He wouldn't force me if I didn't feel like it, and he would prefer I didn't use 'Daddy'—it smacked of juvenility— but if I could call him Father, he would call me Erzi.

"I remember bursting into tears. First, because he'd ordered steak and it was tough as leather and I couldn't manipulate the fork and knife with my little hands, and I thought for sure Mum would be mad at me. Second, because I'd long outgrown toy cars—and Mum had promised me that, if I went to the dinner with him and behaved, I would probably get a nice electronic game or something. Toy cars were a total letdown, and I felt as if the sky had fallen on Chicken Little."

My smile is grim. "Well, don't feel too bad. When Father came to introduce Cassandra to me in South Ken, he brought me a Barbie doll. I was already learning how to put on make-up from friends at school; and he bought me a Barbie doll! It was playthings for adults he was good at. When it came to kids, he was clueless."

We are silent together for a moment. I voice the question swirling in my head. "So, how was Cassandra involved?"

"Maybe as the letter said. She found out through the P.I. and threatened to expose Evelyn and Oriole."

"Yes, she did say that she found out about Mother's affair when she was looking into Father's courtship of Peony. But why expose Mother and Oriole? What would she gain from that? Was she not afraid that something could tarnish the Sze-Toh image? Or did she change once she became a tai-tai?"

Sebastian shrugs. "Perhaps what she meant was that she would expose them to Father. She'd been with Father only a few years then. Think about it. Evelyn was legally Father's wife. Cassandra was just the mistress. Because she cares so much about image and security, being a mistress could be untenable for her. Mistresses could be discarded, wives not so easily."

"Are you saying it was to get Father to divorce Mother? No, wait, Cassandra has always said Mother chose to abdicate. She gave everything up of her own accord when she asked for a divorce. She chose to move to London with me."

Sebastian and I lock eyes. *Click.* Emotional blackmail. I almost hear it in my inner ear, that voluptuous sound as the pieces of the puzzle interlock. Sebastian and I might have distrusted Cassandra, but I had still assumed that everything she told me about Mother and the past was the truth. In the absence of Mother's own words, Cassandra's words gave me something about my mother to hold on to.

Here, then, is an alternative truth: What if Mother hadn't willingly left? What if it was Cassandra who forced her to leave by threatening to expose her affair to Father? Emotional blackmail: in return for not exposing them, she made Mother ask for a divorce. She made her abdicate her position as wife, so that Cassandra could usurp her. In this way, Cassandra could have it all—although, in one aspect, she was sadly deficient. Despite all her shenanigans, she had not been able to secure Father's affections.

I lay it all out for Sebastian. He rubs his brow. "Certainly plausible, Charlie," he says. "Cassandra is more than capable, but is she culpable? We have no proof that it happened exactly like that."

"What other plausible theory is there?"

Sebastian sits up, draws up his knees, resting his hands on top. "Why did Evelyn readily agree? Everything she loved was here. Her position. Oriole. You. Her friends. Her hobbies. She gave all that up because of Cassandra's threat? Father was having an affair too."

A memory pops into my mind: Peony, in her sick bed, telling me not to begrudge my mother too much, that happiness comes from within and not from status. *It doesn't come from being loved; it comes from loving yourself and another without expectation of return.*

Peony must have known about Mother and Oriole. Why else would she have said that? She had been intimating something to me, even then.

"Do you suppose it was to protect me from scandal?"

Sebastian inclines his head, thinking. "Possibly. Oriole writing the letter to break off the affair must have devastated Evelyn."

Sebastian is right. There could be other possibilities. Why did Oriole break things off? Did that have something to do with Cassandra, too?

"Did Cassandra know Oriole?"

"I wouldn't know. If Evelyn met Oriole through Peony, it's possible Cassandra did as well. You need to confront Cassandra," Sebastian says, and his demeanour changes, his voice too. "Don't back down." He straightens his legs, elongates his spine. "You must get at the complete truth."

The thought of confronting Cassandra about this sends me spiralling.

A shift in his glance. A kind of cloudiness. He holds his arms open. "Come here," he says.

The secrets of the past are voluptuous. Some truths, once broken into, are nested within bigger truths. Some truths coming into the light alter everything within their rays.

A Brief Intimacy Without Past or Future

What is love? What is longing? Does it travel in wide wavelengths and high amplitudes? Does it displace as much as it fills up any vacuum? I see it happen, like static fuzz, that moment between Sebastian talking about seeking the truth, and the next, asking me to come to him. The first moment belongs to Sebastian, the next belongs to Wang Tian Wei. A cold whisper slides through my mind: *Is this wrong?*

There is a strange light in Sebastian's eyes as he turns towards me. The scent of hypo-alum is prominent now.

"You've come a long way," I say, softly.

"At the lake, I didn't want to leave you," he says.

"So you stayed." It isn't a question. "What did you see?"

"Everything since that moment. I met your family. You love your brother Sebastian so much."

"He's not my brother, technically."

"Aiko is not my sister, technically."

My laughter rings ghostly in the room. How surreal to be looking at Sebastian's face and know that it isn't him. It's not just the luminous light in his eyes, everything else is different: the cast of his expression, the timbre of his voice, the way Wang Tian Wei carries Sebastian's body.

"I don't know how long I can stay." He is looking around at all the things in the room.

I imagine seeing it through his eyes: the modern chandelier, the soft Persian carpet, the diffuse yellow light, all the cameras in the room—a dozen eyes watching us watching them, as if the room were a stage. Of course Tian Wei would materialise in this room, as if trickster deities were fooling around with mere mortals.

"This is all very strange," he says. "I don't know what I expected." He examines the hands he now has. "Your brother has smooth, pale skin."

"The benefit of rich lotions," I respond dryly.

"We must beat hay while the sun shines." He smiles wryly. A reference to our letters, and something passes between us, fragile, tender.

I ask if I can lie down beside him. We face each other on the bed, our hands pillowed beneath our heads, simply gazing at one another, communicating silently. So much to say, but we're awkward and shy.

He lifts his hand towards my hair. "May I?" At my nod, he tucks a strand of it behind my ear. "In the photograph you sent, I wanted to tuck away that stray hair across your brow," he says, "and now, I can touch you." There is marvel in his voice.

"Having a body has benefits," I agree.

He laughs. His laughter is a supple, rounded, wholesome sound.

He gestures towards my face; I rest his palm against my cheek and hold it there. Warmth and the hardness of a man's hand. His thumb caresses away a tear that has risen at the edge of my eye, catching the single drop.

I ask him if I can read him Oriole's letter. He listens to it, not for the first time, and also for the first time. He repeats the last line, "I love you truly, madly, deeply." But it doesn't sound like a repetition. It sounds like a cry from the heart.

His gaze reflects the words I've uttered. I place his hand on top of my head, an implicit plea to be touched. He complies: beginning with the top of my head, his hand strokes my hair, wanders to my face, cups one cheek, and then his index finger traces my eyebrow, eye, nose, lips, chin; his hand outlines my neck, shoulder, the length of my arm, and when it reaches the hollow at my elbow, it rests there—as if to say, *Here is the key to unlock the hand*—then his hand reaches mine, grasps it. He intertwines our fingers.

A simple touch that takes its time. Especially when we have so little time. A brief intimacy, intense and full of yearning. The distance between us is reflected in his eyes, a distance more than just the span of a hundred years. He shakes his head in wonder.

Our meeting is a beginning that contains also the seed of its destruction. Just as my mother's death and Oriole's letter have opened up my understanding of their story, I realise that every beginning is also an ending. The moment after the discovery of the heart's desire is a threshold. Full of infinite possibility. Immediately after a decision is made, the possibilities narrow: that which is accepted becomes fact, that which is refuted falls away and is no more. All it takes is a tiny switch in register, a gesture more definitive than customary behaviour. In this case, one raised eyebrow with an implicit question—*Would you like to try?* In reply, a half-nod of the head—*I would.*

Damage Control

I hear a loud scream and wake. A tray clangs, porcelain breaks. Atalina is in the room, her eyes outsized, her mouth a round "O"; scattered all over the floor is breakfast. Sebastian half rises beside me, rubbing bleary eyes. Both of us are naked and pale on top of the coverlet. The scene registers.

A hodgepodge of emotions daubs his face: dismay, consternation, confusion. And then, anger. Pure, unadulterated shame and horror. That, more than anything else, feels like disembowelment.

Atalina scuttles out, but her scream and the clang of broken crockery have already alerted the other helpers. Not five minutes later, as Sebastian and I get dressed—very awkwardly, with our backs to each other—there is a rap on the door. Atalina's voice from the other side of the door says, "Mam wants you both downstairs."

Sebastian grits his teeth. "You let me do the talking."

*

Cassandra is seated in a straight-backed chair—the Chinese Chair of Judgement—a cup of oolong on a tall side-table beside her. The urge to sink down on my knees is incredible (oh, let the floor support me at least), and I desist only because that would be tantamount to admitting fault. I am at fault, I've done something unpardonable, we've done something unpardonable, but this sin that Cassandra is about to accuse us of—do I deserve to be excommunicated for it? Lovers must do what love compels. Is it a fiction we cling to while pretending there aren't caveats? The looks on all present—Linton and Madeleine, Laurent and Eloise (all still in their PJs; Linton even has his chamomile eye-mask pushed into his hair)—are enough to flay flesh from bone. The horror, the disgust, the calumny. In place of verbal ridicule and loathing, which would be preferable, the clan looks ready—no, probably dying—to pelt me with the clementines from the Lunar New Year tree still adorning the living room. The Chinese punishment for transgressions is to *fan xing*—self-reflect, self-flagellate. Shame coats me like grease. Behind Cassandra, the helpers whisper. Miles Wee Jun stands between his parents, flicking a finger against the inner wall of his mouth, making a disgusting plopping sound.

Cassandra sips from the cup of tea, presses her lips together. Her eyes are pinpricks of accusation. Her voice has a deadly calm. "I'm afraid I don't understand. Explain, please, why you have done this despicable thing in my house."

A parade of emotions works Sebastian's face. His jaw clenches, unclenches—a series of movements suggesting a swell of undisguised emotion lurking underneath. "It is not what you think, Yi-Ma. Emphatically not what you think. Nothing happened."

I cast a quick glance over at him. He'd been so baffled and confused earlier, but, as if he senses my glance, he squares his shoulders, lifts his chin infinitesimally higher. I understand: *Do not quail, do not grovel, do not show the chink in your armour.*

Cassandra's eyes drill into us. "How, then, do you explain this situation where you are in bed together? Do enlighten me. We must all seem a bit dim to you."

Linton frowns, as if holding in a bowel movement; Laurent smirks.

Sebastian says nothing. I sneak another glance at him. His brow is furrowed.

Cassandra trains her ice-cold gaze on me. "Well, Charlene, what do you have to say for yourself?"

Madeleine and Eloise look as if they wish the floor could swallow them up—they are dying from the patina of shame which has tarnished them.

I suck in a lungful of air. "I…" And the words once again clog my throat, held captive before Cassandra. "I'm so… uhm…so…ah…sorry…" I can't continue; my thoughts flap with the rapidity of a bat. How to even begin to untangle this mess? Wang Tian Wei, *tangki*, spirit possession… Should this narrative be served up with oolong and a slice of *kueh lapis*? Would telling the truth shame the devil? What if the devil is inside me? And how should Sebastian be absolved? His body was not his; he was simply not there, doing a *wan yau sei kai* in the spirit world. Even as I struggle for words, a memory shard pierces me in its sweetness. That moment when I had asked to be kissed. He had leaned in close, hovering, drawing out the moment to a breaking point. The press of his lips against mine. This explosion of feeling. The physicality of pressing against yielding flesh, but it was also cold, like my lips against glass. A residual tingling sensation moves along my spine. *Thraptured.* That word again. An electric spark had conducted itself, making us spring apart briefly, the pain of a tiny jolting charge. That trace of a burn on the lips. And then, undeterred, he had leaned in again. That long, long moment, when kissing could continue forever. I know I will remember that moment for all my years to come.

The sweetness evaporates. "It is not what you think." I take a deep breath, my words of denial sounding fake in my own ears. "I would not…I would never…" which is a half-truth, half-lie. It's fraught and ambiguous emotional territory, and I confess to being confused in the past. "Sebastian would never…" At least this part is true. It wasn't Sebastian.

Sebastian steps in. "Yi-Ma, we haven't done anything to be ashamed of. That's the truth."

I look at him. Does he even know what we did? No matter, he is charging ahead, making a broad guess based on the circumstances. The image of both of us naked on top of the bed sears itself into my brain.

"What we did isn't something to be ashamed of." What is he saying?

Cassandra's gaze swivels from me to Sebastian, disbelieving. "One merely trusts what one sees. Both of you will be the death of me. Did you not spare a thought for us?"

"I have to stop you there…" The tremor in Sebastian's voice is more pronounced. "None of you saw anything. It's what you heard."

"Do you think I enjoy hearing something so scandalous from the servants first thing in the morning? Oh, the shame." Cassandra fans a hand at her chest.

Miles Wee Jun cranes his neck up to look at his dad. "Why is Ku-Ku in trouble? Did she steal the Godiva chocolates from Grandpa's altar, too?"

Sebastian holds firm, though his voice notches up. "You have no proof of anything. This is a joke. All you have is hearsay."

"Hearsay? The proof is in the pudding. What you've done is wrong. The family honour is in a shambles. Your father will turn over in his grave. We are destroyed. How could you?"

I am trying hard to hold my composure, not letting tears spill forth. Her hyperbole could go on ad infinitum, and sooner or later, we would be forced to sink to our knees. Or kowtow before Father's portrait. I sense Sebastian rapidly working out the situation in his head. Repeated denial won't get us anywhere, not unless some form of explanation, no matter how false, is offered.

He ad-libs, "I was ill. Charlie was taking care of me."

Cassandra quirks one eyebrow, clearly disbelieving.

"All she did was give me a sponge bath because of my fever. What's wrong with siblings taking care of each other? Why is that strange?"

It's such a paltry excuse that even Laurent is sending him a look of, *C'mon bro, try harder.*

"Look—" Sebastian runs a hand through his hair, mussing it until it forms a peak— "whatever it is you think we did, why is that wrong? We aren't related biologically; we aren't actual brother and sister. This charge I can see you'd love to stick on us—incest? Try again. It won't hold up."

That word—*incest*—spoken so baldly makes them all flinch. It's the great irony of "face"—accusations and insinuations are far more damaging than bald-faced reality plainly stated.

Conversely, the truth won't mollify—but, oh, a lie somehow does. In a split second, I understand: Cassandra doesn't care what we do, but by staging this farce, she saves face in front of the help, because no sinner would state their shame so blatantly—it's akin to ripping off one's own face.

"A sponge-bath?" She contemplates us. "For this sponge-bath, Charlie also has to take her clothes off?"

Sebastian fumbles, "Uhm...she's..." then pushes on, "Oh, come now, Yi-Ma, what's a little nakedness for us arts people? We are unorthodox. We enjoy spectacles. And we're certainly not prudes. Where is the savoir faire of the Sze-Tohs? A little nakedness and it's a major calamity. The sky is caving in. Hell has frozen over."

Brilliant Sebastian: the way to make Cassandra back down is to fire back.

Her expression changes.

Sebastian delivers the coup de grâce. "I have Adnan, remember?"

Cassandra casts her eyes around. Sebastian's sexuality is no secret, but it isn't mentioned in front of the help, because of "face". "That's quite enough. I've heard enough." She calls out, "Atalina, get breakfast ready for the others. I've had enough excitement to put me off my jook this morning. What a palaver." She addresses us: "You two, please go. Sebastian, I must say, I'm disappointed. First, that forgery scandal, now this. Is this how you win my trust? Leave now. However it is you both like to have your fun, do it out of my sight. Please."

Like a photograph and its negative, the war is won when the truth is blended with a lie. Love is also sin, beauty is also horror, happiness is also tragedy. Why did we ever believe otherwise?

*

Sebastian refuses to talk to me. He answers none of my calls or texts. When I show up at his apartment, he refuses to answer the door. I can't eat or sleep. I can't do what I did in the past—plaster his windows with apologies—because his Marina Bay apartment is a penthouse. I drag myself to work like a zombie; Mahmood and Yoo-lin front for me with the museum director without demur or explanation.

Fan xing: by crossing the unspoken line between us, I've damaged my relationship with Sebastian, perhaps irretrievably. He has forgiven me once before (but it wasn't really my fault then). Would he forgive me a second time (when the fault is indubitably mine)? When events steamroll past our expectations and engender heaven and hell both, how should we take responsibility for those we have injured along the way, how should we account for what we were willing to sacrifice for the hope of paradise? When Chang'e stole the elixir of immortality from her husband Hou Yi, did she know she would be separated from him forever? When Weaver Girl was seen naked by Cowherd, and made him marry her, did the sin of marrying a mere mortal eclipse all else? Was this why she carved a cosmological river to separate the two of them forever? In the end, have I become my mother, suffering the same fate, separated from the one person I really care about?

Will the days of Sebastian refusing to talk to me turn into weeks, months, and years? It makes me want to lie down and never get up again. What is the nadir that a body can reach? Thorns plant themselves everywhere in my heart. I must make amends, but what do I do?

Analogue

These days in the news: a railway explosion near Mukden, Japan invading Manchuria. Speculation is rife: some say the incidents are not related, some say it is the outbreak of war; what's the truth?

In 1929, a new governor arrives in the Straits Settlements. Not only does this distinguished gentleman resemble the don of a prestigious top-flight academic institution, he is reputed to be proficient in Cantonese and Mandarin, having had extensive experience working with the Chinese as Governor of Hong Kong. Feng Yu tells Tian Wei that the new governor was born in India. "Asian underneath the skin. One of us." Feng Yu winks and clicks his tongue. Feng Yu is now the father of a baby boy, whom he dotes on to the point of insanity. Two years ago, by virtue of some new law, Si Nian declared that Feng Yu too was a Chinese national, despite Feng Yu never having set foot in China.

But Sir Cecil Clementi immediately sets to work suppressing Kuomintang activities. The ban against the Kuomintang is again actively enforced, all fundraising activities for the party in China to cease immediately, and quotas imposed on the immigration of Chinese male immigrants. In Chinatown, policemen and officers of the Chinese Protectorate chase after anyone suspected of political activities, arresting them and putting them in prison.

Tian Wei reads in *The Straits Budget* that a Comintern agent by the name of Joseph Decroux, also calling himself Serge Lefranc, has been arrested and sentenced to eighteen months in prison. There follows a report that this key arrest is part of a number of round-ups crucial in "the breaking up of a widespread plot" engineered by Soviet Communists to stir up red uprisings in important Far East cities. The speculation in the reading rooms is that the Communist and the Kuomintang have definitively parted ways.

Business is poor on account of the Depression, the prices of tin and rubber keep plummeting, and Tian Wei is daily preoccupied with concerns about rent and the possible foreclosure of his studio. He isn't afraid of striking out on his own, but what about all the mouths he feeds? Peng Loon has married a lovely Hakka young lady and moved to new lodgings on Pagoda Street. Kee Lung and Kee Mun are grown; Kee Lung takes over the camera for Tian Wei occasionally, while Kee Mun works the darkroom with Peng Loon. Ah Seng disappeared, running from a huge debt that Tian Wei eventually paid off by selling photographs he took of Cantonese opera troupe singers to a postcard souvenir shop in Bras Basah. In Ah Seng's place is a newcomer from Amoy—a tall, strapping lad by the name of Foo Lum, who is immediately smitten with Kee Mun, his eyes perpetually dogging her movements.

Construction everywhere: new shophouses, new shopping areas. Yet another amusement park has opened: Great World in River Valley. There are as many cars now on the streets as rickshaws. Electricity in all the shophouses in the centre of town. Water gushes through newly installed pipes, to the astonishment of Kee Lung and Kee Mun. Many businesses have telephones installed. One can buy freshly baked bread from Cold Storage. Tian Wei buys his first gramophone from a European colonial administrator moving back home. In the evening, a progression of music notes slips and slides through the shophouse. Tian Wei hears about this new music called blues from Feng Yu; when he listens to his first record—Bessie Smith—it is as if thunder is striking his soul. Blues and jazz. Unfamiliar names becoming familiar—Louis Armstrong, Jelly Roll Morton, Count Basie, Beale Street Blues. Tunes that weave into the heart and colour it dusk.

He is once again dreaming about her—his woman from the future. Ever since that fateful night, their letters have ceased. His dreams turn murky and labyrinthian, and he often awakens feeling that his soul has journeyed through chambers of time in search of something irretrievably lost. In search of her and a piece of his own soul. When he had possessed her brother's body, possibly an error was made. Perhaps it was something that never should have happened, and it affected the quantum entanglement. He's gone back to Chung Cheng Lake to no avail. His letters, deposited in the 1152 box, remain unsent. A cosmological river of separation has been carved. Still, he keeps writing. Feng Yu jests, "By Jove, the way you pound hammer and tongs on that old faithful typewriter of mine, who are you writing to?" He doesn't answer, but he keeps all the letters he writes to her tied as a bundle with twine.

If one must believe in something as unlikely, as heartbreaking, as mythological as love, then he believes longing can circumnavigate the celestial realm in search of one's love. It had happened when he appeared in front of her as a mirage and saw her with the schoolgirls. And that one night in a room full of cameras. It happened because his soul in dreamland had time-travelled far and wide to reach her. The memory of that night contains unbearable sweetness. Her poses on the bed, the photographs he took. All he has as evidence that it wasn't a figment of his imagination is the sheaf of letters he can't bear to discard. If mythological lovers are allowed only one night together, will the beauty and tenderness be sufficient to last a lifetime? Will it overflow into other lifetimes? For a moment, Song-dynasty poet Qin Guan's poem about the Cowherd and the Weaver Girl drifts across his mind: *If two hearts are united together, what need is there for two persons to stay together, day after day, night after night?*

Tunnelling the Historical Fantastic

I waylay Sebastian at The Squawk Box. The sun is blinding, it's thirty-two degrees out, and he emerges with a take-away box, a bottle of juice clamped under his arm, taking his fob out for his Porsche, parked nearby. We are creatures of habit, and even though the cafe is only five minutes away from his apartment, he would rather drive ten than walk five, because in a sweltering city, managing sweat under the armpits takes strategy. He sees me make a beeline for him from behind a hibiscus bush, slips his shades on and tacks in the opposite direction at unflagging speed. He hasn't spoken to me in months. Not one call, not one text, when I used to receive a dozen from him in a day.

"Sebastian, we need to talk," I call out. "If you don't talk to me, I will simply howl from here."

He stops mid-track. Does a U-turn. Face to face, he refuses to remove his shades, but a complex mix of pique and resentment and embarrassment edges out around the frame and marks his features. We return to The Squawk Box, where I've been lunching the past few months in the hope of catching him. By now, I have pretty much sampled the entire menu (another açai bowl and I'd turn berry-purple myself). I order a coffee. Being eco-conscious, he asks for metal cutlery to eat his lunch.

"Charlie," he says, then takes a swig of juice. He winces. "I would rather we didn't talk about what happened. Ever. If we don't talk about it, it never happened."

I blow out my cheeks. "If we don't, does that mean you forgive me, and we go back to the way we were?"

He stills, paper straw dangling from his mouth. It's obvious—there is no return to the way we were. There is only forward (do not collect £200, go straight to Chinese hell). That afternoon, after leaving Cassandra's, he refused to look at me and adamantly waved all my explanations aside. He didn't want to hear a single word. I had never seen Sebastian so bloody livid. He took hold of one of Laurent's golf clubs, went up to the Camera Room, and smashed several of the cameras.

"Are we going to get past this? Will you give me a chance to explain? To make amends?" The question emerges as a choked cry. I'd wanted to appear composed, but I have been all but a wreck these past few months. "Please, Sebastian," I beg. "I need you in my life. If you block me, my life is over."

He looks at me finally. A small twitch in the upper corner of his lip. Histrionics between us has always been used to downplay situations. "That bad, huh?"

The question that has been eating at me can no longer be suppressed. "Do you remember anything that happened that night? Or was it a complete eclipse of the mind?"

He pauses. "Maybe not talking to you for a while is a good thing. I get a new perspective on you. You're so anachronistic in your turn of phrase, Charlie. 'Eclipse'? You need to spend less time in a photography labyrinth, get out more. Join the course of humanity."

Yes, be less naive. Less foolish. I've just spent months thinking that my relationship with the one person who cares about me, and whom I care about most, is irreparable. The fact that we are now seated across from each other is nothing short of a miracle. I start talking fast. I need to make things right between us. The whole story pours out in a deluge. How it began one rainy night with a spectral encounter with a scanner, coinciding with Sebastian's return from Shanghai. Two strange letters I cannot account for that popped up from a Chinese photographer named Wang Tian Wei in search of a Japanese girl called Aiko. Then the letters jumping back and forth between Wang Tian Wei and myself. How I wasn't sure sometimes if it weren't a fantasy concocted in my own imagination, dovetailing with the reams of research I was doing in connection with the exhibition. Somewhere in the middle, it began to change, overtaking and becoming more powerful than reality. A vision appearing from a domed skylight during a tour I gave. A mirage at Chung Cheng Lake. Who would believe me? A supernatural correspondence between a Chinese photographer from a century ago and an archivist. But it happened.

It is a story that trips the historical fantastic. In a way, although I hadn't willed the possession, or known how it would change everything, or even suspected what damage it could bring, I was much to blame. I had sought out a *tangki*'s help, hadn't I? Though it was no excuse, the secrets unleashed about my mother had turned my world upside down. The ground on which I stood was breaking up, nothing seemed certain, my whole being felt like it was being torn asunder. Mired in confusion, I didn't know how to accept that I could develop feelings for someone living a century away, someone I'd never met, and yet, there the feelings were. As solid as a giant boulder, as torrential as a waterfall. What was I to do? Perhaps I wasn't just seeking spirit possession; in my subconscious, I was also seeking an exorcism. Like a camera keeping me honest, I was just trying to show my own heart a way out.

"Sebastian, you mean the world to me. I love you. You're my best friend. I will never forgive myself if I have hurt you in any way."

Sebastian listens without speaking. Throughout my retelling, he eats his salad, spearing his asparagus, taking crunching bites, making it an exercise of sheer will for me to continue talking. His irises turn an impregnable slate. He rocks a little, then he says to stop talking, he needs to think. He shields his face. Those minutes of silence feel like an eternity.

When he looks up, there is no hatred nor fury. Just indescribable sadness. "But you did hurt me, Charlie. What you did, how is it different from a form of colonisation?"

The accusation pierces me straight to the core. It's horrendous, what he is saying: I am as guilty as those who reaped and sowed the labour and sweat of others through conquest, who exploited the bodies of others unjustifiably and for their own benefit. People like Hudson Tay, who pivoted according to the winds of fortune, and blithely stole freedoms and futures in the name of love. People like Cassandra, who capitalise on circumstances, even if it means trampling on others, to enable their own version of happiness.

I'm horrified, and struck dumb. Sebastian is saying I'm no different, yet I'd dared to consider myself a cut above them. How despicable of me. I start to seep at the edges, tears I rapidly blink away.

Sebastian stabs at a grape, which rolls away. The dimples in his cheeks groove. "Of that night, I hardly remember anything. I remember discussing Oriole's letter with you, and after that, there is a black void. To be honest, I don't care. If it was indeed spirit possession, I wasn't there. I might as well have been dead, my soul abdicating completely to travel God-knows-where, and what you had was only my carcass." He gives a shiver.

Then his tone turns indignant. "A ghost—or, as you tell it, someone from a parallel dimension—kidnapped my soul. Took over my body. You guys had a fun time. What about me? I think about this, and I'm not sure whether to be enraged or laugh my guts out. Charlie, this is what you allowed to happen. How do you expect me to feel about it? You say sorry and it blows over? Goddamn you, Charlie—grow up."

Tears leak down my face unheeded. Compared to the humiliation Cassandra made me feel, this is a thousand-ton wrecking ball that punches out my inner core. If my life could be extinguished this minute, it wouldn't be a bad thing. "I'm sorry, Seb, I truly am so very sorry. I want to make things better. How do I make amends? Tell me, I'll do it."

"Are you kidding?" His hands curl around each other, kneading his knuckles. "Make amends? Like wave a magic wand and tesseract it away?" He shakes his head. "I've never felt so humiliated in my life, and in front of the Sze-Tohs. Remembering Linton and Laurent's faces still gives me nightmares. This is something you and I have to accept and live with. I don't know that we can go back to the way we were. I'm sorry, too. Right now, I don't know what we can be for each other. You have to give me time."

My throat is so bunged up, it feels like a sharp object has lodged there. "Oriole wrote that there is no shame in love."

Sebastian looks at me, confused for a second. Then, he rests his forehead on a bier of three fingers. "There isn't, of course there isn't. You loved this man from a hundred years ago. You wanted to make the impossible happen. It's crazy as fuck, but as I told you before, don't ever give anyone this much power over you."

Dumbly, I state, "Everything has changed, hasn't it?"

"Yes, it has."

I swallow the wrecking ball and all. "Because of that night?"

"Yes. We've crossed a line we shouldn't have, and now I simply can't look at you the same way."

"Because I've sullied myself? And us?"

"No." Then it hits him, the full import of what I'm saying. "NO! Oh, Charlie, don't internalise that Marcus Lo narrative."

Just like that, the storm breaks. No going back now, the vale of tears won't be stopped. I start sobbing with huge, ugly, gasping breaths.

Sebastian rubs the flats of his palms against the sides of his head. "I care about you, Charlie, and I know that what we have is a very special bond, and if it has misled you…" He stops, uncomfortable.

The waterworks become a flood. All I seem capable of doing is mumbling and repeating how sorry I am, and asking him to forgive me.

He doesn't react. Calmly, he sits there and lets me cry it out. Then, he reaches over and hands me a napkin. His used napkin. "Wipe your face, squirt. Crying makes you look ugly."

"You're the squirt." I throw his napkin into his unfinished salad bowl.

He rises and goes up to beg for more napkins from the eco-conscious cafe. Comes back, this time sitting right beside me, pushing the napkin into my hand. "Dry your tears, before everyone chases me out of here for being a hun dan—a bastard who bullies women. Look at all those dagger eyes, like I've wronged you instead of the other way around. Sheesh." He waits a beat. "By the way, about Wang Tian Wei—ripping yarn, is there more?"

We're not out of the woods yet, this is Sebastian's way of letting me know; but perhaps we've moved just a step away from being estranged forever.

Reckoning

Package warning for unwrapping the psyche: some truths, once revealed, may take the rest of your life to unravel. By making amends, it is my hope that Sebastian and I can get to a new normal.

I've asked Cassandra for a meeting. For emotional fortification, I requested the Camera Room. *Locus delicti*. I'm not sure she will agree, but lo, she does.

Waiting for her, I throw open the terrace doors to the belvedere. A memory drops like a stone: all the things that had transpired in this room. That moment when his finger had touched the hollow of my elbow. So tender it was.

The tap of heels behind me. When I turn, Cassandra is framed within the doorway. I have always admired Cassandra's sense of fashion, and today is no different. Her salt-and-pepper bob is ultra-chic. She is wearing a scarf dress with an uneven hem length, its pattern a riot of colours: carmine, fuchsia, lilac, carnation pink, clementine orange.

"Charlene," she says, twirling her long strand of pearls around one finger. "You're looking pasty." Her trademark bull's-eye style. "I have a new spa I can recommend for a facial."

"Hello, Yi-Ma." I take a deep breath. I've done a mind-fake to prep for this confrontation: I rehearsed what I would say in my mind so many times, it's become a meditation mantra; I mastered the art of deep breathing so well, I'm practically a yogi. I even perform a pelvic-floor clench, before I say, "I want to show you something." Part of the strategy also involves using more action, fewer words. I hand over the photograph of Peony, Oriole, and my mother with their arms around one another.

Cassandra peruses it. Wariness: good. "What's this about, Charlene?"

"Mother, Peony, and Oriole were friends."

. Her lips twist. "They were certainly tight, those three *kawan*, as if being an opera singer is a class above being a KTV lounge girl."

I frown. I'm on to something, though I'm not sure what. I give her Oriole's letter.

She doesn't reach for it. "I don't have my reading glasses with me."

I have foreseen this. Thus, I have recorded myself reading it, the way I read it to Sebastian, with thickly lathered emotion, as maximum war cry. I play the recording for Cassandra.

She listens, arms folded across her chest. A momentary pinch of pain before the wall comes down. Score. She takes an involuntary step back. Another score. "What is this now, Charlene?"

"I want to know the truth. Oriole's letter mentions your threats. Did you threaten to expose Mother?"

Cassandra turns away with a shrill laugh. She heads towards the belvedere. "Why would I do such a silly thing? I wanted to be their friend." She leans against the balustrade, and the blinding light bathes her; she outside, me inside, two different spheres of existence. It is hard to see her clearly, hard to discern the truth when visibility is opaque. Sometimes there is such a thing as too much light. Her tone is airy. "You are so predictable. I knew one day you would come running to me with this. I'm glad to see you picked up finally on all the hints I've dropped. You're not a lost cause yet."

My mouth hinges open. I'm never quite able to gauge the things that she will say. "You wanted me to…to…to find out? Was that why you mentioned the P.I.? I thought you said… uhm…some secrets aren't yours to divulge."

Her hands splay out, palm side up. "But I didn't divulge anything. You found out all by your resourceful little self. I have nothing to hide, Charlene. I didn't threaten your mother, as you say. I merely confronted her with the truth. Your father had no knowledge of her affair to the day he died. I kept her dignity for her."

"You kept her dignity?" That's so rich, I almost choke on my saliva.

"He thought she wanted a divorce because of me. I didn't want him lied to."

"Let me understand this…" I'm seeing red. Deep breath. "At the end of the day, was it about not wanting him lied to, or was it about getting rid of the competition, so you could have it all?"

Cassandra smiles, bitter. "You've got it wrong again. I was trying to help her. I said to your mother that, if she agreed to leave, if she agreed to move far away, I would make sure she got a big fat settlement in London. One that would last her a lifetime. In return, I would ensure the secret stayed with me. That he would never know."

"You were doing Mother a favour? Guardian of Mother's secret?"

"Oh, more than a favour. Do you think your father would view that kind of scandal kindly? He'd look a right cuckold. It would tarnish his patrician image. Linus Sze-Toh's wife in love with an opera singer and a woman. Husband and wife: two peas in a pod with their extra-marital affairs. The ba gua za zhi would muckrake with glee."

The double standard: Father kept two mistresses—he had two full-fledged extra-marital affairs—but this wasn't scandalous enough for the tabloids. "So, you broke them up, Oriole and Mother? You must be so proud of yourself."

Cassandra smirks. "You give me too much credit, Charlene. Those three artsy-fartsy friends thought they were better than me, the Malaysian bumpkin, so ulu. They snubbed my friendship. I could have retaliated, but, in fact, I didn't have to do a thing. The P.I. told me Oriole and Evelyn were separating anyhow. Dearie me, your father was such a stud—in the midst of seeing me on the sly, he was also courting Peony, and he managed to impregnate your mother. She became pregnant with you, and this was just too much for Oriole, I guess. She decided to accept an offer to join a theatre group in Hong Kong. So glum for Evelyn—to mooch around after Oriole left. A change of scenery would do her good. Your mother accepted London as a choice not long after that."

"You forced her to move to London. You wanted her out of your sight."

"No, no, no. Merely a suggestion." She pats her coiffure. "How can I force her, the wife, to do anything? Honestly, you give a mistress too much power. You don't understand the concept of qing di, do you? That's not to say Evelyn was a love rival." Cassandra laughs. "After all—what is this saying Linton told me about the other day?—she bats for the other team, doesn't she?"

All those digs and insinuations at Sebastian—it clicks—all those dropped hints for me. She has been dying to let me know since I moved back five years ago. How she must have enjoyed my blithe ignorance. But how little she knows me. Mother's secret, if revealed at that time, would have been a cause célèbre, but to me it was a cause for celebration. Discovering her love gave me the courage to face my own. It's high time, as Sebastian has been urging me these many years, to beat Cassandra at her own game, and I have a plan.

"You had a lot to gain from Mother leaving. After the divorce, your status changed from mistress to wife. You became legitimate, finally. Not to mention you got hold of all that wealth."

"Oh, sure," she says. "I never said I had a Buddhist nun's heart. Of course I wanted Evelyn out of the way. But you're wrong if you think it's all about face. Or money. I'm not all that calculating. I was also willing to make sure she wouldn't be hard done by. I too am a woman, and I know just how hard it is to try to survive on my own. When one is used to all this luxury, it isn't so easy to live without it." She sweeps her hand across the belvedere, and, out of the corner of my eye, I spy the saguaro cactus with its raised spindly, needled arms. "But do you know what your mother did? She acted all high and mighty. She said she didn't need anything from me, certainly not my help in making sure she got a large divorce settlement. In fact, she merely wanted the house in London, and enough of a monthly settlement to get by. I told her she didn't know what was good for her. Do you think acting sacrificial towards your enemies makes them think kindly of you? But she had made up her mind. She said she would finance her own freedom. She would get a job in London. Imagine! How preposterous. If she chose to lie on a bed of thorns, who was I to stop her? She willingly walked away from all she could have had in Singapore, to live almost a pauper's life in London. I didn't force her. I didn't have to threaten her. She refused my help."

For the first time in my life, I'm proud of my mother. It fills me almost close to bursting. It must have cost her something dire to give all of it up, regardless of whether she did it for me or for herself. As if Mother were watching from above, what I have to do next appears in a new light. A curious symmetry in action and consequence, a karmic chain reaction. Tit for tat.

Deep breaths. The words flow like water spilling from a drum. There is a roar inside my head. The room is spinning. "I didn't know you had acted so nobly, Yi-Ma, looking after my mother's interests. Gosh. Darn it, on second thought, let me express myself more clearly. What you did to my mother is…is…despicable." I use the same word she used against me a couple of weeks ago. "I don't know what you were trying to pull, nor do I think I shall ever understand your twisted logic that you were trying to do right by her, but I'll tell you this now. Never again. Your hold over me ends here."

Stripping a Chinese person of their face is a battle of wits, of seeing who holds on to theirs last.

"I…I'm going to move out as soon as I find another place to live. And, like Mother, even if I have to live in Pulau Ubin, I don't want any of this." I sweep my hands towards the courtyard, the enormous chess set, the lone cactus. Cut out its heart, sever its limbs, and it will grow full again. Cassandra and my mother have taught me this at least: love binds you and it doesn't sever easily—not by death (Cassandra's love for my father), and not by separation (my mother's love for Oriole). "Keep your treasures. I don't want them. I don't need them. Thank you for returning my mother to me." How ironic that it is the one thing she hadn't wished to give. A weight lifts off me.

"One condition," I add. "You must give Sebastian what is rightfully his. If you had so much influence to parlay, you could have said something to Father about Sebastian's inheritance. If Sebastian is expected to fulfil the legal responsibilities of a son, then he also has a right to the bounty. Right now, his business is floundering, as I am sure your P.I. told you. He needs a tranche of cash immediately to buy Adnan out. I'm sure you know what to do."

Cassandra eyes me long and hard. "Are you threatening me?"

I turn up my palms, shrug. "Yi-Ma, I'm an orphan in this house. Where would I have the status or right to make threats? I'm just stating the truth."

It takes her a couple of moments to see how I've turned the tables on her. She mock applauds, soundlessly. "I see. You've grown up, Charlene. The audacity to threaten me." She suddenly peals with laughter, which makes me furrow my brow. "So help me, I'll make a tough nut out of you yet." Armour. Get hurt, get shot, get damaged—if you don't perish, you heal. It forms a keloid. That's your armour. I get it now. Still trying to manipulate me.

"So, will you do right by Sebastian?"

She picks non-existent lint off her dress. "You need to learn how to speak to your elders, Charlene."

"That's what Sebastian says!" Filial piety, the primacy of face, family honour. Within Chinese families, brutal, unforgivable truths are seldom flushed out, dramas remain unresolved, precisely to save face, to preserve family harmony. Because family harmony, like hideous jade sculptures, is irreparable once shattered. Parents become estranged from children, siblings refuse to talk to each other, all because of an inopportune, inappropriately phrased word that cannot be redacted. Strip a Chinese person of their face and you carry victory home.

That is precisely what I'm about to do. Carefully now, enunciating clearly: "I'd hate to think what would happen if the tabloids were to get hold of…oh, I don't know, my mother's secret affair with Oriole, or your manipulation of it, or…" I cover my mouth with my hands in mock horror. "Goodness, what if they got hold of what happened between Sebastian and me? Imagine!"

A small hitch in her breath. Not even a hiss. She merely stares at me for a full minute, her eyes scouring my face, as if a veil has lifted finally and she sees me for who I am. Then her expression changes: capitulation—and, surprisingly, a twinge of respect.

On Cecil Street

Laurent's office is in a swanky building in the Central Business District, soaring into a dazzling blue sky filled with cirrus clouds. Two stone lions sit on pedestals in front of the building. The Sze-Toh Group and Linton's offices are here also. Laurent: the lawyer in the family. Linton: the financier.

Laurent has asked Sebastian and me to come over to his office to sign the paperwork for the new tranche of loans to Sebastian's atelier.

At first, I was confused. "Why do I have to come? Isn't it between TAV and the Sze-Toh Group?"

"Oh, I think you want to hear this. There's a condition in the contract."

Of course there is. Did I think that Cassandra would fork over money without strings attached? How gauche of me.

Sebastian calls me at work. "I heard you confronted Cassandra. I heard you did it in the Camera Room. Wow. Pair it with a killer outfit and it would have been a total power move. A blow-on-your-smoking-gun move."

While things are still awkward between us, Sebastian has called me of his own accord. And he is back to making the same lame-ass jokes as before. I grab Mahmood walking past and try to waltz with him. It alarms Mahmood very badly. Back on the phone, I say, "She takes a person seriously only when they act mean and tough."

Sebastian pauses. I hear him swallow. "You saved me from having to grovel to her. I heard you boomeranged the incest charge at her." He chuckles. "Bet she didn't see that coming."

"Well, you were always quoting that Cantonese proverb at me about not being spineless. I got me some kuat hei. The best defence is offence."

"Good grief—" a deep grimace in his tone— "it's time to be afraid: Charlie's handing out football cliches. Anyway, let's go see what Laurent has to say."

And what Laurent has to say is all good. The sum is enough not just to buy out Adnan, but also for the second developmental phase of Sebastian's atelier; it will cover all operational and technological costs: the move back to Singapore, a new office lease, office renovations, algorithm upgrade, client development, marketing budget, staff recruitment, legal fees—all of it and then some.

The fly in the ointment is that there will be closer supervision by Laurent, on Cassandra's behalf. Sebastian nods: he can live with that.

Laurent pushes his glasses up his nose. The windows on one side reveal a commanding view: the two humps of Gardens by the Bay, like a sea monster cresting the waves. Little red buoys bob amid the swells of silver. A huge black painting adorns the wall behind Laurent's desk—thick slabs of black impasto in whorls and hurricanes, craters and swirling debris. An image of antimatter. The cosmos bristling with dark energy. I can't stop staring at it; it calls to me.

Laurent clears his throat. "There is one more condition here that I should draw your attention to. TAV is required to seek partnerships for collaborations with the philanthropic organisations where Ma sits as a board member. Of course, there should be a rigorous selection process, all above board, but if you should choose one of the charities the Sze-Toh Foundation actively supports, we would look favourably upon future funding requests. I trust this is not onerous?"

Sebastian shakes his head. A boon, more like: Laurent and Cassandra are helping him reach a goal he has always aimed towards—a social impact art business model.

"Ma would like Charlie to be TAV's advisor for this, particularly focusing on the selection of these philanthropic collaborations."

"Come again?" Sebastian says.

Laurent leans forward, steepling his fingers. "It was Ma's suggestion." He sighs. "You have the wrong idea about Ma. Both of you have this chip on your shoulder about your status within the family. Ma is actually fair."

Sebastian and I trade a barely veiled glance.

Laurent continues, "You never bothered to get to know her. She may be sharp-tongued, but she is also an astute businesswoman, and she sees what both of you can bring to the table." He adjusts his glasses. "If we can put aside our differences for a moment, you will see that this current financial arrangement benefits you hugely. Everybody wins."

I don't contradict Laurent. Each of us spins our own fiction. In this world, there are those whose entire raison d'être is extraction; they do not see skin and bone, gristle and flesh, what their gimlet eyes pierce through at a glance is another person's innate worth and how that worth can best be converted into financial advantage or social capital to benefit themselves. In colonial Singapore, this was how compradors, merchants, and magnates alike made their lucre: through a phenomenal extraction ability, now embedded in our collective DNA. Because of what I've done, I no longer judge them so harshly. Love is pure, but what we want out of love is selfish.

Laurent is looking directly at me as he says, "Ma is more maternal than you give her credit for. If you could see how she remade herself, how she clung to life and made use of her talents, you would be amazed. She didn't grow up with riches, you know."

Sebastian and I trade another glance, but Laurent is oblivious. He continues, "Her family was dirt poor and living hand to mouth. Ma grew up in one of those Chinese resettlement villages from the sixties and seventies, a legacy of the colonial plan battling the Malayan Emergency."

It sounds suspiciously like a prepared speech. Laurent goes on to talk about his paternal grandmother being *zong nam heng nui* (Cantonese for preferring sons over daughters), and how

Cassandra's schooling was discontinuous and sporadic. She went to technical college, managed to secure a job as a clerk in an accounting firm in KL. As with women of that generation, whatever she earned had to be sent home to help out with family expenses. "A young woman making her way in a big city like KL in the eighties is not easy. Without money, she didn't have any sort of life, and she certainly couldn't afford to be fashionable. To make ends meet, she worked at a KTV lounge for a while, which was how she met Father. It wasn't until she met Father that the tide turned for her. So don't judge her too harshly. You don't know the whole truth."

Sebastian jiggles his leg in impatience, but I receive a newsflash: ah, the KTV lounge was a reference to herself. Cassandra was the KTV bar girl. I have nothing against KTV bar girls, but evidently she does. Another flash: she takes such pains with her wardrobe because her psyche is still trying to exorcise its past. Everything that happens to us in the future, how we decide what to do or how to act, is tied up with what has happened to us in the past.

Laurent rises from his chair. "Let's give each other a chance, shall we?"

In a more charitable mood, I warrant Cassandra is right: we don't need to be *sayang-sayang* with each other, but we can tread softly on each other's dreams, as the poem goes.

I don't shake Laurent's hand; I let Sebastian do it for the both of us.

After the signing, Laurent asks for a photograph together. We pose in front of a floor-to-ceiling scroll of Chinese calligraphy in the lobby. Instead of the words on the scroll (and it irks me that I can read most of them except for a couple of characters, making me feel defeated by the language), a quote from photographer Gordon Parks comes to me: the heart, not the eye, determines the content of a photograph. I put on a raggedy smile. Me in the middle, flanked by Laurent and Sebastian, who makes bunny ears on top of my head at the last second as the photo is snapped by Laurent's secretary. In memoriam, siblings who love and help each other.

The Emotion of the Land

At a Tung Teh gathering in February 1932, Si Nian, back from Malaya, beckons him over. While waiting for the talk to begin, Si Nian hands over an article. Tian Wei scans it quickly. It is from a Chinese publication published in Nanjing, which Si Nian must have had someone smuggle in via Shanghai. It publishes in full what is allegedly the Tanaka Memorial—Japan's overarching plans to conquer Asia—and the Taiwan Occupation and Russo-Japanese War are phases one and two, respectively, of this grand plan.

"Are you sure this isn't *fei wen*?" Tian Wei exclaims. Can such a plan, if indeed true, be so easily leaked that it is published in a Mainland Chinese paper, no matter how redoubtable?

Si Nian's upper lip curls. "Believe what you want, comrade, but when *mi zhu cheng fan*, you will regret inaction."

"I'm not sure what you mean."

Si Nian turns, one arm snaking round the back of his chair, the other grasping the chair in front, in this way trapping Tian Wei within his circumference. "Debts must be repaid, don't you think? We Chinese must always remember that integrity first and foremost lies with honouring one's promises. It is a matter of face. Without face, a Chinese person might as well disappear, be turned into ashes."

Dread rises from his sternum. Tian Wei understands what Si Nian is alluding to: his help regarding the whole business with Aiko; the Ghee Hin's assistance. Because of Si Nian, the Ghee Hin left his business alone even as they terrorised and demanded protection payment from others. They didn't harass Kee Mun on her way to People's Park to buy meat and vegetables. They didn't bust into his shop to demand repayment of Ah Seng's opium debt and lay a wave of destruction over all that he owned. Over the years, Si Nian has periodically mentioned their botched rescue attempt in Penang, but he has never used the word *debt*. Not until now. Plain speak: Si Nian is reminding him that it is time to pay up.

Violence in China. Skirmishes, casualties. The *Nanyang Siang Pau* begins publishing a Sunday edition, delivering the latest about China, which he reads avidly. Si Nian has said that the overseas Chinese communities in Nanyang must solidify and unite towards this common cause. Indeed, this is exactly what is happening.

Perhaps there is no such thing as chance. Si Nian has said he will rue inaction. One must continue believing in compassion, love, truth, justice, honour, righteousness. The Confucian ideals *ren ai zheng yi* (仁爱正义). The principle of *li* (礼). Everything is governed by the natural law of rites. One must continue to hold on to these things even when the human body is flawed. Aiko too had once written: a debt of gratitude is carried unto the grave. He owes Si Nian; Si Nian coming to collect is destiny waiting to happen.

Digital Mythology

I am waiting for my Mandarin tutor at the Blue Mouse, drinking my usual Kurasu black, and I overhear two young women (one with two pigtails like a manga character, the other with pomegranate-red hair) having a conversation about online long-distance dating. Neither of them has met the person they are in a relationship with, other than online.

Pigtails moans that she doesn't have the money to fly over to see him, even though they have been in a relationship for sixteen months. Pomegranate tries to comfort her by saying physical intimacy is overrated. What's more romantic is casual intimacy. Being on the same wavelength, two beings so different from one another, able to share identical thoughts and feelings through a waveform signal across vast fields of space—if that is not a miracle, what is? Feelings are soldered together when a smile full of heart is shared. The feeling of being able to tell the other person anything at all. Freedom. Long conversations when time just flies. Pure delight. Warmth cocooned in the soul. Falling asleep while the other person watches from a different time zone. Safety. Sanctuary. How they occupy your thoughts every hour of the day. It reminds you of your capacity for love, the engine that drives everything. These are little overlooked things, irreplaceable. They nod solemnly. That's what love is. The little things.

I think to myself: what if you don't have even this?

"I don't need a grand gesture," Pigtails says.

"I don't need love confessions," Pomegranate says. "I only need that look in his eye. When he looks at me, I am the centre of his world."

The eye is a window. Famed photographer Steve McCurry's *Afghan Girl* travelled the globe on this premise.

That look in his eye, I remember it.

Depth of Feeling, Not Depth of Field

Mahmood is working from home, but Yoo-lin is nose-deep within the folders, on the major clean-up and reorganisation I've instructed her to do. She glances up when I enter our basement office. "Oh, good," she says. "Charlie, question."

"Go ahead."

"What do you want me to do about all the Sook Ching articles you've collected? Technically, they don't belong anywhere. We don't have a folder for Second World War photographs."

"Oh, but we will."

"So, what would you like me to do for now?"

"Let me see." I lean over Yoo-lin's shoulder, grab her mouse to direct the pointer.

Many of the articles are open on her desktop. I scan each one, and then I come across one that I've read before. It stops me cold. *Nanyang Siang Pau*—the shooting of a Chinese photographer by the Kempeitai using the *genchi shobun* method. His name, Tang Si Nian, was on the Kempeitai wanted list. Upon hearing the charges arrayed against him, he had laughed maniacally and hung his head low for execution. As if it is happening in slow motion before me—the ringing shot to the head, the body dropping, glasses cracked and smeared with blood—the killing had taken place right outside the Japanese photography studio of Junji Naruto on High Street at 11:11 a.m. on 13 March 1942.

Today is 13 March.

Yoo-lin's computer time: 11:11 a.m.

A feeling of sparks running along a wire, hot and cold settling in my bones simultaneously. Déjà vu. Time is on a loop, and somewhere, across the celestial realm, someone is calling my name.

A tableau flits across my vision. The Camera Room. The terrace doors to the belvedere are thrown wide open, curtains stirring gently in the light breeze. *Click*, I hear the sound. A hand holds a camera. A Rolleiflex MV EVS, encased in a handsome tanned leather case. The hand holds it like a baby.

Myself on a bed. The two top buttons of my blouse undone, the collar pulled down to reveal one shoulder. Two fingers are directed at my lifted chin, and my eyes hold uncommon desire. Only my grin, that of a Cheshire cat, spoils the supposed sexiness of the pose. *Click*.

Another pose, my two arms draped over one raised knee, the skirt ruched up where my thighs cross, the shadow of an aperture.

Standing on tiptoes by the bed, hands reaching towards the ceiling like bare trees.

Legs curved underneath me, like a cat on a bed.

Reclining on the bed.

He watches me undress, remove every piece of clothing. Naked as a lamb now in the wild. I muss up my hair, and he catches a shot of me with my hands in my hair.

The atmosphere becomes charged and thick.

He comes close, the camera almost grazing my thigh. What he's catching isn't the whole outline, but parts of me. A form of memorisation. A shoulder rounding like a hill. A hip undulating like a desert landscape. A breast like a temple bell. A belly button like a sinkhole in an expansive field of flesh.

Hello, hills like white elephants.

Hello, Holly Golightly in dark glasses without a stitch of clothing on, showing a love bite on her shoulder.

At the word *kiss*, his eyes question mine. My eyes respond. He leans in close, hovers, the moment feels drawn out to a breaking point. He presses his lips against mine. This explosion of feeling. The physicality of pressing against yielding flesh, but it is also cold, like my lips against glass. A spine-tingling sensation settling along my spine. Then an electric spark conducts itself, making us spring apart briefly, the pain of a tiny jolting charge. That trace of a burn on the lips. He leans in again, and the night becomes ours. What we explore. How we explore. Instants of forever, and time is at once eternal and too brief.

On the horizon, light blushes the sky, a faint wash of seeping orange. The early sound of a bird chirp. That gentle cradle of wan light in the room. I did not see Tian Wei go.

The Eye Is A Window

Early morning curator's tour: 9:30 a.m. sharp. Once again, standing before Sophia Blackmore and her group of girls.

I begin the tour. The group today is composed mostly of European tourists, huddling close around the famed photograph. Heat brings out different perfumes from bodies at close range—hidden underneath the fragrances is the animality of a woman's body, sometimes subtle, sometimes bold, never not intoxicating. Have the frontiers of art ever tried to capture the alchemical responses of women's bodies to weather? If the scopic regime were to incorporate the olfactory as well, what would it tell us? Korean artist Lee Bul's artwork at the Hayward had involved decomposing fish; she tried to incorporate the olfactory into the scopic. But that's the problem with fish—they stink. The gallery had to be closed and the guards became physically ill. For whatever reason, this reminds me of Cassandra. Ah, perhaps the realisation that I've never been, and now never will be, close enough to her physically to know what she smells like. If I had, would it have been the beginning of a different conversation? Can redemption begin with an olfactory first step rather than relying on visual perception?

Some part of me feels sorry for her. It's not pity, it's the kind of sorry that I would feel for myself. Bits of our interaction come back to me. I think about Cassandra's revelation of the cyst in her breast that had necessitated surgery. How she'd thought she'd psychosomatically taken on Peony's illness. Whether she admitted to it or not, that was empathy, and she was capable of it. But our empathic pathways are pruned off by life's vicissitudes and exigencies. Cassandra as she is now and Cassandra as she might have been naturally—the psychic distance between them reveals how life has pruned her. Were all those barbs and digs at me a plea for understanding? In her truncated, reluctant fashion, she had revealed that it was friendship she wanted from Peony and Mother, not rivalry, but she hadn't known how to ask for it. Her way of getting their attention was emotional blackmail and sabotage, power brokering and advantage.

A woman raises her hand. Shades are perched on her head, reading glasses dangle from a chain around her neck. "I thought this tour was about women's fashion. Why are we looking at school group photographs?"

I've received a scout offer several weeks ago for a position back in London. At first, I thought I would turn it down immediately; although this town does not invoke in me cosy feelings of hiraeth, I'm not quite done here. But then, a whisper from the ancestral ionosphere: *It's time.* In the end, I think I will accept.

Patiently, I explain to the woman who asked about school photographs that, during my stint as junior curator at the South-East Asia Museum (SEAM) in London, one thing I quickly realised was that Asian-themed exhibitions were about the exotification rather than the discovery of its histories. Garments were more important than the hands that produced them. We hint at the inequities and iniquities of imperialism, or we anoint even as we critique an inglorious past. The spotlight is seldom, if ever, shone on the nascent female emancipation movements in the far-flung colonial territories, similarly impacted by the tides of emancipation sweeping through the metropoles of social change. There is an edge of conviction in my voice that wasn't there before. "In this exhibition, one of our goals is not just to showcase the social history of dress and the changing of fashion, but also the bodies that inhabited the clothes. In effect, how women in the early twentieth century clothed their minds. Education was where that story began."

Heads nod within the group. This tour is of fashion proper: from the *baju panjang*, to *baju* Shanghai, to *baju kebaya*, to *qipao*, to Western frocks—the hybrid fashion in the Straits Settlements, where one woman might have all these styles hanging in her wardrobe. It's about how fashion and dress communicated women's self-idealisation and grafted on new identities that conflated tradition with modernity. The fantasy and self-making in front of the camera's eye. These historical photographs, like costumes, are arranged like accordion folios in my mind: a chorus of steadfast, consistent friends.

"You will see as we proceed through the exhibition two things. One: how women used fashion, as men did, to claim 'modernity' and exercise a 'limited agency'. Even then, without being able to articulate it, women projecting themselves before the camera recognised that *woman* is an idea; *woman* is a space of desire and fantasy, and this space is permeable. Two: early efforts towards female emancipation, female education specifically, also acted as a driver to modernise society at large and redefine the Chinese identity of the Straits Chinese community. This re-Sinicisation was considered a huge threat by the colonial government at specific junctures before the Second World War, evidenced through their policies towards Chinese education, and their clampdown on Kuomintang and fundraising activities of the Chinese clan communities."

I conclude with a photograph of a young woman wearing a swimming costume, perched on rocky steps against a backdrop of a lake fringed by trees, explaining how the sporty woman was a signifier of a modern woman. "The nascent female emancipation movement in the Straits Settlements was much influenced by the May Fourth or New Culture Movement happening in China in the 1920s and '30s, as attitudes towards female education and gender roles changed. Women began holding jobs outside the home; they demanded marital and spousal rights in divorce; they wrote in to magazines and newspapers to express their views on the length of hemlines, hairstyles, their rights to choose their own spouses, become educated, free their minds. From being exoticised as *qipa*, or rare flowers, they became *xiandai nüzi*, modern girls."

The women in the group are nodding. The nods are gratifying, but it is the lift of their shoulders, the elongating of their spines that speaks to me of impact. The women are nodding not because I have appealed to their minds—although it is that, too—but because I have tapped into our collective spirit.

*

By tacit agreement, Sebastian and I have stopped attending the monthly ritual dinners. Since moving out to Bishan, it's easier to avoid Cassandra's barbs. Or perhaps I've stopped noticing them and have finally formed my keloid shell.

I don't hear much from Sebastian these days, even though we live in the same metropolis, and the neighbourhood of Bishan is but a skip, hop, and jump from Marina Bay. I tell myself he is busy moving his atelier to Singapore, making new business contacts, getting all the legal details sorted. I hadn't known how much I cleaved to the idea of symmetry until I accidentally ran into Adnan outside the Singapore Art Museum. He was there for a meeting, and I had just finished mine. While waiting at the street corner for the green pedestrian *walk* sign, we caught up on news. I learned that he and Sebastian remained in regular contact. "We're friends," Adnan stated flatly, and the words pricked me. I'd been part of every stage of Sebastian getting together with Adnan, but it seemed I had been removed from that intimacy for their break-up. My relationship with Sebastian is morphing, our previous kindred connection broken, and it was I who wielded the sword.

Back at SCoP, I walk through the gallery halls and the ancestral photographs whisper: what is a photographer? What is a photograph? What is the relationship between photographer and subject, self and camera? What lurks in the shadows, that one misses by a hair's breadth? What memory has the eye forgotten? What longing pierces the eye like a ley line? What if the camera is not something that shoots, nor an extension of one's arm and eye, but a spectral membrane through which one enters the world?

The eye is a window, but it forgets that it is a window. It forgets it is an intersection, a meeting point with the world. It forgets that it is a place where the self becomes permeable, allowing itself to be punctured, allowing the world, too much world, to enter.

Genie

13 March 2020

Dearest Tian Wei:

I have to warn you.

Do not for any reason go to Junji Naruto's studio on 13 March 1942 at 11:11 a.m. I implore you.

Forget Imperial Advisor Han. Forget a citizen's duty. Do not agree to anything Si Nian asks of you. It will cost you your life. Please listen to me. I am sorry I never told you this when I had the chance. I love you. I miss you.

Yours forever,
Charlie.

He hadn't expected to hear from her again. She goes like a puff of air, arrives like a whirlwind. After a thunderstorm the night before, the dawn air on 29 November 1939 is light, even breezy. Outside, the trundle of a mosquito bus. The cries of hawkers. Children walking to school, their voices chirpy, their lunches and books swinging against their legs. Birds chittering in the rafters overhead.

The letter has appeared on the last remaining glass negative in the 1314 box. He reads it and feelings carefully preserved spill forth like a genie released from a bottle. A kaleidoscope of buffeting emotions. To be so alive and to expend that life far from the one he loves. It is torture.

He must act; the urge is strong to leave something for posterity. Love requires no proof, yet leaves traces and residue. Despite nursing a cold, he lugs out Feng Yu's typewriter. Begins typing, snuffling into his handkerchief, typing. Feng Yu would call this barmy behaviour.

What of it? Who among us isn't barmy in some way, broken in another? All-encompassing love is as barmy as a box of frogs. Or toads. As long as their Milky Way allows, he will write for them both.

Chinese Time Is Circular

Since 1932, Tian Wei has been following news about the skirmishes between the Japanese Imperial Army and the National Revolutionary Army. On 7 July 1937, the Japanese bomb Marco Polo Bridge near Peking, and matters escalate quickly. In August, a Japanese naval officer is shot dead in Shanghai. Full-scale fighting breaks out in various places in China.

Later, it will be billed as the outbreak of the Sino-Japanese War. When news of the fighting reaches Nanyang, social activities abound with new purpose: lectures and community get-togethers, the fundraising activities organised by the various *hui guan*. Calls and rallies for the overseas Chinese to do something become vociferous. Tan Kah Kee, the Henry Ford of Malaya, is devoting his energy towards the China cause. The Singapore Chinese Chamber of Commerce calls for a disaster-relief convention—one that will unite the various Chinese clans. It is organised for late July. On the eve of it, the British colonial authorities enjoin the Chamber to call it off. Tian Wei hears about it through the Tung On *hui guan*, which he frequents because of his fascination with Cantonese opera. Something dark has been set in motion. Daily, the sky is sodden with thunderclouds. A flock of pigeons circles above, their cries sawing the air.

A massive convention takes place in August. Hundreds of Chinese representatives participate. The Singapore China Relief General Association comes into being, with Tan Kah Kee as president, headquartered at the Ee Hoe Hean, which becomes the central nervous system for fundraising activities.

Once again, Japanese goods are being boycotted in Chinatown, led by youths banding under the Red Blood Brigade. They picket and distribute leaflets. In the *kopitiam*s, horse races, clubs, and associations, epithets are slung about.

"Dwarf bandits!" people cry. "Japanese businessmen and professionals: all spies." Even a game of mahjong can result in tables upended and tiles flying everywhere as people argue about what is happening in the mother country. At Tung On, Tian Wei feels himself drawn into arguments with old-timers over each violent incident in China, everyone talking in strident voices, staking their families' honour, stamping feet, raising fists. Some praise Chiang Kai Shek's handling of the Japanese. Others say this would be China's weakness: "Watch out—see how the Japanese slice through defences, pillage homes and rape women." Young lads in *hui guan* meetings stand up and deliver speeches denouncing the various Japanese aggressions, fanning the fires of patriotism by singing the "Three Principles of the People". Some days, he sings along. It gives him a measure of relief from the burn in his throat. Other days, he takes photographs.

Feng Yu keeps himself aloof from all the political turbulence; his family's business concerns are tied up with British and Nanyang Chinese interests both. Dual loyalties. In the English papers, a Straits Chinese person writes in: *How can one remain loyal to Malaya and China at the same time?* It sparks a counter-editorial: *Why not call himself Straits British instead of Straits Chinese and be done with it?*

Tian Wei follows the principled Dr. Lim, now returned from his post as principal of Amoy University. Dr. Lim is openly involved in Chinese salvation activities. Dr. Lim can't be wrong. But the more strident voices within the various *hui guan* say his power is limited. At night, sleep is difficult. Tian Wei reads his classics; with all that reading, his eyesight has deteriorated, and he now has to wear glasses. He writes letters, he runs his business, he takes care of his employees, but none of it feels enough. The words in Charlie's last letter are stuck inside him like *susuk* needles. A clock ticks silently. Getting older and feeling older, he realises, are two different things. In the last year, he has not only become older, he feels older. Tian Wei isn't superstitious; he isn't afraid of death either. One could walk outside tomorrow and be run over by a motor car; it is happening often enough with all the cars pootling around, sounding their horns too late, and the lack of traffic lights. Refraining from acting and from doing the right thing, valuing one's life—as he ages, these questions seem more perplexing, not less. Si Nian's words come back to him: *You will regret inaction.*

In 1939, war breaks out in Europe. If one reads *The Straits Times*, one comes away with the impression that these disasters are far away, nothing to do with the East. If one reads the *Malaya Tribune*, one concludes exactly the opposite. To many, life carries on as usual in the sleepy paradise of the tropics. The Japanese brothels close. The Japanese prostitutes are repatriated. People find other amusements. A portion of the Japanese community remains—barbers, shipping clerks, provision store owners, and photographers like Junji Naruto. Ask the general populace and many believe that the British have things well under control. The British sing: "Oh, these Japanese—they got these matchbox aeroplanes, can't do much harm! Consider the Changi Fortress with its heavy artillery and anti-aircraft defences. Consider the newly opened King George V dry dock, the new airfields in Tengah and Sembawang. The Gibraltar of the East! Singapore is impregnable. Even if Singapore comes under attack, the enemy will be swiftly repelled by the vastly superior British military forces."

At night, Tian Wei scans the night sky, infinite stars spangling across a dark dome like crushed ice. He sees once again that room with the belvedere and cameras and the four-poster bed. He sees her, lying down beside him, her face so close it allows him to trace her brow to her eye to the ridge of her nose to the shape of her lips, stroke the downy fuzz of her cheek, hear again the sweetness of her voice, hold again that feeling of insatiable want. What can compare to it? Nothing. Not a thing.

*

Si Nian drops by one morning. He waves his fan at Kee Mun, asking her to run along and get him three *cha shao bao* from the hawker stall down the road. Kee Mun grimaces—she is no longer a kid but a young lady. Tian Wei, in the midst of opening all the shutters, purses his lips. What to do with Si Nian these days? Damned if you do, damned if you don't. Si Nian, who keeps calling him "old buddy", confiding in him about his amours. Si Nian closed his studio during the Depression, and Feng Yu said Si Nian was spending time upcountry, even bought a motor car to enable easy travelling to shepherd his new business interests. Tian Wei did not ask what these new business interests were.

Si Nian takes a seat in a rattan chair, closes his fan with a snap. In his hand is a package. He unties the raffia rope, unwraps a stack of printed handbills. "Need your help, old buddy." It isn't a request.

Chinese characters are scrawled in red: 抗日救亡。 *Resist Japan and Save Our Dying Nation.* "What's this?"

"Handbills to be posted everywhere."

"What do you mean, everywhere?"

Si Nian has grown a slender goatee, and caresses it like a pet mouse. "Everywhere. Shophouse doors. Lamp posts. Vacant walls. Like I said, everywhere."

"Isn't this illegal?"

"I would do it either late at night or early in the morning. And watch behind you for mata-mata."

He has no wish to get entangled with the police. "Do I have a say in this?"

They hear Kee Mun's footsteps. In a minute, she brings in tea and the requested buns. Si Nian drinks his tea and consumes the buns rapidly. He rises, flaps his long tunic to straighten it.

"I must be off. I wouldn't force you to do anything, but I hope you will help me out." He doffs his hat at Tian Wei, and says, "Honourable friend."

It marks the first of several such visits from Si Nian. The next favour is to help the Cantonese leaders who are designing relief boxes to collect donations from Cantonese hawkers and businesses, and, since Tian Wei speaks Cantonese, his help will be indispensable. Another time is to collect donations during a

Cantonese opera performance, and, given his interest in opera, it is difficult for Tian Wei to say he won't be there.

Next, a fundraiser for the Ee Hoe Hean Club.

More handbills with slogans: *Come Together At A Time of National Calamity. Donate in the Name of Nationalism.*

In each case, Tian Wei obliges, hoping that Si Nian will consider the debt repaid. Increasingly, he feels conflicted. Doing more is no bad thing. There are victims of bomb explosions in China, those run out of their houses, those who die on roads and are left as unburied corpses. If standing outside an opera performance collecting money means a child getting food for another day in China, how can this be wrong?

Si Nian asks Tian Wei to stand outside a Japanese provision store and stop people from going in and patronising it. Strong-arm tactics. This is what a number of other Chinese protesters do to embargo Japanese businesses. Tian Wei draws a hard line. What did these Japanese businessmen ever do to him? Junji Naruto trained him, shared with him important publications like the written guidelines by esteemed Japanese photographer Matsuzaki Shinji. Junji Naruto gave him a new lease of life. Without him, there would be no Wang Tian Wei the photographer. So, he refuses. Si Nian's eyes carry a warning: *I'll remember this.*

Even women are mobilised to help. The Chinese Women's Association, comprised of distinguished wives of the Straits Chinese elites, spearhead major fundraisers, no longer just organising language or home economy classes. Other women's groups do the same, organising drama troupes and social activities, going door to door to solicit donations. Kee Mun becomes active in them, far more strident than Tian Wei when it comes to the China cause. Now that she reads fluently, she begs him to get her the magazine *Xi (Play)*, a theatre journal put out by Yuan Muzhi, the lead actor of *Roar, China!* at the Shanghai Theatre Society. A version of this play has been adapted and is being staged at one of the Chinese schools in Singapore, and

Kee Mun has a prime role in it. These days, she spurns the attentions of Foo Lum, declaring she has no wish to get married.

It is Kee Mun who drags Tian Wei to some of the speeches at Tung Teh about marriage reform along Western lines. The colonial government is making concessions for the legal support of concubines and their children left stranded because of a father's death. Meanwhile, missionary societies are agitating for the abolition of the *mui tsai* slavery system and traditional Chinese concubinage practices. Change is in the wind. Up above, the heavy clouds break. Rain descends in sheets of water. Birds, soaked in the flame trees, fall silent.

Young women come to his studio, red-lipped, hair done in marcelled waves, dressed in Western frocks and heels, sporting cigarette cases. They ask to pose in front of mirrors, not looking at the camera, looking at themselves instead. Tradition and modernity, he realises, are not opposed, but rather they tango together as in a fire dance.

He continues writing those letters in service to his dreams. According to the logic of exponential maths, he will not receive any letter from her until the year 1948. And if the warning in her last letter isn't heeded, he will not be alive to receive it. In the harsh sunlight of the tropics, his dreams dissolve like smoke, returning to origin: a place of intense yearning.

1942

War comes first to Malaya, then Singapore. Soldiers swarm across the causeway on bicycles. They swim across the spit of water separating Singapore from peninsula Malaya. Within seventy days, on 15 February 1942, Singapore surrenders to the onslaught of the 25th Japanese Army under the command of General Tomoyuki Yamashita. Tian Wei hears the broadcast from Governor Shenton Thomas on the radio.

It is over. The last month: the cascade of leaflets like rain, acrid black smoke in parts of the city, the screams of air raid sirens, the *rat-a-tat-tat* of strafing artillery fire, the explosions that shake foundations like loose teeth rattling within a dark maw, the dark hulks of bombed buildings, the cracked crevasses in roads, the bodies, the bodies, the bodies. Streets empty of vendors and pedestrians overnight. Windows are blacked out. Those who can do so head north to hide in remote kampongs and encampments. Tian Wei tells his employees to leave for cover if they feel safer elsewhere, but Kee Lung and Kee Mun remain with him. Kee Lung, out to reconnoitre for news every day, tells him that, right after the surrender, the Europeans who remained—men, women, children—were all gathered in the Padang, inspected, and marched off to places unknown. Japanese soldiers in jeeps circle the town, hooting and waving flags. The clock on the Victoria Memorial Theatre has been blown off.

A few days after the surrender, while Kee Lung is out, this time to queue for food before it is all gone, Japanese soldiers walk into Tian Wei's studio and confiscate all his equipment, film, and frames. They requisition the gramophone, the radio, even his silver cigarette case and lighter. "No radios allowed," they bark. Anyone with a radio will be shot. After the looting, they aren't quite done. One of the soldiers seizes Kee Mun by the arm, and she whimpers. Tian Wei rushes to block him and is swiftly knocked out by a rifle-butt. He is lucky that is all they do to him. Kee Mun isn't quite so lucky.

Certain events, when they happen, swallow time. A lifetime rushes by in an instant. *Click.* Thereafter, life is extinguished, though the body remains. A husk housing a wandering spirit.

In the streets, life appears to return to normality. All civil, economic, and administrative functions, all public utilities, return to normal. But life isn't at all the same. For many, it is a canvas of black. Whorls of debris, a mass of seething dark energy. The deep heart of magma, of intolerable fires, is devoid of light. It is the beginning of Occupation.

*

Following the soldiers' visit, Tian Wei sends Kee Mun and Kee Lung up north to Seletar with Si Nian's help. It hurts to think of Kee Mun. He can't do it without wanting to kill something, to destroy with his bare hands. Rage, he understands finally, is murderous; revengeful thoughts engulf and shrivel the soul from within.

One morning, Tian Wei walks outside to get breakfast. The morning sun touches the surface of his skin with filigrees of warmth. The silence is unusual. Even the birds, usually chirping raucously in the morning, aren't to be seen. Except for a lone crow pecking at a sliver of red by the side of a rubbish dump. The shophouses opposite shimmer in the light. There are no Chinese newspapers other than the renamed *Straits Times* as the *Syonan Times*, the *Sin Chew Jit Poh* as the *Syonan Jit Poh*. Without radios, there is no communication with the outside world.

Tian Wei changes his mind about breakfast. Going back indoors, he looks at the date: 8 March 1942. That same morning, an order had arrived from the Japanese administration, saying Wang Tian Wei was to report to a screening centre off Jalan Besar. What is this about? There is of course no breaking the order. He could consult Si Nian, ask him what to do, but Si Nian has requested that communication between them be kept to a minimum—for Tian Wei's own safety. Three months ago, Feng Yu sailed with his family to Jakarta, days after the Japanese soldiers landed in Kota Bahru. The order states that he should prepare provisions for a week to take with him. His studio is on its last legs: the roll-top desk lies on its side, a downed beast; his props a mess of broken chattel; chairs half punched out; broken crockery a rubbled heap in the corner. Kee Mun has swept up, but he hasn't the heart to throw anything out.

A presence in his shophouse doorway. As he turns, the silhouette of a woman is backed by light: the outline of a kimono, a hairbun with large pins threaded through it. She comes into the shop gingerly, her kimono flashing black and gold, its motif of dragons shimmering, as if fireflies are dancing within the folds. She shuffles in her clogs. Shock ripples through him. Aiko-chan.

It couldn't be. And yet it is.

"Tian Wei Ge Ge—" the expression in her eyes deep and intense, a tunnelling back in time— "how have you been keeping?"

"Aiko?" Tian Wei shakes his head to clear it. "How…what… why are you here?"

Aiko is so close, the bags under her eyes are evident. There are tiny moles on her face that weren't there before. "I wasn't sure if your studio would still be here." Her face—the cupidity in it still traceable despite a hardened quality of stolen innocence—is this a mirage? Is Aiko really standing before him as this voluptuous young woman in a kimono? "Everything is still here as I remember it," she says, indicating the broken furniture. "Well, mostly as I remember it."

Tian Wei wants to weep. Puny mortal: he has been unable to protect anybody or anything. The presence of Aiko is karma. When rage recedes, what is left?

"I have such fond memories of this place. Do you remember you used to teach me stories from *Chrita Dahulu Kala* here? Sitting right at this roll-top desk?"

Tian Wei's eyes fill with unshed tears. He nods. "Did you visit your mother and father?"

A small laugh escapes her. "My father and his other wives have sailed for Sumatra. They intend to weather Syonan from there. My mother went back to Japan."

Tian Wei slowly processes this.

"I work now for the Japanese administration as an interpreter. See, all those languages do come in useful. Thanks to you, I can read Mandarin and Bahasa Melayu well."

"You work for the Occupation authorities?" Tian Wei's face pales.

Aiko bows her head. "Remember you once told me that we must do whatever we can to survive. If one is drowning, one must grab on to whatever floats, don't you think?"

Tian Wei is unable to speak.

"I asked for the posting. My husband is a colonel in the army. He leads one of the regiments in the 5th Division under General Matsui."

For a moment, there is nothing to say. Images of destruction and war swim before Tian Wei's eyes, memories that return to haunt and freeze the soul. "Do you want to sit?" he says, recovering his manners finally. "There are a couple of chairs from the third floor I can bring down…"

She shakes her head. "I can't stay long."

"How about coffee? Shall I make tea? I don't have any kueh…"

She bites her lower lip. "I don't need anything. And I have no appetite to eat anything. We don't have time to reminisce." Her voice hushes. "This is probably the last time we will meet, Tian Wei Ge Ge." Tears moisten her eyes again. "I've come to warn you. There will be a mass purge of all those who helped spread anti-Japanese resentment, or participated in activities supporting the China cause. Chinese men between the ages of eighteen and fifty, especially those who helped fundraise for the China Relief Fund or for the Ee Hoe Hean Club, or those who are members of the Kuomintang. Tian Wei Ge Ge, I saw your name on the call-up list, to report for registration. I've come to warn you to go hide."

They stare at each other long and hard. He wants to protest his innocence. Fundraising activities? He hadn't willingly done them. But then, he hadn't refused either, had he? Compliance was proof. "You shouldn't be here then, Aiko-chan. You are putting yourself in danger."

She smiles, sad. "You once risked your life for me. It's a debt I want to repay. Please. Save yourself."

Tian Wei shows her the order he received that morning. "It may be too late."

She grabs his hands. "It is not too late!" Her tone sharpens. "Go north."

"I can't just abandon everything."

Aiko becomes urgent. "There is nothing left for you here, don't you see? You do not have a shop left."

No shop left. No business. No camera, no glass negative. She is absolutely right.

Their leave-taking is abrupt. In wartime, one either indulges in too much banality or too little. Social niceties are not conducted for social reasons. Aiko leaves hurriedly when they hear a battalion march outside, the order in Japanese short and staccato. He watches her disappear and feels a pinch in his gut. Yes, why not save himself? Disobeying the order will put him on the run. But perhaps his days are numbered anyway.

Si Nian is likely hiding in a death house on Sago Lane. Si Nian might be able to help. How ironic—he once feared Si Nian's help, now he seeks it. The Kuomintang operatives or the Ghee Hin will have a way to smuggle people upcountry into the jungles in Malaya. With the Occupation, the Kuomintang and the Communists are once again forced to work together.

He waits until nightfall, sets his affairs in order, writes a letter each to Peng Loon, Yip Kee, Ah Seng, Foo Lum, Kee Mun, and Kee Lung, deposits them in the 1152 box. He packs some clothing and food in a cloth bundle. At the last minute, his eyes fall on the packet of letters he has written to Charlie. His heart seizes; he can't simply leave these behind. He places them in his cloth bundle, padlocks the shop, and hurriedly walks away. He doesn't look back, not once. A turtle is the perfect metaphor for peregrinations; it carries its memories on its back.

The night sky is a vault of velvet, no stars. The air is humid, thick with smoke, although he isn't sure where the smoke is coming from. All the shopfronts are shuttered, the streets deserted. A black cat slinks across his path, hisses, then disappears.

When he reaches Sago Lane, he quickly walks up the side staircase. Inside, a lone tungsten bulb glows a wan yellow. He hears voices. He knocks. When Si Nian opens the door, a cigarette dangling from his lips, dressed in a white singlet and shorts, he sees there are three other men inside. Rough cut. Sallow faced. A bottle of cheap rice wine being shared. A meeting in progress. He has never met these men before.

Si Nian pokes his head out to scour the street behind him, then quickly pulls him inside. "What are you doing here?" he says, roughly. "Are you trying to get us killed?"

"What's going on?"

Si Nian doesn't answer. Tian Wei shows Si Nian the order he got served. Si Nian smirks. All the men around the table do the same, each producing his own order. Si Nian taps his shoulder. "Don't worry, brother, stick with us. See, didn't I tell you? Didn't I say you should join us? We leave in a few days."

"Where are we going?" Tian Wei asks.

Si Nian pushes him down on to a rickety chair. Tips his chin at one of the fellows, who gets up immediately and brings a plate of rice, a hard-boiled egg, some anchovies marinated in sambal paste, smeared on a stamp-sized banana leaf. "Don't worry about the details. Eat, keep up your strength. You'll need it."

*

The day they are meant to leave is the thirteenth—coincidence? That morning, Si Nian packs up his meagre belongings, collects the shirt he has washed from the line and pulls it on. The men staying in Si Nian's lodgings come and go mysteriously; whenever Tian Wei tries to ask, Si Nian makes a motion of two fingers pinching his lips closed. *Understand this*, the gesture says, *the less you know, the better.* If caught, he won't be able to give away what he doesn't know, even if they break all his knuckles and tear out his tongue.

But he has ears and eyes; he suspects these men are all K.M.T. members in hiding. The plan is to leave that day on foot. They will walk to the border, where a small boat will row them across the Straits to Johore. That is all Si Nian is willing to say.

Si Nian scoots out first thing in the morning, but at about ten, he comes back with newspapers, food, and cigarettes. Packets of rice with rancid soya sauce, a measly slice of *char siu*—poor rations. But the men fall upon it, slavering like wolves. The last few days, Tian Wei has tried to talk to some of them, sandwiched between them on thin bedrolls at night, but they are not a talkative lot, preferring to smoke, drink, and play cards. One of them has a bad squint, another has rotting teeth. Coolies, roped into the K.M.T. because of families back in the homeland. One of them, though, notices the letters that Tian Wei keeps on his person at all times, notices that he even sleeps with them. "What are them? Sweetheart letters?" The man grins and hawks up spit. Tian Wei sees no reason to enlighten him.

Si Nian walks in with a limp. Is he hurt? His glasses are broken, hastily taped back together. A bad bruise on his wrist. "Listen, I need a favour. There is a provision store run by a Kumamoto-san. A man named Mamoru Shinozaki has prepared false papers for us—Kumamoto has them. Can you go collect them for me?"

"Why me?"

"The Kempeitai is keeping tabs on me. I don't want to send any of the others—" he indicates them, one sitting with a leg up, pinching off his overgrown toenails, another lifting a butt-cheek to fart—"it is critical this mission doesn't fail. You understand? Our lives are depending on you now."

Tian Wei says nothing, his chest stuffy and uneasy.

"We leave under cover of night. This evening. We need those papers. With those papers, and dressed as Malays, we may have some hope of being let go, even if we are stopped. You speak Malay; we need you with us."

Tian Wei hesitates.

"Trust me, please," Si Nian finishes.

10:30 a.m. on the clock. What choice does he have? A Chinese philosophical concept comes to him: *wu wei* (无为). The way of Tao dictates that the best action is to flow like water, to bend like bamboo in the wind. All action in compliance with the natural flow of the cosmos.

He nods. As he walks out the door, one of the men opens a *pintu-pagar* shutter and the dim, squalid interior is flooded with stabs of light, leaving him momentarily blinded.

*

At Kumamoto's provision store, no papers. Kumamoto-san frowns. "This some mistake?" he asks. "Papers collected yesterday, ne?"

It throws Tian Wei into confusion. Did Si Nian send him here as a ploy so he and his comrades could leave without him? He, not being a staunch K.M.T. member, is deadweight Si Nian doesn't need to carry around while they are on the run. Or is it a different kind of trap? Is Si Nian in trouble of some kind, coming back as he did, all bruised and dishevelled?

On his way back, a jeep full of Japanese soldiers in khaki uniforms screeches to a halt, cutting off his path. Three soldiers jump out and a rifle digs into his ribs. They drag him off to the side. Dimly, he realises that his puzzled mental condition has led him straight up High Street, and now he is standing not far from Junji Naruto's studio. They push him down to his knees, reading various charges against him. They call out the name Tang Si Nian. The truth dawns on him then, the irony of it, the craziness of destiny, the madness of fate which cannot be avoided. Charlie had sent a desperate letter to warn him, but without the various pieces of the puzzle, he couldn't have known how to avoid it. When he met Si Nian, he had been struck by the similarities between them and their photographic journeys. Now it looks like those similarities have finally caught up with him. Laughter bubbles up his sternum—bitter, hyena-like—Tang Si Nian he is not, would never wish to be; they have the wrong body, but it is no use, he won't be believed. Instead of being buried in an unmarked grave, what does it mean to be buried under a false identity? Is this how we die, with burning questions on our lips?

He doesn't feel it coming. There is just a whistling in his ears. A woodenness in his head. The last cry in his heart: Charlie. The last thing he sees is a tiny black ant, crawling its way to the sanctuary of a crack in the paved road. The ant makes it. Tian Wei doesn't.

Theatre of Light

I have moved back to London, but periodically I am lucky enough to be invited to work with museums in Singapore. This stint as chief curator of an exhibition at SCoP entitled "Fashion and Dress in Early Twentieth Century Nanyang" is a big step up for me. I'm conducting the Curator's Tour when I hear the call of a name behind me. A name that has sailed across the stars and jolts me so much I stop in my tracks.

I turn.

Two young friends are walking together: one in a long-sleeved denim shirt and khaki chinos, another in a blue suit with a Hawaiian shirt inside. The sleeves of his jacket are pushed up to his elbows, and he is easily six foot two. His physique is that of a rugby player: broad shouldered, cabled muscles along his forearms. A crew cut. Cheekbones, chiselled jaw. I thought I heard someone call him Wang Tian Wei.

I stare with such intensity that they can't help but notice me. I put a hand out. "Excuse me for my odd question. Is your name really Wang Tian Wei?"

He gives a start. "No—" his expression is bemused— "it's Benedict."

His friend looks at me as if I were possibly insane. Probably I am, conjuring an auditory hallucination like I did. Benedict's eyes take me in. I watch it happen in slow time: something ancient like recognition, forgetting to blink, his silent swallow, the stillness overtaking his body.

My hands come together. "This sounds crazy, but would you like to join my tour? I'm an archivist, also the curator of this exhibition. I promise you the tour will be interesting."

He looks at his friend, then again at me.

Please say yes, my eyes beseech him.

His nod is slow, but it isn't reluctance, it's hope. Fear of future bliss.

After the tour, he asks if he can have my number.

Our first date is by the bank of the Singapore River, near Robertson Quay, where one late summer evening, we see an incongruous gaudy pink pavilion set up in a broad green field. A bridalwear trade show, the huge sign announces. At least fifteen brides in white billowing gowns are floating about like lost swans. And as many gawky penguin grooms. A stunning floral archway hangs across the entrance.

银河系—Milky Way in Chinese. So corny.

My cheeks flush red. "I didn't plan this route, I'm not suggesting anything."

His head swivels towards the sounds of wild bird cries in a nearby flame tree. A flock of them are roosting, hidden deep within its leaves. A sense of déjà vu invades. We barely see the birds, but we hear them. A small aircraft arcs across the blue sky, drawing a huge heart in white plumes, skywriting in Chinese, 一生一死, 独一无二。

More cheesiness. Because the Chinese are so restrained when it comes to expressing emotions, the vocabulary for romantic love is studded with cliches and shorthand. I've finally learned the cliched homophones of 1314—"in life and death", and 1152—"only you and no other". These are numbers couples might text to each other to say these *rou ma* hackle-raising things. But here's the thing about numbers I've just come to realise: there is a connection in how numbers are invoked. A photograph stored in SaneCloud is a medley of numbers; each stroke of a Chinese character is a number; time is measured by a basic unit of numbers; a photograph is a unit of time. Or several units. Connect it in zig-zag, a photograph can also be a measure of numbers. If love had to be represented by a number, then the Q.E.'s numeral coincidences were telling me that certain moments in our lives were prime numbers, divisible only by itself and one, like the number thirteen—unique, alone, unsolvable by other equations. There may never be an explanation for how Tian Wei and I were able to connect, to feel this avalanche of feelings, to experience the watershed of events that tumbled my world.

Benedict and I don't end up dating. But his appearance in my life is not coincidental. His great-grandfather was Wong Yip Kee, who worked in a photographic establishment on Hill Street in the 1920s before marrying and establishing his own studio in Ipoh. His great-grandfather always felt he owed a great deal to his kind and generous employer, a man he deemed a *wen ren*, which was what this employer had aspired during his life to be. When this employer died—he was executed by the Occupation authorities during the war—they had found a fat bundle of letters on him. It seemed that, for a period of at least a decade, he had corresponded with a certain Miss C., and they had always assumed he was a confirmed old bachelor!

Benedict hopes to piece together the story behind the letters. Not all the letters have survived intact—some are sentence fragments, others are yesteryear postcards.

I ask, with my heart in my mouth, if I can see them.

He says yes.

*

21 September 1933

Dearest Miss C.:—

Since last year, the newspapers have been
reporting on the Japanese attacks in Shanghai.
With few friends or family left in Shanghai,
I have no use for such news. Nevertheless,
they sink my spirit. I continue to dwell
on your notion of "beauty". I believe it is
something the writer Lu Xun wrote about. Not
all densities are the same, not all have the
same grain. Light and dark together form a
theatre. A photograph is a theatre of light.

7 January 1936

Dearest Miss C.:—

I had a dream of you today.

In it, we were both in Shanghai, sneaking
into Whiteaway, Laidlaw on Nanjing Road — we
weren't going to take anything. Five floors
in this Emporium, with unbelievable offerings
of foreign goods—you tried on a cloche hat, I
watched an electric train go round and round on
its track for a good hour. We held hands, we had
a fine cream tea in the lovely art-deco cafe on
the top floor, sunlight streaming in from one of
the tall windows and bathing us in gold.

In my dream, you sipped from your cup and
asked me if I'd ever been to London.

I remembered you'd told me you had grown
up there.

We talked for hours that day. We talked until the sun set and dusk arrived.

I asked if we should go, but you smiled and said, "We have all the time in the world."

11 January 1940

Dearest Miss C.:—

What does it mean to have memories of your childhood come back to you on melancholic days? Is this acute nostalgia? Is it a sign that death is coming?

There was a noodle stall on Bubbling Well Road. The noodle-seller there would always spare a bowl of noodles for me. Squatting in a corner, I would watch well-dressed ladies step in and out of broughams and phaetons. Melodies floated out of windows and doorways, sometimes Russian, sometimes French. Once, a white lady came out of a church, saw a stray dog and said, "Shoo," then saw me and said, "Shoo!" again. Life was very hard, and I often went to sleep hungry. I sometimes thought dying would be easier.

Dreams of you come rarely, but when they come, I wake up feeling as if the dream was long, that it went on and on, and I never want it to stop. Fragments come back to me, such beautiful, cherished fragments that warm me from within my soul: how you slept in my embrace, snuggled up close; how ...

11 November 1939

Dearest Miss C.:—

I remember that moment when you fell asleep
— you were in the middle of a sentence you
didn't finish, your lips still parted, but I
could feel your measured breathing. I sensed
I had to go; if I stayed any longer, I would
never leave. As I floated out through the
terrace doors, I looked up at the night sky.
The stars above were tiny points of light. I
turned back towards you, to imprint you in
my memory. You stirred, you mumbled in your
sleep, but though I strained to catch what you
said, I couldn't. I was already too far away.

5 February 1942

My dearest Miss C.:—

Much bombing outside. These days, I wake
at four a.m. It is a curious hour, in between
night and dawn — and I long for you so much it
feels that the song from my heart must dance
through the celestial realm to get to you. I
wonder then if you will remember me. I wonder
what stories you will tell of me. I love you,
and always will.

*

For a couple of years after I sent the warning letter to Tian
Wei, I waited for a reply. He never wrote back. Every day, I
checked the newspaper archives to see if the article about a

photographer being killed by the *genchi shobun* method would miraculously vanish. But it never did.

Now the truth is revealed.

A photograph on glass is indeed a sedimentation of time—sand transmuting itself into glass that captures light. Through the sands of history, an image is retained. Tian Wei, I have dreamed of you, too. In one dream, you are dressed as always: sharp cream linen suit, a fedora on your knee, hair neatly combed. You have aged slightly, and you wear glasses. Black squarish frames, they make you look stylish. A *wen ren*. Next to you on the simple rustic bench is a book. Perhaps a book of Tang poetry. Together with this book is a hand-drawn picture of a woman. She poses on a bed, legs tucked underneath her, the collar of her shirt pulled down to reveal a rounded knob of shoulder, one hand tossed into her mussed hair, the other cradling her cheek. Her eyes shine. It is a picture about desire, about the slow dance of seduction, pure and innocent. It is a picture about seeing a woman. Seeing, truly seeing, with the eyes we all have in our hearts, that which cannot be named or easily pinned down. The woman in it glows. The woman is me. I am glowing.

All The Lost Futures

Of all the surprising coincidences one might find in life (and I certainly have had my fair share)—I'm scheduled for the midnight flight back to Heathrow from Singapore, and who should I meet while going through airport security? Matt Sharpe. We seem destined to bump elbows in airports.

An Asian woman is going through the checkpoint with him, rapidly stuffing laptop and iPad back into her rucksack, her iPhone into the back pocket of her jeans. Matt is looping his belt and recognises me immediately. I had heard he moved out of the Guest Lodge shortly after I moved to Bishan. We text periodically, but we did not meet up again.

He introduces me to his girlfriend, Sam Teoh. They're bound for Machu Pichu, on holiday. He asks about Sebastian, and I tell him that Sebastian's business is now doing remarkably well. "Adnan?" Matt enquires. I tell him they speak every once in a while; they are still friends. But Sebastian is now dating a woman from a wealthy Indonesian Chinese family, as fickle as he when it comes to hobbies. Matt laughs. I don't mention that Sebastian is thinking of settling down—not with this Indonesian woman, but with a house. He has plans to do a complete renovation of Peony's *lao jia*. I don't tell him that, even though Sebastian and I are good, something was lost— an innocence. Our bond has been strengthened as siblings, weakened as best friends. The line we drew has hardened, cementing our dealings with each other. We've never spoken about that night again.

As Matt and I part ways, I watch his disappearing back with a feeling akin to regret. All our lost futures. How many relationships have begun in the last few years, while an epidemic raged and swallowed time? How many have ended? As relationships morph, become new connections, they engender new pathways. Whether that connection becomes something more than touch, sidle, bump, or collision, is that destiny or choice? Does anyone really know the truth of the matter?

*

The light is grey; it's early dawn when I let myself back into my mother's apartment, the place I grew up in, which I now call home. When I first moved back here, I found traces of my upbringing in unlikely places. Tucked behind the accordion radiator was a fallen cartoon drawing of mine. Up the chimney, hidden in a nook, a Barbie doll's blond head of hair that I ripped off in a fit of pique when I heard what the nanny said about me on the phone: *spoilt brat, crybaby*.

Looking out through the tall French windows, I remember my mother taking me to the garden square opposite. She wore a sunhat, sat on one of the benches and read. Puppy-like, I ran back and forth, fetching curious offerings I found: a leaf, a funny-shaped pebble, a ladybird, and once a used condom. These memories puncture me, settle in my body like warmth from the sun. When feelings change, memories do too.

What are memories but coincidences you've forgotten? The chimney of the fireplace needs a proper sweep. In mid-sentence, while talking to the engineer, I remember sitting in my mother's lap, being read to from a book of Chinese mythology. I'd snuggled in like a little cub, pillowing my hands in the cradle of my mother's neck.

I no longer refer to her as Mother, with a capital M, she is "my mother". This is a suggestion from my therapist, whom I've been seeing the last three years—on Zoom, if we can't physically meet. They mentioned that personalising my experience of my mother might continue the journey of letting her reveal herself to me.

At the centre of what Tian Wei means to me is the photograph. Some say that a photograph is inherently and ultimately performative. As object, phenomenon, and transaction, the camera tells and shields the truth simultaneously. But it is also true that, in front of it, I have been reconstituted, (re)framed. The camera keeps me honest.

I have come to terms with what transpired between me and Tian Wei and Sebastian. To say this is to learn to live with ghosts. To express the silent text of the psyche. For me to open myself to all my possible futures, I had to move beyond the third space—that small, lit space—between us.

Here I am. A woman left with intense longing. An intense longing for love from another time and place, love impossible to fathom. Uncontainable and mysterious. What is real isn't always physical. Our past prepares us for all the love we are able to receive in the future. There once was someone who opened up the pastures of my heart and prepared me for the return of wound and fire and a 从头到尾 kind of love that slips time and boundaries.

List of Characters 2019–23

Adnan, Sebastian's boyfriend and business partner
Atalina, Cassandra's helper
Benedict Wong, Wong Yip Kee's great-grandson
C. Sebastian Sze-Toh
Cassandra Sze-Toh, stepmother to Charlie and Sebastian
Charlene ("Charlie") Sze-Toh
Derek Tsai, a Chinese spirit medium
Eloise Sze-Toh, Laurent's wife
Evelyn, Charlene's mother, deceased
Laurent Sze-Toh, Charlie's second stepbrother
Linton Sze-Toh, Charlie's stepbrother
Linus Sze-Toh, Charlie's father
Madeleine Sze-Toh, Linton's wife
Mahmood, Charlie's archival assistant
Marcus Lo, Charlie's first boy-crush
Mason Wee Sun, Linton's second son
Matt Sharpe, friend
Miles Wee Jun, Linton's son
Oriole, fellow theatre actress, friend of Peony's
Peony, Sebastian's mother, deceased
Xueling, Zhou Zhen's wife
Yoo-lin, Charlie's second assistant
Zhou Zhen, photographic artist

List of Characters 1920–42

Ah Lan, *mui tsai* girl-slave working at Cherry Blossom
Ah Seng, photograph retoucher
Aiko, adopted Japanese daughter of Hudson Tay
Aw Boon Haw, tiger balm merchant (historical figure)
Bibi Gemuk, matchmaker
Dr. Lim Boon Keng (walk-on historical figure)
Foo Lum, Tian Wei's new assistant
G. R. Lambert (historical figure and renowned studio)
Hatsumoto-san, photographer and proprietor of Nikko Studios, Penang
Hudson Tay, Chinese Baba and mercantile owner of many businesses, Aiko's father
Kee Lung, shophouse assistant
Kee Mun, shophouse assistant, twin sister of Kee Lung
Lin Feng Yu ("Philip"), Tian Wei's friend
Master Ouyang Shizhi and Powkee Studio (historical figure and studio)
Mr. Ki, the hired gangster who held Aiko captive by order of her father
Ohatsu-san, *mamasan* at Cherry Blossom Brothel in Penang
Pastor Cheng Ping Ting (walk-on historical figure)
Peng Loon, darkroom assistant
Reverend Goh Hood Keng (walk-on historical figure)
Sansan, Tian Wei's childhood friend in Shanghai
Sister Yuk, Aiko's chaperone
Sng Choon Yee (historical figure)
Tan Kah Kee, the "Henry Ford of Malaya" (historical figure)
Tang Si Nian, fellow Chinese photographer
Teo Eng Hock (historical figure)
The Coroner
Tomoko-san, Aiko's mother
Wang Tian Wei, a Chinese photographer
Wong Yip Kee, glass negatives assistant

Explanatory Note on "Foreign" Words

Words not found in the Oxford Dictionary are italicised, except when these words appear in dialogue (the speaker in this particular setting would not have regarded them as foreign words) or in the letters from Tian Wei (as these words would not appear italicised on a typewriter).

The main text uses Roman pinyin throughout. Mandarin characters are written as they present in letters, text messages, sky-writing, cast as a sculpture, embroidered on a hankie, emblazoned across a floral archway, or written as a note. In other cases, except in dialogue (where Mandarin is sounded), Mandarin characters are inserted in brackets for Chinese philosophical concepts (because they reference a realm of tradition and knowledge); as historical reference, such as *zhi shi fen zi* (referencing a literati of a time and place); and cultural reference, such as tangki practices and symbols, and the art of portraiture (*chuanshen xieying*). All other Mandarin phrases are included in the Glossary, followed by the Mandarin characters.

Lastly, the Glossary is provided here as a tool of convenience for global readers; undoubtedly, the Internet can provide far more comprehensive explanations (complete with images).

Glossary

*ah beng (*Hokkien/Singlish)—pejorative term for uneducated or lower class youth

*ah lian (*Hokkien/Singlish)—female equivalent of *ah beng*

*ah-ku (*Cantonese)—Cantonese word for woman or lady, irrespective of age, but in this context, it is a polite term of address for a Chinese prostitute in colonial Singapore

amituofo / 阿弥陀佛 (Mandarin)—Chinese transliteration of the Sanskrit "Amithabha" that Buddhists use to greet or well-wish and means "immeasurable light and immeasurable life"

*anak dara (*Malay)—unmarried young girl

*angpau (*Hokkien)—red packet filled with money usually handed out to children or unmarried sons and daughters during the Lunar New Year. It is also handed out as a wedding gift or during other auspicious occasions, such as moving into a new house or opening a new business

*ayam buah keluak (*Malay)—mildly spicy traditional Peranakan dish of chicken, tamarind paste, shrimp paste, galangal, lemongrass and candlenut

ba gua za zhi / 八卦杂志 (Mandarin)—gossip tabloids

Baba (Malay)—Peranakan male. The female is referred to as *nyonya*.

*babi pongteh (*Malay)—traditional Peranakan dish of braised pork in fermented soybean sauce

bai jiu /白酒 (Mandarin)—liquor

*baju (*Malay)—shirt or blouse, but in colonial times, referred more generically to tailored garments for the upper body, both male and female

*baju kebaya (*Malay)—female Peranakan style of dress involving a short cotton or chiffon blouse and a sarong skirt of batik. It is more form-fitting than the *baju panjang* and signified modernity when it was first introduced as fashion. It is still worn by Peranakan women today as cultural dress.

baju Panjang (Malay)—long cotton blouse paired with a long sarong skirt (often batik) worn by women that was typical of an older era of Malay dress which gave way to the kebaya in the 1920s and 1930s

ban tu er fei / 半途而废 (Mandarin)—Chinese idiom that means "giving up halfway"

bawang puteh (Malay)—white onion

becak (Malay)—rickshaw

belachan (or *belacan*) (Malay)—condiment made of shrimp paste as an accompaniment to Malay, Eurasian and Peranakan meals

betul sekali (Malay)—right you are

bomoh (Malay)—witch doctor or Malay shaman

bubur chacha (Malay)—sweetened coconut milk dessert containing usually pearled sago, tapioca jelly, sweet potato, yams, and bananas, and can be served hot or cold

chap ji kee (Hokkien)—"Twelve cards", an illegal lottery widespread in colonial Singapore, based on an old Chinese game, believed to have started in Johore in the 1890s

char kway teow (Hokkien/Teochew)—stir-fried flat noodles with chicken or shrimp, and cockles, of Southern Chinese origin and popular as a dish in Southeast Asia

char siu (Cantonese)—roast pork Cantonese style

cha shao bao / 叉烧包 (Mandarin)—roast pork bun

chee cheong fun (Cantonese)—steamed rice roll with different inserted ingredients such as *char siu*, prawns or beef, also known as *cheung fun*, which is served in dim sum restaurants

chin chai (also spelled as *cincai*) (Manglish/Singlish)—"loose" or "easy"

chinchalok (Malay)—Malay condiment originating from Malacca, tracing back to Portuguese origin, made from fermented shrimp or krill

choi! (Cantonese)—expression to dispel bad luck

cong tou dao wei / 从头到尾 (Mandarin)—from head to toe

chope (Singlish)—Singaporean slang typically meaning "reserving a place" in a restaurant or eatery by putting a packet of tissues on the table. Here, used as a metaphor to bag a name

chuanshen xieying / 传神写影 (Mandarin)—transmission of the spirit by depicting shadow image or reflection

dabao (Cantonese/Singlish)—takeaway or doggie bag

daging babi (Malay)—slab of raw pork

du dou / 肚兜 (Mandarin)—an embroidered diamond-shaped cloth panel that drapes over the bare chest of the *tangki* during a ritual possession, also called a "stomacher" as worn by a baby to prevent colic. This is because a *tangki* is known as a child spirit medium, a half-filled spiritual vessel, though he may physically be an adult.

er nai / 二奶 (Mandarin)—mistress

erzi / 儿子 (Mandarin)—son

fan tian fu di / 翻天覆地 (Mandarin)—earth somersaulting with sky

fan xing / 反省 (Mandarin)—to self-reflect

fatt-gow (Cantonese)—pink-coloured buns made of rice flour

fei wen / 绯闻 (Mandarin)—fake news or false reportage or rumours

feng xian hua / 凤仙花 (Mandarin)—*Impatiens glandulifera*, a kind of herb used in traditional Chinese medicine to dispel wind.

fu lu / 符箓 (Mandarin)—Taoist incantation or magic symbol, translated roughly as "talismanic script", written or painted with red cinnabar ink on yellow paper as a talisman to ward off evil, usually issued by a Taoist priest or practitioner at a temple

fu pin / 福品 (Mandarin)—lucky items that may be sold following a spirit possession ritual to raise donations

garang (Malay)—ferocious, fierce

Ge Ge / 哥哥 (Mandarin)—elder brother

genchi shobun (Japanese)—a method of killing called "disposal on the spot" through shooting employed by the Kempeitai during the Japanese Occupation of Malaya and Singapore

gin pahit (Malay)—alcoholic drink made with gin and Angostura bitters popular in colonial Malaya among planters and civil service officers

guazi lian /瓜子脸 (Mandarin)—face shaped like a melon seed

gua jia / 国家 (Mandarin)—country (here used with nationalistic overtones)

hancur hati (Malay)—my heart is crushed

hong dou tang /红豆汤 (Mandarin)—red bean soup dessert

huang hua li /黄花梨 (Mandarin)—yellow flowering pear (to describe a certain type of wood)

huat-soh (Hokkien)—the process of purifying or cleansing an area of evil spirits prior to the commencement of a *tangki* spirit possession ritual

hui guan/会馆 (Mandarin)—association or society

hun dan / 混蛋 (Mandarin)—an arsehole

hutong/ 胡同 (Mandarin)—ancient city lane or alleyway in China

ikan masak merah (Malay)—Malay dish of fish in spicy red sauce

jing shui bu fan he shui/井水不犯河水 (Mandarin)—Chinese proverb meaning "well water does not cross river water", mind your own business, or do not interfere in each other's business.

jook (Cantonese)—rice porridge, usually eaten for breakfast

jou gai (Cantonese)—pejorative term for "becoming a prostitute"

kacang puteh (Malay)—tasty treat sold by street vendors in Malaysia and Singapore comprised of an assorted mix of salted nuts as a snack

kai wan xiao / 开玩笑 (Mandarin)—Are you joking?

Kak (short for Kakak) (Malay)—elder sister

karayuki-san (Japanese)—Japanese term that literally means "going to China" used to describe rural women from the Amakusa island and Shimabara Peninsula who headed to Southeast Asia to earn a living; it became the form of address for Japanese women prostitutes in colonial Singapore

kawan (Malay)—friend

kaypoh (Singlish)—busybody

kim zua (Hokkien)—paper items burned for the dead

kolek (Malay)—Malayan traditional canoe rigged with a rectangular sail

koon sah or *baju* Shanghai (Hokkien/Malay)—Chinese style blouse or top paired with a long skirt worn by women that was typical of the pre-1930s era before the advent of the *qipao*

kopi (Malay/Singlish)—the local coffee in Malaysia and Singapore, and it comes in different versions, e.g. *kopi c, kopi c kosong, kopi siew dai*

kopitiam (Malay/Hokkien)—local cafe/diner in Malaysia and Singapore

kuali (Malay)—frying pan that's essentially a wok

Ku-Ku (Cantonese)—paternal aunt

kuat hei (Cantonese)—"bone gas" or courage

kueh (Malay)—sweet pastries and cakes

kueh lapis (Malay)—of Indonesian-Dutch origins, it is a layered cake (up to 18 layers!) made with spices, and very rich. There is a steamed Chinese version with nine layers, called *jiu cheng gao.*

kueh pie tee (mixture of Hokkien and Malay)—a Peranakan appetizer (also called "Top Hat" in Malacca) which is comprised of a crispy pastry cup and filled with delicious sauteed jicama, carrots, fermented soy bean and/or prawns

lan gwai (Cantonese)—Cantonese expletive roughly translated as "damn ghost" or "fucking ghost"

lao jia /老家 (Mandarin)—hometown, or childhood home

lap ngap (Cantonese)—Chinese waxed duck or cured duck dish, served in a variety of ways, especially during Lunar New Year

li / 礼 (Mandarin)—proper custom or ritual

lor mei (Cantonese)—an olden-day dish of red stew made with pork offal, cuttlefish and tofu puffs

lou ban (Cantonese)—boss

Luo Shu / 洛书—The Luo Shu is the magic map of the seven stars received by Yu the Great, founder of the proto-Chinese Xia dynasty (2070-1600 BCE), from heaven. Imprinted on the shell of a turtle from the Luo River, it sets out the Eight Trigrams or bagua (八卦) in which numbers connect in a zig-zag pattern to a central number. Yu the Great danced this zig-zag pattern unceasingly for thirteen years to combat the demons of a great flood.

luo ye gui gen / 落葉歸根 (Mandarin)—fallen leaves must return to their roots

ma fan (Cantonese)—bother or bothersome

majie /妈姐 (Mandarin)—women, predominantly from the Shunde area in Guangdong, China, who worked as domestic helpers in colonial

Singapore or Malaya, identifiable by their hair buns and traditional samfu outfit of white Mandarin-collared top and black trousers. These women had taken an oath never to marry. The term means "mother, sister" and references their role of taking care of children as well as the household.

ma la huo guo /麻辣火锅 (Mandarin)—spicy Sichuan hotpot dish into which you dip raw veggies and meat to cook at table

malu (Malay)—ashamed

mamasan (Japanese)—brothel hostess

mambang (Malay)—spirit or ghost

mata-mata (Malay)—police

mee udang (Malay)—prawn noodles

mengkuang (Malay)—screw pine or palm from the genus "pandanus" local to the coastal Southeast Asia and Pacific Islands regions and used often to weave mats and baskets in local arts and craft

mi zhu cheng fan / 米煮成饭 (Mandarin)—rice grain has become cooked rice

mui tsai (Cantonese)—girl-servant or girl-slave

nasi lemak (Malay)—rice made with coconut milk that comes with a choice of anchovies, curried or fried chicken, peanuts, sambal, hard-boiled egg and cucumber

nasi ambeng (Malay)—dish containing usually steamed rice with curry or soya-sauced chicken, boiled egg, tofu, *sambal*, and a salad of steamed vegetables; most popular in Indonesia, but also within Malay communities in Malaysia and Singapore

nian gao / 年糕 (Mandarin)—glutinous rice cake, usually served during Lunar New Year

nipah (Malay)—a species of *nypa fruticans*, also known as mangrove palm, which grows on the shorelines of Southeast Asia

obi (Japanese)—sash tied around the waist to fasten a kimono

okasan (Japanese)—mother

okonomiyaki (Japanese)—pancake sold as popular street food; the name literally means "grilled as you like it"

ondeh-ondeh (Malay)—made of pandan-infused dough, the inside is filled with gula melaka or palm molasses and covered with desiccated coconut. It's a cake/dessert and popular in Malaysia, Singapore and Indonesia.

pantang (Malay)—taboo

piao piao lang lang / 飘飘朗朗 (Mandarin)—to be adrift at sea, buffeted by waves

pilu (Malay)—melancholy

pintu-pagar (Malay)—double-panelled wooden doors in colonial style shophouses in Nanyang *po-po* / 婆婆 (Mandarin)—maternal grandmother

qing di / 情敌 (Mandarin)—love rival

qipa / 奇葩 (Mandarin)—rare flowers

qipao / 旗袍 (Mandarin)—Chinese form-fitting dress for women

ren ai zheng yi / 仁爱仁正义 (Mandarin)—Each character embodies a Chinese philosophical concept, and here, represented together as a saying encompassing the Chinese notions of benevolence (or compassion and love of humanity), love, justice and righteousness.

rou ma / 肉麻 (Mandarin)—so corny or sentimental as to raise the hackles

samisen (Japanese)—three-stringed musical instrument played with a plectrum called bachi

samseng (Singlish)—hooligan or gangster (the word is derived from Hokkien)

San Qing / 三清 (Mandarin)—triumvirate of Pure Ones, the highest deities in the Tao pantheon

sanggul (Malay)—chignon or hair bun

sapu tangan (Malay)—handkerchief

sayang-sayang (Malay)—lovey-dovey

sei foh (Cantonese)—expletive meaning "we are doomed"

sekejap sahaja (Malay)—only for a little while

seong-tai (Cantonese)—matchmaking meeting between prospective bride and groom

sibuk (Malay)—busy

sin tua (Hokkien)—makeshift home temple or altar

sinkeh / 新客 (Hakka converted to English)—guest people or new Chinese immigrant

sireh (Malay)—betelnut

stengah (Malay)—popular drink with British subjects made with half whisky and half soda water served over ice in colonial Malaya (the word *stengah* means "half" in Malay)

susuk needles (Malay)—charm needles used by Malay shamans as talismans, made with gold or precious metals

tai-tai / 太太 (Mandarin & Cantonese)—wealthy married woman

tak boleh (Malay)—cannot

tampal kasut (Malay)—cobbler

tangki / 乩童 (Hokkien)—Chinese spirit medium, also known as a "child diviner"; they may physically be an adult, but are considered a child spiritually

taufufah (Cantonese)—sweet bean-curd dessert or snack

Taukeh Besar (Malay)—Big Boss

tieguanyin / 铁观音 (Mandarin)—variety of Chinese oolong tea also called "Iron Buddha" originally from Fujian Province, China

tikar (Malay)—mat

toh tao (Hokkien)—main assistant of a *tangki* in a spirit possession ceremony/ritual

topi (Malay)—hat

towchang (Hokkien reading of the Mandarin *bian zi* / 辫子meaning queue)—a hairstyle for men during the reign of the Manchus, where the front and sides of the head were shaved, but the back was a long-plaited queue (also known as the pigtail)

tsuzumi (Japanese)—Japanese hand drum with a wooden body shaped like an hourglass

tutup (as in mode of dress) (Malay)—male colonial style of dress involving a white jacket top

ulu (Malay)—backward

wan yau sei kai (Cantonese)—to travel the world

wen ren / 文人 (Mandarin)—a cultured person or literati

wo de tian ah / 我的天啊 (Mandarin)—an expletive similar to "My God" or "heavens"

wo ai ni /我爱你 (Mandarin)—I love you

wu wei / 无为 (Mandarin)—a Chinese philosophical concept from the Tao that perhaps can be translated as "inaction" or following the order of nature or the universe (quite impossible to summarise as a definition)

xian shui mei /咸水妹 (Mandarin)—salt-water maid (derogatory term for prostitute)

xian dai nü zi / 现代女子(Mandarin)—modern women

xiao san /小三 (Mandarin)—little three, or mistress

Xifu (Cantonese)—Master, used as a term of respect similar to "Teacher"

yat ji (Cantonese)—calendar date

Yi-Ma (Cantonese)—Second Aunt

you tiao /油条 (Mandarin)—long, fried piece of dough, or "fritters", usually had for breakfast along with rice porridge

yukata (Japanese)—summer kimono, usually made of cotton

zhang san li si / 张三李四 (Mandarin)—any Tom, Dick or Harry (closest equivalent)

zhi shi fen zi / 知识分子 (Mandarin)—learned person (a person who could be considered part of the Chinese intelligentsia)

zong nam heng nui (Cantonese)—to privilege sons over daughters

Author's Note

Toni Morrison famously said, "If there's a book you want to read, but it hasn't been written yet, then you must write it."

This is that book for me.

I was first drawn to the period of the 1920s and 1930s in Singapore through the history of photography, looking at how the invention of photography changed the world then, just as digital technology has changed ours. Scouring through thousands of photographs in the National Archives Singapore as part of an early historian grant, particularly delving into the Lee Brothers Studio archive (which alone had over 2,500 photographs), I was much affected by the gazes panned back at me by the subjects in front of the camera, ghostly and yet with a solidity that breathed, *The past is alive*. It thrummed with truths we have not deciphered. Their gazes were different from the colonial gaze that much colonial era literature about Malaya has hitherto offered; this gaze wants to tell a different story, a micro-narrative that historian James Warren has called "intimate viewpoints of history".

In trying to understand this gaze, I began to read, and I began to understand. The Japanese Occupation might have been a cataclysm that cleaved time into a Before and After for Malaya, but war is seldom a singular happening, and the research showed me a world in upheaval, in the lead-up to the Second World War and the Occupation. Fiction tends to spotlight the dramatic "firework" events, but I was more drawn to historical facts I didn't know much about, e.g. that there was a lively Japanese community in Malaya pre-Second World War, and that one segment of this community was in the brothel business; that photography studios were majority-owned by Cantonese photographers; that these Chinese photography studios were in turn influenced by how studios were run in places like Shanghai and Hong Kong; that, besides advocating for Chinese causes and political issues, much anti-imperialist propaganda was spread through not just the Kuomintang, but also a network of Chinese reading societies, becoming a distinct threat to the colonial government. These side views of history showed abundant life, emotionally resonant, lived through the eyes of inhabitants under the shadow of empire.

As a diasporic person, the realisation that I am also a child of diaspora, a beneficiary-descendant of the waves of Chinese migration to Nanyang (the Southern Ocean, as the region was nostalgically and romantically referred to), meant a parallel in our search for identity and belonging, then and now, though a hundred years apart. Just as we are grappling with these questions now in contemporary Britain, so were my ancestors in Nanyang as the issue of Chinese identity came to the fore for the *sinkeh*, new immigrant Chinese, vis-à-vis the Peranakan Chinese, who had settled far longer there. These questions are age-old, I knew that, but age-old in exactly what ways? What does history show us? This book hopefully shines a tiny light through the angle of photography.

Singapore was not just a colonial entrepôt, it was also a metropole that harnessed the winds of change, regional and global, from the arrival of new technologies such as the motor car and refrigeration and moving pictures, to the rise of feminism, anti-colonialism, re-Sinicisation, cultural movements, and, yes, Communism. Sun Yat Sen made nine visits to Malaya to raise funds and support for his new government; but I was more drawn to what this meant in terms of political activity via the local Kuomintang chapters and the search for Chinese identity and belonging, and how the Peranakan Chinese leadership, taking a leaf out of China's book on modernisation, similarly instrumentalised the nascent female emancipation movement as wider cultural reform.

Dickens' famous opening to *A Tale of Two Cities* comes to mind, but, once again, I'm drawn not to the best or worst when writing about eras, but rather to the wisdom and foolishness that swept through, how we believed and were also incredulous at the same time, how we hoped and also despaired, and the question of what was good or what was evil could not be a measure of the time, but like photographs as time-stamps of the past, only evident in hindsight.

Acknowledgements

I owe much to several people in this project, researched and written during a raging pandemic (to those separated from loved ones, it must have felt like a separation of eons): to Dr. Zhuang Wubin for all the fascinating discussions about photography, and for being a mentor to a fledgling historian; to the LASALLE College of the Arts and the Singapore Chinese Cultural Centre for the early historian grant that enabled the research; the librarians at National Library Singapore, particularly Michelle Heng, for all the research surrounding Chung Cheng Lake; to the Oral History Centre (all those hours listening to archived recordings of real life photographers from that era and post-Second World War now casting a romantic glow in my mind) and the National Archives Singapore, and all the different people who assisted; and finally, to historians I consulted, without disclosing the nature of the project because I felt too daunted by it sometimes.

I have writers and good friends to thank for comments on specific sections: Gabriella Otty, Melissa Fu, Yin F. Lim, Mahita Vas, and Yvonne Adhiambo Owuor, and especially to Candida Lacey, who had to read the first 25,000 words in a hurry as a subsequent submission for the longlisting with the Cheshire Novel Prise (my gratitude also to Sara Naidine Cox and the readers and industry professionals at C.N.P. for the longlist, which really boosted my confidence for the project, and not least provided valuable feedback, like the proverbial fire under the tushy, to finish my first draft). To my daughter Teia, my first and most trusted reader, always and forever—Mummy loves you. To Sadiq and Zac, who had to endure endless conversations as I exclaimed over historical findings, often without context, and my ill humour, as the narrative stumped me.

This book could not have reached you without the monumental labour of the entire team at Neem Tree Press:

Archna Sharma, its founder and also one of the first to read the whole novel, Kat, the publicity team (Divia, Lisa, Yasmeen, and Amy), and all who helped champion it at Neem.

To render the past alive, I owe much to sources far and wide, all of which are catalogued in the bibliography for the academic paper I wrote for the Singapore Chinese Cultural Centre, "Self-Fashioning Towards Modernity: Early Chinese Studio Photography of Chinese Women" (full bibliography available on my website), but below is a listing for readers keen to explore further:

Barthes, Roland. *Camera Lucida: Reflections on Photography*. London: Vintage Classics, 2006 (which inspired many chapter titles in the novel).

Cody, Jeffrey W. & Terpak, Frances, eds. *Brush and Shutter: Early Photography in China*. Los Angeles: Getty Research Institute, 2011.

Heng, Terence. *Of Gods, Gifts and Ghosts: Spiritual Places in Urban Spaces*. London: Routledge, 2020.

Kenley, David L. *New Culture in a New World: The New May Fourth Movement and The Chinese Diaspora in Singapore, 1919-1932*. New York and London: Routledge, 2003.

Lee, Peter, ed. *Amek Gambar − Taking Pictures: Peranakans and Photography*. Singapore: Asian Civilisations Museum, 2021.

Liu, Gretchen. *From the Family Album: Portraits from the Lee Brothers Studio, Singapore 1910-1925*. Singapore: National Heritage Board, 1995.

Singapore: A Pictorial History 1819–2000. Reprint. Singapore: Editions Didier Millet in association with National Heritage Board, 2000.

Song, Ong Siang. *One Hundred Years' History of the Chinese in Singapore*. Annotated by Kevin YL Tan. Singapore: National Library Board Singapore & World Scientific, 2020.

Turnbull, C. M. *A History of Modern Singapore 1819–2005*. Singapore: NUS Press, 2020.

Warren, James F. *Ah Ku and Karayuki-san: Prostitution in Singapore, 1870–1940*. Singapore: NUS Press, 2003.

Gartlan, Luke and Wue, Roberta. *Portraiture and Early Studio Photography in China and Japan*. London and New York: Routledge, 2020.

About the Author

Elaine Chiew is the author of *The Heartsick Diaspora* (recommended in *The Guardian*, *The Singapore Straits Times*, Book Riot, and *Esquire SG*) and compiler/editor of *Cooked Up: Food Fiction From Around the World*.

Her stories have won prizes, notably twice in the Bridport International Short Story Prize, and been anthologised in the U.S., U.K. and Asia, with BBC Radio 4, and in *The Best Asian Short Stories 2021*.

She mentors, teaches creative writing ad hoc, writes freelance and has worked as an independent researcher in the visual arts. She has an M.A. in Asian Art History from Goldsmiths London. In a former career, she was a U.S. trained attorney with a degree from Stanford and worked in New York, London, and Hong Kong. *The Light Between Us* is her first novel and has been longlisted for the inaugural Cheshire Novel Prize.

You can find more information on www.epchiew.com and find her on X (formerly Twitter) @ChiewElaine, Facebook @epchiew.921 and Instagram @epchiew.

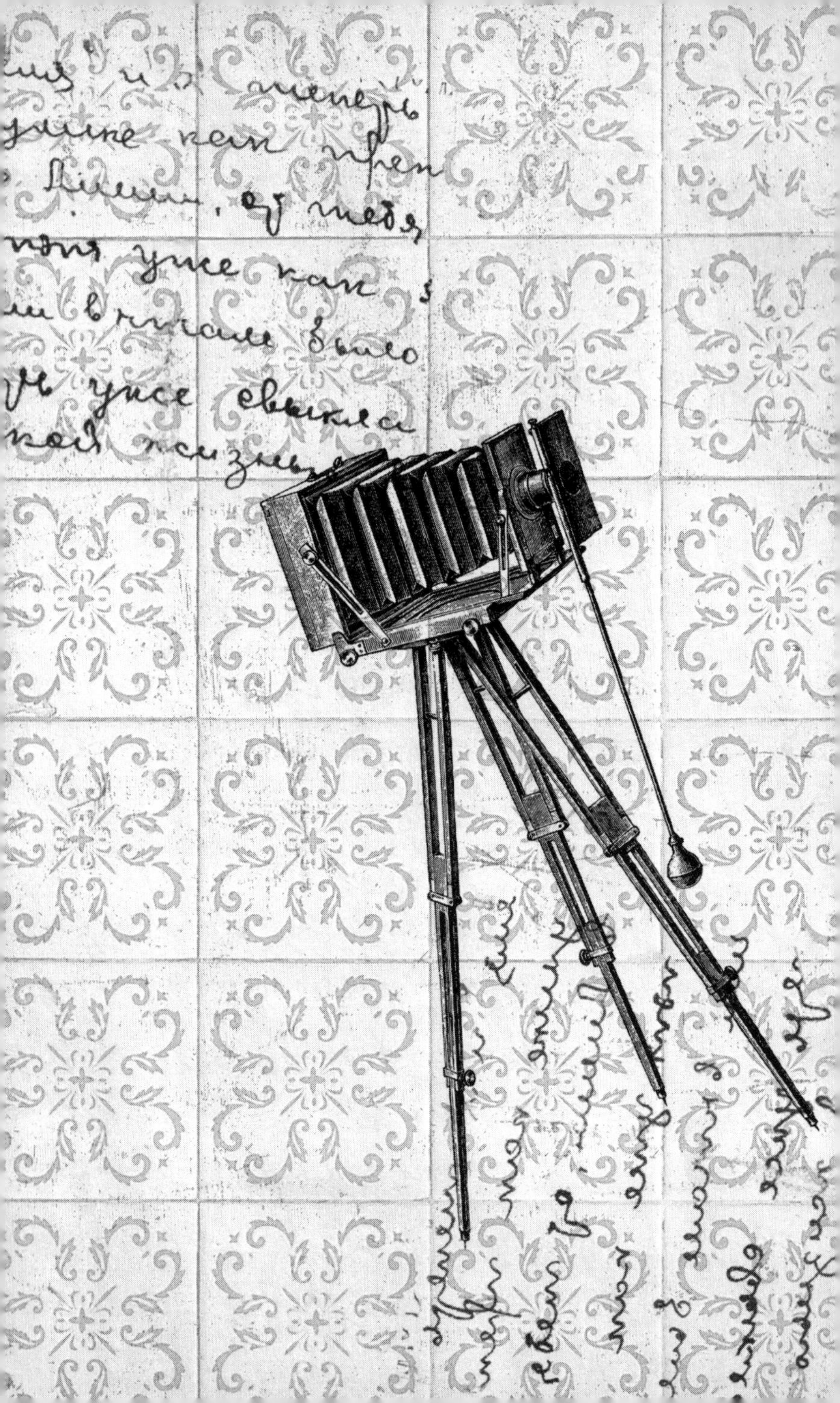